STILETTO D'ORO

STILETTO D'ORO

I HOPE YOU ENJOY . . .

James Thomas

A NOVEL BY
JAMES THOMAS

Library of Congress Control Number: 2006902158
ISBN 10:   Hardcover   1-4257-1146-4
                Softcover   1-4257-1145-6

ISBN 13:   Hardcover   978-1-4257-1146-7
                Softcover   978-1-4257-1145-0

This book was printed in the United States of America.

To order additional copies of this book, contact:
Xlibris Corporation
1-888-795-4274
www.Xlibris.com
Orders@Xlibris.com
33422

PROLOGUE

F t. Lauderdale, Florida is a waterfront city that has long been a playground for the rich and famous. Million dollar homes nestle alongside multi-million dollar estates, all of which are built along interconnecting waterways. It is a city where boats number in the tens of thousands. Naturally, such a concentrated abundance of wealth has served to upstart a vast number of waterfront cafes and bars from which party goers and fine diners alike may watch the nightly parade of expensive yachts as they transient the Intracoastal Waterway. It is a parade of affluence and decadence at its finest.

The Gold Coast of Florida is an area where wealth goes beyond measurement and is perpetual. There always has been, and always will be, someone bigger and faster—someone with a larger yacht, a faster car, a sleeker jet. The possibilities are directly proportionate to desire and the sky is the limit. Competition is fierce, perhaps even audacious. Yet, that only serves to attract the wealthy. It is a melting pot for the rich. However, for many it has also been their waterloo. Trust Fund Babies—young recipients of inherited fortunes—flock from near and far to jockey into position as potential suitors for devastatingly beautiful women. Those in the know often refer to those beauties as *Zoologists*. When referred to in this context, a Zoologist is one who is on the hunt for four particular species—a jaguar in her garage, a mink in her closet, a tiger in her bed, and a jackass who will pay for it all without questions asked.

Unfortunately, those not in the know must learn. Many a wealthy man has relocated to Ft. Lauderdale, Florida to, *show them how it is done*, only to find himself well laid, but penniless, some three years later.

Of course, as with any game of desire, the *have nots* are always figuring a means to compete with the *haves*. Enter crime, cons, strippers, smugglers, gambling . . . it would be necessary to update the list daily, for imagination and desire know no holiday. There is but one desire . . . one goal . . . and that desire knows no discrimination whatsoever. In order to compete with the *haves* one needs nothing more that a burning desire to become a *Player*.

This is a story of some of those *Players*, so please, read on . . . if you dare!

CHAPTER ONE

T he cloudless, robin's egg-blue sky allowed the tropical sun to blaze down upon the afternoon sunbathers positioned around the bar's pentagon shaped swimming pool. Between the hours of 3 p.m. and 5 p.m. the five-sided pool is so crowded that it is impossible for one to walk its perimeter. Lounge chairs are parallel parked against one another, and for the most part, stranger beside stranger. Saturday afternoon revelers stand three deep at the bar hollering their drink orders across rows of fellow drinkers to one of the five bartenders on duty. Bathing suits and shorts are deemed acceptable attire, while tops range from one hundred dollar beaded sequined T-shirts to skimpy bikinis so tiny that they barely cover the overflowing D-cup sized breasts beneath them. This was just another typical weekend at Pegleg's, a favorite waterfront watering hole.

A wooden-planked dock stretches the full length across the pool and bar then continues north alongside the adjoining establishment, Shylock's. For all practical purposes, the two are one in the same—same owner; both serve food and drinks, and are jointly connected by the swimming pool and patio area. Yet, the two bars that have been widely renowned as famous Ft. Lauderdale hot spots could not be more different. Pegleg's caters to a more casual crowd, while the sophisticated drinkers favor Shylock's.

On this particular Saturday the patrons were standing three deep at Shylock's. Thick gold necklaces adorned nearly every neck, male and female. Heavy bracelets offset the weight of solid gold wristwatches—preferably a Rolex Presidential, its face surrounded by a platinum and diamond bezel. The jewelry is far more than an expensive ornament made from precious metals set with gems and worn for personal adornment. It was a statement. Not a fashion statement, yet a statement that identified its wearer as a *Player* to others. In today's world of imitation knock-offs, every wanna-be and his brother is sporting a *Rolex* watch. It is their ticket into the big leagues. However, for the most part all it buys them is a comfortable seat from where they may observe just how the game is really played.

The dock that runs the entire length of both restaurants was completely full. As a matter of fact, boats were rafted one off the other until they stretched seven across into the Intracoastal Waterway. Neatly dressed young men scurried from boat-to-boat, bow-to-stern, while they frantically adjusted lines and fenders. Meanwhile, as many as ten boats at one time lingered nearby, their positions maintained by the careful jockeying of the throttles on their powerful twin-engines, their owners anxiously awaiting the next available slot at Shylock's. These beautiful boats are commonly referred to as *go-fasts*, and regardless of the brand they all share one common nucleus—they cost upwards of hundreds-of-thousands of dollars.

If owning one of these big boys' toys were to be placed in terms more familiar with baseball, a go-fast would be a ground rule double. At Shylock's a go-fast automatically advances the owner to second base without hesitation. These boats pre-qualify prospective catches for the women, it is common knowledge that it takes a lot of liquid cash to own and run one of these toys.

Precisely at 4 p.m. the sunbathing area alongside the swimming pool was cleared of sunbathers, at least enough to allow a walk through pathway completely around its five sides. The four-piece band stopped playing when the announcer took over the microphone. Seconds later his voice boomed across the bar and the Intracoastal Waterway when he announced, "Ladies and gentlemen, could I have your attention, please. In fifteen minutes we'll begin Pegleg's famous bikini contest. Could . . ." ***HONK! HONK! WHOOP! WHOOP!*** The master of ceremony's voice was immediately drowned out by the blaring of the many boat horns, along with the exuberant yells from the excited bar patrons. Once the noise receded to a moderate roar, the M.C. continued, "Could I have today's contestants come forward to the stage. Judges, I'll need you up front in ten minutes, please." The applause suddenly became deafening. Finally he was able to add, "Ladies and gentlemen, on behalf of the management here at Pegleg's and Shylock's, I would like to thank you for choosing us as the place to spend your Saturday afternoon. Thank you." This time the crowd broke into an applause that sent waves of noise echoing from the high rise condominiums across the waterway. The go-fasts repeatedly blew their horns while those aboard raised their drinks high in a ceremonial gesture. Within moments, the world famous bikini contest would commence.

As a bevy of bikini clad beauties slowly worked their way toward the poolside stage, Vincent Panachi signaled the bartender. Vincent was a regular at Shylock's waterfront bar, and, as a result of his patronage, he had struck up a friendship with one of the bartenders, Tony. Now being a regular in an establishment as popular as Shylock's does have certain advantages, one of which is being able to immediately get a bartender's attention. For the most part the people behind the bar are constantly *in the weeds*, an industry term that denotes their sections are full and their orders behind. However, when Tony was not buried in the weeds he made it a point to linger in front of Vincent's seat and fill him in on who's who. It made for an amiable relationship. Tony took care of Vincent with drinks and information while Vincent made certain that Tony always had a good financial day.

Vincent had appeared on the Ft. Lauderdale scene five years earlier, and Tony vividly recalled the first time he had seen him. Vincent had been sitting at his section and had ordered a magnum of Moet Chandon champagne. Tony had routinely prepared a sterling silver bucket with crushed ice, and then had carefully placed the large bottle in it. However, one time Tony had placed it in front of Vincent and Vincent had waved his hand in a brushing manner and had replied, "We don't need all that flash and pizzazz. Why don't you just stick the bottle in the ice bin and chill the glasses behind the bar. Okay?"

Tony remembered that he had simply nodded and had answered, "Sure."

The scene had made a lasting impression upon him though, mostly because it had been his experience that everyone that spent a hundred plus dollars on a bottle of champagne wanted the entire fanfare that accompanied such expenditure. It was as if they wanted everyone sitting at the bar to know what was being consumed and by whom. Initially Vincent had appeared no different to the seasoned bartender, yet time had proved that assumption wrong. Unlike the mass majority of champagne drinkers, Vincent had proved that he could afford the game and Tony had witnessed it over the years. High rollers; big shots; tourists in town for a well deserved two-week vacation, trying their absolute damnedest to spend the limit on their credit cards. Most did, and then returned home where they could lick their financial wounds for another fifty weeks before attempting another go at the high life. That was by far the rule rather than the exception. Vincent Panachi was that exception, he sat there year after year at Tony's station regularly ordering expensive bottles of champagne. Vincent never seemed to hit that financial lull that others inevitably experienced. As Tony had once commented to one of his fellow co-workers behind the bar, "The man definitely has financial staying power."

Tony stopped in front of Vincent's seat and queried, "Is that it, Vince?"

The handsome Italian replied, "Yeah, that's enough damage for today."

Vincent grinned as he casually tossed an American Express Platinum Card on top of the brass-covered bar, just as he had done countless times before. Tony returned the ingratiating smile, and then disappeared with the credit card. While he was gone Vincent reached into his trouser pocket, removed the money clip and peeled a fifty dollar bill from the folded wad he always carried. Heedful not to attract the attention of the fellow drinkers around him, Vincent raised his champagne glass by its narrow stem and slipped the bill beneath it. Tony reappeared a moment later with the credit card receipt, and Vincent signed it with a flourish. They exchanged a handshake while assuring one another, "I'll see you tomorrow."

That exchange had not gone unnoticed. An attractive woman in her early thirties was sitting across the bar from Vincent and witnessed the transaction.

Long blond hair flowed past her shoulders and swept to one side exposing a glittering one-carat diamond earring. A half-full glass of chilled champagne set on the bar in front of her.

She carefully watched while Vincent pocketed the credit card, turned around and began weaving his way through the crowd toward the dock. While doing so Vincent inadvertently glanced her way and noticed her looking at him. It wasn't her attractiveness that initially grasped his attention. It was the afternoon sun reflecting off the diamond bezel on her lady's Rolex Presidential that sent a dazzlingly colorful spectrum of light in forty directions. Vincent noticed a small red lipstick mark smeared across the top of the champagne glass where her lips had gently rested. The pose was one that had obviously been well rehearsed. Vincent smiled to himself, yet afterwards he was certain that she had assumed he was smiling at her. At any rate, the very attractive woman flashed him a radiant smile in return. It took Vincent five minutes to wriggle through the crowded bar, but after a series of turns and twists, he reached the dock.

Meanwhile, a swarm of dockside drinkers steadily moved toward the swimming pool area while the boats in the waterway formed a semi-circle around Pegleg's. The announcer's voice boomed, "Ladies and gentlemen, let's give a really big hand to our lovely contestants before we begin today's contest." The sounds that followed were earsplitting.

"Going to watch the contest?" asked one of the young dockhands as he approached Vincent.

"Not today." Vincent shook his head. "Unfortunately, I have to leave early. I have plans this evening."

"I'll get your lines for you, Mr. Panachi," said the dockhand smiling.

The dockhand stepped from the dock onto the stern of a Cigarette Café Racer, across the stern of a Sea Ray Express Cruiser, then across the aft deck of a Fountain Lightning. Vincent followed the younger man's footsteps while they traversed three more go-fasts before finally reaching Vincent's boat, the beautiful thirty-eight foot Scarab Thunder.

The young dockhand quickly scrambled to the bow of the boat and manned the forward line. Vincent inserted the matching keys and fired up the powerful engines, one at a time. Full racing cams rumbled while cylinder head temperatures quickly rose. Vincent released the aft line and signaled the dockhand to do the same with the bowline. Afterwards, Vincent skillfully held the Scarab in place with differential power while he handed the young man a folded ten dollar bill. The dockhand stuffed the bill into his shorts and thanked Vincent with a nod, and then stepped onto the adjoining boat. Vincent gently eased the Scarab into the waterway. No sooner had the space become vacant, another go-fast gently slid into the spot.

Vincent carefully maneuvered the watercraft through the flotilla of pleasure boats until he was safely free from the danger of collision, then he glanced toward

Pegleg's. A bathing beauty was strutting around the perimeter of the swimming pool while loud wolf whistles and boisterous cheers demonstrated the crowd's approval of her shapely figure. The woman glided across the concrete in five-inch heels that seductively hiked her buttocks high while the angle of her feet flexed her lengthy leg muscles as she walked. A thong bathing suit left little to the imagination, particularly from the rear view. Her muscled back sloped upward and only the sides of her large breasts overflowing from the restraint of the tiny nylon bikini top disturbed that perfect slope. The beauty swung her shoulder-length hair from side-to-side in rhythm with her every step while the crowd went wild. These women were not bimbos off the beach. They were seasoned professionals—exotic dancers enjoying a day of sun and fun, where the lucky winner would pick up over two thousand dollars in cash and prizes. Besides, there was no better way for them to see and to be seen. Aside from a shot at the cash prize, there were always the boys in the go-fasts. All things considered, each contestant became a winner.

Vincent watched the beauty parade a lap around the pool before he eased the engines' transmissions into gear. The Scarab slowly idled away from the crowd and away from the noise of Pegleg's and Shylock's.

The blond seated at the lower bar had been watching Vincent the entire time. She observed that his movements were completely relaxed, and it was obvious to her that he was comfortable with who he was by the auspicious manner in which he handled himself. Naturally, her trained eye had not missed a trick—the Rolex watch on his wrist, which ironically matched hers, the two-carat diamond on his left ring finger, the ten dollar gold piece surrounded with diamonds that served as a money clip, and the Scarab Thunder speedboat.

This one was a prime catch, she mused, someone worth pursuing.

The woman caught the bartender's eye and signaled him. Tony stopped in front of her seat as she leaned across the bar to be heard over the roar of the bikini contest next door.

"Tony, I'll have another glass of champagne, please. But, before you pour it you must tell me, who was that handsome gentleman seated across the bar?"

"His name is Vincent Panachi. He's a local." Tony grabbed her glass and smiled.

"Thank you." The blond returned Tony's smile.

When Tony walked away the blond turned to search for Vincent's Scarab, but the sleek speedboat had pulled out and was already in the distance. "That's him," she mumbled under her breath.

* * *

Across the Intracoastal Waterway directly west of Shylock's stands a ten-story condominium whose large sliding glass doors overlook the drinking establishment. The penthouse apartment on the far left has a breathtaking southeast view that encompasses the beach area all the way south to Port Everglades. The condominium's living room has a tinted protective film that prevents the blinding morning sun from glaring through the glass doors. It also averts any curious eyes, because the reflective film functions like a two-way mirror; one can see out, but not in.

Inside the condominium's living room area were four agents of the Organized Crime Task Force who had set up shop there two months earlier. Along the sliding glass doors stood nearly a dozen 35 millimeter (mm) cameras mounted on aluminum tripods evenly spaced along the wall of glass. Some of the cameras protruded further into the living room than others because of the various lengths of their telescopic lenses which ranged in size from 200 mm to 600 mm, with the latter being nearly twelve inches long. A 600 mm lens can discern the writing on a pack of cigarettes from a distance while the less powerful lens will produce a larger, less detailed image. One of the cameras had a wide-angle lens attached that encompassed the entire waterfront area of Pegleg's and Shylock's. All cameras were trained on the waterway.

Today's assignment, just as it had been for the past two months, was to photograph the go-fasts and their owners sometime during their stay at the waterfront bars. Every boat, along with its occupants, would be photographed. Once the agent manning the cameras finished a roll of thirty-five photographs, he would reload the camera and pass the exposed film along to the darkroom specialist. The specialist would develop the roll of film in one of the bedrooms that had been converted to a specially illuminated room for processing photographs. Within hours, the photographed subject's image would be reproduced on photosensitive paper, and then categorized and filed by boat name into one of the many file cabinets banked alongside one wall.

The agent manning the cameras systematically moved from left to right down the row of cameras. After two months on the job, his movements were down to a science. His left hand made minute lateral adjustments to the camera with the 300 mm lens until the aim in the view finder was directly centered and focused upon the Scarab Thunder. The agent held his breath for a split second while his right index finger gently depressed the camera's shutter switch. He smiled, then carefully backed away from the tripod and exclaimed, "Got ya!" A perfect image of Vincent Panachi's face at the helm of the Scarab Thunder had been captured on film. Several hours later, the agents were all in agreement that the Scarab shot had been the best of the day.

*   *   *

SIX HOURS LATER

Vincent Panachi stood on the aft deck of the 112-foot Broward yacht and peered into the dark water below. The rhythmic vibration of the ship's two huge diesel power plants gently massaged his feet, yet the vibration was not enough to disturb the effervescent flow of the rising bubbles in his champagne glass. The yacht had departed Pier 66 one hour earlier and was slowly making its way along the Intracoastal Waterway north through Ft. Lauderdale. It was a black tie affair that included sixty guests, more or less, most hailing from the northeast United States. The soiree was this year's annual social gathering of the Vitale crime family, and its date could be predicated a year in advance because it was always held on Anthony Vitale's birthday. Vincent leaned over the yacht's massive transom and watched the phosphorescent trail of tiny luminous flecks left by the slow churning of the huge bronze propellers. As the flecks slowly blended into the dark waters Vincent mused that the past year must have been a very profitable one for the crime family. Last year's yacht party had been thrown on a 90-footer, and this year's yacht was twenty-two, absolutely gorgeous feet longer.

Vincent ran his finger along the inside of the buttoned collar on his pure silk dress shirt. A black butterfly bow tie stood perfectly centered along the neckline of the snow white shirt. His jet-black, Italian designed tuxedo was custom fit by the finest tailor in Ft. Lauderdale. The shoulders on the jacket hugged Vincent's broad back and the jacket's sleeves stopped exactly one inch from the shirt's French cuffs. The jacket's lapel tapered across Vincent's forty-two inch chest and exposed three of five diamond studs that matched the cuff links. The remaining two were hidden beneath the jacket's cummerbund. The matching trousers had an immaculate, knifelike crease that stopped precisely at the top of a pair of expensive Italian loafers and covered a pair of thirty dollar socks. A blood red pure silk handkerchief neatly tucked into the breast pocket of the tuxedo jacket accented his formal attire. The dark tuxedo made the moderate five-foot ten-inch, Vincent Panachi appear much taller. It also accentuated how handsome he was.

Vincent had been living in South Florida for so long that he had almost forgotten that these people were from his hometown in Newark, New Jersey. Yet they were quick to remind him of his roots, with their wisecrack comments shortly followed by abrupt slaps on his back. Their coarse New Jersey accents were even more pronounced than he had remembered.

The guest of honor at that evening's gala was Anthony Vitale, affectionately referred to as the *Old Man*. Not so affectionately, Anthony Vitale had also been referred to for a great number of years as *The Shark*. He was the undisputed head of the Vitale crime family who had ruled Newark for more than four decades. It was understood that the Capos regularly siphoned off enough funds during the course of the year to finance the lavish annual party. The head of the crime family knew it, but acted as if he had never noticed the shortages during the respective cash deliveries. He let it slide because the money had been skimmed with good intentions and would be used to help boost the family's morale. However, Anthony Vitale could have told you precisely how much was missing and from whom.

Anthony had made his bones in the early days by taking care of those individuals who had stolen from the crime family, and it had been those vicious collections that had earned him his nickname *The Shark*. His reputation had grown within certain circles so rapidly that it had become infamous among the underground economy of Newark. Those legendary days were once summarized by an older Capo appeasing Vincent's curiosity when he had explained, "Many a thief of the family tried to steal more chain from Anthony than he could swim with." Vincent had understood perfectly—thieves sleep with the fish!

Vincent's father had also been a distinguished member of the Vitale crime family, and had risen through the ranks rapidly. Vito Panachi was still a very young man hustling the streets of Newark, New Jersey when he had become Tony the Shark's right hand man. Vito had shown such promise for the family that Tony the Shark had personally taken him under his wing as his protégé. Vito Panachi was destined to be the crime family's youngest Capo, the leader of a section of the family's ruling territory. That was thirty years ago when the old man himself had been a Capo.

Unfortunately, Vincent's father had taken a bullet meant for the shark during a hit attempt by a rival crime family. Vito had saved Anthony's life, but had lost his own. Ever since that day Anthony had taken responsibility for the life and well being of Vito's only son. The future for Vincent Panachi had been sealed.

Vincent was afforded every opportunity to further his education. He attended the finest schools and became polished. He also learned about the world outside the inner city of Newark, New Jersey. But, it had always been understood between mentor and protégé that Vincent would return and become part of the Vitale crime family. Even then the Shark was laying the groundwork for decades down the road.

Twenty-five years later the Shark was head of the crime family. It had been his destiny, his family heritage, and he had been expected to do better than his predecessor. Anthony had eventually expanded the family's territory to include the Gold Coast of Florida. His particular business interest was in Ft. Lauderdale, and by his orders Vincent had been sent south to oversee the family's financial interests.

That had been five years ago, but to Vincent it had seemed much longer. During the past years Vincent had flown once a month to Newark in a chartered Learjet to meet with Anthony Vitale. Anthony would playfully muss Vincent's long but neatly trimmed hair while discussing future business strategies. Inevitably, during the course of their meetings, Anthony would query, "And is there anyone special in my nephew's love life?"

Vincent's eyes would avert the elderly gentleman's when he replied, "No, sir . . . not as yet." No doubt it was one of the old man's favorite subjects. Vincent was in charge of delivering the proceeds from the family's many businesses in and around Ft. Lauderdale, yet sometimes Anthony would ask the routine question even before he inquired about the millions that Vincent was personally delivering.

The faint sound of a band playing carried through the panes of glass that separated the Broward's main salon from the aft deck while muffled voices of several dozen people talking at once blended with the music. Suddenly, the salon door opened and the music blared through the open doorway. Vincent casually turned to see who had joined him, and saw that it was one of the family's most trusted Capos. The middle-aged man gently placed his hand on Vincent's shoulder.

"Vincent, what goes, huh? You don't like the party?"

"Just grabbing a breath of fresh air," Vincent smiled as he replied.

"Well, better make it quick because the old man wants to speak to you," the Capo announced while patting Vincent's shoulder then walking away to return to the party.

"Where is he?" Vincent queried after he took a swallow from his champagne glass.

"He's downstairs in the master stateroom," the Capo replied over his shoulder as he turned reentering the main salon.

Vincent nodded his head in acknowledgement, but it had been a futile move. The Capo was already through the doorway. A minute later, Vincent followed.

The salon area was crowded, just as Shylock's had been earlier that day. As soon as Vincent entered the lavish salon a white tuxedoed waiter, supporting a sterling silver tray full of crystal glasses brimmed with Dom Perignon, placed a fresh glass of bubbly in Vincent's hand. The women in ultra-expensive designer gowns made an interesting contrast to the numerous identical penguin suits that most of the men had rented for the annual occasion.

Vincent held his champagne glass high to prevent it from being bumped while he slowly made his way across the main salon. The Broward was the most beautiful yacht Vincent had ever seen, and being a boater himself, he enjoyed the privilege of having been aboard several spectacular vessels. Shades of pale beige and maroon predominated throughout while the bulkheads were veneered with white oak that contrasted against peach carpeting. Along the port side a spacious C-shaped divan curved around two small tables. Opposite, a round card table with four chairs nestled in the corner. Further forward, a glass topped dining table provided seating for a dinner party of eight. Across from that, along the starboard side, was a white oak bar with a brass trimmed ecru marble top. As Vincent moved through the jubilant crowd, his eyes wondered toward a woman in a strikingly beautiful, ruby red dress. Straight blond hair cascaded the length of her back and stopped alluringly short of the roundness of her hips. Vincent knew a little something about women's dresses, or at least enough to recognize a Halston original when he saw one, and that the designer's dress most certainly cost close to two thousand dollars. The woman was leaning against the bar in a position that prevented Vincent from seeing with whom she was talking. After Vincent moved forward another five feet he was able to identify the mystery man. The stranger in the red dress was talking to Slick Nick, a transplanted New Jersey con man who had risen through the crime family's ranks enough to manage a restaurant the family owned in nearby Boca Raton.

As Vincent approached the couple, Slick Nick caught Vincent's eye and signaled for him to join them. Had it been only Slick Nick standing there, Vincent would have begged off by saying, "I'm on the way to see someone . . . we'll talk later." Of course later would have never come, because Vincent did not particularly care for Slick Nick. However, the woman in the red dress had captured Vincent's attention, and he was curious to see what she looked like without being so gauche as to turn around and gawk at her after passing by.

Vincent joined them and extended his hand to shake Nick's.

"Nick, good to see you."

"Yeah, same to you."

Vincent caught a quick glimpse of the woman. To his surprise, the woman standing before him was the attractive blond Vincent had seen earlier that afternoon at Shylock's.

"Vincent Panachi, say 'Hello' to Jennifer Swords," Nick said as he shifted his eyes toward the woman.

"Nice to meet you, Vincent," Jennifer replied as she extended her hand to him.

"The pleasure is all mine, Ms. Swords." Vincent smiled while their eyes locked into a lengthy stare. Vincent felt the spark in her gaze and the blond returned his smile. Suddenly, conversation came easily.

Jennifer had plenty to smile about, because she had put up with Slick Nick's pawing and crude behavior for weeks while patiently waiting for just this moment. Meeting Vincent Panachi was NOT a chance happening.

CHAPTER TWO

Jennifer Swords stood naked before a full-length mirror and carefully critiqued her body. The master bedroom of her ocean front condominium had a dressing room with a three-sided mirror, similar to those found in the shops where she had frequently made expensive purchases. The angled mirrors allowed Jennifer to view herself from three different sides at once—a frontal view along with either quarter side. Her skin was still rosy from a lengthy steaming hot shower.

Jennifer was in her early thirties, but had a body that could compete with any twenty-one year old. Of course, Jennifer had an unfair advantage. She had cheated father time by going under the knife each time her body had begun to show the telltale signs of aging. It hadn't begun that way, but once Jennifer had been introduced to the world of cosmetic surgery she found access into a world she had long dreamed of, the life she had always imagined that only the beautiful people experienced.

Almost overnight she had been transformed from an ugly duckling into a beautiful swan. With the exception of one operation, all of her numerous cosmetic alterations had been performed by the hands of Dr. Mitchell Swords. Now, it was as if the woman who once was had never existed. If it were possible for the past and present Jennifer to stand along side one another, one would swear that they were two completely different people. The alter ego inside that voluptuous body remembered all too well who she was and where she had come from. Jennifer Swords had not always been Jennifer Swords. Before she moved to Ft. Lauderdale from a small town near the Jersey shore, she had been Marie Castellano, the daughter of full-blooded Italian parents. Marie had always favored her father's side of the family. She had his dark eyes and hair, and unfortunately, a rather large, hook nose. During Marie's puberty it had become her greatest complex, but not her sole obsession.

In Marie's eyes, psychoanalysis was a luxury which only rich people could indulge. Nonetheless, she certainly could have profited from extensive counseling during those painful years, but treatment had not been an option. Instead, Marie withdrew further into herself while her life's wish list grew. Like all teenagers who experience the pain of growing up, Marie was the person most critical of her own physical imperfections.

Magazine advertisements featuring beautiful women with perfectly sloping noses seemed to attract more attention to her imperfections. As the obsession over her own profile grew she began a desperate search for alternative solutions. It had been during those solitary moments of soul searching that Marie discovered the sophistication incorporated in photographs of jewelry, fur coats and designer dresses.

Soon an idea formed. Money would cure all of her problems. With money she could afford all of the luxuries she had yearned for in those magazine advertisements. But, just as psychological treatment was expensive, so were the finer things in life that Marie now viewed as a solution. Every night she would lay in bed and ponder a solution until the answer came to her. Late one evening, Marie ran across an advertisement for career nurses.

The full-page color advertisement had portrayed young nurses performing various duties. By now Marie had become very adept at scrutinizing every detail of a photograph. While she scanned the scenes of nurses one thing became obvious in each photograph. No matter where the nurses were or what they were doing, doctors—doctors that made tremendous amounts of money—surrounded them. Later that evening she formed a plan. Marie would change her name, become a nurse, marry a doctor, then live the life of luxury she was certain was her destiny.

Marie Castellano remained steadfast and focused during the pursuit of her goals. Marie graduated with honors in the top five percent of nursing school, and then left New Jersey the next day by Greyhound bus bound for Florida's Gold Coast. The thousand-mile bus ride provided plenty of time for Marie to search her soul. Her decision had been made years before, but now the reality was in motion. By the time the bus arrived in Ft. Lauderdale, she was no longer Marie. Her new identity was to be Jennifer, and she would not use her last name socially. It would have been impossible for her not to use her real last name while she sought employment. Nevertheless, her name change from Marie to Jennifer was enough to satisfy her peace of mind.

Jennifer it was and she immediately found employment at a Ft. Lauderdale hospital and was able to get a small furnished apartment nearby. She began work immediately, and that was when she met Dr. Mitchell Swords, a renowned plastic surgeon.

Dr. Swords was introverted and shy. He was an "early to bed, early to rise" type who had developed a very successful practice as a plastic surgeon in Ft. Lauderdale and Boca Raton. His routine, however, hampered his ability to socialize; it earned him a reputation as a workaholic and something less than a lady's man.

Jennifer sensed Dr. Swords' behavior right away and viewed him as easy prey. The two were married within three months after meeting, and in retrospect there had been individuals close to Dr. Swords that felt he had temporarily taken leave of his senses. After that blissful union, Marie Castellano legally became Jennifer Swords. Suddenly the confused little girl from New Jersey was now the wife of a prominent doctor, and had every opportunity that she had ever dreamt of.

Within a matter of weeks the cosmetic transformations had taken place. After nine hours of surgery Dr. Swords had completed the rhinoplasty correcting Jennifer's nose. Next, Jennifer's jagged teeth were capped with white porcelain, and the contact lenses that replaced her glasses dramatically changed the color of her eyes from dark-brown to sea-blue. Her mousy brown hair became bleached blond while she had acrylic fingernails applied at the same time. Finally, electrolysis removed the dark shadow above her upper lip.

Dr. Swords either performed or coordinated all of her cosmetic improvements, and the end result was a wife as pretty as any he had ever imagined. Even Jennifer could not believe the transformation. But, there was one cosmetic addition that Jennifer had wanted badly.

Ft. Lauderdale is full of bathing beauties with perfectly shaped, surgically enhanced breasts. Jennifer utilized her professional connections to research which doctor was renowned to be the best at breast enhancement surgery, and then booked a consultation appointment. Jennifer had the surgery performed while her husband was out of town at a two-day convention and the result was stunning. Within one afternoon, Jennifer's chest size increased from a 32B to a voluptuous 36D.

When Dr. Swords returned from his trip Jennifer was seductively waiting in their bedroom to surprise him. What a surprise it had been. Dr. Swords entered the dimly lit bedroom and found Jennifer sitting cross-legged on their king-size bed, clad only in a sheer silk negligee. The cool sensation of the thin, transparent fabric lightly brushing her nipples had created small hard protuberances. The firm roundness of her breasts angled her nipples upward causing the near nothing of a negligee to limply drape. For a split moment Dr. Swords' mouth hung agape at the sight of this beautiful woman. Until now, any woman that had looked that sexy would not have given Dr. Swords the time of day, much less a pleasurable evening he would never forget.

The meek and mild mannered surgeon could not get enough sex. They made love once a day, but his appetite for sex became insatiable. During the following weeks they engaged in sexual intercourse with such frequency that it became an obsession for the doctor.

Jennifer's lifestyle changed drastically. Her voluptuous figure required a complete new wardrobe which required a substantial amount of time spent shopping. Jennifer patiently waited for an evening when her husband had experienced a particularly throbbing orgasm before she unveiled her dilemma. Dr. Swords did not hesitate before he told her to quit her job and go shopping.

Jennifer did not bother with the customary two weeks' notice. She quit her job as a nurse the following day. Full days were spent shopping and within two weeks Jennifer ran up nearly twenty-five thousand dollars on Dr. Swords' Gold American Express card. Even though she had quickly become a clotheshorse, the transformation had been worthwhile to the doctor. If there had been any consolation for the doctor it was that Jennifer was now stunningly gorgeous. A new, improved Jennifer Swords emerged.

Within a short period of time the days at the mall were replaced by long lunches at a nearby country club where Jennifer befriended several wealthy socialites—The Ft. Lauderdale-style wealth, where many are filthy rich beyond money. It had not taken Jennifer many luncheons to realize that she was nothing more than the wife of a high-salaried worker; a commoner who's parvenu had been discovered. In spite of her newfound exterior beauty, Jennifer lacked the cultural taste and social grace of her socialite companions.

Desire flared once again and Jennifer Swords became a quick study. She studied the women daily, particularly those who were older and more sophisticated. They talked candidly about their lives, their husbands, and their husbands' businesses. Jennifer learned many things. Unfortunately, one of them was that she was only pacified in her marriage, not satisfied. This marked the beginning of the end for Dr. Mitchell Swords.

Soon tremendous arguments began to take place between Jennifer and Dr. Swords, until eighteen months after their wedding Jennifer and Dr. Swords were divorced. The day her divorce became final some of Jennifer's divorced, middle-aged, and very wealthy socialite friends threw her a lavish party at the country club. The occasion was meant to launch the *old* Jennifer into her new and exciting single life, and it worked. What emerged from that champagne-drinking soiree was the *NEW* Jennifer Swords.

Men that were close friends of her socialite friends were thrust upon her nearly daily. Most were handsome but older gentlemen, while all were blue-blooded aristocrats funded by an abundance of inherited wealth. It was the beginning of two years spent living the high life. Even so, the high life lacked things that were significantly important to Jennifer. She had been living off of her generous four hundred thousand dollar divorce settlement during that two-year period. To the privileged minority of ultra-wealthy persons, that figure represents the absolute minimum required to exist during a couple of years on the go.

Jennifer had considered her extravagant expenditures as an investment, and the eventual return on her investment was to catch an aristocratic husband. Available men of that caliber were regularly pursued by a great number of women, and never married unless the female was of equal or greater net worth than their own. As the adage goes among the ultra-rich, "There are never marriages; only mergers." Jennifer had received many wonderful gifts from her suitors that demonstrated their appreciation for her companionship, but there had never been a proposal of marriage.

Jennifer's savings had been substantially reduced to approximately one hundred and fifty thousand dollars before reality set in. She would never catch one of the gentlemen's gentlemen. Jennifer realized that she was nothing more than an expensive vase to these men, something to be enjoyed while on display for others to see. She succumbed to the fact that she would have to lower her standards for a potential catch in order to achieve her goals. She still desired someone with a lot of money, but it had to be someone who would be in awe of her new found sophistication; someone who viewed her as she had viewed those ultra-wealthy men that had so patiently taught her the ways of the world.

Money played a large part in her decisions, but that wasn't all she had to consider for future suitors. There had been another area lacking during Jennifer's flings with the wealthy older gentlemen. Sex. She realized that she would have to satisfy her uncontrollable sexual desires before she could possibly become engaged in the multiple head games planned for potential suitors. Finally, it was time for a major change in her life. It was common knowledge that the players hung out at the many waterfront bars along Ft. Lauderdale's Intracoastal Waterway, and she decided that this would be the area where she would concentrate her pursuit for a worthy catch.

Jennifer moved to a high-rise condominium on the beach centered on the sun and fun activities in Ft. Lauderdale, and then splurged another ten thousand dollars furnishing the two-bedroom condo. Days later she invested another thousand dollars at a made-to-order bikini shop, and the result was a sexual bombshell. Within one week she felt that her new life was established and that she was ready to go out on the town.

That evening Jennifer dressed down by digging into the back of her closet where she found several pairs of tight-fitting designer jeans. She wriggled into her favorite pair and donned a pair of expensive three-inch heeled, snake skinned boots. Then, a deep-V-cut sequined blouse clung to her ample breasts revealing her cleavage. She paused for a moment to critique her image in the bedroom's full length, three-sided mirror, and smiled. Jennifer continued to smile as she walked out the door of her condominium.

Thirty-five minutes later Jennifer strutted into a large upscale country and western bar located in the nearby town of Davie. She wanted to make absolutely certain that whomever she met that evening would not be someone she would run into at the waterfront bars of Ft. Lauderdale. Jennifer was hell-bent on making tonight a one-night stand.

Jennifer was initially stunned by the bar scene after spending the past two years being spoiled in five star restaurants and having attended gala opera openings.

She walked to the far end of a lengthy bar and chose a seat with vacant stools on either side. A handsome man seated across from her watched her every move. He noted that she appeared uncomfortable to the point of appearing frightened, and quite frankly she was. At that moment she was no longer the sophisticated woman who had socialized with the country club set. Suddenly, she became the frightened little girl who hailed from rural New Jersey, and that alter ego remembered the painful years of rejection from the young men she had desired. Jennifer was uncertain of being accepted.

Ten minutes and one drink later the handsome man summoned up enough courage to walk around to the end of the bar.

"Hi, my name is Mark. May I join you for a few minutes?"

"Yes, please do." She shyly offered her hand, "My name is Jennifer . . . Jennifer Swords."

"Murray . . . Mark Murray," he said taking her hand and sensing that she seemed frightened of him being a stranger. "I don't usually make a point of broadcasting my occupation, but Jennifer, you're safe with me. I'm a cop, off duty, of course."

Jennifer listened with raised eyebrows. She had never met a cop before, not even as a driver receiving a speeding ticket. She had this mental vision of cops like the ones around her hometown—overweight, angry, redneck types that were always looking for a confrontation. Now, seated beside her was this gorgeous, well-built gentleman that in no way fit the profile she had envisioned for so many years.

"A cop . . . as in a policeman?"

"Well, not really. I work for the Organized Crime Task Force, and we only chase after the big boys."

"Oh, how interesting. Please, tell me more."

For hours, Agent Murray overwhelmed Jennifer with exciting stories about his life, his goals and his profession. Excitement was something she had longed for during her social outings with the well-mannered, ultra-wealthy gentlemen of her immediate past. The more she listened to Mark, the more convinced she became that he was precisely what she was looking for that night. He was separated from his wife of ten years, and seemed harmless, lonely, and had confided in her that his ex-to-be was desperately trying to catch him with his pants down, literally.

"Unfortunately, I have been celibate for over six months while waiting for this divorce to be finalized," Mark divulged somewhat shyly.

"Mark, if that's a line, it's one that I have never heard," she said placing her hand atop his and staring into his eyes. He returned the smile, and she knew for certain that she would bed him that night.

Agent Murray perceived Jennifer to be elegantly refreshing compared to the "bar bimbos" he had been subjected to over the past several months. She had a dignified richness and grace about her that reflected in her mannerisms.

He realized that this beauty sitting beside him was the type of woman he had dreamt of, and the type of woman that men of his caliber never seemed to meet. Even more attractive was that she seemed genuinely interested in his occupation, something that his ex-to-be had detested with a passion.

Hours passed quickly for both of them while they continued to swap stories until midnight.

"Let's go somewhere where we can be alone," Mark suggested.

"Okay," Jennifer responded after a short silence. She did not want Mark to think that she was easy. But, in reality Jennifer could not remember the last time she had enjoyed really good sex, and tonight this devastatingly handsome stranger had turned her on.

Mark and Jennifer checked into a Holiday Inn within a mile of the bar. Jennifer waited in the car while Mark went inside the small office to register. He reappeared moments later with the key to a room located on the ground floor. Unfortunately, his automobile was not well hidden from the passing traffic, and that made him nervous.

"I have to be concerned about my future ex-wife . . . she is a witch," Mark explained as he inserted the key to unlock the door.

"Don't worry, Mark . . . I understand." Jennifer squeezed his hand. She could not possibly have hoped for more. Mark had no desire to drag her around town on his arm like a showpiece, and at Mark's request, the quality time they would share together would be their little secret.

Jennifer glanced at the king-sized bed and noted the typical Holiday Inn décor where the curtains and bedspread matched while Mark latched the door's security chain. Jennifer turned and threw her arms around his neck, pressing her soft lips tightly against his, her pouting breasts pressed firmly against his chest. Mark felt the heat emitting from her body as he encircled his arms around her back, one hand sliding down past the curvature of her spine until it rested on the roundness of her voluptuous buttocks. Jennifer's right hand slid down Mark's side until she found his belt, then her slender fingers followed the piece of cool leather around to the front of his trousers. Meanwhile Jennifer's tongue expertly swirled inside Mark's mouth, then across his lips, all the while gently massaging his now enlarged manhood. The sensation drove him wild. Mark moaned as he withdrew his lips from hers and began passionately kissing her neck. They did not speak a word. Jennifer continued her stimulating strokes that were driving Mark over the threshold of passionate desire while he slowly kissed his way to her exposed cleavage. Jennifer moaned. The moment had arrived.

Jennifer sauntered to the small bathroom to undress while Mark undressed bedside. He turned down the sheets and slid between them. A small night-light illuminated the room with a dim, romantic glow that was enough for Mark to watch Jennifer's breasts bounce in unison with every step as she approached the bed. When she reached the bed Mark reached up to her. Jennifer leaned forward and gently pressed her hand on his chest to instruct him to stay put while she pulled the sheets away and swung a leg over his body to straddle him. Her right hand found his erect manhood and guided it until they began moving in a rhythmic motion that became one. Minutes passed like hours while Jennifer brought Mark to the brink of heavenly bliss. Their sexual frenzy finally exploded into simultaneous orgasms and afterwards, Jennifer collapsed onto Mark's chest.

That scenario was repeated regularly for the next three months until Jennifer was as sexually satisfied as she had ever imagined, and her passionate lovemaking and insatiable appetite for sex had misled Mark into believing that she was madly in love with him. Agent Murray had fallen hopelessly in love while Jennifer had been venting her sexual frustrations. In addition, she had been laying her groundwork by qualifying potential suitors.

Throughout those three months, hours of pillow talk about Mark's work had followed their sexual interludes. Mark was professionally barred from disclosing details about the task force's ongoing investigations, but what he had divulged gave Jennifer enough information to determine who the big money players were. It was during those intimate moments that Jennifer had learned of Vincent Panachi, the "bag man" for the Vitale crime family.

Vincent Panachi was young, wealthy, and most importantly, single. After careful consideration Jennifer decided that he was perfect. Now she was faced with the perplexing problem of meeting him. Without even realizing he had done so, Mark had provided the answer to that dilemma one evening after they had made love. Mark casually mentioned the name of a particular low-level member of the Vitale crime family while telling Jennifer about the upcoming annual birthday celebration thrown by the distinguished members of the crime family. It slipped that Slick Nick had been under surveillance during the previous year and had led them to the lavish yacht party. It was there that task force had learned of Vincent Panachi. Slick Nick seemed like an easy target to Jennifer and she quickly formulated a plan. She would meet Slick Nick and through him she would meet Vincent.

That evening Jennifer got all the information from Mark she needed to implement her plan. Then, the next evening without explanation and without regrets, Jennifer spoke the most painful words Agent Murray had ever heard.

"It's been nice, Mark, but it's over."

"I feel as if my heart has been cut out with a knife," he confessed to Jennifer.

"Mark it's over. Get over it!" She coldly responded.

The memories of them together continued to burn in his mind on a daily basis. The pain had cut into his soul and he was sent into an emotional tailspin that lasted longer than any of his previous bouts with depression.

Finally in a last ditch effort to make her realize how deeply she had hurt him, Mark contracted a jeweler to design a unique necklace made of eighteen

carat gold that encased pave diamonds that spelled one word in capital letters—
STILETTO.

The gift did not raise a response from Jennifer. Her mind and her heart were set on her financial security, yet she wore the necklace daily only because it served as a reminder of the power she possessed over men. It gave her the confidence she had longed for. Jennifer Swords had absorbed the final bit of confidence she had needed from Agent Murray.

Now, as she stood before the mirror in her dressing room, Jennifer reached around her bronze tanned back and fastened her brassiere. She slipped her slender shoulders into the straps, then reached into each cup and carefully adjusted her breasts. The restraint of the lace-covered fabric lifted her breasts high and pushed them to form a cleavage that few men could avoid noticing. Next, her slender fingers found the clasp behind her neck and fastened the necklace. Jennifer paused from dressing for a few moments while she admired herself in the mirrors. She stood naked from the waist down, but that's not what her eyes critiqued. It was the sparkling reflection from the necklace that caught her eye. She smiled back at her own image. She was happy. That night marked a very special event in her life. Tonight was to be Jennifer Swords' first date with Vincent Panachi.

He had no idea what he was getting himself into.

CHAPTER THREE

L ate in the afternoon of that same day, Vincent Panachi wheeled his Mercedes Benz 500 SL into the valet parking area at Shylock's and stopped it short of fifteen feet from the front entrance. A young, very fit parking attendant quickly approached the high gloss, chocolate brown luxury car the second it came to a halt. Vincent was a regular and the young man did not bother with the customary question asking a preference of keeping the vehicle up front. In this case the question would have been redundant. Vincent Panachi always parked up front, and was reputed to be a good tipper.

"Good afternoon, Mr. Panachi," the valet attendant greeted Vincent.

"Good afternoon to you," Vincent replied as he slipped the transmission into park, stepped out of the automobile, and shook the young man's hand. The attendant swung himself behind the Mercedes' steering wheel and carefully began backing it into Shylock's prime parking spot as Vincent walked away. A moment later Vincent entered through the front door and stopped to say hello to the two hostesses standing at the reception desk.

Meanwhile, a surveillance agent posted in the room of a third-floor condominium directly across the street from Shylock's front entrance snapped two photographs, first from a 200 mm lens camera, then he quickly shifted to a tripod mounted camera with a 300 mm lens for the second shot. The first camera instantly captured a perfect image of Vincent as he exited his Mercedes. The second shot took several minute adjustments before the clarity was tweaked to the agent's satisfaction. The end result was a perfectly focused picture of the Mercedes' New Jersey license plate, and its yellow background made those black registration letters and numbers more legible. The transplanted, southern good-ole-boy agent for the Organized Crime Task Force slapped his knee with joy as he exclaimed, "I got ya' now, you guinea sum-bitch!"

Vincent slowly walked through the crowded restaurant and stopped to speak with some of the regulars along the way towards the lower bar. Tony glanced up from his station and noticed Vincent approaching. Quickly, Tony turned to his bar back.

"Go get me a magnum of Moet champagne, right away."

"One Moet on the way," the younger man called over his shoulder as he immediately headed towards the kitchen area.

Vincent met the bar back on the steps that lead to the lower bar, and the younger man acknowledged him with a quick nod of his head as he scurried past. Downstairs Tony was motioning Vincent to his usual seat that faced the water by placing a cocktail napkin on the bar. Tony waited while Vincent swung himself onto the wooden bar stool, then the two shook hands. Within seconds, the magnum of champagne arrived. Vincent was a creature of habit and Tony was well trained to accommodate.

Tony opened the bottle of Moet. **POP!** It was a sound that Vincent had heard countless times before and intended to hear many more. The bartender filled Vincent's chilled glass and placed it in front of him. Suddenly, the golden, fine wine was filled with hundreds of bubbles racing towards the surface of the glass. Vincent nodded his head in approval. The sparkling, effervescent bubbles denoted the difference between a fine wine and mediocre champagne. Tony placed the large bottle in the ice bin then took care of the rest of the customers seated in his section.

It was five minutes before Tony could break free, and then he stopped in front of Vincent.

"Didn't bring the Scarab today?" Tony queried casually.

"No, I drove. I've got a dinner date in a couple of hours. In the meantime, I thought I'd come down here and see my pal."

"How was the party last night?" Tony asked smiling.

"It was just your usual floating champagne bucket."

"And I suppose you drank your fair share?"

"Naturally . . . and then some," Vincent replied laughing.

"Well, I'm glad you had a good time, but you sure missed something by leaving so early yesterday."

"How so?"

Tony placed his elbow on the bar and leaned closer to Vincent, "You know that hot blond with the chest unit . . . the one in here yesterday?"

"My friend, you just described half the women in Ft. Lauderdale. Could you be a little more specific, please?"

"She was sitting over there yesterday afternoon, directly across from you."

"Yes?" Vincent smirked.

"Well, 'ole buddy, she noticed you. As a matter of fact she even asked me your name after you left," Tony excitedly continued.

Vincent was flattered but continued to play his friend along.

"So, did you get her name?"

"Well, not really, but one of the other bartenders remembered it from her credit card, Jennifer Swords. She's a cute lady. I'm sorry you missed that one."

Vincent could not restrain his smile a moment longer. He gently pushed his champagne glass towards Tony, "Met her at last night's party, of all places, and I'm taking her to dinner tonight."

Tony stared at him for a few seconds, uncertain as to whether or not Vincent was pulling his leg.

"You're unbelievable . . . not to mention despicable. All I know, Vincent, is that I am sure glad I don't have a sister with blond hair and big tits hanging around here."

The two men broke into hearty laughter.

Tony had done precisely what Jennifer Swords had planned, which was to initially divulge Vincent's name to her the day before. Now, according to her plan, Vincent would never suspect their meeting to be anything more than an introduction through Slick Nick.

Jennifer had set the stage, and the bartender's performance had been outstanding.

*   *   *

While Vincent Panachi was sipping Moet at Shylock's, several bottles of Dom Perignon were being consumed in a posh hotel suite five miles south. The Marriott's Harbour Beach Hotel is located on a strip of white beach bordered by a small field of sea oats. Together they separate the magnificent hotel from the vast Atlantic Ocean. Manicured landscaping surrounds the lagoon-like swimming pool that has its water replenished by a tropical waterfall. Balconies offer views of Ft. Lauderdale to the north and views of the entrance to Port Everglades to the south. Late in the afternoon guests enjoy a view of mammoth cruise ships departing the port bound for the azure waters of the Bahamas and the Caribbean.

The drapes across the entire wall in the living room of the William P. Marriott suite were open, and a picturesque view filled the sliding glass doors. An elongated balcony spanned the distance alongside the glass panes. The sliding glass doors remained closed and the air conditioner blew full power twenty-four hours a day in order to keep out the torrid heat. When one pays three thousand dollars a night for an oceanfront, three bedroom suite the management has little concern over the excessive use of electricity. And as a frequent guest at the famous hotel, Anthony Vitale was afforded every luxury.

It was no secret among the hotel's staff that the *old man with the silver hair* tipped thirty percent on everything he ordered, and the room service personnel regularly argued over who would make the next delivery. It was also common knowledge that the elderly gentleman from New Jersey seldom left his hotel suite, and that particular unusual behavior fueled numerous rumors. Some speculated that he was an eccentric like the deceased, mega-wealthy Howard Hughes, while others speculated that there was more to it than eccentricity. There were brutal, goon-like ruffians who spoke with thick, coarse New Jersey accents always around him, and that was the fuel for the hottest rumor that the gray-haired man staying in the William P. Marriott suite was the *Mafia*!

A gentleman from Mr. Vitale's suite placed a room service order for two bottles of Dom Perignon and six chilled glasses. A beautiful twenty-one year old part-time model was selected to make the delivery. She carefully arranged the glasses placing them in a shallow pan of crushed ice accompanied by a decorative bowl of fresh strawberries, compliments of the hotel. As the young woman surveyed her handiwork, she grew increasingly excited from the anticipation of a big tip. In front of her were two large serving trays holding a sterling silver ice bucket filled with crushed ice, two bottles of Dom Perignon champagne, the pan containing the six chilled glasses, and the decorative bowl of strawberries. Satisfied with the presentation of both trays, the enterprising server recruited the help of her best friend to make the delivery. Each woman supported a tray on the flattened palm of her right hand, and hoisted it over her head while the left hand firmly grasped the edge of the tray to provide the necessary balance. The service elevator whisked them to the hotel's top floor, and from there it was only a matter of a few steps to the polished door of the William P. Marriott suite.

The young model gently tapped on the suite's door with her left hand then quickly replaced its handhold. Her friend was in position directly behind her.

"Yes, come in, ladies," a gruff, barrel-chested man with thick dark, curly hair remarked as he opened the door, "Just set the wine down on the dining table."

The overconfident young women immediately became timid, even though there was nothing out of the ordinary taking place in the suite; five men were sitting around the living room talking while the sixth attended to the room service order.

The model set her tray down and her friend placed hers alongside.

"Would you sign the check, please?" the model blushed and asked meekly. The man took the bill, added a thirty-percent tip, and signed Anthony Vitale's name with a flourish. While the Italian was looking down, the model quickly glanced at her girlfriend and noted that her face was flushed, also.

"I brought some fresh strawberries for you. I hope you like them . . . they're my favorite, especially with champagne," the young model blurted. She felt the heat rising off her rosy cheeks.

"Would you two young ladies come over here for a moment, please?" the old man with the silver hair, seated on the sofa softly addressed them.

"Yes, sir," the young women chimed simultaneously.

The elderly gentleman was removing a horse-choker sized money roll from his right trouser pocket as the women walked across the thick piled carpet. They watched him gently peel two, one hundred-dollar bills from the wad.

"You girls are very sweet . . . and thank you for the extra touch. Strawberries are my favorite, too." Anthony Vitale leaned forward, handing each woman a crisp one hundred-dollar bill. "Please accept these as a token of my appreciation. We'll probably need more champagne in about an hour. I would appreciate it if you two girls would deliver them."

Anthony noticed that the young girls were engrossed in their hundred dollar bills. The young model looked up to find the elderly gentleman staring at her, smiling.

"You know to this day I still remember my first hundred dollar tip," he said.

"Thank you," the young model and her friend returned the smile.

"The pleasure was all mine, girls." The head of the Vitale crime family held both hands up, palms facing outward; it had been.

The same barrel-chested man that had let them in also showed them to the door.

The young women clutched their respective one hundred dollar bills and quickly walked toward the nearby service elevator. While they were waiting for the service elevator, the two close friends heard faint, unintelligible voices through the suite's closed door. One thing they identified was that a good deal of the overheard conversation was in Spanish, very rapidly spoken Spanish.

The two young women could barely control their excitement, but did not speak a word in the hallway or in the elevator for fear of being overheard. Once they reached the basement they were safe to gossip. Both women spoke at the same time, which resulted in nothing intelligible. Afterwards, they burst into high-pitched giggles before they tried to speak again.

"What do you think?" the model queried.

"Did you see the South Americans? Do you think they were Colombians?" her friend answered with a question.

"Most definitely . . . three of them. And how about those burly Italians guys? They looked pretty spooky to me."

"Yeah, the one that signed the check gave me the creeps." She paused for a second before she added, "But I really like the older man. He's so sweet."

"Yeah he was sweet. I just can't believe that we were in the same room with the Mafia."

"Do you think he is some kind of Godfather-like boss, or something?" her friend asked lowering her voice.

"Do you?" the attractive young woman countered.

They both held their ground for twenty-seconds before they replied in unison, "Definitely!"

Without another word between them they entered the kitchen area giggling.

*   *   *

Upstairs, the atmosphere was more serious. The room service personnel were correct in their assumption that three of the six men in the suite were Colombian nationals. The trio had made a trip from their Cali, Colombia home specifically to meet with Anthony Vitale for the second time.

The first meeting had been one month to the day earlier in the most expensive suite at Atlantic City's famous Taj Mahal Casino and Hotel. The three bedroom suite was named "Alexander the Great" and cost them six thousand dollars a night for the week. To the head of a Colombian drug cartel that had been a paltry sum.

The meeting had finally taken place after a two day delay for "unavoidable circumstances." Señior Calerro and his two advisors were seated directly opposite Anthony Vitale and his two most trusted Capos. As the six men casually observed each other's attire, it was easy to see that they were from two distinctly different cultures. The Colombians wore silk shirts open at the neck that exposed thick gold chains, and pleated slacks with belts that matched exotic skinned boots. In contrast, the members of the Vitale crime family were impeccably dressed in twenty-five hundred dollar, flawlessly custom tailored Italian suits. With the exception of the slight bulge visible beneath all of the jackets' left armpits, they looked as if their clothing came directly from the pages of the *Gentleman's Quarterly* magazine. To the knowledgeable person it was obvious that the two men were packing a pistol snugly fit into a shoulder holster.

Señior Calerro began the conversation after the proper introductions had been made. The Colombians requested the meeting with the Vitale crime family, and it was proper etiquette for Anthony Vitale to defer from interrupting the designated speaker until the presentation had been completed. Anthony had attended countless meets, and learned to be a courteous and patient listener. Señior Calerro clasped his hands finger tips together, palms apart.

"Mr. Vitale, my advisors and I would like to thank you and your associates for attending this meeting. I would not have asked for it if it were not of the utmost importance."

Anthony Vitale nodded his head, but remained passively silent while he calmly twirled an expensive Cuban cigar between the fingers of his right hand, taking just enough puffs to prevent its glowing red tip from going out.

"First, please allow me to enlighten you with some background information . . . perhaps it will help you better understand our dilemma."

The head of the Vitale crime family nodded his head for Señior Calerro to continue.

"The American Drug Enforcement Agency (D.E.A.) launched a campaign against drug producing countries a couple of years ago. As a result of that thrust, we immediately ceased all operations and took a hiatus from our cocaine shipments. At that time we were of the opinion that your D.E.A. would soon grow weary of chasing small-time producers and move on within the year. Unfortunately, the D.E.A. continued their campaign longer than anticipated, and their continued presence has caused a problem for our organization. We have sustained our normal operating expenses such as farms, farmers, general field workers, etc. in addition to our considerable monthly political payoffs. In summary, the American drug war has depleted our organization of virtually all of its hard cash reserve. Of course we have hundreds of millions of dollars in real estate holdings, but now find ourselves desperately short of liquid cash. To compound the problem, one month ago I learned from our resident representative in Ft. Lauderdale that he is of the opinion that the smuggling groups located in and around the Miami area can no longer operate safely under the pressure that the drug war has created. To be perfectly honest, we have no desire to absorb the loss of another load of cocaine." The Colombian lifted his hands in a dramatic gesture to demonstrate his frustration with the entire situation, and Anthony Vitale obliged him with a sympathetic understanding nod of acknowledgement. It was détente at its finest. Señior Calerro then leaned forward in his seat until his elbows rested upon his knees and paused for a moment before he continued.

"Mr. Vitale, we have come to you with a proposition; a proposition that could not only resolve our problems, but could net your organization a very substantial amount of money." Señior Calerro paused once again, this time out of courtesy.

"You may continue," Anthony Vitale's voice was barley audible.

"Gracias," he continued, "What we propose is a partnership between our two organizations, and it will require a joint effort on each of our parts. Mr. Vitale, it is our understanding that the Vitale crime family controls the state of New Jersey. It is also our understanding that your organization is well respected among the crime families who control New York, in particular, New York City. What I propose is this. Our organization has obtained a secure arrangement where we can ship multiple loads of cocaine via Avianca Airlines directly from Cali, Colombia to New York City's J.F.K. International Airport. Now, what we respectfully request from your family is the connection on the New York end. If your organization could arrange to have certain baggage handlers at the J.F.K. airport in their pocket well . . ." Señior Calerro's voice trailed off while his eyes sparkled with enthusiasm. A minute later the head of the Colombian drug cartel added, "The potential profit during our first year could reach as high as one hundred million dollars. That's fifty million for your organization, and fifty million for ours. And, if I may speak candidly, it will take every bit of our share to meet the overhead expenses we will incur during this upcoming year. We are confident that the

American D.E.A. will finally leave after another year spent chasing their tails throughout South America." That shrewd observation brought smiles to all six men seated in the luxurious suite.

No one spoke while Anthony Vitale twirled his cigar, puffed it, and then exhaled heavy clouds of smoke. Meanwhile, proper etiquette denoted that the Colombians wait as long as necessary until his counterpart responded to the business proposal.

"Señior Calerro, I am honored by your proposition. As the head of an organization, I can sympathize with your situation. However, this important decision is something I cannot make without carefully weighing the benefits, and I require some time. Nevertheless, let me offer this—I will carefully consider your proposal over the next month. I will be in Ft. Lauderdale exactly thirty days from today; perhaps we could meet there and then?"

"Thirty days from today in Ft. Lauderdale, Florida. I will be there," Señior Calerro allowed a smile to form across his face while he extended his hand toward Anthony Vitale.

"Fine. I will be staying at the Marriott Harbour Beach Hotel in the William P. Marriott suite."

"Bueno," Señior Calerro replied.

"In the meantime, if your organization requires some additional cash to carry you through . . ." Anthony Vitale calmly suggested.

"No Señior. That will not be necessary. There will be plenty of money after we reach our agreement," Señior Calerro replied as he held his hands up, palms facing outward towards the silver hair American Italian.

The one common element the six men shared was that their word was their bond. It was an understood code of ethics enforced by all crime families whether they were of Italian or Spanish heritage. Consequently, there had never been a question in any of the gentlemen's minds as to whether or not the "meet" would take place. Thirty calendar days later, the same six men met in the Marriott Harbour Beach Hotel in Ft. Lauderdale, Florida.

The William P. Marriott suite was not nearly as plush as the Taj Mahal's suite, but nevertheless, it was comfortable. Once again, Señior Calerro sat directly across from Anthony Vitale. The other four men were seated on either side of their respective bosses with a glass of chilled champagne in their hands. The Colombians had been speaking rapid-fire Spanish among themselves, but as soon as the head of the Vitale crime family cleared his throat silence fell over the room.

"Gentlemen, thank you for coming to today's meeting." Anthony Vitale directed his soft-spoken comment to Señior Calerro. The statement was a polite way of announcing that it was time to get down to the business at hand.

Anthony Vitale delicately held the long-stemmed crystal champagne glass with two fingers and the thumb of his right hand. Hardly the sort of behavior that one would expect from someone known as *The Shark*, but the years had mellowed him considerably. Now he was all business, and the position as the head of the crime family had kept his aged mind sharp. He was a thinker, a schemer, and every projected operation followed an orderly, systematic master plan. Today Anthony Vitale had a plan for the Colombians.

"It is true what you have heard about our organization controlling operations within the state of New Jersey, just as it is true that the Vitale crime family is well respected among those crime families in control of New York City. Gentlemen, it has taken decades of cultivation to get and keep the right politicians in our pockets. Ours is a people business—gambling, prostitution, loans, etc. It is a protection we have enjoyed throughout decades of political changes, and the politicians in power would not take kindly to our expansion of business interests into the importation of cocaine. I am truly sorry gentlemen, but I just cannot risk the security that is fundamentally the backbone of our operations." Anthony Vitale leaned forward and placed his glass of champagne on the coffee table, then sat back. His hands were flat, palms facing outward and fingers outstretched in an apologetic manner while he stared intently into Señior Calerro's eyes. He continued, "There is certainly no offense intended. Business is business, and I hold the highest regard for you and your business associates. However, I hope you understand my awkward position. I'm afraid the Vitale crime family must pass on your generous offer."

Anthony Vitale's eyes held Señior Calerro's for what seemed an eternity, yet it had been nothing more than a long silent moment. Suddenly a broad smile formed across Señior Calerro's face. No matter what decision had been made, diplomacy, tact, and respect were the rules of the game.

"We thank you for your valuable time while considering our offer, but regret that we could not reach an agreement with the Vitale family. You have our utmost respect for allowing us your audience."

Anthony Vitale returned the smile and slowly bowed his head in acknowledgment for the respect that the head of the Colombian drug cartel had demonstrated. The Colombian's response had been precisely the one that Anthony had hoped for. Señior Calerro had shown him respect, and in return he would propose something that could help them both.

Anthony picked up his glass and casually sipped the fine champagne.

"I did not mean to imply that our families could not reach an agreement profitable to each of us. I am merely stating that your business proposal is not politically correct for the Vitale family at this time. However, perhaps your family would be interested in joining forces in another proposition?"

Señior Calerro quickly glanced first to his right, and then quickly left. His advisors gave him their nods of approval without a single word spoken.

"What did the Vitale crime family have in mind?"

Anthony smiled and turned toward the Capo seated to his immediate left. He instructed him, "Let's open the other bottle of champagne for our guests." Anthony redirected his attention to Señior Calerro and commented, "I think you're going to thoroughly enjoy this." Five seconds later the sound of the cork ejecting from the expensive bottle filled the room.

Anthony gently leaned back and the sofa's cushioned back sank deep from his weight. He was very comfortable with the ambiance of the meeting and was particularly keen on this project. The plan was not Anthony's original idea, but rather an improvement over one that his father had embarked upon twenty-plus years ago. The Capos seated on either side of him remembered all too well as both of them had been soldiers of the Vitale crime family during those days when Anthony's father had put his scheme into action. Now, twenty-plus years later, the Colombians had provided the second generation Vitale with another shot at his father's master plan. Naturally some variations had been made to bridge the changes two decades had brought, yet it was still basically his father's plan.

"If I understand your problem correctly, Señior Calerro, your organization needs somewhere in the neighborhood of fifty million dollars to see it through another year. And it is also my understanding that those funds are required to maintain numerous monthly payoffs, as well as your own organization's fixed overhead costs. May I assume that those persons are all located in Colombia?"

Señior Calerro had absolutely no idea where Anthony Vitale was headed with his train of thought.

"Sí, that is correct. All monies are paid in our country."

"Perfect. Now that we have established that the funds are paid in South America, please allow me to ask you another question. Would you say that it is likely the dollars will remain within your country?"

Señior Calerro shrugged his shoulders, "I suppose so, Señior. These are simple people . . . they do not make overseas investments."

"Very good, my friend. Here is my proposal—your organization needs fifty million dollars. The Vitale crime family will give you those fifty million dollars . . . in flawless counterfeit twenty dollar bills. Currency made so identical that even you could never tell the difference, much less the farmers and policemen of rural Colombia." Anthony paused for dramatics and waited the five minutes it took for Señior Calerro's response.

"And what would the Vitale crime family's take be?"

Anthony placed his hands together like he was preparing to pray, and replied, "Señior Calerro, our family is here to offer our assistance in your time of need. We are not greedy people and would want nothing in advance. The risk of production will be all ours. All I ask in return is that we receive a twenty-five percent payment for services rendered upon delivery of the fifty million dollars. Twelve million five hundred thousand dollars. I think this is an equitable arrangement taking into consideration that we have to bear the expense of production. At any rate, the end result should supply your organization with ample cash flow to resolve your current problems." Anthony Vitale now had Señior Calerro's undivided attention while he further explained his plan.

Señior Calerro turned to his advisors for their opinions, and what followed were several minutes of rapid fire Spanish between the three Colombians.

Silence fell over the room, and then Señior Calerro nodded his head in agreement with his two men. The head of the Colombian drug cartel stood and extended his hand toward Anthony Vitale. Anthony instinctively stood and accepted the gentleman's hand.

"Mr. Vitale, we have reached an agreement. We will do business together."
"Excellent. My nephew, Vincent Panachi, will represent the Vitale family during our business transactions.

"Then I'll be looking forward to doing business with your Vincent Panachi."

The ringing of six crystal champagne glasses clinking together sealed the deal just as a rap at the door sounded.

"Room service."

CHAPTER FOUR

T he orange-yellow sun fell below the horizon and cast a soft, diffused light across the Intracoastal Waterway. The go-fasts were rafted off one another three deep towards the center of the canal. Vincent Panachi savored one last look at the golden sunset before he cashed out and left the bar. When Tony returned with his check he queried, "See you tomorrow?"

"My friend, I try my very best to come here only on the days that end in the letter Y," Vincent grinned.

"Sunday, Monday, Tuesday . . ." Tony reached Thursday before he realized that he had been had. He laughed and waved off Vincent as if to dismiss him and remarked, "Tomorrow then."

"Tomorrow," Vincent smiled. He slipped a twenty-dollar bill underneath the long-stemmed champagne glass, and then slid off the barstool.

As soon as Vincent reached the restaurant's upper level, Tony grabbed the telephone that hung beneath the cash register at his station. He quickly punched in a three digit number for an in-house call, the valet captain answered and Tony instructed him.

"Vincent Panachi is on his way out the door. Bring his Mercedes up front, please."

"Right away, Tony," the captain said.

The valets knew that having Vincent's car out front waiting for him when he exited the building was good for a guaranteed ten-spot. When Vincent came through the front doors of Shylock's his Mercedes Benz was fifteen feet from the doorway, idling. True to form, he palmed the parking attendant a crisp ten-dollar bill as he gracefully slid behind the Mercedes' highly polished wooden steering wheel. Darkness had already fallen, and the luxury automobile's glossy finish brilliantly sparkled beneath the canopied lights of Shylock's covered entranceway. Several attractive women watched as the handsome Italian pulled onto the roadway and sped away. They were not the only ones who had shown interest in the wealthy young man.

From the window of the third floor condominium across the street from Shylock's, an agent from the Organized Crime Task Force snapped four more pictures, two from each camera. He continued watching Vincent's car until it turned the corner at the stop sign and headed north. The agent grasped the cheap ballpoint pen he kept in his shirt pocket and made a quick notation of the surveillance time on a yellow legal pad. Afterwards, he walked through the darkened living room of the condominium to the kitchen where a telephone was mounted on the wall. Quickly he dialed a cellular telephone number. The phone rang twice before a voice on the other end answered bluntly, "Yeah."

"The guinea sum-bitch is on the road," the agent informed him.

The agent who received the call was positioned in a strategic location where he could photograph the incoming automobiles and their occupants as they valet parked at Slick Nick's restaurant.

"I'm ready. Since it's the old man's annual party, don't you think it's only right that he should have some pictures to remember it by?"

Twenty minutes later, Vincent Panachi pulled up in front of Jennifer's condominium. He glanced to the side and saw her through the clear, highly polished plate glass window. Jennifer's blond hair cascaded over a red leather dress that stopped midway down her muscular thighs. Above, the soft calfskin firmly held her breasts together to form a sensual cleavage. She waved to Vincent with her left arm, and the movement sent reflective rays of light from her Rolex watch's diamond bezel. Jennifer walked towards the front door while Vincent watched through the Mercedes' passenger window. The lobby had two large circular tiered crystal chandeliers that shown down upon her as she gracefully moved across the marble tile floor. Vincent noticed the glimmer from her necklace and its reflection caught his eye a number of times as she approached his automobile. Vincent leaned across the seat and pulled the door latch at the same moment she reached for the passenger's door handle. He gently shoved the door open while he greeted her. Jennifer replied, "Hello, Vincent" as she slid onto the leather seat, closed the door, shifted herself in the seat, and turned towards him. The headlights from a passing car suddenly reflected off her necklace and Vincent's eyes instinctively shifted toward the shimmering piece of jewelry. It was then that he first laid eyes upon Jennifer's "trophy"—*STILETTO*. The word seemed a bit strange to Vincent, but his inquisitiveness quickly passed. It had never been his nature to be unnecessarily curious for he certainly did not fancy people prying into his personal affairs. He reasoned that she would tell him when she was ready for him to know. Slick Nick had thought that very same thing. Now he knew.

*   *   *

It had been ten days since Slick Nick made love with Jennifer, but to him it had seemed longer. No one had ever been so amorous with him, and Jennifer had given him the finest sexual moments ever. He was certain that she had fallen madly in love with him. On the contrary, Jennifer found Nick to be crude and inexperienced in bed. She had gone through with it only to hold his attention until she could meet Vincent Panachi, and nothing more. Jennifer was in full control over the lovesick spell she had cast upon Nick. She finally realized just how far-gone he was when he had called early that morning and asked her out. Nick had been appalled when he had learned that Jennifer was going out with Vincent Panachi. There was no logical reason for her to have told Slick Nick that she had a dinner date with someone else. However, under the circumstances, she had no choice because dinner that evening was being hosted at Slick Nick's restaurant. The event was the annual *landlubber* party celebrating Anthony Vitale's birthday, and as usual, it was being held the following evening of the boat party in order to give those who had missed the gala event a second chance to pay their respects to the old man.

It took Vincent and Jennifer a half-hour to drive from her condominium to Slick Nick's restaurant in Boca Raton. Conversation came easily and the two talked during the entire drive. Meanwhile, the agent from the task force was busy snapping pictures of the valet parking entrance to the Italian restaurant. One after another, limousines pulled beneath the covered valet area and dropped off their passengers. The agent had expected a good turn out for the annual bash, yet the sudden frequency momentarily overwhelmed him. He exclaimed aloud, in spite of the fact that there was no one there to hear his excited statement, "God damn, there are so many of the guinea bastards I don't know if I can load the camera fast enough." The task force agent snapped one particular photograph that captured the perfect image of Anthony "The Shark" Vitale and his two most trusted capos as they exited a long white limousine. They were all smiles, almost as if they had posed for the picture. Of course the agent involved had no way of knowing that they were all smiling because of the outcome of the meeting with the Colombians.

The agent's camera steadily clicked away until two rolls of film had been exposed. He was three-quarters through the third roll when he captured four perfect shots of Vincent Panachi and an unknown female companion exiting Vincent's Mercedes Benz. Ordinarily he would not have taken four pictures of the same subject, but Jennifer looked absolutely stunning that evening. Consequently, her face had been perfectly centered in two of the four photographs.

Slick Nick positioned himself at the restaurant's front entrance. Even Jennifer had to admit to herself that Nick looked rather dapper in his jet-black tuxedo. Nick greeted Vincent and Jennifer at the doorway and complimented both of them on how nice they looked. "Thank you, Nick," Jennifer purred. Nick flashed a smile in return, yet inside he was in pain. Knowing that he would see her tonight with someone else was one thing; actually seeing her was entirely another matter. Once again, Jennifer Swords had cut deep into his heart.

Inside the Vitale crime family was assembled in the private dining area where several four-top tables had been placed together to form an elongated T-shape that was deemed the "Table of Honor" among the Vitale crime family. Anthony Vitale was seated at the top of the T and was flanked on either side by his capos.

Within an hour the private dining room filled to capacity. The champagne flowed freely and it seemed that a long-stemmed, crystal glass was permanently attached to Jennifer's right hand. Her left arm affectionately intertwined Vincent's right arm. They were the perfect picture of a couple falling in love, even though it was only their first date. Anthony Vitale noticed it, and so did Slick Nick. To say that Nick was jealous would have been an understatement; he was resentfully envious.

Dinner began with an appetizer of tortellini covered in Nick's specialty pink sauce. This unique blend of white and red sauces was so delicious that the old man himself had once suggested the unorthodox blend for a marinara sauce to the owner of his favorite restaurant in New Jersey. How could the proprietor refuse such a request from the head of a crime family? That very same week it had appeared on the menu, and much to his surprise had been as well accepted in New Jersey as Mr. Vitale had told him it was in sunny South Florida.

Anthony Vitale kept tabs on his favorite nephew throughout the entire four-course dinner by observing Vincent from the corner of his eye. It was obvious to the old man that Vincent was infatuated with this blond bombshell, and he made a mental note to ask Vincent about her during their after dinner talk. Anthony was not the only person interested in this new affection; Slick Nick was unobtrusively noting their every move and every reaction. Pangs of jealously shot through Nick's body with the force of an adrenaline surge while he watched Jennifer's fingers affectionately stroke Vincent's forearm. Somehow Nick managed to contain the jealous pain while he mingled among the capos and top soldiers attending the dinner. However, no matter whom he was talking to, he could not help but glance toward Jennifer and Vincent.

Vincent noticed Nick observing them several times during the five star dinner, yet it was not something Vincent was uncomfortable with. Nick had always looked at Vincent with eyes filled with longing and desire, but fate had not dealt the cards that way. He would never be Anthony Vitale's favorite nephew. Slick Nick was as far up the ladder in the Vitale crime family as he could ever hope to be, and he knew it. So did Vincent.

After the white tuxedoed waiters served a dessert of Italian cheesecake, Anthony Vitale stood. He gently clanged the side of his crystal glass with a spoon, and the ringing immediately silenced the private dining room. All eyes turned toward the head of the table, and Jennifer's long blond hair swung as she turned to face the elderly gentleman. Vincent also swiveled to face the old man but was somewhat distracted by the lustrous sheen of Jennifer's hair.

Anthony cleared his throat once, a habit he was known for, before he began, "My family, I'd like to propose a toast." Anthony raised his champagne glass to eye level as he continued, "To health, love and money!"

The crowded dining room burst into cheer while raising glasses high into the air, "Salute."

When the noise receded the head of the Vitale crime family added, "And I think I speak for all of us when I say we're in business for the money."

The crowd went wild with applause. Every member of the Vitale crime family had become a part of organized crime for just that reason. There were others in the room who may not have taken the toast in the same context, namely Jennifer. At least that was what Vincent had believed; he had absolutely no idea that Jennifer knew who he really was and what he really did for a living. The elderly gentleman set his glass down as he motioned towards the capo seated to his immediate right.

"There are several of you present that I would like to speak with individually after dinner. Mr. Pillegi will summon you when I am ready. Thank you for a wonderful birthday surprise."

The dining room exploded with applause before Anthony had time to sit down. Vincent swore to himself that he saw the old man blush. Finally, Anthony broke the enthusiastic applause by holding up both hands, palms facing outwards, and said, "Thank you . . . thank you all!" before he took his seat.

Jennifer turned towards Vincent and flashed him her best radiant smile. Vincent returned the smile and winked at her. She leaned over and kissed him ever so lightly on the check and even so, her pouting, glossy lips left a red lipstick mark on the side of Vincent's face. Jennifer giggled as she wiped the smear from his cheek. It was a move meant to get Vincent's attention.

Anthony turned and whispered to Capo Pelligi. Vincent just happened to be looking in their direction when the Capo leaned forward and looked directly at Vincent. Their eyes met while Anthony continued whispering in Pellegi's ear. Finally, Vincent broke the stare by glancing back at Jennifer. Seconds later, Anthony Vitale stood and all eyes turned toward the old man in anticipation of another toast. Instead the head of the crime family held up his hands and said, "If you will excuse me, please, Mr. Pelligi will begin summoning a few of you to the special dining room now. Thank you all for attending this evening. It makes an old man's birthday very special."

Once again the whole room burst into an earsplitting applause that lasted until Anthony made his way to the secluded dining room at the rear of the restaurant. Slick Nick watched from across the room as the head of the crime family entered the posh dining area.

An interior designer of Anthony Vitale's choosing had decorated the special dining room. Moreover, the middle-aged woman he had chosen had been his mistress at the time. Now a year had passed since that affair ended, and Anthony remembered her with fond memories every time he sat among the custom built furnishings. Eight black lacquer oriental chairs surrounded a one-inch-thick, smoked glass, rectangular table. The heavy piece of glass was supported by a pair of black angular pedestals that sunk deep into thick, piled carpet made from velvety, emerald green yarn loops. Dim accent lights shown concentrated beams upon expensive artwork that adorned the grass-cloth-covered walls. The room made the ultimate statement of wealth and sophistication, which was a far cry from the way Anthony had lived among the streets of Newark, New Jersey thirty years ago. The head of the Vitale crime family used this special dining room as his location for conducting family business. He would have never agreed to meet with the Colombians in this room, yet for the elite members of his crime family the back dining room at Slick Nick's was the favored location. Slick Nick was aware of these meetings, but due to his relatively low ranking within the upper management level of the crime family, he had never been invited to attend one of the exclusive gatherings. Nick was paranoid by nature, and felt that it was he that they were talking about behind closed doors. Those thoughts haunted him to the point that he could no longer accept the not knowing. One night after all the employees had left, Nick had an electronic eavesdropping system installed in the special dining room. Its receiver was carefully hidden in his office which had always been off limits to all employees.

From that night forward Nick had eavesdropped on every meeting and had satisfied himself that the boys were not talking about him. Nick found the meetings to be extremely interesting and could not resist the temptation to continue eavesdropping with his new toy. He learned a lot about the inner workings of the Vitale family's business, probably enough to get him killed if the old man ever found out. When Slick Nick saw Anthony Vitale enter the private dining room, he graciously excused himself from the party and headed toward his office. Once inside it took him less than a minute to uncover and turn on the hidden receiver. Immediately, the covert transmitter began transmitting.

Meanwhile, Capo Pillegi walked over and placed his hand on Vincent's shoulder. In a gentle voice filled with a heavy New Jersey accent, the Capo said to Vincent, "Mister Vitale would like to speak with you, in private. He is waiting in the private dining room." The heavy-set, full-blooded Italian turned to Jennifer and politely said, "He won't be long, Miss. I'll make sure of it."

Jennifer smiled as she looked over at Vincent and replied, "That's quite all right . . . I'm a big girl." Jennifer flashed her blue eyes up at the Capo and continued, "Besides, you would protect me . . . wouldn't you?"

Vincent smiled as the fireplug-built man blushed and agreed, "But of course, Miss."

Vincent excused himself from the table and walked towards the dining room. Along the way he stopped and briefly spoke with a few of the family members.

However, the conversations were kept to an absolute minimum because Anthony Vitale did not like to be kept waiting.

Five minutes later Vincent entered through the double, carved oak doors. The old man was seated at the head of the table, on the far end away from the door. When Vincent saw the old man sitting across the plush room, the strangest thought came into his mind—for a split second Vincent pictured himself when he was a much younger man, being tutored in the ways of the world by his Uncle Anthony. Now, twenty years later, he could still hear his uncle's voice echoing somewhere from deep within his memory, "Vincent, never, never sit with your back to the door. Always know who is entering the room . . . any room. Remember this for as long as you live and you will live long."

Anthony Vitale placed both his hands on the chair's armrests and pushed himself up. Vincent called out from across the room, "Please, don't stand on my account. I am the one who is honored to be here."

The elderly gentleman released the tension in his frail arms and smiled as he said, "My favorite nephew . . . come in, come in."

Vincent walked past the chairs surrounding the elongated dinner table and outstretched his hand toward Anthony. The head of the crime family accepted Vincent's hand with both of his and vigorously shook it. Vincent marveled at the strength of the frail old man's grasp and met its force with half the invigoration. Anthony released his grip and made a waving motion with his right hand toward a chair. "Sit down, Vincent, and talk with me for a few minutes."

Vincent gently pulled out one of the Oriental chairs and replied, "Thank you, sir. I'd like that."

Anthony's eyes smiled with pleased approval at the polish and good manners his favorite nephew displayed. Vincent was worlds away from the streets of Newark and the rough neighborhoods that he and Vincent's father had roamed decades before. To Anthony, Vincent was a representation of what was to come of the Vitale crime family during the next generation, long after his demise.

Once Vincent was seated, thirty seconds of silence fell between the two while he curiously watched the elderly gentleman's eyes. They were aged and the crow's-feet along the sides emphasized that. However, Anthony's eyes were also clear and cold. Vincent knew for certain that those eyes were windows to a very shrewd, calculating, analytical mind. Finally, Anthony Vitale spoke.

"Vincent, we had an opportunity to talk on the yacht about your private life, so tonight we are going to talk business." The elderly gentleman paused for a second.

"Yes, Sir," Vincent responded.

"The family is taking on a new project . . . and interestingly enough it is something that your father had a hand in nearly thirty years ago, just before his death."

The statement took Vincent by surprise and he caught himself leaning slightly forward in anticipation of what Anthony Vitale might say next.

"You see, my boy, your father and I were involved in a counterfeiting scheme that would have distributed the funny-money through the family's numbers runners. It was a beautiful plan, but unfortunately, one that never became reality."

"Why? What happened?"

"There is a printer that your father knew very well. He's not Italian, but he can be trusted. You may be wondering, 'How am I so sure of that?' Well, it is because he has already taken a fall for the Vitale crime family and didn't squeal on anyone. Just before this 'artist,' as your father affectionately referred to him, was arrested, he worked on the counterfeiting operation with your father. He could have very easily implicated your father, yet instead held his tongue. The printer did not rat on anyone . . . even after the Feds sentenced him to twenty years in prison."

"What happened to him?" Vincent asked.

Anthony cracked a half-smile, "He was released from Leavenworth Penitentiary eight years ago, and the family has been taking care of him ever since. The years that the government stole from him have left him angry inside. He knows that he would never have to work again if he so chose, yet he still has this desire to complete the plans we made decades ago. Nevertheless, I have always turned him down . . . even though I know full well that he is still capable of producing the most realistic looking twenty dollar bills one has ever seen. At that time the Vitale crime family had no resources available to distribute enough funny-money to make the operation feasible . . . until now.

Anthony paused for a few seconds while he crossed his legs, right over left.

"Counterfeiting? As in print your own?"

"Precisely. I have just cut a deal with some Colombians to give them fifty-million dollars in counterfeit, twenty dollar bills. Upon delivery they will give us twenty-five percent—twelve and a half million in real currency. It is an inspired deal—they get to meet their expenses; the money stays out of the country; and we get to make a tidy profit."

"Twelve point five sounds like a big number."

The old man laughed a good belly laugh, "Yeah, big number." After the smile left his face, he leaned forward and placed his wrinkled hand on top of Vincent's and said, "I want you to handle this operation for me. This will be your first big operation for the family, and with that responsibility comes your first big piece of the action. You handle this right and make me proud of you, and I will see to it that you receive two and a half million dollars for running the operation."

Vincent did not know what to say. For a few seconds his mouth involuntarily hung open. Even when you work for the crime families it is not every day that one is offered a two point five-million dollar payday. Vincent quickly gathered his composure.

"I'm honored that you have chosen me for such a delicate undertaking. However, I recall you claiming that you would never work with the Colombians."

"That statement pertained to drugs . . . this is money, and money knows no bias."

"Never a truer statement spoken. Cash is king."

It was another of the elderly gentleman's philosophies that he had often shared with a much younger Vincent Panachi, and now, it warmed his heart to hear his protégée apply it to real world economics. Anthony Vitale affectionately patted Vincent's hand as if he were patting the son's he never had.

"Then it's settled. Capo Pelligi will put you in touch with the Colombians."

"I do have a couple of questions, if you don't mind."

Anthony Vitale raised both his hands from the table top and held them palms up, "Of course you may ask."

"What about the printer?"

"We call him 'The Quill,' and I will personally speak with him. Capo Pelligi will know what to do. And your other question?"

Vincent paused for several seconds, for dramatics, before he asked, "Will my two and a half million dollar payment be REAL money?"

Anthony Vitale burst out laughing, just as Vincent had hoped. Vincent always tried to make the elderly gentleman laugh; it was something Anthony Vitale had rarely known.

Meanwhile, across the restaurant in Slick Nick's office, Nick was hunched over the electronic receiver. For some reason, the transmissions had not come in entirely clear and most of the conversation had been completely unintelligible, which pissed Nick off to no end. Anybody else and it probably would not have mattered. However, since it was Vincent Panachi conversing with the old man, Nick desperately wanted to know everything that took place behind those sacred closed doors. The conversation between Vincent Panachi and Anthony Vitale had faded in and out, soft then loud while Nick cursed the sophisticated piece of electronic wizardry. He painstakingly fumbled with the receiver's silver knobs until one statement blared through loud and clear—*I'm going to see to it that you receive two and a half million dollars for running the operation."* Seconds later, the receiver had gone dead again.

Nick's full attention was focused on the problem with the receiver and he did not hear the persistent, knocks on his office door. The restaurant's Maitre d' heard voices through Nick's closed office door and immediately recognized Anthony Vitale's voice from the toast he had given earlier that evening. Finally, Nick heard a knock at his office door and hurriedly switched off the receiver. Nick jerked open his office door and growled, "Yes, what is it?"

"I'm sorry; I did not realize you were with someone."

"I'm alone, you fool. Now, what is it that you want?"

The Maitre d' despised the subservient manner in which Slick Nick treated his employees, and he had always told himself that he would screw him at the first opportunity. The Maitre d' smiled as his mind quickly accessed the voices he had just heard. He knew that the head of the Vitale crime family was in the special dining room.

"The guests are asking for more champagne. Shall I crack open another case for them? You told me to check with you first."

"That order was for normal patrons, NOT Anthony Vitale's birthday party, damn it."

The Maitre d' stood there and silently took the verbal abuse. He was not listening to Nick. His thoughts were lost deep in the satisfaction of knowing that finally he had a means to get Nick, but good. The Maitre d' smiled at Nick, then turned and walked towards the wine cellar.

CHAPTER FIVE

M onday mornings in Ft. Lauderdale begin with a capital M; the entire city of "Liquor-dale" is in slow motion from the partying weekend. Sunday winds it all up, and then it's back to the daily grind that supplies the party funds. Whether it is hustler or hairdresser, Monday mornings are dedicated to the pursuit of the all mighty dollar, and activities are extremely slow along the waterfront bars and restaurants. Very few boats are seen on the Intracoastal Waterway, and liquor sales drop dramatically. It is almost as if the city of the rich and famous is in mourning, but not to worry; Wednesday will begin a whole new surge of energy into the party circuit.

It was 11:30 a.m. when Jennifer entered the prestigious hair salon. The hair stylist smiled as she walked towards the reception desk, and then greeted Jennifer.

"Hi. Right on time, as usual," Darlene said.

Jennifer flashed a smile, "Hi. Are you ready?"

"Of course," the stylist replied as she motioned Jennifer towards her station.

Jennifer crossed the elegant salon and casually nodded at the faces she recognized, although she did not know their names. The same women were there every other Monday, just like Jennifer, to get their hair colored. It was a routine that both the hair stylist and the patron had repeated countless times, and each knew exactly what to do. Jennifer placed her Gucci purse on the counter top then gently slipped into the cotton robe. At the same time, Darlene slipped into a pair of rubber gloves to protect her hands from the harsh chemicals. Within a matter of moments, the stylist was busy applying the concoction that kept Jennifer Swords' lengthy hair blond.

As with all hair stylists, the next two hours were filled with small talk. Girl talk. Gossip. Who's doing who; when and where. Hair salon gab, supreme. In order for the hair stylist to keep gossip current, she must eventually ask the question, "Anybody new in your love life? Someone special?" One must be extremely careful how that question is answered, because within a matter of days the information given in the fullest confidence will be flashed about the salon's elite clientele. Collectively, these women could make or break a relationship. Many torrid love affairs have caused nasty divorces because of the rumor mill. On the other hand, the salon's gossip train provides an avenue to travel should someone *want* to broadcast their new found loves. This ploy is often used to let potential competitors know that a certain man is being actively pursued, and nothing quite rivals a cat fight between two women in it for their future security. It is a society where the word *work* is referred to as, "That four letter word."

Jennifer and Darlene gabbed during the entire two hour session, and when 1:30 p.m. rolled around the stylist knew all about Jennifer and the handsome man she was dating, Vincent Panachi.

"Dah-ling, you know whatever you tell me stays right here," Darlene made a point of repeating several times.

"But, of course, that's why I can tell you," Jennifer remarked.

Jennifer told her all about the exquisite party on the yacht and how they met, then about the dinner party the following evening, and how she and Vincent had kissed long and passionately, like teenagers, when he dropped her off at her condominium. By the end of the two hours, the stylist had enough information to spread the word, and Jennifer knew exactly who Darlene would call first with the hot news flash—Slick Nick. Nick was not as slick as he thought because the hair stylist did not hesitate one moment to tell Jennifer that Nick had pumped her for information.

"To think that he thought he could pry confidential information from me by offering me money . . . Dah-ling, it's absolutely appalling."

It was not until several nights later, when Nick and Darlene had champagne and dinner that the hair stylist's tongue loosened. After two bottles of Moet, she had told all; all that Jennifer had led her to believe. Without knowing, the hair stylist had helped Jennifer shrewdly manipulate Nick, and now, Jennifer had given her just enough information to pass along to Nick. That juicy gossip combined with the fact that he saw her with Vincent Panachi would put an end to his pestering pursuit of her.

Jennifer looked in the mirror as Darlene held a handful of hair high above her head. Her dark roots were blond once again. Jennifer looked in the larger mirror to check the overall coloring, but it was not her hair that caught her eye. Without realizing she had been doing so, the fingers on Jennifer's left hand were playing with her necklace while she was lost deep in thought about Slick Nick and the hair stylist. Almost as if she were inserting pins into a voodoo doll, Jennifer slowly ran her fingers across the diamond studded word *STILETTO*. When she averted her eyes from the necklace, she smiled. Her hair was the perfect color.

*   *   *

Lunch hour at Shylock's on any Monday is slow, but this particular Monday was extremely dead. Tony did not mind, however, because it gave him a chance to restock the bar with supplies. The weather was clear, and the temperature pleasant; a beautiful South Florida day. The sliding glass doors were opened all the way so that the patrons seated at the waterfront tables could enjoy the slight sea breeze. There were no boats moored at Shylock's lengthy pier to block the view of the Intracoastal; an event that very seldom happened, and when it did, inevitably it was a Monday. Absolutely no one was seated at the lower bar, Tony's bar. Mondays were a breeze.

The lack of traffic up and down the Intracoastal Waterway, as well as the lull experienced by Shylock's every Monday, did not go unnoticed by the Organized Crime Task Force. They shut down their surveillance on Mondays, but the agents would meet at the condominium across the waterway from Shylock's at about 11 a.m. where they would discuss their strategy for the upcoming week. Mondays were also the day set aside to develop the numerous rolls of film the surveillance teams had snapped during the busy weekend. The multitude of exposed film was developed in the condominium's converted bedroom, a specially illuminated room for processing photographic material.

Senior Agent Mark Murray and the agent who had been assigned to the valet entrance at Slick Nick's restaurant were seated on a long sofa in the condo's living room. It was a few minutes past noon, and the other agent's day off. The only reason he had stopped by the condo was to drop off the rolls of film he had shot the evening before at Anthony Vitale's party. When he walked through the door he tossed a sack full of exposed thirty-five millimeter film into the darkroom then swung through the kitchen on his way towards the living room. The agent plopped down on the sofa with a cold beer in his hand. Agent Murray looked him up and down before he remarked.

"A little early for a drink, isn't it?"

"It's afternoon, and it is my day off," the agent replied with a grin as he rolled his left wrist so that he could read the time on his watch.

"So it is. What are you doing here?"

"I shot a bunch of film last night, and I thought you might want to develop these in a hurry. A lot of biggies showed up. Got some beautiful shots." The agent took a swig from the long-necked bottle.

Suddenly Agent Murray became interested, mostly because the other surveillance cameras had shot nothing but routine pictures of go-fasts and expensive, luxury cars. Mark pondered the thought for a moment then called out across the condominium.

"Hey, I want you to develop those restaurant shots, now. Put everything else on hold, and let's have a look at those."

"Yes, Sir," a voice hollered out from around the corner.

Mark and the other agent spent twenty minutes telling lies and swapping tales before the darkroom operator delivered the first batch of photographs. His timer was running in the darkroom, so he casually tossed the photos onto the coffee table while he explained, "Timing is everything with this photosensitive paper." Without waiting for a reply to his remark, he turned and hurriedly walked towards the converted bedroom.

The agent who shot the pictures leaned forward and set his beer on the coffee table. In the same movement, he scooped up the photographs with both hands, and then leaned back until he was pressed firmly against the sofa. The agent propped one foot on the edge of the coffee table, then used his knee to support the photos while he methodically flipped through them one at a time. The darkroom specialist had developed one of the first rolls of film the agent shot the evening before, and ironically, it happened to be the photos of Vincent Panachi and Jennifer Swords.

When the agent came across the picture of Jennifer centered in the photograph, he plucked it from the others. The agent handed the photograph to Mark while he explained, "Take a look at this bimbo. See, crime does pay. If we had money to blow like the boys do, then we'd be humping girls like this. My God, look at those tits."

Senior Agent Murray barely comprehended the last words the other agent said. A burning pain ricocheted between his eyes, brain, and heart while he desperately struggled to maintain his composure. Nevertheless, he couldn't help the audible gasp he emitted. The other agent heard it and remarked, "Yeah, you should have seen her in person. She takes your breath away."

That statement sent another searing pain shooting deep into Mark's heart. "Jesus," he mumbled under his breath, he knew that he was not over her. Jennifer Swords had been very special to him; no one knew about the affair.

Senior Agent Mark Murray gathered his composure then laid the photo of Jennifer on the coffee table. The other agent reached for it to replace it back in the stack with the others, but Agent Murray grabbed his hand, almost as if it were an involuntary movement. Before the agent could question him, Mark Murray ordered, "Get me a couple of eight by tens of this picture. Color."

The other agent merely smiled and remarked, "You're a real cock-hound, Sir."

The statement was meant to be a compliment—a crude compliment, but nevertheless, a compliment. Agent Murray managed to flash his subordinate a smile in response, but inside he was hurting.

* * *

At precisely 2 p.m., a pearl-colored, DaBryan, stretch limousine pulled up in front of the Marriott's Harbour Beach Hotel. This particular limousine was constructed with the discriminating individual in mind, and was uniquely prestigious. It was Anthony Vitale's favorite of all the limousines on the Gold Coast of Florida. The automobile's wide body offered ample seating for six, but only three passengers entered the luxurious interior—the two capos, and Anthony Vitale. Vincent Panachi was already comfortably seated in the rear of the DaBryan when it pulled up to the Marriott's front entrance.

Vincent handled all the travel arrangements for Anthony Vitale when he visited South Florida. The Gold Coast was considered Vincent's turf, and it was taken for granted that he would know what was best for the family. Vincent made it a point to have the newest, most luxurious, limousine readily available for the head of the Vitale crime family. Anthony noticed those little things.

A black, plexiglass, partition separated the driver from the four men he was chauffeuring to Walker's Cay Jet Center at the Ft. Lauderdale International Airport. The partition made the limousine's passenger compartment totally soundproof. "Just as well," the chauffeur had told the captain of the Marriott's valet parkers during their conversation about what is was like to drive the Mafia around. Now that the driver was en route to the airport with his passengers, he pondered that question once again. "What the hell," he said out loud, "they're the biggest tippers I haul." Vincent Panachi made a point of taking care of the chauffeur, and requested the same driver every time. The chauffeur made a concerted effort to be punctual and confidential. It was an agreement that worked well for both parties.

Sophisticated travel arrangements take considerable effort to coordinate, and when things don't run smoothly they fall apart quickly. On the other hand, when everyone is on schedule, travel arrangements will run as smoothly as a Swiss watch. When that happens, it makes Vincent Panachi look that much more efficient in Anthony Vitale's eyes. This afternoon, it happened.

The limousine pulled through the fenced gate at Walker's Cay Jet Center then slowly crept across the asphalt ramp towards a gleaming Learjet. The door to the Learjet was open, and an auxiliary power unit sat along side the sleek wing, its heavy-duty electrical cord connected to the aircraft's external power plug. Within minutes the pilot would call upon the ground crew to power up the huge generator that would supply the electrical current to fire up the turbine engines.

The capos were first to exit the limousine, cautiously scanning the area, out of habit mostly, before Anthony Vitale leaned his head through the open rear door. Following a brief exchange of words, the head of the Vitale crime family exited the luxury automobile and headed for the Learjet, which was less than ten feet away. The pilot stood beside the sleek jet's split door and cautioned the approaching elderly gentleman, "Watch your head as you enter, sir." Anthony Vitale nodded his head in acknowledgment then seemed to carry the same movement slightly lower as he ducked his head and entered the business jet. The two capos followed him, and then Vincent followed them. Anthony Vitale sat in the divan seat by himself while the much larger capos chose individual seats across the aisle from one another. Vincent sat in a seat facing backwards, directly across from Capo Pelligi. Vincent flashed a smile at Anthony, who returned it, then his eyes diverted to Capo Pelligi. The thick, fire-plug-built man held Vincent's stare for a couple of seconds before he reached forward and gave Vincent a "love-tap" slap on his cheek.

"Take care of yourself, kid. I'll be in touch . . . very soon."

"I'll be looking forward to it," Vincent replied as he nodded his head.

The men remained silent for a minute until the quiet was broken by a voice from one of the cockpit's radios, "Learjet 30 Tango Papa, you are cleared to Newark, New Jersey via Atlantic Route 1 to Wilmington, North Carolina, then radar vectors direct Newark. Climb and maintain niner thousand, expect flight level 450 ten minutes after departure. Maintain runway heading and contact Miami departure on 119.70; squawk 5173. Have a good trip, and contact ground on 121.90. Good day."

"Looks like you're on the way," Vincent said as he slid to the edge of his seat.

Anthony Vitale lifted his right hand and waved good-bye. Just then, the radio blared, "Good afternoon to you, Learjet 30 Tango Papa. Taxi to runway 9L. Information 'Romeo' is current."

Vincent did not notice the light-off of the Learjet's right engine while he bid the capos farewell. It was not until he exited the aircraft that the shrill of the high speed turbine engine attacked his eardrums. The captain shook Vincent's hand then started up the stairs. The pilot did a half twist with his upper body while his left hand clung to the upper portion of the Learjet's door. It was a practiced move, because the door seemed to gently follow his body into the aircraft until the door's halved pieces became one. No sooner did the door to the aircraft close than the left engine began spooling up. The turbine engine emitted a low, growling noise for several seconds while its razor sharp blades spun faster. Vincent walked towards the limousine. Suddenly, he heard what sounded like the flash explosion of a match that had been tossed onto lighter fluid soaked charcoal lying in a barbecue grill. *WHIFF!* The turbine engine reached a thunderous roar within seconds.

Vincent stepped into the limousine and quickly closed the door behind him. The chauffeur pulled the elongated, wide-body, Lincoln forward. At the same moment, the Learjet began its taxi to runway 9L.

*   *   *

The Maitre d' at Slick Nick's restaurant was scheduled to report to work at 3 p.m., even though the captains and waiters did not show up until 4 p.m. The extra hour was supposed to give him ample time to check the evening's dinner reservations, to determine which captain would best suit a given station, and to pull the selection of fine wines specifically requested by guests when they had made their reservations. All in all, the duties took approximately forty-five minutes to complete. Even so, the Maitre d' reported to work fifteen minutes early, at 2:45 p.m., to make certain he would have enough time to make his phone call.

First things first, and this was something the Maitre d' had thought about all night the night before. He let himself in the restaurant with his own key, just as he did six days a week. The professional cleaning crew that came in nightly, during the wee hours of the morning, had long since gone, leaving only the familiar scent of spring pine lingering in the air as testimony to their having been there. The restaurant was spotless; but then again, it always was. The Maitre d' crossed the darkened dining room, stepping around the tables by memory, until he reached the utility room located in the rear of the building. A flick of five switches illuminated the entire restaurant.

The Maitre d' nervously checked his watch and noted that the daily routine had taken five minutes. Slick Nick NEVER arrived earlier than 3:15, and usually didn't appear until closer to 3:30. This allowed the Maitre d' a little cushion to do what he had contemplated during the night. Quickly, he crossed the restaurant. The door to Nick's office was closed, but not locked, because the cleaning crew came in nightly to empty the trash and wipe off the desk top. That necessary evil bothered Nick, but the daily accumulation of dirt and dust bothered him even more. Reluctantly, Nick had ceased locking his office door nearly six months ago.

The Maitre d' turned the doorknob, and the solid oak door easily swung open on its well oiled hinges. His hand reached inside the darkened office and flicked on the light switch. A pair of fluorescent tubes mounted on the ceiling blinked twice before they emitted steady streams of light that completely illuminated the office. Unbeknownst to the Maitre d', the light switch also provided power to a voice activated tape recorder hidden in the office's suspended ceiling. Even though Nick's office was off limits to all employees, his paranoia would have never allowed him to keep it at just that—a rule. Instead, he had the recording device installed when the electronic eavesdropping system was put in; and even though Nick made a nightly ritual of checking it, he had yet to hear a voice on it.

The Maitre d' sat down at Nick's desk and quickly flipped through the metal Rolodex file. The 2-¼ by 4 inch, white cards were alphabetically indexed A through Z. His hand trembled ever so slightly as he flipped the Rolodex to the letter *M*. The words *MARRIOTT HARBOUR BEACH HOTEL* were neatly typed across the card. Beneath the heading was an area code 954, Ft. Lauderdale. The Maitre d' lifted the telephone's handset with his left hand while his right dialed the number on the card. Seconds later, a friendly voice answered.

"Marriott's Harbour Beach Hotel, how may I help you?"

"Front desk, please."

Certainly, sir. Just a moment while I connect you."

The Maitre d' noticed his palms perspiring during the twenty seconds he waited before a pleasant sounding voice answered, "Front desk."

He swallowed hard, "Do you have an Anthony Vitale registered there?"

"Just a moment while I check that information for you." The name did not register until after the words had already escaped her mouth. Two seconds of silence passed, as if she were busy checking the register, before her voice returned on the line. "I'm sorry, sir. The Vitale party has already checked out."

The Maitre d' held the phone to his ear, but said nothing in response. His mind whirled with the possibilities as he questioned his decision to call in the first place. Finally, he gathered his thoughts and replied, "Thank you for the information." The Maitre d' hung up the handset then looked at the phone for a couple of minutes while he planned his strategy. Quickly, his fingers flipped through the Rolodex files until he reached the letter *V*. There it was, the first card in the index—*VITALE, ANTHONY*. Alongside the head of the crime family's name were two phone numbers—one home, one private—and both were prefixed with the area code for Newark, New Jersey.

The Maitre d's hand was shaking so badly that he could hardly write the numbers legibly. Nevertheless, this was the opportunity that he had waited years for, and nothing would stop him from hanging Slick Nick. The Maitre d' pulled a black, ball point pen from the mahogany desk set, then carefully copied the two telephone numbers onto a sheet of memo paper. He replaced the pen and folded the paper. When he stood, he placed the information in his trouser pocket, then checked the desk top for any signs that he had been there. Once he had satisfied himself that all was in order, the Maitre d' quietly slipped out of the office, switching the lights off on the way. A quick glance at his watch verified he was running on schedule. It was 3:04 p.m., and there was no sign of Slick Nick.

*   *   *

Vincent thoroughly enjoyed the luxury of the DaBryan limousine. In order to charter the prestigious automobile, one must agree to a six hour minimum. Six hours was just about enough time for Vincent to be alone and think. After they departed the airport, Vincent instructed the driver to motor along A1A, the highway that parallels the ocean. Vincent referred to it as his "therapeutic roadway," and the limousine provided the ultimate therapy.

A row of crystal champagne glasses were neatly arranged within arm's reach and Vincent selected one from the end. The glass accidentally touched another while he lifted it from the teak rack. The high-pitched, chime rang for a second before Vincent touched the side of the glass to silence it. The driver had Vincent's modus operandi down pat, and the fact was evident by the chilled bottle of Moet champagne in the sterling silver ice bucket. Vincent grasped the bottle with one hand while he held the cork with the other. Slowly, he turned the bottle of fine champagne, careful to keep his thumb on top of the cork, lest it fly off and hit something. Within a couple of turns of the bottle, Vincent heard a hiss rather than a pop and smiled—a proper uncorking.

The limousine continued north of Boca Raton towards West Palm Beach. It was Vincent's favorite part of the beach cruise. He poured himself a glass of champagne and watched the scenery whisk by at thirty miles per hour. Out of habit, Vincent checked his watch for the time. It was 4:45 p.m. Estate after estate began passing by the limo's windows as the elongated automobile approached West Palm Beach, but it was not until they reached Palm Beach proper that the ultra-wealthy estates began. The owners of these homes were beyond money, elite members of a self proclaimed, "Plutocracy"—a group of wealthy people who control a government. Never was a truer statement spoken.

Vincent marveled at the wealth these people openly displayed. These multimillionaires openly taunted the Internal Revenue Service; the same IRS that cowered Anthony Vitale in the corner. The difference was that these millionaires could account for their wealth through generations of inheritance, whereas Anthony Vitale could justify only tens of thousands. Not that the Vitale crime family couldn't buy and sell these people any time, they just couldn't write a check for it. Vincent pondered this dilemma while the homes of the rich and famous swept past the limousine's tinted windows. The thoughts brought him around to Anthony Vitale, to the amazing job he had done at running the family's business through the years. Vincent took a swig from his champagne glass while his thoughts continued about the head of the Vitale crime family.

*   *   *

By 7 p.m., Slick Nick's restaurant was packed, even though it was a Monday night. The posh city of Boca Raton enjoys an economy of its own. Regardless of what the neighboring cities are experiencing, Boca's spending is perpetual. Those seemingly endless lines of credit on their American Express Gold cards keep the restaurants busy year round, and Nick's was one of the most frequented. It had proven to be one of the best investments the Vitale crime family had ever made.

Now that all the employees were busy with the patrons, Slick Nick turned to his Maitre d'.

"Keep an eye on things. If you need me I'll be in my office."

The Maitre d' managed a compulsory smile when he replied, "Certainly, sir."

Nick walked away without another word to his employee, but he did mumble under his breath, "Ass kissing little prick." It was Slick Nick's typical demeanor.

Nick found his office in order, just as he had each evening. The trash can was empty, the desk had been dusted, and the carpet showed telltale signs of a vacuum cleaner having been tracked across it. Of course, there were also footprints, but that was nothing out of the ordinary. There were footprints every time the cleaning crew vacuumed. Nick pulled out his desk chair and sat at his desk. He leaned back in the seat to rest a couple of minutes, and clasped his hands behind his head. The chair reclined until the back was at a forty-five degree angle to the floor. Nick was comfortably staring at the ceiling. Less than a minute passed when his thoughts turned to his toys. Looking at the ceiling reminded him of the voice activated recorder carefully hidden in the suspended ceiling. Nick leaned forward then stood up. He had to stand on top of his desk to reach the ceiling, but he knew precisely where the recorder was. Nick had the electronic unit in his hand within ten seconds, and then carefully stepped down from the desk top. He laid the recorder down while he turned around to adjust his chair. The chair's overstuffed seat bottom made a whooshing sound when Nick plopped onto the cushion. He slid the wheels across the carpet until he was within reach of the recorder and rewound the tape. The fact that something had activated the recorder did not excite him in the least, because he had listened to a high quality recording of the cleaning crew in his office a hundred times. Nevertheless, the not knowing would have driven him crazy, perhaps even crazier than he already was. Once the rewind mode stopped, Nick pressed play, then leaned back in his chair.

The tape played several minutes of the cleaners rumbling around in his office. Nick played a little game in his mind by matching the sounds with their imaginary movements. He could discern the dumping of the trash can, then the start up of the vacuum cleaner. Nick thought he was pretty sharp at identifying those sounds, and he was. He smiled. Suddenly, there was a familiar voice on the tape. Immediately, Nick leaned forward with breakneck speed, the smile removed from his face, *"Front desk, please."* There was a pause where the recorder had cut itself off and on again then the voice continued, *"Do you have an Anthony Vitale registered there?"* Again, the tape machine clicked off and on. Finally, the identical voice remarked, *"Thank you for the information."* The words ended with the sound of the telephone handset being placed in its cradle. Slick Nick could not believe his ears. He desperately wanted to rewind the tape and listen to the voice again, but his sense of danger alerted him that there could be more. Nick listened. There were no more voices, however there were unexplained sounds. Quickly, Nick depressed the rewind button for only a second and the tape began replaying the two noises. Nick listened while his mind played the game he had played so many times before. His eyes followed the moves his imagination envisioned. He saw the pen being removed from the desk set and the paper being torn from the memo pad. Nick let the tape continue to run while he reached for the memo pad. He grabbed it and tilted the paper towards the overhead light. Involuntarily, he gasped. The light struck the paper at an angle and revealed indentations of the name *ANTHONY VITALE*. Two telephone numbers followed it.

Like a madman, Nick flipped through his Rolodex file until he reached the letter *V*. His eyes scanned the file card then he compared the numbers on the memo paper. They were identical. Nick's mouth fell open, "What the HELL is going on here!" He slapped his palms flat onto the desk top and yelled, "The fucking Maitre d'!"

CHAPTER SIX

A s a rule, agents of the Organized Crime Task Force do not receive phone calls while on surveillance duty, and they never receive personal calls. That would constitute a breach of security because the condominium across from Shylock's does not exist, or at least that was their official position. Otherwise, photographs taken from the bank of surveillance cameras aimed at Shylock's would be developed at the agency's downtown laboratory, rather than in the condo's back bedroom. This operation was working under a cloak of secrecy, and its leader had learned the hard way years ago that the tendency to keep things secret was directly relative to the culpability of the subject. Somehow, by someone, various groups under investigation by the Organized Crime Task Force had been pre-warned during past investigations. Consequently, the investigation of the Vitale crime family was initiated on a need to know basis.

The telephone hanging on the kitchen wall rang seven times before Agent Mark Murray finally picked it up. The caller knew that the phone was not manned but the condo was, and eventually someone would pick it up.

"Yeah." It was not exactly a cordial greeting, but that was okay. Mark knew his oldest and most trusted friend, Karl Spalding, was on the other end. Karl was also Mark's immediate superior, and no one else, at least to Mark's knowledge, had the phone number to the condo.

"Just the man I wanted to speak to. How are things going?" Karl asked.

"Slow, but that's all right. Wednesdays always pick up. Tuesday will be slow."

"Get any good photos last weekend?"

Murray winced at the memory of the picture of Jennifer before he answered, "Yeah, got some beautiful shots from Anthony Vitale's birthday bash. As a matter of fact they're still being developed. God damn chemical smell is killing me."

"Well, you're going to get some fresh air. Meet me down stairs in twenty minutes."

"What's up, boss?" The head of the task force had long since hardened about deaths, and as far as he was concerned he could care less if the, "Guinea bastards," as he referred to the Italian heritage that was prevalent amongst the Northeastern United States' crime families, "can kill off one another . . . as long as they don't scatter dead bodies all over Ft. Lauderdale."

"I got a call from the West Palm Beach County Sheriff's department early this morning. Said they found a body out in the sugar cane, and they suspected it was some sort of gang related killing."

"What led them to that assumption?"

"I don't guess they get too many corpses dressed in black tuxedos in Belle Glade."

"No, I wouldn't think so," Mark replied.

"Twenty minutes, down stairs. We'll grab some lunch on the way out of town. Something tells me we want to take a look at this one."

"Twenty minutes, down stairs. Got it."

Both men hung up the phone at the same time. No, "Goodbyes." Just a click.

A dark-blue Ford sedan pulled up in front of the waterfront condominium exactly twenty minutes after Agent Murray hung up the telephone. Mark was standing out front when the automobile turned into the circular driveway. Karl Spalding pulled right to the building's entrance, and Mark slid onto the front seat.

The traffic in and around Ft. Lauderdale moves at a snail's pace, but once one gets free of the city everyone drives at a minimum of fifty-five-miles per hour regardless of the posted legal limit. The two agents traveled north along State Road 441, a four-lane highway that runs north and south, paralleling the shoreline approximately ten miles inland. It traverses some of the most beautiful subdivisions in Broward County then blends into horse country when it enters Palm Beach County. Karl had been true to his word when he told Mark that he would be getting some fresh air.

"Jeez," Mark told his long time friend, "I cannot remember the last time I was this far inland. We are out in the sticks."

"We're not in the sticks yet. Just wait until we reach Belle Glade." Two miles later, the Ford sedan turned west onto Highway 27.

The large, elegant homes and white-fenced, horse ranches were quickly replaced by sugar cane fields that stretched as far as the eye could see. Fields of tall, olive-green sugar cane swayed gently to the rhythm of the blowing wind. Compared to the Gold Coast of Florida, the area portrayed all the differences of night and day and that made for an enjoyable change. Of course, the fact that the two men were en route to see a brutally murdered body did not add to the ambience, yet still a day in the country was nice. More than likely it was nicer for Agent Murray's superior than it was for Agent Murray, because he could have cared less about the body. "A mere formality," was how he termed it when asked. At any rate, it was obvious to Agent Murray that his hardened superior was enjoying the countryside, because they never stopped for lunch as planned. Before they knew it, a wooden sign announced, *WELCOME TO THE CITY OF BELLE GLADE, FLORIDA.*

Karl Spalding glanced at his watch as the sedan passed the road sign, then remarked, "It's a good thing we didn't stop for lunch. We would have been late for our meeting."

Agent Murray decided against calling him on the obvious afterthought. On the other hand, lunch and a trip to the coroner's office just did not sound appealing to Mark, so he let the subject slide. It was Karl who broke the momentary silence when he changed the subject. He turned his head so that he could see Murray's expression when he asked, "Had any good humps, lately?"

Mark looked in his direction just in time to catch the sly grin on his friend's face a second before his eyes quickly diverted back towards the road. Mark laughed, "I've hit a dry spell. No action."

His boss slapped the steering wheel with the meaty portion of his palm while he remarked, "Bull shit! You can tell me. What about the broad you were shacking up with?"

Mark knew his friend was referring to Jennifer Swords, even though he did not know what she looked like or the first thing about her. Just the thought of it pained Mark, and that pain made the picture of her with Vincent Panachi flash into his mind. Agent Murray informed his friend, "That's history, and so is this line of questioning." But, the kidding continued. Finally, the barrage of quips ceased when the Sheriff's substation came into sight a hundred yards ahead on the right. The division head wheeled the sedan into the parking lot and parked alongside one of the unmarked cars. Ironically, it was a dark-blue Ford sedan, as well. The only distinguishing difference between the two automobiles was that the task force's had tinted windows so dark that no one could see inside the car.

The concrete block building was covered with beige stucco and long, narrow windows stretched across the side facing the parking lot. Once Agents Murray and Spalding turned the corner, panes of glass the size of picture windows brightly reflected the midday sun off their mirror-like, golden tint. The concrete walkway led to a pair of metal framed glass doors centered along the street side of the building. Two official seals were embossed on the double doors, one on either side. As Mark approached the doors, he read the seal on the left first. The letters encircled the outside diameter of the seal and formed the words *PALM BEACH COUNTY SHERIFF'S DEPARTMENT.* Below the seal, the words *BELLE GLADE SUBSTATION* were hand painted in gold leaf. Mark's eyes quickly shifted to the right door where yet another colorful seal was embossed upon the glass door. This one read, again with letters formed in a circular fashion, *PALM BEACH*

COUNTY CORONER'S OFFICE. Mark was still looking at the seal when his superior's hand reached past him and opened the left door. Mark heard, "After you, my friend." The two men entered the Sheriff's substation.

A plump secretary with an outdated beehive hairdo looked up from her small desk and asked, "May I help you?"

"Yes. We are with the Organized Crime Task Force, and we're here to see Detective Polk. He's expecting us," Agent Spalding answered.

The woman shifted several times in her chair as if she were gaining the momentum necessary to stand. When she reached her feet, she said, "Just a minute, please. I'll tell Earnest ya'll are here."

Mark tossed his boss a quick glance, but the look went unnoticed. His superior was still looking the secretary in the eye when he replied, "That will be fine. Thank you."

Minutes later, she returned with Detective Earnest Polk; a heavyset man, wearing snug polyester. The tops of his brown loafers showed evidence of lots of polishing, but the sheen on the sides were dull and dirty. He extended his hand, "Welcome to Belle Glade. I'm Detective Polk."

The division head introduced himself and Agent Murray, then the three men shook hands. Almost as if Detective Polk had read Mark's earlier thoughts, he pointed at his lackluster loafers and commented, "Damned sugar cane field muddied my hundred dollar shoes." Mark met the detective's eyes when he looked up, and they shared a smile between the two of them. If the heavyset man could have read Mark's thoughts then he would have read, "Is this guy for real?" Mark's sarcastic thoughts were interrupted when Detective Polk addressed the question to him, "Agent Murray, what do you want to see first . . . the murder site or the body?"

Before Murray could answer, his superior jumped in.

"Let's see the site first, while the sun is still high overhead. I imagine the sugar cane casts some shadows late in the afternoon."

"Well, I can see that you city boys didn't come out here with straw in your hair. That's damned brilliant thinking. That's exactly how I stepped into that God damned mud puddle early this morning. Sum-a-bitch was hiding in a shadow."

Mark smiled, but it was more out of being polite rather than enjoying the detective's coarse sense of humor. Detective Polk started through the double doorway, "Let's go in my car. Damned tires are dirty already."

This time it was Agent Murray who beat his superior to the punch. He quickly motioned towards the door with his left arm and said, "After you, my friend."

The ride to the murder site was informative, but the information had nothing to do with the killing—it was more of a "Who's Who in Belle Glade" sort of discourse. Both agents took Detective Polk's one-sided conversation in stride until finally he turned off the two-lane highway onto a dirt road. It was then that the heavyset man switched from tour guide back to a detective.

Tall stalks of sugar cane flanked the narrow dirt road on either side. The dirt was hard packed and showed signs of frequent travel. As the sedan traveled down the road, Agent Murray noticed several small pathways that led from the dirt road.

"Detective Polk, what are these paths leading off the roadway?"

It was not necessary for the detective to remove his eyes from the road because he knew this rural region like the back of his hand. Without glancing sideways, the detective said, "Them are cuttin' paths. The workers cut the cane with machetes then drag the stalks along them paths 'til they get 'em to this road. Trucks pick it up from there . . . that's why this dirt road is so packed hard-packed down."

Agent Murray nodded his head in acknowledgment, as if to say, "Makes sense to me," but he kept his thoughts to himself.

The sedan traveled another fifty yards then the detective slowed to less than five miles per hour. He turned the automobile left, into an opening in the sugar cane no wider than the sedan. As a matter of fact, bright green leaves swept past the windows, some of which were pressed firmly against the glass. Thirty yards into the bush the pathway widened somewhat, then two cars became visible. A closer look determined that they were unmarked police cars. Detective Polk quickly confirmed that deduction. He said, "We've been here all morning searchin' for clues."

"Find anything?" Agent Spalding asked.

Detective Polk stopped the car then his right hand placed the gear selector into park. His pudgy neck folded into several wrinkles when he turned his head sharply to answer. "Well, let's get out and ask 'em. Damned shadows did not help, earlier."

Detective Polk's partner was a local country boy by the name of Jack Farmer. He obviously took his investigative duties seriously, Murray noted. He was removing a pair of rubber surgical gloves from his hands while he walked in their direction. Detective Polk smiled as he introduced everyone. "Detective Farmer, this is the division head of the Organized Crime Task Force, and one of their top agents, Mark Murray."

The country boy shook their hands while he addressed them individually, "It's a pleasure. Welcome to Belle Glade."

Agent Murray was the first to turn the conversation towards the investigation when he asked, "Have you turned anything up . . . anything solid?"

Detective Farmer nodded his head as he replied, "Yep, sure did. Got some tire tread prints near the blood stained dirt, and a trail of blood leads across the dirt into sugar cane. Looks to me like he was killed somehweres else, then dumped here."

Agent Spalding turned toward Detective Polk and confirmed, "Coroner got the body?"

"That's affirmative, sir. He should have the official cause of death and the approximate time of death ready for you by the time we get back to the office."

Detective Farmer interjected, "The plaster cast of the tire treads should be dry, real soon. I'll get an identification of those as soon as possible, hopefully before you leave this afternoon."

Karl Spalding nodded his head, "That would be very helpful. Thank you, detective."

"Shucks, it ain't nothin'," replied the country boy.

The four men walked over to the site where the body had been found. Sugar cane and weeds were squashed flat where the body had lay, and blood stains left a gruesome trail from the pathway. Agent Murray made a general observation, rather than addressing the comment to one person, when he said, "There is way too much blood present for him to have been shot here. I believe we can all agree that the body was dragged from the point where the tire treads left their indentation into these bushes." Mark turned to face Detective Farmer when he asked, "What did the body look like? Any signs of a struggle?"

Detective Farmer made a grimacing face when he replied, "You know, I've seen some violent killings in my time, but I ain't never seen a man beat up as bad as this one was."

"How so?" Agent Spalding queried.

"His face was beat to a pulp. It is so bad that we're gonna have to identify him by prints," the detective remarked.

The description sent a shiver up Agent Murray's spine. Gangland style killings were particularly gruesome for a reason. In general, the murder was a message for the surviving members of a given crime family. It was for that reason that Karl Spalding was so adamant about making the trip out to Belle Glade to assess the situation himself.

Detective Polk broke the uncomfortable silence by asking, "You boys want to look around a bit?"

Agent Murray answered even though the question was not necessarily directed toward him.

"Yeah, I'd like to scour the area, if you don't mind."

The heavyset detective remarked, "Hell, that's what I brung you out here for. Be my guest."

"Thank you," Agent Murray courteously replied as he turned toward the rectangular, wooden-framed, plaster cast. Mark Murray thoroughly searched the area in and around a twenty foot diameter of the tire print, but turned up nothing more than Detective Farmer had already found. The search took him the better part of an hour, and he looked it. The height of the sugar cane prevented any breeze from reaching ground level, yet the early afternoon sun had no problem blazing down on them. The humidity made the temperature torrid, but it was a necessary search. Finally, Agent Murray satisfied himself that the detective had done a very thorough search, and told him so.

Detective Farmer remained behind while Detective Polk drove the two Organized Crime Task Force agents back to the Belle Glade sub-station. Naturally, the three men speculated about what took place the night before, but at that point it was precisely that—speculation. Their first bit of conclusive evidence would come from the Coroner's office, which was their next stop.

The unmarked Sheriff's department sedan turned quickly into the parking lot, and its tires squealed in protest to the fast rate of turn. Mark firmly grasped the automobile's dashboard with his left had while the muscles in his forearm strained to counteract the centrifugal force generated by the sharp turn. Even so, he leaned forcefully against his superior. The ride back through town had been considerably quicker than the trip to the murder site, or at least so it seemed. Of course, the fact that the three men discussed the murder rather than the history of Belle Glade could have had some bearing upon it.

Detective Polk parked the automobile in a reserved space that had the word *DETECTIVE* stenciled with black spray paint over a yellow barrier.

"Why don't I take you fellars in to see the coroner," the detective suggested, "then I'm gonna slip over to my office and check my messages."

"Sounds like a plan. Let's do it," Agent Spalding replied.

The heavyset man led the way as the three men followed the concrete walkway toward the double door entrance to the building. This time, however, the agents from the Organized Crime Task Force entered the right side of the double glass door. Detective Polk announced their entry by hollering, "Dr. Kramer, I brung you the agents from Ft. Lauderdale."

A voice called from the rear of the building, "Yes, I've been expecting you. Bring them back, please."

The heavyset detective smiled as he motioned with a flabby arm, "This way, gentlemen." Agent Murray and his superior walked through a partially opened door, then waited until the detective goaded them by adding, "The autopsy room is all the way back. Just follow this hallway. I'm gonna run next door for a couple of minutes. Dr. Kramer will answer any questions ya'll may have." Agent Murray led the way down the lengthy corridor to its end and his boss followed.

A short, elderly gentleman dressed in lime-green surgical garb greeted them with an ingratiating smile. He said, "Don't be frightened, gentlemen. Come in, please . . . Come in."

Both men were veterans at viewing violent deaths, but nobody ever learned to enjoy it. Never. One may grow numb, like Agent Spalding had, but even he did not look forward to it. Inevitably, dead bodies and spilt blood meant trouble to follow, and that was the reason the division head had come out here to judge for himself what the repercussions may be. Was it a simple murder, or was it only the beginning of a bloody trail of crime family bodies? Dr. Kramer's professional opinion on the cause and manner of death definitely shed some light on the subject, but the future was not as bright as it could have been. The initial diagnosis fit the bill for a gangster style killing.

The body of the deceased was covered up, but traces of blood on the white sheet served testimony to the violent nature of his death.

"The facial area has multiple contusions and several deep cuts. The facial features are distorted beyond recognition," Dr. Kramer confirmed.

"From what?" Agent Spalding asked.

The doctor shifted his eyes to Agent Spalding and held his gaze while he answered the question. "Through the years spent as a coroner I have had the displeasure of seeing a great number of faces beat to a pulp. Migrant workers kill one another over jealous rights, whether it is a woman or cane fields, with such frequency that it's scary. These farm laborers don't have guns. They just beat each other to death with something." Dr. Kramer nonchalantly motioned towards the corpse with his right arm when he added, "In my professional opinion, this man was severely pistol whipped before he was murdered. The beating may have killed him anyway, but clinically the cause of death was two gunshots, point-blank to the skull." A moment of silence followed, during which time the doctor walked over to the murder victim and turned the sheet back far enough to allow the two agents to view the head of the deceased.

Agent Murray nearly vomited at the grotesque sight. As it was, he was not able to control himself when he blurted, "God damn."

The doctor appeared to be totally unphased by the gruesome appearance of the disfigured face. Instead, he quipped, "I believe it's a little late for that now. It appears that the Lord already has."

Agent Murray's superior made no comment, but he did stare at the body with a disgusted look on his face. There was no doubt that someone had pistol whipped the deceased, probably for information. Without another word, the coroner unfurled the sheet and covered the dead man's face.

The official report was hours away from completion, or so the coroner informed the two agents. There was nothing more they could do in Belle Glade so they decided to head back to Ft. Lauderdale. The sight of the bloodied body confirmed Agent Spalding's suspicion that the murder was somehow Mafia related. For nearly a half-hour, the two men tossed a few hypothetical motives about.

Karl reasoned, "Whoever killed our mystery man wanted some information from him before they did him in. He's not a 'snitch' because they didn't shoot him in the mouth. No, someone wanted him to be able to talk up until the final moment of his life." The head agent paused for thirty-seconds before he spoke again, as if he had just remembered something else that bothered him. He averted his eyes from the road long enough to catch Mark's, then added, "Another thing that just doesn't figure here is that damn black tuxedo."

Mark did not say anything, but that statement jarred his memory and sent his investigative mind into overdrive. He thought out loud when he mumbled, "Mafia style killing; black tuxedoed body." Several seconds passed while he blankly stared at the passing countryside, then his mind flashed the memory of the eight-by-ten photographs taken at Anthony Vitale's landlubber party. Shot after shot of the black tuxedoed members of the Vitale crime family had been photographed entering the Italian restaurant. "Of course," he said out loud.

"What was that?" His boss queried.

Mark slapped the top of the backrest with his left hand while he swung his leg around so that he sat sideways on the front seat. Enthusiastically, he said, "I've got a hunch I'd like to follow."

Karl raised his eyebrows as he turned his head and replied, "Well, are you going to share it with me?"

"Not yet," Mark replied, "give me a couple of days, but I will tell you that if it pans out you're gonna love it."

A moment of silence followed, Karl said, "Follow it."

From that point forward Agent Murray did nothing but eat, sleep, and breathe the Vitale crime family. Investigations must start somewhere, and it was that black tuxedo that led Agent Murray to Slick Nick's restaurant, the scene of the "black tuxedoed affair."

*   *   *

The crystal clock on Slick Nick's desk top was a gift from one of the restaurant's regular patrons. Nick had eyed the piece himself at a very high-classed jewelry store in the Town Square Mall, and ironically, one week later the patron presented it to him during their dinner. Nick placed it on his desk top that evening and it hadn't left since. Aside from keeping perfect time, the clock served another purpose. When laid flat on its face, the smooth, clear, brilliant glass made a perfect surface for chopping cocaine into lines.

It was 2:47 p.m. when Nick seated himself at his desk and last looked at the clock. He locked the door to his office behind him, even though there was no one else present in the restaurant and would not be for at least another hour. Slick Nick's nerves were all but shattered and his paranoia had reached an all time high. The rims of his eyes were tinged with red where the small blood vessels had broken, and the edges of his nostrils were raw and inflamed. Two parallel lines of finely chopped, ninety percent pure cocaine lay on the crystal glass, and a tooter lay diagonally across the bottom of the lines. Slick Nick had just snorted two identical lines of cocaine moments before and was enjoying the momentary fire in his brain.

The restaurateur's mental disorder had been characterized by delusions. His paranoia brought with it vast waves of persecution, particularly when he was coming down from his coke high. However, there was a flip side to his personality disorder and it shown through when he was flying on cocaine. A quick toot could make the problems in his life simply disappear. Visions of grandeur replaced delusions of persecution in a matter of seconds. ***CHOP, CHOP! SNIFF, SNIFF!*** "Aha . . . I'm the man . . . the one."

Slick Nick had arrived earlier than he ever had at his restaurant for a very good reason. There was no question in his mind that the Maitre d' would not show up for work that evening, or any other evening. Nick was certain of that fact. Dead certain, because twelve hours prior Nick had pistol whipped the Maitre d' until he had beat a confession out of him. During his raging fury, he had crossed the point of no return and decided to finish it. Two, earsplitting cracks from his .38 revolver did the job. The lugs made contact from a point-blank range, instantly killing the Maitre d'. Afterwards, Slick Nick dumped the body in a sugar cane field so far away that he was certain it would be days, maybe weeks, before the murder was discovered. A couple of toots along the ride there and back kept his mind focused and sharp, or so he thought, and he had continued snorting cocaine throughout the following morning. Now, the afternoon following the murder found him in high spirits. He was infallible, even though his nerves were on edge from staying awake all night. He was certain that he had made no mistakes, left no clues.

Suddenly, the private line on his desk phone rang. The unexpected ringing of the phone's bell startled him so bad that he jumped. Instinctively, Nick's right hand reached for the handset and removed it from the cradle. Very few people were privy to the number, yet he hated not knowing who was on the other end. Nick's heart raced as he spoke into the mouthpiece. "Yeah?" he said.

A squeaky, high-pitched voice responded from the earpiece "Nick, dah-ling, is that you?" Before Nick could even reply, the voice continued, "This is your good friend, Darlene, the hair stylist . . . I just wanted to let you know that I talked to Jennifer Swords yesterday. Honey, have I got some gossip for you . . ."

CHAPTER SEVEN

T wo days had passed since the discovery of the Maitre d's brutally murdered body.

*   *   *

The tinted, sliding glass doors in Jennifer Swords' condominium were partially open, which allowed the gentle sea breeze to waft through the living room. Sheer drapes made from raw silk danced in whiffs of clean sea air, their bottoms swinging several feet above the carpeted floor. The mid-morning sun shone brightly through the clear sky and sent shimmering reflections across the ocean's placid surface. It was a picture perfect day in South Florida, and the flat-calm ocean was ideal for power boating.

Vincent Panachi did not enjoy a view of the ocean from his home in the Las Olas Islands, but the gentle breeze rippling across the canal behind his house did indicate that the ocean was calm. Business had occupied the first half of his week, but now Vincent was caught-up. It was one day over hump day, and Thursday mornings were perfect for boating because the waterway traffic was minimal. Fridays, however, unleashed a swarm of weekend warriors hell-bent on venting the week's frustrations out on their runabouts. Saturdays and Sundays spent along the Intracoastal Waterway were pandemonium, to say the least.

Vincent had not seen Jennifer since Anthony Vitale's landlubber party, but he did speak with her on the phone late Monday afternoon when she had called him.

"Just wanted to thank you for a wonderful evening, last night," she cooed.

The desired effect of the polite call was instantaneous when Vincent remarked, "How nice of you to call."

The two talked for nearly a half an hour, and Jennifer kept the conversation light with lots of laughs; lots of sophisticated flirting. Jennifer was a master at that and there was no question in her mind when she hung up from the conversation that she had successfully mentally tantalized Vincent. He may have been a powerful member of the Vitale crime family, but the art of seduction was her jungle—a jungle that lived by survival instincts which Vincent Panachi had not yet honed. When Jennifer hung up the telephone she was smiling. It was an expression of confidence.

Vincent had thought about her for the past several days, but he did not want to scare her off by hounding her daily. On the other hand, Vincent did not want her to think that he wasn't interested in her either. The day after hump day seemed timely enough. It was just a few minutes past 9 a.m. when Vincent dialed Jennifer's home number. The voice that answered was soft and sexy.

"Good morning," Jennifer said.

"Yes, it is a good morning. This is Vincent."

"Oh, Vincent, I've missed you. How are you?" The somewhat sleepy voice gushed.

"Fine, Jennifer. I have been busy . . . business." He let the comment drift off, mainly because it was a subject he did not care to discuss. Even the most innocently asked question could have put him in a bad position, so rather than lie Vincent chose to avoid the subject. Jennifer was one step ahead of him. She knew precisely who he was and also avoided the subject like the plague. Jennifer picked up the conversation.

"Well, now that you have a break in your business duties you should enjoy yourself."

"You know, that's not a bad idea. As a matter of fact, I was thinking about going boating today. Would you like to come along?"

"Oh, Vincent, could we really go? I just love boating." Jennifer was careful not to let on that she already knew Vincent owned a Scarab Thunder, the same go-fast she had seen him in at Shylock's.

Vincent laughed. Her obvious excitement brought a smile to his face and naturally boosted his ego.

"Going fast on the water is my favorite therapy, and something I try to do at least a couple of times a week, whether I need it or not. I'll tell you what . . . I realize that I just sort of dropped this in your lap, so why don't we do this—I'll get the boat and bring it around to the beach in front of your condo. The tide is high this morning and I should be able to get in real close, but you'll probably have to wade in knee deep to get to the boat, so wear your swimsuit. Does that sound like a plan?"

"Are you always so well organized? I could never think that fast first thing in the morning."

"Well, actually I've been up for a few hours. I bicycle ten miles every morning. Relieves the tension, don't you know."

"You are a pretty amazing man. I'm flattered that you asked me to spend your leisure time with you. What time will you pick me up?"

Vincent paused for a second while he figured which inlet would best suit his purposes, "How does between eleven and eleven-fifteen sound? I'll enter the ocean through the Hillsborough Inlet, and if you'll keep an eye out from your condo. You'll see me coming. Okay?"

"It's a date. Between eleven and eleven-fifteen. Bye."

"I'll see you then. Bye." Vincent quietly stared at the phone after hanging up. At that moment it was he who became aware of the powerful draw this mysterious woman had over him. Yes, he had entered into her web.

Jennifer sat staring at her phone as well, but her thoughts were entirely different from Vincent Panache's. Vincent was pursuing Jennifer in more of a courtship fashion, one which would have allowed their relationship to develop naturally, while Jennifer's pursuit of Vincent followed premeditated stages. Now that she would have Vincent's undivided attention on a boat for the afternoon, it provided a perfect opportunity for her to begin their sexual relationship. She would orchestrate it so that Vincent made the final move, but not until she had tantalized him throughout the day until he could resist no longer. Sex had proved to be her most powerful strength, and she wielded her sexual prowess like a self-seeking, aphrodisiac drug. Jennifer had witnessed its withdrawal symptoms once she divorced her plastic surgeon husband, but it was not until she terminated her affair with Mark Murray did she really realize the power she possessed. Now, Vincent Panache was to be her next conquest. The only term to describe her motives would be premeditated fortune hunting.

Jennifer glanced at her Rolex and noted that she had an hour and a half before Vincent was due to arrive. Realistically, she would need every moment of it to get ready.

Jennifer entered the bathroom adjoining her bedroom and turned on the bath's faucet. A quick check of the water temperature aided by a slight adjustment of the hot water yielded the desired warmth. Sounds of cascading water echoed off the tiled walls of the bathroom as the tub filled. Meanwhile, Jennifer laid out several bikinis on her king-sized bed and began selecting the swim suit she would wear for Vincent. All were custom made and fit her body as if they had been sprayed on. Like all women she had her favorite, and naturally, that was the one she selected. The bikini was brief. The top was low cut and pressed her breasts together to form a very sexy cleavage, while the bottom, from the rear, left little to the imagination. No doubt Jennifer Swords had several, together with matching visors and sandals made from the same material as the bikini to complete the ensemble. Finally, a change in the tone of the splashing water announced that the tub was full.

Jennifer walked into the bathroom and turned the faucet off with her right hand while her left hand pulled a towel from the wall rack. A flick of her wrist fluffed the bath towel while she bent over, her long, blond hair almost touching the floor. A practiced movement swiftly wrapped the towel around her hair and piled it on top of her head. Jennifer stepped into the tub then submerged neck-deep in the warm water. The ledge behind her head held shampoo, conditioner, shaving cream, and a razor. A portable telephone lay on top of the closed lid of the toilet within arm's reach. A large bottle of expensive liquid soap sat on the ledge closest to the faucet, and Jennifer pushed three times on its plastic dispenser. A golden stream of soap quickly mixed with the bath water while she paddled her feet, and the result was a soothing bath which softened Jennifer's skin. Jennifer luxuriated in the tub for ten minutes before she began shaving her legs. The strokes were long and she followed the razor blade with her free hand as it slid up her shapely legs, careful not to miss a spot. It was her full intention to wrap those legs around Vincent Panachi before the day was over.

A gurgling sound came from the bathtub as the water raced down the drain. Jennifer stood beside the tub and patted herself dry with a towel. Her naked body glistened with beads of water and the sudden temperature change made her nipples hard. They jutted forward to their full erectness while the soft touch of the towel only served to make them harder. Wonderful thoughts of Vincent filled Jennifer's mind while she dried herself.

Jennifer wasn't expecting any callers, yet out of habit she picked-up the portable telephone from the toilet lid while she walked towards her dressing table. Out of habit she laid the phone next to her cosmetics. Jennifer was busy applying the foundation of her makeup when the telephone rang. She laid the brush down and picked-up the phone.

"Hello," she purred into the telephone, thinking that perhaps it was Vincent calling with a last minute thought.

A male's voice replied, but it was not Vincent's.

"Sweetheart, this is Nick." His voice was trembling, and if Jennifer had been capable of seeing through the phone she would have realized why his voice quivered.

Nick was propped up in his king-sized bed. The nightstand beside the bed had an ashtray which overflowed with cigarette butts. A glass half-full of Crown Royal whiskey sat next to that, and the combined stench of the two made the room smell like a bar rather than a master bedroom of a luxurious, waterfront home. Slick Nick looked like warmed over death. He had slept less than six hours in three days, most of which had been more of a drugged-out, alcohol induced nod. His eyes sunk deep into their sockets and his hands were shaking. Slick Nick's nerves were totally shot. This morning's crash had been much worse than the previous day's, and his increasing immunity to the cocaine was not helping him reach the level of high he desired. The more he did, the more he wanted; but cocaine is an evil mistress—the more he did, the more it took. Now, Nick's mood swing had him deep into his subconscious where all he could think about was Jennifer Swords.

Another drink and a couple of lines had not distracted those desires. Instead, all he could visualize was "his" Jennifer with Vincent Panachi. Jealousy burned in his head like the cocaine that ran through his veins.

It had been a while since Jennifer had heard from Nick, and she really hadn't expected to. At least not after the way she had dumped him for Vincent, and certainly her hairdresser would have said something to Nick by now. She sensed something wrong in his voice, right away.

"Good morning, Nick. I'm surprised to hear from you."

Immediately, Slick Nick's drugged out mind translated that remark into a sarcastic one which placed him on the defensive, and he attacked. His paranoia had him believing that everybody and everything was involved in a conspiracy against him.

"You don't even care if you hear from me or not, do you?"

"Nick, what do you mean?" Jennifer calmly responded.

The days spent talking to himself during his coke binge brought forth a flurry of words, and he spoke so fast that some were totally unintelligible.

"You know damn well what I mean. How could you come to my restaurant with Vincent Panachi? Besides, you were my girl when he met you. Another thing, I heard from the grapevine that you two are a hot item now. God damn it, you're mine . . ."

Jennifer cut him off before he could continue his rage. Slick Nick had allowed the drugs, jealousy and booze to bring him to the point where he was being manipulated by uncontrollable anger. Jennifer, on the other hand, was as cool as anyone could have possibly been. She had what she wanted—a shot at Vincent Panachi. Also, Nick was correct in his assumption—Jennifer Swords could care less if she ever heard from Slick Nick again. Jennifer was ruthless.

"I am not yours; never have been yours; and never will be yours."

There was a silence before Nick spoke again.

"What about us making love together?"

Jennifer's voice was as cold as ice, "I may have fucked you, okay. But I NEVER made love with you."

That statement went through Slick Nick's heart like a knife. His mind turned those words into fuel for a jealous rage, and he exploded into the telephone, "You bitch, I better not see you anywhere around with any guys . . . especially Vincent Panachi!"

Jennifer coldly replied, without raising her voice, "I will go anywhere I please, with anyone I choose . . . and if you can't handle it, then that's your problem. Good-bye, Nick."

She slammed the portable phone down onto the dressing table, and the noise echoed through Slick Nick's receiver.

He sat in total silence for a half minute before a monotone voice carried through the telephone's receiver, "If you would like to make a call, please hang up . . ."

Nick's temper blew, and he pulled the telephone from the wall. "That bitch!" he screamed at the top of his lungs. In his twisted mind he had turned to Jennifer in one of his weakest moments, and she had spit in his face. Nick was infuriated! He was also a drugged-up, emotional cupcake. Suddenly, with no warning, Nick flung himself on the bed and began crying. Somehow, within a matter of days his life had turned to shit, and he knew it.

Slick Nick's emotional state did not affect Jennifer in the least. On the contrary, the more she thought about it the happier she got. As a matter of fact the phone call boosted her already inflated self-image. Jennifer was now enjoying a power that she had dreamt of throughout her adolescent years. It had been an emotionally enduring climb for her to the top, and now she had a chance at the brass ring. She knew that if she captured Vincent Panachi she would be set for life, and no amount of sniveling could distract her from that goal. She smiled at her reflection in the mirror.

While Jennifer carefully critiqued her makeup application in the mirror, Vincent skillfully steered his Scarab Thunder underneath the Hillsborough Bridge. The idle speed zone extended through the sheltered harbor, and it wasn't until he reached the rocks that he powered up the Scarab's engines. The dual throttle controls vibrated in his hands while the throaty engines idled at one-thousand rpm. However, no sooner had he reached the rocks, the throttles advanced and the powerful engines responded. The Scarab Thunder shot two rooster tails eight feet high until the thirty-eight foot hull lifted from the water onto a plane. The vibrating throttle controls quickly became rock-solid handles in his right hand as the engine's rpm wound higher. Instinctively, Vincent looked behind the boat to check the water exhausts. The powerful engines were shooting two streams of water through four inch exhaust stacks, which meant the cooling systems were functioning properly. Vincent's left hand found the hull's trim tabs, and his fingers lightly danced upon them. The Scarab Thunder responded as the bow lowered closer to the water and the rooster tails trailing behind the go-fast diminished to a normal wake. Within a minute, the Scarab was skimming across the ocean's placid surface at over sixty miles per hour. It hadn't fully registered when it happened, but now that the Scarab was properly trimmed and the engines were screaming, Vincent recalled seeing the end of Hillsborough's rock jetty zip past in his peripheral vision.

The Scarab Thunder was south bound at the same moment Jennifer Swords was stepping into her skimpy, T-back, bikini bottom. Her ample breasts swung back and forth as she bent right then left. The top fastened from the rear, but in order to form a seductive cleavage it was necessary for her to reach inside the top and cup her breasts, one at a time, to set them properly inside the custom fit bikini. Jennifer checked her figure in the bedroom's full length mirror and smiled. One thing was certain—if no one else was in love with her, she most certainly was in love with herself.

Jennifer glanced at her watch; it was 10:48 and Vincent would arrive anytime, so she walked into the living room where she could view the endless miles of the Atlantic Ocean. A concrete pier jutted into the ocean just to the north, and Jennifer had often used it as a division mark when she searched for a particular boat. This time it was not hard for her to discern Vincent's Scarab. A quick search of the area south of the pier had not revealed anything resembling his go-fast, but once she shifted her field of vision to the north, Jennifer quickly identified the Scarab Thunder right away. The unmistakable, multi-colored stripe down the center of the deck was unique in that it was the only one she had ever seen. It blended from yellow to green to blue to purple, and extended from the tip of the bow to the wraparound windscreen. Silver, bold, block letters angled at the bottom of the windscreen reflected the morning sun and spelled the word *SCARAB*. It was beautiful watching the sleek watercraft glide silently across the ocean's surface.

Jennifer figured that the go-fast was closing in on her condominium at a very fast rate, and within minutes Vincent would be in front of her building. Quickly, Jennifer grabbed her purse from the kitchen counter. The elevator was just outside her door, and she pushed the button to summon it. Apparently, someone on the condominium's upper floors must have just used it, because the elevator was there within seconds. Jennifer entered the elevator and pressed the appropriate button for the ground floor.

Meanwhile, Vincent's Scarab passed the concrete fishing pier. Vincent glanced to his right and watched as the huge pilings blurred past the go-fast. Ahead, Jennifer's high rise condominium towered above the beach. Vincent's right hand gently pulled the throttles back reducing the fuel flow to the two powerful engines. Instantaneously, the rpm began winding down. Even so, the Scarab was traveling so fast that it remained up on the plane, its hull smoothly skimming across the placid surface. In less than a minute, the Scarab approached Jennifer's building. Vincent reduced the throttles even further, and the sleek hull settled into the water. The engines idled and the shoreline was one hundred yards away. Vincent turned the wheel to the right until the bow of the Scarab pointed directly at the high rise. Several sunbathers, complete with their umbrellas, coolers and chairs, dotted the beach area in front of the condominium building. Nevertheless, it only took seconds for Vincent to discern which bikini clad beauty was Jennifer. She was standing in ankle-deep water waving her outstretched right arm high above her head. Her long, blond hair swung in rhythm with her every move. Vincent waved back with his right arm then quickly replaced his curled fingers around the throttle quadrant. The powerful engines rumbled while the exhaust stacks coughed and spit gallons of water through the chrome twin pipes, as if in defiance of being starved their precious fuel. These engines were thoroughbreds designed to run fast, not idle. Vincent placed the gear selectors in neutral, then raced the engines to prevent them from loading up. Once the rpm dropped, he pushed the handles back into forward. The beach was twenty-five yards away and Jennifer was knee-deep in the water. Vincent gently laid his fingers on the power trim and began raising the stern drives. Within seconds, dual, three-bladed, stainless-steel propellers were whipping the water behind the stern into tiny whirlpools. Vincent placed the gear selectors into neutral and killed the ignition. The Scarab Thunder gently glided towards the smooth, sandy shore.

The elongated bow of the sleek go-fast made contact with the shoreline's sandy bottom, and the thirty-eight foot boat came to a halt. Jennifer was standing midway between the end of the bow and the windscreen.

"Walk just past the windscreen where I can help you aboard," Vincent smiled and instructed her.

"What a nice boat, and Vincent, you look so sexy in it!" Jennifer returned the smile and began walking towards him.

"Thank you, Jennifer."

Vincent crossed to the other side of the Scarab and reached his hand over the gunwale. Jennifer extended her arm to meet his while the water reached her upper thigh. Vincent took her purse with his free hand and laid it on the passenger's seat, then grabbed her with both hands. Gently but firmly, Vincent pulled Jennifer into the boat. As the upper portion of her body came over the side of the Scarab Vincent could not help but notice her breasts, and with her arms outstretched forward it helped accentuate them. When Jennifer was safely in the boat, Vincent leaned over and gave her a kiss. Their tongues found one another as their lips pressed together in passion. Vincent could feel the heat rushing to his loins and knew that he had better end the kiss or be prepared for an embarrassing moment. Jennifer closed her lips and sucked on his tongue as he withdrew it from her mouth. Vincent looked into her eyes and they held a momentary stare. He was thankful that his embarrassing moment had passed. Jennifer knew what was going through Vincent's mind and that was precisely the reason she had clamped her lips down on his tongue.

Vincent led Jennifer through the companionway to the cabin space below. She ducked her head as she carefully stepped down the two steps, her right hand resting on Vincent's shoulder. Once Jennifer was in the cabin, Vincent motioned toward a small settee.

"Why don't you leave your purse and sandals here?" Vincent suggested. Jennifer laid her Gucci purse against the back of the seat and Vincent added, "You'd better leave your visor here, also. More than likely it would blow off." Jennifer did not verbally reply, but she removed the matching visor and laid it beside the sandals. She shook her head and her lengthy mane of hair swung from side-to-side. Afterwards, there were no crease marks where the visor had been. Jennifer had the movement down to a science. She looked around the cabin and complimented Vincent.

"This is so nice."

"Thank you."

Jennifer saw his head turning and averted her eyes from where she had been looking—the queen-sized, V-berth in the bow of the cabin. His eyes met hers, and he asked, "Are we ready?"

"Let's go fast," she replied as she flashed him a radiant smile and reached for his hand.

Vincent barely touched the keys when he fired-up the powerful engines. With the exhausts spewing water and the finely tuned engines rumbling, Vincent placed the gear selector in reverse and gently backed the deep-V hull off the sandy bottom. The Scarab went straight back until Vincent determined there was sufficient room to turn the thirty-eight foot boat around. He placed the port engine in forward while the starboard engine remained in reverse. The differential power spun the Scarab on its axis, and Vincent allowed the bow to swing around until the compass had swung a full one hundred and eighty degrees. Jennifer did not know anything about compass bearings, but she did notice that Vincent had not even turned his head to look during the turn, yet the bow of the Scarab stopped turning precisely when it pointed towards the open ocean. Vincent gently brought the starboard engine from reverse to forward with such smoothness that Jennifer had not noticed the gear change. Once the bow became stabilized, Vincent advanced the throttles. The roar of the engines was deafening as they began guzzling high octane fuel as fast as it could be sucked into their carburetors. Vincent's right hand was curled around the throttles while his left firmly held the steering wheel with such force that his knuckles flushed white in color. Instinctively, he glanced over to check Jennifer. She was in a relaxed position, safely encased in the stand-up, wrap around seat, her left hand resting on the side of the boat. Within a minute, the Scarab was skimming across the placid Atlantic Ocean at seventy miles per hour. Jennifer's long, blond hair trailed behind her head like a flag in a stiff breeze. The Scarab's engines were screaming as the distance between the go-fast and the shoreline grew farther apart. Finally, after almost ten minutes of hard running, Vincent slowly inched the throttles back to idle. The sleek hull that had been standing on the props now settled into the calm water beneath it. The deafening roar of the engines was replaced by the irregular rumblings of idling racing cams. Vincent turned the steering wheel to the left, and the bow of the boat responded accordingly. Both he and Jennifer looked towards landfall and saw that her high-rise condominium appeared to be no more than a small scaled model on the horizon. Jennifer looked around the Scarab then flashed Vincent an erotic smile. Whether or not he had planned it this way didn't matter, because it certainly fit her plans to the tee. There was not another boat in sight.

"I have some suntan lotion in my purse. Would you like some?" Jennifer asked. She had already begun to move towards the cabin before Vincent could answer.

"No, but would you get me a beer, please? I shoved a six-pack in the ice maker this morning." Vincent replied.

"Okay. I found them."

While she was below, Vincent turned off the motors and secured the stern drives in neutral. Immediately, the silent serenity of the open sea replaced the rhythmic, mechanical, rumbling of the Scarab's idling engines. Gentle, rolling swells from the Gulf Stream lapped against the elongated, fiberglass hull while Vincent breathed in the clean sea air. He loved the peace and quiet that only the ocean provided, although this was a love that neither Anthony Vitale nor Capo Pelligi shared. The extent of their boating experience consisted of motoring up and down the Intracoastal Waterway on a floating condominium.

Jennifer squeezed a thin line of lotion along the length of her extended arm then set the bottle down on the countertop. She gently rubbed the lotion into her skin until its presence was untraceable. Systematically, she repeated the procedure with her other arm, then applied the lotion to both legs and set the lotion back on the countertop so that she could reach into her purse for her hairbrush. Long strokes untangled her wind blown hair until it was silky smooth. A quick check in her compact mirror verified that her makeup was still intact, even after the high speed ride. Jennifer replaced everything back in her purse except the suntan lotion. Instinctively, she glanced toward the companionway to see if Vincent was watching her. From her position in the cabin, he was not in sight. Quickly, Jennifer reached behind and untied the knot in her bikini top. Within a split second, the thin fabric slid from her rounded breasts. Jennifer rolled the bikini top into a small ball and stuffed it into her purse. The ice maker was on the same side of the cabin, next to the countertop. Jennifer pulled the split-door open and saw the necks of several Heineken bottles protruding from the ice. She grabbed one and tugged as it slid effortlessly from the surrounding ice. The green, glass bottle was chilled to the point of nearly freezing the beer inside. The coldness of the bottle against her hand reminded her of something she used to do that drove her ex-husband into an erotic frenzy. Jennifer reached into the ice bin and removed a piece of ice. Slowly, almost torturously, she encircled the tips of her nipples with the frozen water. Jennifer gasped slightly as she slid the smooth ice crosswise against her now throbbing nipples. The procedure took less than two minutes, but the results would last an hour. When Jennifer looked down she smiled. Her nipples stood out half an inch from her D-cup breasts. She knew that this little trick would have the same effect on Vincent as it had with Dr. Mitchell Swords. Yes, Jennifer knew all the tricks.

Jennifer popped the top off of Vincent's beer. With suntan lotion in one hand and a bottle of Heineken in the other, she stepped through the companionway. Vincent had been looking the other direction until he heard her coming up the steps from the cabin. His eyes met hers just as she came through the hatch. A smile was on her face, her hair reflected the sun, and her naked breasts jutted forward. Vincent did not stare, but his eyes worked their way down from hers. When his eyes shot back to hers, he found her still smiling. She said, "Here's your beer, and would you rub some lotion on me, please?" Who was Vincent to refuse such an invitation?

That is exactly how it began, and before the day was over they made love three times. When the afternoon sun hung low on the horizon, Vincent Panachi could not ever recall having been so well satisfied. As for Jennifer Swords, she knew exactly what her emotions were, and what his were.

CHAPTER EIGHT

I t was a two man operation to swing open the huge, iron gates that separated Anthony Vitale's New Jersey estate from the rest of the world. Two soldiers of the Vitale crime family were stationed along the cobblestone driveway, and they had been given word that the old man was holding a meeting that morning. The wind howled and drove the temperature well below freezing which chilled the men to the bone, but the two maintained a vigil watch over the entrance to the estate. Before dawn that morning a car had driven off, and although they weren't certain, the passenger was thought to have been Capo Pelligi. If so, and he returned to find them not at their assigned post, the ass-chewing of the century would shortly follow. Therefore, the two soldiers stood beside the iron gates with the collars on their winter coats turned high to break the relentless wind. Shoulder holsters harnessed cold, steel, automatic pistols beneath their coats, and machine pistols rested against the stone walls that supported the heavy iron gates, their steel-blue frames bearing a color resemblance to the obscured sky above. It was a typical miserable winter morning in Newark, New Jersey.

The whistling of the wind prevented the two solders from hearing the Limousine as it approached the estate. It was not until the elongated Cadillac was upon them that they realized it was there. Fortunately one of the men saw it before the driver blew the horn signaling to open the gate. The side and rear windows of the limousine were tinted, which prevented them from seeing anything more than a silhouette when the car had previously departed. Now that the limousine was sitting at the gate, the soldiers had a clear shot through the windshield. Their suspicions were confirmed when they saw Capo Pelligi with an unidentified passenger in the rear of the limousine. The two guards removed their hands from their coat pockets and acknowledged the driver's identity by waving. The driver merely nodded, never removing his hands from the steering wheel. The soldiers swung the heavy iron gates open, and the driver sped through the entranceway as the limousine's exhaust spewed a cloud of smoke when the warm exhaust met the cold outside air. The soldiers watched as the limousine followed the curved, cobblestone driveway towards the old-brick mansion. Neither of them questioned the other, but both men wondered who the unidentified passenger might be. Silently they closed the iron gates, and resumed their vigil watch.

The more aged Anthony Vitale became, the more he disliked the frigid winter temperatures. It had been one week since his return from the balmy, sun-drenched skies of Southern Florida, but even still he had been overheard complaining that a week in the tropical sun had thinned his blood to the point of not being able to handle the God forsaken cold winter days. Consequently, the old man spent his days comfortably nestled in the library of his spacious mansion. Capo Pelligi served as Anthony's legs as he was dispatched on the most trustworthy of missions. Today's mission had been to bring the infamous printer to Anthony Vitale.

The library was Mr. Vitale's favorite room. It had mahogany paneling, a wet bar, a huge marble fireplace, built-in bookcases, and views of the pool area and manicured grounds. The vaulted ceiling allowed for a twelve-foot Palladian window, which, at a great expense, had been custom-built of bulletproof glass. Anthony Vitale's favorite chair sat directly in front of the huge pane of glass, perhaps to entice those who would wish to see him killed. It was from this chair that the head of the Vitale crime family spent many mornings pondering the strategic moves of the syndicate. It was also from this chair that the old man watched as the Cadillac limousine approached the mansion.

The cobblestone driveway paralleled a line of hardwood trees as it serpentined its way through the estate. Even though Anthony Vitale was closely watching the approaching vehicle from his chair, the weaving of the limousine and the poor lighting from the obscure winter sky made it impossible for him to get a good look at his long-term associate. The driveway led into a huge, round area completely covered with cobblestones. An old-brick planter stood directly in the center of the circle and encased a huge oak tree—Anthony Vitale's favorite. He watched the elongated hood of the limousine as it slowly circled the planter, then stopped at the front entrance to the mansion. The right, rear door opened and Capo Pelligi stepped out. Anthony Vitale leaned forward in his chair and strained to see more clearly as he peered through the library's large window. A pair of legs swung from the opening in the side of the Cadillac, while the old man looked on in anticipation. Suddenly, the figure appeared—the Quill.

Although they had spoken many times during the years since his release, Anthony Vitale had not physically seen the Quill in nearly twenty years. It had been understood that the Vitale mansion was just too "hot" for the Quill to frequent, especially in light of the fact that he was then completing a term of supervised parole. Now, with all that behind him, Anthony Vitale waited with open arms to welcome one of his most trusted friends. The head of the Vitale crime family watched as the two figures approached a pair of circular stairways that lead to a columned, circular portico. Without realizing he was doing so, Anthony Vitale nodded his head in approval of the way his associate looked. The years had been good to him, even if so many of them had been spent behind bars. In actuality, the closer the Quill got, the more Anthony thought that the aging process had remained stagnant during his years in prison. Anthony had seen that same sort of thing before where one of his soldiers had taken an extended "Roman Holiday," compliments of the federal government, only to return well rested, alcohol free for years, and in excellent physical condition. In some cases, the soldiers had looked years younger upon their return to the family. Anthony watched from the window while the two men entered the double-door entranceway that opened into a stunning front-to-back marble foyer. Anthony could not see the Quill's reaction, but he envisioned the scene in his mind—the Quill was standing in the center of the magnificent foyer, and ever so slowly, his head would tilt upwards as he viewed its twenty-foot, vaulted ceiling and its enormous chandelier. It was a scene the head of the crime family had witnessed many times, and the Quill was no different. His movements were precisely as the old man had envisioned. From the corner of his eye, Anthony saw the limousine pull away. Instinctively, Anthony stood and shook the wrinkles from his wool trousers, then tugged at the bottom of his cardigan sweater. To the unknowing the head of the Vitale crime family may have been mistaken for the chief executive officer of a major corporation, relaxing at home on a cold winter's day, causally dressed. A large, mahogany desk sat in the middle of the floor and was positioned in such a manner as to allow the person sitting at the desk a breathtaking view of the estate's forest-like hardwoods. As Anthony walked toward the desk, he visually checked the briefcase Capo Pelligi had placed there earlier that morning. The slim, executive-style, leather case laid on top of the polished, mahogany desk. Inside the briefcase were eight, individually wrapped packets that contained twenty-five thousand dollars apiece—two hundred thousand dollars, all in one hundred dollar bills. Seed money for the counterfeiting project.

Anthony Vitale patted the case as he walked by it on the way to the library's door. His timing was impeccable. Just as he reached the door he heard footsteps approaching across the imported-Italian-tiled hallway leading to the library. Three distinct sounds; Capo Pelligi, the Quill, and the butler. The butler tapped lightly on the solid mahogany door, in his usual manner. Anthony responded, "Enter." The library's door opened inwards, so Anthony stepped to the side and stood next to the doorway. The butler opened the door then stepped aside. His extended arm showed the two men in.

The Quill was first through the doorway, and his eyes immediately met with Anthony's. The two elderly gentlemen stared almost in disbelief that they were truly looking at each other in the flesh. It had been some twenty years since the two friends had physically met. Anthony smiled as he held his arms out to embrace his long-lived friend and associate. The Quill mirrored the movement, and the two elderly gentlemen embraced. The head of the Vitale crime family craned his neck from side to side as he kissed his friend on the cheeks. The cordial greeting was far more than just a practiced custom. An Italian-style kiss on the cheek from the head of a crime syndicate reflected honor and respect, both of which the Quill had earned by not implicating any of his fellow conspirators when the Feds had nabbed him some twenty, irrecoverable years ago. Now the two men stood together, no more than an arm's length apart. Anthony grasped the Quill by the shoulders and held him with outstretched arms while he commented, "My friend, the years have been kind to you."

The Quill had both his hands lightly resting on Anthony's elbows, almost as if he were supporting the weight of the elderly gentleman's outstretched arms. The Quill smiled as he replied, "And you . . . you haven't aged a bit. My friend, the Shark."

Anthony playfully slapped the Quill's shoulders as he laughed. The head of the crime family quipped, "And you still know how to lie with a straight face, just like you did to the Feds."

A moment of silence followed while the two men held a stare filled with admiration. Finally, it was Capo Pelligi who broke the silence when he said, "Mr. Vitale, I'll have to get going if I'm going to be there when the Learjet arrives."

Anthony dropped his arms and glanced at his watch. He turned his head slightly so that he could address his most trusted Capo face to face when he said, "Yes, you will. Bring him directly back here to the library." Anthony grabbed the Quill by the elbow and turned to lead him into the room, then, almost as an afterthought, he instructed the Capo, "Send the butler back with a bottle of brandy and two snifters . . . and cigars . . . several cigars." Capo Pelligi did not have a chance to acknowledge the order, one way or another. Instead, Anthony Vitale continued speaking to his friend as they walked towards the sofa. "We've got a lot of catching up to do." Capo Pelligi did however overhear his boss tell the Quill, "I have someone very special coming to meet you. Someone you will recognize, right away, but have yet to meet." The Quill looked at him with a curious expression, but all the old man would tell him was, "I'll give you a hint—he is the spitting image of his father." The hint only served to befuddle the Quill, for it had been over two decades since he had seen any of the boys from Newark. At any rate, the two men sat down, the Quill on the sofa and Anthony in his favorite chair. The mystery man would appear soon enough, and in the mean time, there were years upon years to talk about.

The first few minutes of conversation were awkward. There was so much that had happened during the past twenty years that Anthony did not know where to begin. The men sat across from one another, and both noted the Cadillac limousine leaving the estate. The Quill broke the moment of silence when he remarked, "I suppose the man Capo Pelligi has gone after has something to do with our deal."

The statement was meant to serve as an icebreaker or at least place them on a common ground—the making of money. It was a subject whereby neither of them was ever at a loss for words.

Anthony smiled at his friend and replied, "Yes, you are correct. As a matter of fact, he will serve as the family's liaison for the largest production project you have ever been involved with."

The statement raised the Quill straight backed in his seat. "How interesting. Please tell me more."

Actually, the Quill's excitement was difficult to keep self-contained. Time and time again since his release, the head of the Vitale crime family had rejected any and all plans that the Quill had proposed. It had never been a question of quality, for it was a well-known fact that the Quill was the best reproduction specialist available. Anthony Vitale had always blamed his reluctance to do anything on distribution, or more to the point, the lack of it.

Anthony's eyes shined with a gleam. "It is time for you to go to work, my friend. I have cut a deal for the delivery of fifty million dollars in counterfeit twenty-dollar bills."

Involuntarily, the Quill whistled. *PHEW!* "Fifty million dollars!"

Anthony chuckled, "Nice, round number, wouldn't you say?"

The Quill laughed, as well, "Hell, I guess so." He paused for a couple of seconds while his mind played with the large number, then he confirmed, "You've got somebody that can move all that? That's a lot of paper . . ."

Anthony's voice was soft, almost soothing, when he replied, "Yes, my friend. The Colombians will take it all."

The Quill could not hide the surprise in his voice when he asked, "The Colombians?"

Twenty years ago, when he went to prison, Drug Lords had not even been heard of, and Colombia was a South American nation that supplied the world with fresh mountain coffee, not a seemingly endless supply of marijuana and cocaine.

Anthony sensed the uncertainty his long-term friend must have been experiencing, so he added, "Don't you worry about those details. That will be the responsibility of the young man on his way here. All you need to concern yourself with is doing what you do best . . . print the money."

Unlike the subject of Drug Lords operating out of remote sectors of South American countries, this was familiar turf. Even during his "stretch with the Feds," the Quill kept abreast of the technological changes within the printing industry. The advancements made during the two decade span were astonishing. Antiquated printing presses had been replaced by high-tech computers and full-color, high-speed, color copiers. Every process had been automated from the point of inserting the paper, all the way through the tedious task of cutting the printed matter into the appropriate size. As a matter of fact, some machines even separate and package the material. No matter how advanced the technology became, however, one thing that could not be duplicated was the knowledge the Quill possessed of making false currency. As the adage goes, "They broke the mold when he was born." Perhaps because there were not, and never had been, any as good as the Quill. He was in a class of his own.

The Quill looked out the window and stared at the hardwood trees while he contemplated the figure. Suddenly, he turned his head back towards Anthony when he asked, "How soon do you need it?"

Anthony clasped his hands in front of him with fingers entwined. He laid them on his lap and queried, "How soon can you deliver?"

The Quill was cool when he replied, "Given 'Carte Blanche' to purchase the necessary equipment, three months on the outside."

The head of the Vitale crime family confirmed, "Fifty million?"

The Quill did not even flinch, "In flawless, twenty-dollar bills."

The men shared a smile, and were holding that smile on their faces when the butler sounded his familiar *TAP! TAP!* on the library's solid, mahogany door. Anthony turned his head and hollered, "Enter."

The butler walked backwards through the doorway, both hands underneath a sterling silver tray. As he pivoted through the opening, the Quill saw that the tray supported a full decanter of fine brandy, two crystal glasses, a crystal lighter with a matching ashtray, and a wooden box of Cuban cigars.

The butler said, "Your brandy and cigars, sir."

Anthony unfolded his hands and made a sweeping motion towards the coffee table while he instructed the servant, "Put them over there, please."

The butler carefully placed the silver tray on the table, then turned to his boss and asked, "Will there be anything else, sir?"

"Not at the moment. Just show Vincent in when he arrives. Thank you," Anthony Vitale replied.

The butler did a half-bow, half-nod, then left without another word. When the library's door had closed, the Quill queried, "Vincent?"

Anthony reached for the decanter of brandy and poured an inch of the dark liquor into each of the glasses. He turned his head and smiled at his long-term friend as he offered him a drink. Seconds of silence passed before he responded to the name, then he said, "Yes. Vincent Panachi."

This name Panachi triggered memories from as far back as the Quill could remember. The Quill and Vito Panachi had been much more than close friends. They had shared their hopes and dreams with one another on a daily basis.

It was tough living in the neighborhoods of Newark, New Jersey during those times, but Vito Panachi had proved to be quite capable of handling anything that got in his way. His loyalty had earned him the position of Anthony Vitale's right hand man, himself a Capo at the time. Anthony Vitale carried with him the family heritage of being a Vitale, so when a street war broke out between the Vitale crime family and a rival crime family, it was Capo Vitale who had been targeted for a hit. The contract was placed with the rival gang's best shooter, but he screwed it up. One evening, the rival crime family's foot soldiers spotted Capo Vitale and Vito Panachi entering a theater. News traveled quickly, and eventually found its way back to the shooter. He waited across the street from the theater's entrance, cloaked by a veil of darkness. Capo Vitale and his most trusted soldier, Vito Panachi, emerged from the theater. The shooter fired from his concealed position and watched as a body dropped onto the pavement, then ran like hell through the dark alleyways between the buildings. It was not until the following day that the rival crime family learned of the shooter's mistake—he had gunned down Vito Panachi, Vincent's father, instead of his intended target, Capo Anthony Vitale. It was a mistake that cost them dearly, for that attempt on Anthony's life started an all out war between the two families. Bloodshed filled the streets of Newark at an unprecedented rate. Killings took place nearly everyday for months on end until finally, a truce was called. The Quill learned of his best friend's demise shortly after he entered Leavenworth Penitentiary. It was a very sad day, and like all tragedies, one that was branded into his memory, forever.

There are those who share the belief that one's life flashes before their eyes seconds before they pass away. The memories of Vito Panachi and those days decades ago flashbacked through the Quill's mind with the same speed. As a matter of fact, the chain-thinking had happened so quickly that Anthony was not aware that his friend had just time-traveled through the past. The thoughts did serve to remind the Quill of some of the good 'ole days, and gave him fresh subject matter to rekindle his long-term friendship with Anthony. Immediately, the subject of the impending counterfeit operation was changed to the good times they had enjoyed together, and before either of them had realized it half the decanter of brandy, as well as an hour of time, had disappeared. The magic spark in their friendship was rekindled while the two gentlemen talked and laughed as they reminisced the turbulent years of their youth. Meanwhile, the Quill had yet to correlate the names Vincent with Vito.

Anthony Vitale was the first to see the Cadillac limousine as it approached the estate. He smiled to himself, because he knew within a matter of minutes that the Quill was going to see the perfect likeness of a younger Vito Panachi when Vincent entered the library.

Several minutes passed while the two men talked, then the butler's familiar knock was heard at the door. Anthony leaned forward in his chair as he said, "Excuse me," to the Quill.

The interruption silenced the Quill, who had been in the midst of a story. Anthony stood then crossed the room to the door. Rather than blurt out his usual command of, "Enter," the head of the crime family opened the library's door himself. The Quill could not see past Anthony, but standing in front of Anthony

Vitale was Vincent Panachi, well dressed and well tanned. The two men hugged, and Anthony kissed Vincent on both cheeks. The Quill watched from across the room and instinctively stood in preparation for an introduction to this mystery man. When Anthony turned around, Vincent Panachi's face came into the Quill's view. What he saw shot a surge of adrenaline through his veins. As Anthony and Vincent walked towards the Quill, he riveted his eyes on the much younger man. He could not believe his own vision. Vincent was identical to his father, or at least as the Quill remembered him. The Quill's eyes shifted momentarily to Anthony's face, whose expression was one of utter delight. The old man had waited decades for this moment, and he was going to thoroughly enjoy himself.

Once the two men were standing in front of the Quill, Anthony said, "Vincent, say hello to a gentleman known only as the Quill."

Anthony turned his head slightly to address the Quill when he queried, "Haven't you two met before . . . perhaps in another time?"

The Quill remained silent for several seconds, dumbfounded by the shocking resemblance, before he answered, "It is Vito . . . Vito Panachi."

Tears filled the elderly man's face as he bypassed Vincent's offer to shake hands. Instead, he bear hugged the younger man, much to the shock of Vincent. Vincent could feel the wetness of the man's tears of joy as the Quill lovingly pressed his cheek against Vincent's. Finally, it all became clear when the Quill half-spoke, half-whispered, in Vincent's ear, "Your father was my best friend . . . I would have died for him . . ."

The rest of the day was spent in an atmosphere worthy of a family reunion while the three men reminisced about the good 'ole days. As the cold, winter day turned to night, the conversation lead to business. It was this meeting that sealed the deal. The Quill was to work underneath Vincent's command, and Vincent was to cater to the Quill's every need. It was an inspired arrangement, because in the end they would all get what they desired—money . . . lots of money.

CHAPTER NINE

T echnically, it was just a few minutes past sunrise in Newark, New Jersey, but one could not tell from the lackluster sky. The low-pressure system that had engulfed the northeast area several days earlier still lingered, and consequently, the first light of the new day was shrouded by low level obscure clouds. Even though Vincent Panachi had been in New Jersey almost twenty-four hours, there had been no measurable change in the weather. The sky was still the same winter-gray, dismal color he recalled every winter ever having been. As much as Vincent enjoyed spending time with Anthony Vitale, he was always glad to be headed back to the Sunshine State. He no longer wanted anything to do with the cold winters of New Jersey.

The three men in the library had been joined by Capo Pelligi the night before, shortly after 9 p.m., and a good time had been had by all. Vincent was the youngest of the group yet he had begged off first, just prior to midnight, when he reminded Anthony Vitale, "You do remember that the jet is picking me up in the morning, don't you?"

Anthony Vitale was somewhat inebriated. He looked at his nephew with admiring eyes, and smiled. "Yes, I remember."

The elderly gentleman stood and walked over to Vincent. Vincent also stood; not out of courtesy, but to steady Anthony's wobbling walk. Anthony placed a hand on Vincent's shoulder, and then looked into Vincent's eyes. Perhaps the liquor had made the hardened man soft, but Vincent swore he saw tears in the old man's eyes. Anthony pulled Vincent towards him enough so that he could crane his neck and kiss Vincent on the cheek. Vincent smiled, and when the head of the Vitale crime family leaned back, he was smiling, also. The hand that had rested on Vincent's shoulder slid down to his elbow, and with no explanation, the elderly gentleman led Vincent towards the desk in the center of the room. The leather briefcase had lain on the desk, untouched, during their entire meeting. No one really gave its presence a second thought, because it was nothing out of the ordinary to see a slim, executive-style case lying there.

Anthony patted the briefcase with his right hand while he informed Vincent, "Tomorrow morning, you take this case and the Quill back to Florida with you. The case contains two hundred grand start-up funds for our project. That should be enough for now. Get the Quill anything he needs . . . anything he wants. No questions asked. This man is the best, so keep him happy."

Vincent patted Anthony on the back and replied, "I'll make you proud of me . . . don't worry, there will be no problems."

Anthony smiled as he gave his favorite nephew a love pat on the cheek. He said, "I know."

As with after any night spent drinking, one always feels that they could have gotten more sleep. Vincent Panachi was no different. The alarm clock startled him from a sound sleep over an hour before sunrise. Apparently things began happening early around the mansion, because the sound of the Cadillac limousine's huge motor warming up could be heard through the closed bedroom window. When Vincent looked out he also saw other lights on downstairs. Indeed, the days began very early for the Vitale mansion's staff.

Once Vincent dressed and went downstairs he was greeted by the Quill. The elderly gentleman was sitting at the expansive dining room table, sipping a cup of coffee. Vincent greeted him, "Good morning."

"And a good morning to you," the Quill replied as he looked up from his cup.

"You're up awfully early, aren't you?" Vincent asked.

"A habit from the joint," replied the elderly man smiling as he set his cup down on the saucer. His judgment was a hair off, and the small, round, shallow dish made a clanging noise as the bottom of the cup met it.

"Yes, I suppose so," Vincent remarked.

After all, what kind of intelligent response could be made to offset one's having been awakened at 4:30 a.m., involuntarily, for twenty years. All things considered, the elderly gentleman had retained a remarkable sense of humor.

Vincent tactfully maneuvered the conversation towards happier times, such as the present and the future.

"Quill, have you ever been in a Learjet before?"

"I've never flown before. Today will be my first time," the Quill replied as he looked Vincent straight in the eye.

"You are going to love it," Vincent said as he flashed the elderly man a comforting smile.

The Quill nodded his head with the full belief that he would. A few uncomfortable seconds of silence passed before Vincent attempted to carry the conversation.

"How about Florida? Have you ever been there?"

The Quill looked down at his coffee. Perhaps he was mulling over the years that had been robbed from his life and the things he had never had a chance to do.

"Can't say that I have," the Quill finally mumbled.

Vincent was very perceptive to people's emotions, and he quickly read the Quill's expression like the morning newspaper. Anthony Vitale had ordered him to keep the Quill happy. Happy employees are productive employees. Vincent's mind played back Anthony's statement, and the voice in his head made him react accordingly.

"Well, there is no better time than now to fly to Florida in a private jet. Quill, you're gonna love it. All of it."

The statement hit home. The Quill's eyes lit up with a look of excitement and anticipation not unlike that of a child on Christmas morning. For him it was like Christmas. Today he was getting everything he had hoped and wished for during the past two decades.

The head of the Vitale crime family slept in and did not see the two men depart the estate. The Cadillac's set of dual headlights illuminated the asphalt-surfaced roadway with their high beam. Even so, the blacktopped, winding road was difficult to discern, particularly from the rear compartment of the limousine. The dark tinted windows all but blacked out the automobile's headlights. Apparently, the driver could see all right, because he negotiated the curvy roadway with such speed that the Quill and Vincent leaned against one another, respective to the direction of the curve. Eventually, the rural road intersected with a main highway, and that well traveled road led them to the airport.

The Learjet sat on the ramp in front of the Signature Flight Support office. The same lights that shone upon the front of the large hangar reflected off the polished fuselage of the sleek jet. The limousine drove through the gated entrance then followed a taxiway that went between the office building and the main hangar. When the Cadillac turned the corner of the building, its headlights swept across the ramp. The light beams struck the shiny Learjet and Vincent confirmed that the aircraft's door was open. Vincent knew from his prior experiences with the aircraft's crew that they were ready to go at a moment's notice, and seeing the Lear's open door only served to confirm his thoughts.

Vincent and the Quill were traveling light. Vincent was never gone long enough to require any luggage, and besides, everything he needed was at Anthony Vitale's mansion anyway. On the other hand, the Quill had nothing at their destination. However, it was decided it would be best if the elderly man did not depart the aircraft with enough luggage to stay the winter. "You never know who's watching," Anthony had philosophized to Vincent, the Quill, and Capo Pelligi. Who were they to argue with the head of the crime family? The Quill carried nothing onboard the personal jet. Vincent carried one item—the slim, executive-style, leather briefcase that contained two hundred thousand dollars in hundred dollar bills.

Cold, dense, air is precisely what turbine engines thrive upon. It pushes their thrust to the outside of the performance envelope, and if the pilot is not careful, it is quite possible to create so much pressure inside the various stages of compression that the jet engine will, in layman's terms, blowup. Vincent and the Quill were seated on the divan seat, in the rear of the Lear 25D. Vincent was seated on the right hand side of the aircraft, and from his vantage point he could see the pilot's hand on the throttles. They had just taken off, and the sleek jet was climbing out at a steep angle. Vincent noted that the aircraft's throttles were not advanced forward as far as they could go. A less knowledgeable person would have expected to find takeoff power with the throttles slap against the stops, but Vincent knew better. He had asked the pilot the same question, once before, and the pilot had been patient enough to explain the phenomenon to him: the turbine engines had torqued out before they temped out, meaning compression had overridden temperature. Nevertheless, the Learjet was climbing like a homesick angel.

The obscure sky blanketed the aircraft and prevented the Quill from seeing anything outside the small, porthole-like window, but he looked outside the aircraft anyway. The noise of the engines' raw power whining in the cabin suggested that they were flying, even if, in fact, the Quill had not yet witnessed the earth from above. As with anyone's first flight, it is an experience remembered for a lifetime, particularly if one is fortunate enough to experience something out of the ordinary during that initial flight. The Quill was one of those fortunate few.

Darkness shrouded the aircraft, but less than a minute after takeoff, openings in the cloud deck began emitting intermittent rays of light. Thick, overcast clouds associated with the cold front blanketed the area while the Learjet climbed through a grayish sky. Cold fronts top out relatively low, and then it is clear above. The term best used to describe this is CAVU—Clear Above, Visibility Unlimited. That morning's flight found the top of the cold front at seven thousand feet, and the sky above definitely qualified as CAVU. The Quill was glued to the portside window while the personal jet screamed towards seven thousand feet. The sky was streaked with grazing rays of sunlight as the aircraft approached the top of the cloud deck. Naturally, the change in the ambient light made Vincent look towards the left side of the aircraft, as well.

Suddenly, with the abruptness of a camera's flash bulb, an extremely bright light flickered twice through the aircraft's side window. The Learjet burst through the overcast cloud deck into the clear sky above. Vincent and the Quill were looking towards the east from the left side of the personal jet, and what they witnessed had to be one of the most beautiful sights either of them had ever had the pleasure of seeing. The cloud deck was perfectly flat on top, and snow-white in color. A golden beam of light extended as far as the eye could see towards the rising sun, and the round fireball was half-above, half-below the cloud deck. Aureate rays of morning light blended with the remains of the darkness until the day relentlessly shoved the black sky back into the spectrum of color. The rays from the rising sun turned the heavens above a beautiful hue of amethyst purple.

The Lear 25D was scorching through the sky, southbound. The captain was cruise climbing the aircraft at a speed of 250 knots with a vertical ascent of two thousand five hundred feet per minute. Fourteen minutes later, the Learjet was level at forty-thousand feet, and what had been a colorful carpet of red and orange hues just minutes before, was now a blanket of milk-white, cotton ball, clouds that completely obstructed the earth below from view.

The Quill was experiencing another world, and his expression showed it. He turned to Vincent and said, "Unbelievable."

Vincent smiled as he patted the elderly man on the knee and agreed, "I know. No matter how many times I witness a sunrise from up here, I always see something different."

The beautiful experience seemed to bond the two men together. Perhaps in Anthony Vitale's genius he had planned it this way, for he could have just as easily sent the Quill down to Florida on a chartered jet by himself. But, like the game of golf, traveling in a private plane with someone provides ample opportunity for the individuals to get to know one another. A sort of do not disturb sign that really works. Guaranteed.

An hour and several states later, Vincent felt comfortable with the elderly gentleman; comfortable enough to hit him with an abrupt, direct question. Vincent shifted in his seat somewhat so that he could look the Quill directly in the eye when he queried, "Can you really do it? I mean REALLY do it?"

Twenty years of imprisonment had taught the Quill patience beyond a normal man's understanding. The question directed at his ability did not faze him in the least, mainly because he knew he was the best. When others think you're the best there is, it strokes your ego. But, when *you* know you're the best there is, it provides confidence. There was no question in anyone's mind that he knew the business—the Quill was the best. However, what they thought really did not matter to him, because his work stood on its own merits, and *he* knew he was the very best there was.

The elderly gentleman held Vincent's inquisitive look with one of the most riveting stares Vincent had ever witnessed. The Quill's voice was relaxed when he replied, "You bet I am . . . I'm the best there is. After all, why do you think they call me the Quill?"

Vincent's eyes held the gaze for a few seconds after his response then broke away. Vincent turned towards the window while he pondered the answer. When he turned back toward the Quill he smiled and said, "I find you a very interesting man. I think we'll do well together."

The Quill returned the smile as he remarked, "Just lead the way . . ."

The Learjet touched down at Ft. Lauderdale-Hollywood International Airport on schedule. During the last hour of flight, Vincent and the Quill had mapped out their strategy, and now had a working game plan allocating work and specific deadlines for the project. One other thing . . . the two men had become friends.

*　　*　　*

Later that day, but nearing the midnight hour, Slick Nick stood in the rear of his restaurant, surveying what remained of a fairly busy crowd. The tables along the huge plate glass windows were still filled with patrons, some of whom were loud and exuberant from the consumed bottles of fine wine. It had been an exceptional business night for a Monday. However, Nick was not enjoying himself. His nerves were shot, and he had been on a cocaine binge since the fatal night. Although it had only been one week since he had aced-out the Maitre d', to him it seemed like a month. His mind relived the scene over and over, replaying the horrible memory etched permanently into his brain. It was not his conscious that kept involuntarily recalling the murder. The burning in his mind was caused from uncertainty. Nick was in such a rage that night that he was not one hundred percent certain if he had left the murder scene without clues. He knew that it only took one fact that did not check out, or one unexplainable object found at the scene of the crime, to initiate a thorough investigation. Time and time again during the week Slick Nick cursed himself and his memory. He would do a line of cocaine then stare at his own image in the mirror. Finally, the reflection would win out in the staring contest, and Slick Nick would throw a temper tantrum. During his violent outburst of rage he would scream, "God damn it, I just can't remember."

Sleeplessness became a way of life. Day became night, and night became day, until his drug ridden mind could no longer separate the two. Nick had become nocturnal during the past seven days. The lack of sleep only served to accentuate his paranoid state of mind that much more.

The customers at the table nearest the restaurant's entrance stood, apparently in preparation to leave. At any rate, Slick Nick watched them from the rear of the restaurant. The party of four stopped to say goodnight to the captain who had served them dinner earlier that evening. The laughter and gaiety could be heard all the way in the back of the expansive restaurant, but Nick did not mind. That was good public relations. He watched while the five people talked by the front door, but their presence there prevented him from seeing the well-dressed man that entered the restaurant at that same moment.

Nick did not discern him from the others until he was between the group and himself. The stranger had a purposeful walk about him, and as Slick Nick looked closer, he noted that the man's eyes were filled with aim and determination. It was not a look that Slick Nick was unfamiliar with; he had learned to recognize another player early on in the game of life, lest his life expectancy be shortened. The look was so familiar to Nick that he immediately checked the gentleman's suit jacket for any unusual bulges. After so many years in the crime business the cursory glance came as second nature, but usually to no avail. However, this particular time Slick Nick swallowed hard. His eyes involuntarily widened at the recognizable sight of the bulge beneath the man's finely tailored suit jacket. "Shit . . . he's packin'," Slick Nick mumbled out loud to himself. Nick's heart pounded in his chest like a Polynesian drum while the stranger walked directly towards him. The man's eyes were riveted on Slick Nick, and his presence reflected self-assured confidence. Whatever was going down, Slick Nick knew it wasn't going to be pleasant. Instinctively, he reached inside his coat pocket for the security of his own pistol, only to find that he had left the .38 revolver in his office. The stranger approached within ten feet of Nick. The restaurateur's palms were perspiring profusely now, and his legs actually began to quiver, much to his own surprise. His mind ran rampant with the possibilities, one of which was that this well dressed gentleman with the hardened look was there to snuff him out. One thing was certain—he was not here to hand-deliver an invitation to one of Boca Raton's elite parties.

Slick Nick and the approaching stranger held one another's stare even after the man stopped directly in front of Nick. The days of snorting cocaine had left the pupils of Slick Nick's eyes dilated. Consequently, the contractile circular openings resembled dark, lifeless pools rather than a beautifully colored source of vision. Even so, the darkness of Nick's widened pupils did not compare to the coldness he found in the stranger's peering eyes. Whoever he was; whatever he wanted; this man was driven by a force much more potent than any sniffable drug, and Slick Nick knew it. The man's stare was piercing to the point of rendering the restaurateur motionless, at least on the outside, yet inside Slick Nick was shaking. The stranger did not blink an eyelash as his right slowly disappeared inside his suit jacket. Involuntarily, Slick Nick drew a deep breath; he fully expected to see the stranger's hand withdraw with fingers curled around the handle of a piece. It was weird, almost to the point of being eerie; the way Slick Nick's mind never considered retreat, but rather questioned what type of pistol would fire the fatal shot. Will it be a .22, .25, or a .38 caliber? The uncanny part about this was the inevitableness that the long-term street hoodlum made good felt once he resigned himself to the fact that he was about to meet his maker. Slick Nick watched through widened eyes as the stranger's hand effortlessly slipped from underneath his jacket. Without realizing, Nick winced when he saw that the man's fingers were indeed clutching something. The stranger never removed his eyes from Nick's. The well-dressed stranger's hand made quick flickering movement. A sharp sound followed. *SNAP!* Involuntarily, Nick flinched, but a split second later, his mind identified the sound as not being a gunshot. The stranger stepped closer while he held his right hand at chest height. Slick Nick registered the movement in the corner of his eye and instinctively looked down. What he saw made him gasp, for in his unstable frame of mind he would have almost preferred a bullet. Inside a crisp, leather case—crisp enough to have made the snapping sound when the stranger flung it open—was a silver and gold badge. Slick Nick's mind ran rampant as his brain sent the message to his mouth. "A fucking badge," he blurted out, before he could bite his tongue. The restaurateur's eyes darted upwards, and met with the stranger's unwavering stare.

The stranger was cool, calm, and collected as he spoke in a low voice, low enough that unwanted ears could not eavesdrop on their conversation. "I am Agent Mark Murray of the Organized Crime Task Force. Let's you and I have a little talk in your office."

Without waiting for a verbal response, Agent Murray grabbed Slick Nick by the elbow with his left hand and gave it a slight tug in the direction of the restaurant's office. Nick did not attempt to fend off the agent's grip. Instead, he began walking towards the office with Agent Murray in tow. Mark Murray snapped the badge wallet closed with a flick of his thumb and forefinger then replaced it in his suit jacket pocket. Just to be absolutely certain, he rechecked the restraining catch on his shoulder holster. If it became necessary for him to draw his weapon, it was unlatched and ready for action.

Slick Nick nodded at several of the restaurant's patrons as the two men crossed the floor towards the office. He maintained a smile on his face to better accent a relaxed poise. The last thing Nick needed was to have his customers suspect that something was wrong. The intricate windings of the Boca Raton grapevine would have news like that spread all around the posh community before sunrise. Instead, Nick walked calmly toward his office. Although he never looked back, Slick Nick was one hundred percent certain that Agent Mark Murray was on his heels, and his assumption had been correct.

Nick turned the doorknob on the solid oak door, and it easily swung open on its well-oiled hinges. His hand reached inside the dark office and flicked the wall switch. Twin fluorescent tubes flickered twice before they fully illuminated the room.

"After you, Agent Murray," Slick Nick said as he jauntily turned his head.

"I wouldn't consider it . . . after *you*, please," Mark Murray smiled at Nick's comment.

Nick shrugged his shoulders as he entered the office. Instinctively, Agent Murray's right hand slipped inside his coat jacket, next to his pistol. When Slick Nick turned to sit at his desk, he noticed the Napoleon Bonaparte-like pose. Agent Murray followed Nick's eyes with his own, then commented, "Just so we understand each other, it's a Walther PPK."

Slick Nick raised his hands in a mock gesture as he sat down in his desk chair. His heart rate had calmed. A sudden, unexpected rush from the cocaine in his system gave him a quick high, and he immediately fell back into his usual cocky, rude self. Slick Nick taunted the agent in an aggressively self-confident manner by saying, "Oh please, Mr. Policeman, don't shoot me."

Slick Nick sat there grinning, certain that his cute comment had caught the agent off guard. On the contrary, Agent Murray used Nick's rudeness to his advantage when he replied, "I'm not going to shoot you, Nick . . ." For effect, Mark paused for several seconds before he continued, "Anthony Vitale is going to shoot you."

Slick Nick's mouth fell open and his arms dropped to his side. Agent Murray calmly sat down in the chair across from Nick's desk then smiled. It was an unnerving smile. Slick Nick recognized the confidence Agent Murray was displaying, and that alone told him the man knew something. Something strong. It was common knowledge among those savvy in the shrewd mannerisms of the street that the most dangerous persons were not the lunatics screaming, "I'm gonna kill ya, mudderfucker!" almost unintelligibly at the top of their lungs. No, it was the meek and mild mannered, completely calm individual that tells you, usually only once, "I am going to kill you," that, by far was the most dangerous, because these people are not emotionally frazzled when they make the threat.

Immediately, Nick went on the defensive. He raised his voice when he queried, "Wha? . . . Wha? . . . What the hell are you trying to pull here?"

"That's a nice tuxedo you're sporting there, sport," Agent Murray remarked after waiting several seconds. The sarcastic compliment caught the restaurateur by surprise, and without thinking, caused him to look down at his black tuxedo. Before Slick Nick could rebut the comment, Agent Murray added, "Found a corpse dressed in one just like that one week ago in Belle Glade."

Agent Murray stared directly into Slick Nick's eyes and watched his reaction. The blood rushing into Nick's face was completely involuntary while the agent from the Organized Crime Task Force watched his face flush beet-red. Nick squirmed in his seat, because he knew that Agent Murray knew. Slick Nick gathered his composure the best he could before he offhandedly remarked, "So wha? Wha's that got to do widst me?"

Agent Murray used his moment of weakness to move in for the kill. Mark Murray leaned forward and raised his right hand, as well as his voice. His hand viciously slammed onto the desktop while he spoke loudly and clearly, "I'll tell you what, you little guinea bastard . . . I know that you did it."

The deafening sound of the earsplitting slap against the wooden desktop more than startled Nick's drugged senses. The crack was similar to that of gunfire, and scared the hell out of him. Slick Nick jumped in his seat while Agent Murray sat back in his chair and waited.

"What proof do you have to come into *my* restaurant and make an accusation like that?" Slick Nick finally queried.

Agent Murray crossed his legs, left over right, and comfortably slouched in the chair. His relaxed position only added more dramatics to his confident posture. It was a move meant to thoroughly rattle Slick Nick's already shattered nerves. Calmly, Agent Murray answered Nick's question.

"Well, let's see. First off, let me tell you that you made some mistakes . . . and I found them. We got a beautiful tire print from the murder scene, and guess what? The tread just happens to match the Michelin tires on your Mercedes. Of course, I'd have to compare tailors, but I'd put my money on the fact that your tuxedo was made by the same designer as the one the murder victim was wearing . . . which brings us to another interesting point. We ran the victim's fingerprints in hopes of identifying him. Turns out he had a record . . . small-time, petty street crimes, but nevertheless, his arrest record supplied us with the information we were after. Not only did we get an identity, but that led us to his last known place of employment. Imagine my surprise when I learned that you had hired someone with a lengthy police record as your Maitre d'. Goodness, what is this world coming to?"

During the past minute, Slick Nick's face had gone from beet-red to ashen-white. It was much worse than he had imagined during his coked-out nights spent wondering what clues he had left behind. The unexpected excitement triggered a torpid ulcer in Nick's stomach, and a sharp pain caused him to wince in pain. His face grimaced from the pain, but the expression could have been taken as one of disgust. That was the way Agent Murray read it. Agent Murray moved in to deliver the finishing blow, the coup de grâce. He uncrossed his legs and leaned forward. Both hands were placed on the edge of the desktop, but his forearm muscles were relaxed.

Agent Murray spoke softly, "Oh yeah, one other thing . . . those boys over in Belle Glade may be just a little backwoods-like, but their coroner, Dr. Kramer, is on top of things; very knowledgeable in his field of expertise. He determined that the murder victim was pistol whipped before he was fatally shot. In addition, he recovered the two slugs from the skull of the victim, and, in spite of the fact that the bullets were fired from a point-blank range into bone, Dr. Kramer was able to retrieve both bullets, intact. They were .38 caliber . . . but of course, you already knew that, didn't you Nick?"

Slick Nick did not say a word, but his eyes told the truth—they were the size of a quarter.

Agent Murray finished him when he added, "It took me a couple of days before the pieces came together, but it wasn't until I found your gun permit registration that I knew I had you. That's right Nick, the .38 caliber pistol registered to you and licensed as a concealed weapon. After all, owning a fancy restaurant does have its privileges, doesn't it?"

Agent Murray sat back in his chair. Like a salesman who had just completed a presentation to a corporate executive, he sat back and waited. Slick Nick would have to speak first. It was all psychological—the one who spoke first would automatically be placed on the defensive side of the negotiations, and that was really what it was all about. Agent Murray did not want this punk, even if he was a murderer. He wanted what this could give him. If he put this slime ball's nuts in a vice, and torqued down on them with just the proper amount of pressure, there was no doubt in his mind that Slick Nick would turn. He would not hesitate to roll over on his people, and in this particular case, the people Agent Murray wanted to reach were those players in the Vitale crime family. The old man would be nice, but Agent Murray housed a particular dislike for Vincent Panachi. The picture of Jennifer Swords and Vincent Panachi together had been the final blow to the agent's shattered ego.

Slick Nick finally broke the silence between the two men when he figured out, "So that's why you believe Anthony Vitale will shoot me?"

"Certainly. After I arrest you for murder, Tony the Shark will know that it was you who brought the heat down upon his crime family. He will want blood . . . and yours will do," replied the agent as he flashed the nervous Italian a confident smile.

Nick pondered the statement for several minutes. He was a byproduct of the inner city streets of Newark, New Jersey and knew how the games were played. He also recognized the fact that he was in deep shit . . . and sinking.

"Maybe I can do something for you. You know, sort of even the odds," Slick Nick suggested.

Agent Murray knew that he had his pigeon, but wanted to make him squirm a little more before he made him an offer. It was apparent that Slick Nick's balls were in that vise. Agent Murray smiled as he mentally torqued another turn.

"Well, I guess if I were in your position, I think I'd prefer the electric chair to a Mafia-style killing. Rumor has it that Tony the Shark has one hell of a terrible temper. Is that true?"

Nick remained silent for a minute before he spoke again. His breathing had become rapid, almost to the point of hyperventilating.

"Okay . . . okay, how about if I help you get to the Vitale crime family? That has to be worth something to you."

Agent Murray placed his finger tips together and exercised his hands, back and forth, like a spider doing push-ups on a mirror. He did this for thirty-seconds while Slick Nick squirmed. It was the longest half-minute of Nick's life because whatever decision the agent made would undoubtedly drastically affect the remainder of his life. Agent Murray placed both hands on his knees.

"Here is what I want. No negotiations. No questions. You'll do as I say, or you'll fry in the electric chair. Do we understand one another?"

"Yes, sir," Nick became completely subservient.

It was not the affirmative answer that tipped Agent Murray off. It was the fact that he affixed the "yes" with "sir." For a man as crude as Slick Nick, that must have been as painful as anything he had ever experienced. Agent Murray knew with absolute certainty that Slick Nick had folded his tent. Agent Mark Murray owned him.

Now that Slick Nick had resolved himself to the fact that he was willing to cooperate in order to save his own ass, he pressed Agent Murray to be a little more explicit with his demands.

"It's really all very simple . . . I want Vincent Panachi," Agent Murray responded.

The very second the agent said his name, a mental picture of Vincent and Jennifer together flashed through Murray's mind. Vincent's name had much the same effect on Slick Nick, with the exception that his mental picture of the two lovebirds together was in his restaurant. Nevertheless, both men were driven by the same penchant desire, and both had felt the cold blade of her stiletto in their hearts. This time it was Slick Nick who smiled a broad smile.

"Vincent Panachi, huh . . . it would be my pleasure."

It was that evening . . . that conversation . . . that created the mole in the Vitale crime family.

CHAPTER TEN

As Agent Mark Murray drove over the Intracoastal Waterway on the Oakland Park Boulevard Bridge, the blazing fireball that had risen above the Atlantic Ocean just a few minutes earlier temporarily blinded him. His face made a grimacing expression while his eyes instinctively narrowed. Without thinking, Mark switched his grasp on the steering wheel from his left hand to his right then slid the freed hand into the suit jacket's right hand inside pocket. His hand found his sunglasses with little effort. After a quick practiced flick of his wrist, Agent Murray flung open the wire framed temple and placed the teardrop Ray Ban's on his face. The relief from the UV-400, dark-green lens was instantaneous upon his bleary eyes.

It had been quite some time since Agent Murray had pulled an all-nighter, and the sleepless night was now taking its toll. Mark was no stranger to the ways of stool pigeons. Once Slick Nick had resigned himself to the fact that he was boxed in and needed to fully cooperate with Agent Murray's ongoing investigation of the Vitale crime family, Mark knew that it was vitally important for him to immediately extract some sort of information from the informant. The idea was to establish the playing field early on in the game. For instance, should Slick Nick have a change of heart the following day, and he had not really divulged any information to Agent Murray, chances are that Murray would lose him forever as an informant. The reason could be any of a vast number of possibilities—the most obvious being that someone had gotten to him, threatened his life or his family's, etc. On the other had, if the informant had already spilled his guts he was committed. In his mind, he was already a dead man . . . that is if anyone in the crime family were to discover that he had talked. Consequently, Agent Murray had used his expertise during the early hours of that Tuesday morning to extract a vast wealth of knowledge from his frightened stool pigeon, Slick Nick.

Slick Nick was also very well versed in the ways of self-survival, especially when it pertained to the ways of the streets. Yes, he agreed to "fully cooperate" in exchange for his immunity from prosecution for the murder of the Maitre d', but he was not stupid. His silent thoughts during the initial stages of the interrogation said it all. Cooperate . . . yes; fully . . . no way! Slick Nick was more than happy to assist Agent Murray in dismantling Vincent Panachi's world in any way he could, and he did. Throughout the wee morning hours, Nick outlined the chain of command of the Vitale crime family beginning with Vincent Panachi and working down. Once the coked-out restaurateur got fired up, Agent Murray had to quickly scrawl almost illegible notes in order to keep up with Slick Nick's confessions. However, afterwards Agent Murray roughed out a sketched graph of the South Florida players, with Vincent at the top of the diagram. Slick Nick certainly told him a lot, but he did not tell him all that he knew about Vincent Panachi. Nick's streetwise ways told him to hold back the most important information. The culpability of the soldiers beneath Vincent denoted that they would get federal time, more than likely at one of the country club prisons. They didn't kill anybody, he did, and that was a completely different story all together. Unlike racketeering, a federal crime punishable by years at a federal facility with tennis courts and salad bars, murder-one brought an eternity in a living hell-like state joint, and under no circumstances was that an experience that Slick Nick felt he could handle. He had a buddy who was doing time in a state facility back in New Jersey, and the guy had told him, "Man, I was there less than a week 'fore this big, buck nigga bent me over a weight bench and drove it home." Slick Nick shuttered at the thought. Hell no, he wasn't about to subject himself to that treatment. Slick Nick reassured himself during the debriefing that everything would be all right, at least for him, because he was going to take measures to make certain that it did. He silently told himself, *Murray, you can have that back-stabbing, woman-stealing Panachi . . . but not before I rip-off that two point five million he's gonna have. That ought to keep me in the lifestyle I'm accustomed to living. Costa Rica, maybe.* Slick Nick provided the agent with enough information to bury Vincent Panachi, but held back on the money. Eventually, that would be his. Period.

The bridge spanning the Intracoastal arched thirty feet above the waterway before it sloped. Instinctively, Agent Murray glanced to the right as his sedan rolled toward the bottom of the steel incline. There they were, Shylock's and Pegleg's, their docks and patio dining areas motionless in the daily appearance of the sun above the vast blanket of water on the eastern horizon. An odd thought quickly passed through his mind when, for a split second, Agent Murray pondered just how much time he had spent watching the two drinking establishments from the task force's surveillance condominium across the canal. By the time he had finished with the thought, the sedan had reached the bottom of the bridge. A Denny's restaurant was situated in a hard to reach by car location at the end of the Oakland Park Boulevard Bridge, on the same side as Shylock's and Pegleg's, and had become a traditional breakfast haunt for tourists and locals. It was not uncommon, particularly during the wee hours of the morning, to see everything from formal attired patrons who arrived by limousine, to sandal footed bridge dwellers, all having breakfast. To some its central location served as a meeting spot, halfway between Ft. Lauderdale and Lauderdale by the Sea, the adjoining city along the beach to the north. For the Organized Crime Task Force, Denny's also served as their breakfast meeting spot.

Agent Murray turned the sedan at the traffic light south bound onto Highway A1A, and circled the block so that he could enter the Denny's parking lot. Two beer delivery trucks sat in front of Shylock's despite the fact that it was barely sunrise. Murray pulled into the lot and maneuvered the sedan into a narrow parking spot. Weariness had dulled his mind, and it wasn't until the beams from his headlights illuminated the bushes in front of his sedan that it registered to turn off the automobile's lights. He exited the car, then glanced over his shoulder while locking the driver's door. Agent Murray saw Karl Spalding's sedan parked beside his then he checked his watch, 6:35 a.m., five minutes late for his scheduled appointment. Not bad, all things considered, as his boss was unaware of what had just transpired with Slick Nick.

Agent Murray entered the restaurant and immediately looked down the row of booths that lined the street side of the restaurant. Karl saw Mark and signaled him by holding up a menu above eye-level. Agent Murray walked toward the booth and the two men shared a smile before Mark sat down.

Karl Spalding was well rested, and his quick wit reflected it when he quipped, "Traveling incognito this morning?"

The question went over Murray's head for a second before he realized his friend was referring to the fact that he had forgotten to remove his sunglasses. Mark simultaneously removed the tear drop sunglasses as he slid onto the seat across from his boss. He looked sheepishly at his boss when he grinned and joked, "Daylight already?"

Karl laughed a hearty laugh as he remarked, "Get the fuck outta here." The two men stared at one another for a couple of seconds before Mark's boss exclaimed, "Jeez, Murray, your eyes look like two piss holes in the snow. Wha'd you stay up all night, for Christ's sake?"

"As a matter of fact, I did . . . and you're going to love this," Mark replied.

Just then a waitress came to the table with a coffee cup in one hand and a menu in the other. She cheerfully greeted them. "Good morning. Coffee?"

"Sure. He'll have a black. Better make it two . . . and I'll have a refill," Karl answered.

"How about if I just bring you a small pot of coffee?" the waitress suggested.

"That would be great. Thank you," Mark interjected.

The waitress nodded, smiled then disappeared as fast as she had appeared.

"So, are you planning to share this good news with me anytime soon?" Mark's boss queried.

"Yes, I am . . . just as soon as I have a cup of coffee," Mark smiled.

The waitress reappeared with the pot of coffee and poured the two men a cup. While he sipped his morning coffee, Agent Murray gave his superior a systematic summary of the night before. Karl listened without interruption while Mark outlined Slick Nick's debriefing. Step by step, Mark informed him of the details surrounding the Vitale crime family's South Florida operations. When Mark had finished, both coffee cups were half full. His superior grabbed the small pot of coffee and refilled them. When he set the steaming pot back onto the hot pad, Mark could sense that his boss' mind was evaluating the information. He had not become the head of this division by being slow, and his next remark reflected that quick thinking.

"Well, your boy may not be as slick as he thinks he is."

Mark was in the midst of a sip of coffee. After he swallowed he asked, "How so?"

"As a point of law, we've still got him by the short hairs. While he may be well versed in the ways of the street, he obviously doesn't know shit about the law. If he did he would have kept his mouth shut. He would have known that you do not have the legal authority to grant him immunity from prosecution. He just fucked himself . . . big time."

Mark looked puzzled as he attempted to clarify his boss' statement. The confusion was apparent to Karl by his friend's expression, so he explained, "We'll use Slick Nick for everything we can get out of him . . . then we'll throw him to the prosecutors. They will tear him up like fresh meat to a pack of hungry wolves."

"What about my verbal agreement with him to not prosecute in exchange for his cooperation?"

Karl shrugged, "What verbal agreement?"

The silence that followed said it all—Slick Nick was to be used, then abused. Mark merely nodded his head in acknowledgement of his superior's wicked plan. The coffee was strong, but not strong enough. Screw the Vitale's . . . all I want is to go to sleep were Mark's thoughts. Just then, the cheerful waitress appeared and asked, "Are you gentlemen ready to order?"

*　　*　　*

That particular sunrise Agent Mark Murray wasn't the only one bleary eyed, for both Vincent Panachi and the Quill looked quite fatigued. They also had pulled all-nighters. Crime does not recognize a nine to five work schedule. Consequently, Vincent and the Quill, along with three of Vincent's underlings, had worked around the clock to get the Quill set up and in business. Finally, after a white, unmarked van had made a total of three deliveries, the sophisticated equipment was in place.

When the vehicle pulled away from the rented house for the final time, Vincent watched it leave through a crack in the living room's ceiling-to-floor curtains. Once the van's taillights were out of sight Vincent turned toward the Quill, who was standing beside him. The elderly man looked like he was totally exhausted, and rightfully so. Neither of them had stopped since this time yesterday morning, and things had really become frantic after the Learjet had touched down in Ft. Lauderdale. The Quill had done his homework during his Roman holiday because he knew precisely what equipment he needed to successfully complete the job. Within a matter of one day, Vincent Panachi went through ninety thousand of the two hundred thousand dollars Anthony Vitale had given him.

Vincent placed his left hand on the Quill's shoulder and the Quill turned to face the younger man. Vincent asked, "Are you okay?"

"Yes, I'm fine, but like yourself, I imagine, I'm tired," the much older gentleman replied.

"Yeah, I can relate to that," Vincent smiled and agreed. After a few seconds Vincent continued, "Well, you have everything here that you have requested. No doubt, we're both going to need some rest . . . so what would you like for me to tell Capo Pelligi about the time schedule?"

"Tell him I will begin the operation tomorrow. Today, I sleep," the Quill replied without hesitation.

"Fair enough. Done," Vincent said as he patted him on the shoulder with the same hand.

Finding a bedroom to sleep in was not a problem at the house Vincent had rented, it had five. The expansive house was located in the city of Coral Springs, slightly northwest of Ft. Lauderdale, on the fourteenth fairway of the Coral Springs Country Club. A local realtor had handled the listing, and the house was owned by a well-to-do couple from Ohio that was unable to winter in Florida that season. The realtor gave Vincent the address over the phone, and then they met at the house an hour later. More than likely, Vincent would have taken the place sight unseen. However, knowing that he was going to utilize the house for illegal purposes, Vincent thought it best that he squash any suspicions the realtor may have right from the beginning. His charming personality had done just that. The New Jersey accent, accompanied by an out of state driver's license, sealed her confidence that she had indeed rented the house to a wonderful young man in town for the winter. That was precisely how she described the new tenant to the owners up north. In addition, she gushed over the phone, "And, I have collected all six months rent in advance, cash. So there will not be any waiting period for the check to clear. My check to you will be in the morning's mail. I'm so happy for you." Needless to say, the realtor was happy herself, because the advance payment allowed her to collect a season's commission, up front. Fair is fair. They were in business; she was in business; and now, the Vitale crime family was in business.

Getting tooled up for the project was time consuming, but ran equally as smooth. The Quill was like a kid in a candy store when he got inside the warehouse sized computer sales center. Computers. Who would have imagined some thirty years ago that technology would have taken us as far as it has? The Quill stood at the front entrance of the store and relived the days of old in his mind as he looked around in awe. The customers in the store spanned three generations, from eighteen to eighty, all sharing the same common interest. For the Quill, it seemed that time had stood still. Twenty years spent in the box had not slowed technology, though. What had once taken the Quill days to reproduce some thirty years before on an offset printing press, a dinosaur-sized relic piece of equipment whose only surviving factor has been the mass production of wedding invitations, could now be done in a matter of minutes by computer.

While the Quill was still incarcerated, he had subscribed to *P.C. World*, a trade magazine focusing on the computer industry. It had not taken very long for the extremely intelligent man to learn the ins-and-outs of the computer world. Through the informative articles in the magazine the Quill was able to determine precisely what equipment and programs he would need to do a job. There was no time wasted when he and Vincent went to purchase the appropriate equipment.

Vincent Panachi knew a whole lot about fast horses, fast boats, and fast women, but admittedly, knew nothing about the sophisticated equipment the Quill had purchased. However, he was astute to the fact that it took money to make money. Vincent did not even flinch when the bill had reached in excess of sixty-five thousand dollars. One couldn't say that about the two sales clerks. They had never witnessed anything quite like the Quill's spending spree. As a matter of fact, they both helped load the equipment into the cargo van Vincent had purchased, which to the clerks was somewhat out of the ordinary, but there was no way that either the Quill or Vincent wanted anyone to know the exact location where the equipment was to be delivered. Delivery was included in the price, but Vincent had quipped, "Cash and carry, thank you."

Vincent's boys delivered the equipment to the rented house, concealed from view by the shroud of midnight darkness. The upper-middle class neighbors were none the wiser when the morning sun lit the neighborhood. If they had peered through their drapes early that morning, they would have seen nothing more than their new, affluent, well dressed, neighbor leaving in his Mercedes 500SL. In the wealthy subdivision of the Coral Springs Country Club, Mercedes, BMWs, and Porsches were the norm, and Vincent Panachi did not attract one raised eyebrow as the expensive, German built, luxury automobile slowly drove past his neighbors' homes. As he drove away, he glanced over his shoulder for a final look at the house. It was perfect. The plan was perfect and "Perfect . . . ," was the description Vincent would use when he spoke to Capo Pelligi. "That word should appease the Colombians," Vincent remarked out loud as he accelerated past the manicured lawns.

The Quill was fast asleep before the Mercedes was out of the immediate area. "Today, I sleep . . . ," were words to be taken literally. The elderly gentleman's body clock was way off; no doubt, it would take him a full day to catch up on his rest.

Vincent was exhausted, as well, but had one more thing to do before he could join the Quill in dreamland. Just before he turned onto Interstate 95, Vincent pulled into a convenience store parking lot. A freestanding bank of public pay phones stood on the far side of the empty lot. Not another soul was in sight, so Vincent pulled the Mercedes alongside the phones, parallel to the concrete based structure. He turned off the car's motor, then reached inside the walnut covered glove box for a Crown Royal sack full of quarters. His hand found the dark-blue bag without effort.

Vincent dialed a telephone number within the same area code as Newark, New Jersey. The house he was dialing was located within local calling distance of Anthony Vitale's mansion, but the modest home's owner did not have the slightest connection with the Vitale crime family. As a matter of fact, and at the risk of sounding like the used car salesman's old standby line, which in this case was true, the house was owned by a little old woman who was so clean that she had never even had a traffic ticket. A computerized voice was heard through the phone's earpiece, "Please deposit two dollars and forty-five cents for the next three minutes." Vincent listened to the audible tone of the computer language that recorded the number of quarters being inserted into the phone's coin slots. Once the computer registered that the proper amount of change had been deposited, the call was placed. Within seconds, the touch of Vincent's fingertips put him in touch with a house outside of Newark, New Jersey. However, the call did not stop there. When the call reached the modest home in New Jersey, it clicked twice, then call-forwarded to a local New Jersey telephone number—the telephone number for Anthony Vitale's mansion.

Capo Pelligi had been expecting a call from Vincent, and answered the phone himself. "Yes?" he asked in a sleepy voice.

Although Vincent felt secure about talking over Anthony's telephone line— mainly because Capo Pelligi had it swept once a week for listening devices—it was understood among those involved with the crime family that you never, never discussed business over the telephone lines. Vincent Panachi lived by those words of wisdom.

"Perfect," was Vincent's reply in response to Capo Pelligi's greeting.

"Thank you. Tomorrow?" replied the Capo. The meaning was apparent.

"Tomorrow," was Vincent's single word answer.

"Ciao," the Capo said without hesitation.

"Ciao," Vincent replied in his father's native tongue.

Vincent hung up the phone, which disconnected the call as well as the telephone company's time and charges computer. It did not ring back which signaled Vincent that his telephone call had fallen short of the three-minute credit, and no additional quarters were to be deposited. The call left no paper trails, whatsoever, on either end, yet Capo Pelligi now had up to date news for the Colombians. Vincent, on the other hand, was all caught up. No calls. No errands. Only sleep.

As he turned the key and restarted the Mercedes, Vincent smiled when he thought about the Quill. He shifted the automobile into drive at the same time he laughed and said, "Today, I sleep."

*   *   *

Less than an hour later, in a beautiful, hillside villa on the outskirts of Cali, Colombia, Señior Calerro was engaged in an overseas conversation with Capo Pelligi. The two crime family bosses exchanged several ingratiating compliments with one another before Capo Pelligi finally told the head of the Colombian drug cartel the reason for his calling.

"Good news . . . production will begin tomorrow."

Señior Calerro was also not one for discussing details over the telephone. A couple of seconds of silence followed the Capo's remark, but neither of the men was certain if it was due to a delay in the satellite relay of the overseas call, or not. At any rate, there was no reason to expect anything but the best, for either of them.

"Bueno . . . and the nephew? When do I get to meet with him?"

"Soon, amigo. Soon. I will be in touch . . ."

Whether the satellite caused it, or not, the two men stepped on each others words when they both said, "Adios," at the same moment. The overseas connection was terminated.

CHAPTER ELEVEN

V incent Panachi was in a deep, deep sleep; so deep that even the rapid, jerky movements of his eyeballs during the stages of sleep associated with dreaming did not awaken him. His dreams were filled with vivid, colorful images that seemed almost real. Staying awake nearly thirty hours had totally exhausted Vincent, and he had fallen asleep within minutes of lying down and had not moved.

Suddenly, from what seemed like a long distance away, Vincent heard a noise. *RING!* He did not immediately recognize the sound, partially because his senses were controlled by his tranquil state of mind, and also due in part to the fact that his subconsciousness had conveniently worked the sound into his dream. The sound returned—*RING!*—and found its way deep into his mind. Vincent's groggy senses finally identified the disturbing sound, and before he opened his eyes, his hand instinctively reached for the telephone. It found its mark on the second grope and he placed the telephone receiver to his ear.

"Hello," Vincent answered in a sleepy voice.

"Vincent? Did I wake you?"

Vincent's brain quickly came up to running speed and matched a face to the soft voice.

"Jennifer?" he asked.

"Yes, it's me," she answered.

Vincent slowly opened both eyes before he rolled over towards the nightstand. Immediately, he noticed that it was dark outside.

"Jennifer, what time is it?"

"Vincent, it's only seven p.m.," she laughed. Before Vincent could say anything in reply, she quipped, "You know the saying, Vincent, 'Early to bed, early to rise, and your girl goes out with other guys.'"

The humorous poem struck Vincent as being quite entertaining. He laughed as he sat up in the bed. Vincent twisted his upper torso as he reached to turn on the bedside lamp.

"Well, I was up all night . . . business problems."

It was the key word "business" that alerted Jennifer not to pry any further. Instead, she kept the conversation light.

"You must be starved if you've been sleeping all day. Why don't you come over to my condo and I'll make us both a wonderful dinner?"

Vincent did not consider the Quill, nor contemplate the needs of the counterfeiting project, because he had already thought that out during his ride home. Everything was caught up, so why not relax?

"That sounds like a great idea. Tell you what . . . I'll bring the wine, okay?"

"Champagne all right?" Jennifer giggled.

"Of course. Champagne it is. What time is good for you?" Vincent asked.

Jennifer paused for a moment before she answered. After all, she had to figure not only the time it would take to prepare an absolutely fabulous dinner, but also the time it would take for her to get ready. This was not a normal, romantic dinner for two. It was as calculated a move as one would expect in any game of chess, and the object of both games shared a similar objective—to capture the King. In Jennifer's mind, if she made the right moves, she would capture her King—Vincent Panachi.

"Is ten o'clock too late?"

Vincent was a night owl himself and liked eating late.

"Perfect. That will give me plenty of time to wake up."

"I'll see you at ten o'clock. Bye," Jennifer's said very softly.

Her soft-spoken voice sounded extremely sexy and brought forth a spontaneous flood of memories of the two of them together on the Scarab Thunder. Vincent felt a quick spasm in his loins before he was able to say, "Good-bye."

Vincent hung up the telephone then lay there with his hands clasped behind his head. The memories of Jennifer's exquisite body reminisced through his mind. That moment marked the first true sign that Vincent had indeed entered into Jennifer's web. A smile formed across his face while he pondered what might happen.

Perhaps it was mental telepathy, but Jennifer was sitting on the edge of her bed wondering the exact same thing. If this were a poker game one would have to concede that the cards were stacked in her favor. It was Jennifer who would determine how the evening's sexual activities progressed. She was fully aware of this fact, and she intended to maintain an advantage over the situation, at all cost. Jennifer had seen the power she possessed over men, particularly after she began sleeping with them. She was an expert at playing mind games, and had driven three men—Dr. Mitchell Swords, Agent Mark Murray, and Slick Nick—to the brink of insanity trying to figure her out. However, Vincent Panachi was different from those three, or from any man she had ever been involved with.

Inside of that plastic surgeon's perfectly sculpted body was the same frightened, insecure, little girl who had once lived in New Jersey. Although her exterior had been drastically changed, inside she still lacked the confidence in herself that it took to become truly happy. Dr. Swords had recognized the symptoms that indicated a personality disorder, and had even gone as far as prescribing an anti-depressant drug for her, but he was a plastic surgeon, not a psychologist. She suffered from something far worse than any habit-forming drug—Jennifer's addiction stemmed from the desire to have money . . . lots of money. For her, money was the answer to all of her problems. Never once had she considered emotional love as the answer; only money. With money she could find the security in life that she had never known . . . or so she thought. The problem with that theory was that there would always be someone with more. A bigger yacht; a faster jet; a sleeker car. Even though Dr. Mitchell Swords was a very nice gentleman and a loving husband, he had become a stepping stone—no more than a means of bettering herself. And so the saga continued, through the country club set, Agent Mark Murray, then Slick Nick. The difference now was that Jennifer had focus and that focus was on Vincent Panachi. Vincent Panachi was to be her King and she would use every trick in the book to make certain of it.

All of the men that Jennifer had been involved with in the past couldn't get enough of her, or so it seemed. Once their relationship progressed to the point of having sex, men began relentlessly pursuing her until eventually they smothered her with affection. From that point on, it was down hill. With Vincent, however, things were completely different. This time, it was she who was left wondering about the status of the relationship. While Vincent was out of town and busy with the project at hand, he had not had an opportunity to call Jennifer. Days would pass, not weeks, but Jennifer's insecurity attacked her self-confidence.

Now, as she sat on the edge of her bed, Jennifer planned the evening. First things first. She had three hours to get ready and prepare dinner. She pondered for a few minutes then walked towards the bathroom. Jennifer decided she would get dressed first then make dinner. Her logic was that it would be better to be late with the dinner than late getting ready. Vincent was bringing champagne . . . and wouldn't it just be a shame if they were to have to drink a bottle while dinner cooked? Whatever, Jennifer was going to be certain that she was stunningly attractive when Vincent arrived.

Jennifer turned on the water in the bathtub and stood there for a few seconds while she adjusted the temperature. Once the water was comfortable to her touch, she poured two caps of bubble bath directly into the cascading stream. Immediately, the bath water clouded and bubbles rose from its surface. Jennifer unbuttoned her jeans and peeled them over her rounded bottom with her thumbs and forefingers. Once the top of the cotton jeans cleared her buttocks, they fell to the floor without help. Jennifer slipped her top over her head at the same time her feet kicked free from the legs of the jeans. She tossed her top onto the bathroom floor alongside the jeans. The tub was only half full when she stepped into the warm water. The change in temperature caused goose bumps to form on her skin, but within seconds, she was fully submerged in the warm bubble bath and the momentary roughened condition of her skin disappeared as fast as it had formed. The warm bath was relaxing, both physically and mentally. Jennifer luxuriated in the soothing bubble bath while her thoughts drifted to making love with Vincent on his boat. There was no doubt in her mind that he had thoroughly enjoyed the animal-like sex the two of them had experienced. Perhaps it had been her ice-hardened nipples that had driven him to such levels of ecstasy, but whatever the cause may have been, Jennifer did not want to lose the edge she had gained.

After five minutes of lounging in the warm water, Jennifer reached behind her head and grabbed the shaving cream and razor. She slid forward in the tub until she was submerged neck-deep then lifted her right leg above the water's surface. Jennifer rested her foot against the tiled wall to steady her leg. The tile was cool to the touch, and the warm water dripping from her foot made streaks down the moisture-laden squares. Jennifer lathered her leg with the shaving cream and took notice of the vertical lines streaked through the condensation on the wall. It was almost art deco looking, she thought. The razor began sliding gently up her muscular legs, leaving behind it a clear path swathed through the foamy cream. Out of habit, she ran her finger along the freshly shaved area then smiled. Jennifer's skin was as smooth as a newborn baby's.

It took five minutes to shave both of her legs, but that time was not wasted. Jennifer was scheming. She wanted to grasp Vincent's attention with such a degree of desire that there would not be any question in either of their minds that he was falling for her. An unequivocal, yearning desire. She had had the same effect on other men, so why not Vincent? As a matter of fact, Jennifer's bedroom ploys had reduced her emotionally strong ex-husband to total mush. All she had needed to do to swing a disagreement her way was to cross her legs for a couple of days, if he lasted that long. Jennifer had selfishly experimented with the man's sensuality. Different positions while making love got his attention and lengthy periods of oral sex brought forth animal-like groans from deep within. But, it wasn't until Jennifer tried something completely different that elevated him to wild, frenzied orgasms. From that point on, she had had her husband on an invisible leash. It had been that simple, just like ordering something from a magazine. Jennifer had picked up a *Penthouse* magazine at the news stand one day, and out of sheer curiosity, flipped through the explicit pages. What her prying eyes saw was a voluptuous, extremely attractive, woman who had shaven off all the hair on her love mound!

At first, the picture had been somewhat shocking, but the more Jennifer thought about it that afternoon, the more developed that evening's plan became. When her husband returned that evening, he found a new, improved model of

Jennifer Swords. Later that night, after champagne and foreplay, he reached an unsurpassed orgasm.

Now, as Jennifer reminisced those wild evenings spent with her otherwise meek and mild mannered ex-husband, she could not help but wonder if the technique would affect Vincent in the same manner. The pondering thought turned into a devilish smile, Jennifer had figured out what she would do to capture Vincent's attention.

She raised herself from the bottom of the bathtub then sat on its porcelain edge. Jennifer reached for the shaving cream and razor, lifted her right leg and rested her foot on the faucet, then smoothly applied the moistening cream. Carefully, gently, her hand stroked the razor until finally the job was done. When she submerged herself back into the warm water, the sensation was vastly different. She couldn't help but wonder how different she would feel to Vincent, but tonight she would know. She would make him tell her.

Jennifer soaked in the bath for a few minutes more before she had enough. When she stood up, her body glistened from the therapeutic oils in the bath gel. The temperature of the water made her skin a rosy color. Jennifer reached for the towel rack and pulled down a fluffy, pink one. The heavy cotton towel absorbed the excess water like a sponge while she gently rubbed down her body. Her skin was silky smooth where the towel swept across it.

Tiny droplets of water marked the bath mat where Jennifer stood. Her entire body was dry from the knees up . . . well, almost her entire body. Jennifer placed one leg at a time on top of the lid that covered the toilet while she wiped her shapely calves dry with the towel. When she had dried the last one, Jennifer kept her leg hiked in the air while she placed the fluffy towel between her legs. The soft, warm, towel met her exposed lips and Jennifer let out a soft moan. Gently, she patted herself dry while a smile formed on her face. Jennifer found it ironic that only minutes before she was wondering how different sex would feel to Vincent when she engulfed his manhood in between her freshly shaven lips. Now, as she experienced sensations she had never known just by towel drying herself, Jennifer marveled at how much more receptive she was to sensation. Seconds later, before she even finished drying herself, her shoulders shook with a sudden, involuntary muscular contraction and she became lightheaded. Jennifer steadied herself by leaning her free hand against the tile wall while her raised leg quivered. The smile became a full-fledged, hearty laugh when Jennifer removed the towel from between her legs. Suddenly, it all became clear, due in part to the moist spot on the towel. The softness of the bath towel against her swollen lips had caused her to experience a mini-orgasm. While her body may have been dry, there was no absence of natural moisture in her love mound.

Jennifer stood naked before a lengthy rack of clothes. The fingers of her right hand slowly pushed plastic coat hangers back and forth across a metal rod that ran the full length of the master bedroom's walk-in closet. It was a wardrobe worthy of royalty, all purchased when Jennifer was married to Dr. Mitchell Swords. One by one, Jennifer flipped through the collection of designer labeled dresses while she pondered which one to wear. Finally, her fingers found just the right one. It was silky, slinky, and very sexy. Jennifer smiled as she pulled it from the rack. "This is just perfect," she mused out loud.

The fine, soft fabric swung freely as she carried it into the bedroom and laid it on the bed. Jennifer turned towards her bureau, but hesitated before she pulled out one of the drawers. It wasn't that she was spacing-out. Her indecisiveness was due to the advanced planning that she was doing in her mind. Jennifer wanted Vincent to react with the same shock and surprise tonight that he had shown when she had exited the cabin of the Scarab topless. She contemplated the evening's future scenario then reached for the top drawer. Jennifer selected a very brief, very sexy, T-back pair of panties. She stepped into them then wriggled the tight G-string type briefs snugly over her love mound. The silk fabric clung so tightly to her body that when Jennifer turned toward the full-length mirror, the outline of her vagina lips was clearly visible through the fine, lustrous fibers. She looked at her reflection in the mirror and nodded her head in approval. "This will certainly get Vincent's attention," she mumbled below her breath.

Jennifer carefully removed the expensive, designer, dress from the bed and unzipped it. The zipper ran the length of her back and was hidden from view once the dress was on. Ever so slowly, Jennifer stepped into the dress. Its thin fabric would have torn had she lost her balance and pressed her weight against it with her foot. Her forefingers and thumbs guided the smooth fabric with a firm grasp over her curvaceous body until finally, the soft silk loosely draped from her shoulders. A difficult but practiced movement brought the dress' zipper all the way from the base of her spine to the nape of her neck. Jennifer cupped her ample breasts, one at a time, as she seated them in the dress. Of course, she wore no bra, and that only served to accentuate her thrusting nipples. The soft fabric pressed her breasts together to form a lengthy, deep cleavage that was fully visible through the V-cut of the dress' neckline. Jennifer looked at her image in the mirror—a frontal view first, then slowly turning until she could see herself from the side. Jennifer continued turning while she craned her neck until she could see one side of her back and rear. Slowly, she reached behind her as far as the bend of her elbow would allow and stroked her hand downward against the dress. The pressure of her hand ran the wrinkles ahead of it until there were none. The sensual, silk dress flawlessly clung to her body in the precise manner the designer had imagined it would. Jennifer allowed herself a most gratifying giggle, for there was not doubt in her mind that she was going to drive Vincent Panachi stark raving mad with desire before the evening was through.

Jennifer sat at her make-up counter and carefully applied the expensive cosmetics until they were perfect. Next, came the jewelry, and of course, one piece was selected without thought—it was the necklace that spelt *STILETTO*. Seconds later Jennifer put on her diamond-bezeled Rolex Presidential and checked the time. It would be one hour and forty-five minutes before Vincent arrived. "Plenty of time," she said out loud to her image in the makeup mirror.

* * *

Vincent did not even begin to get ready for the dinner date until 8:15 p.m. An hour and forty-five minutes was more than enough time for him. Now, at the same moment that Jennifer was getting up from her make-up counter, Vincent stood beneath a pulsating showerhead. The rhythmic flow of the steaming hot water beat down upon his head and shoulders. Vincent placed his hands on the tiled wall of the walk-in shower and tilted his head upward so that the water massage would cascade down upon his face. The high-pressure narrow-streams of hot water stung his face to the rhythm of the showerhead's intermittent flow, and awakened Vincent's dulled senses. He allowed his mouth to fill several times while he rinsed and spat. After several minutes beneath the spouting showerhead, Vincent's body temperature returned to normal. Finally, he felt rested.

Vincent dressed quickly. Unlike Jennifer, he was completely fluffed and buffed within forty-five minutes. Vincent was garbed in casual attire—a pair of expensive, Italian designed wool slacks and a V-neck, pullover, alpaca sweater. The trousers had a knife-like crease, and because they had been hung outstretched in the closet by the end of the pants legs, were void of the usual fold mark at the knees. The immaculate crease stopped at a pair of very expensive, Italian-made, alligator loafers. Vincent checked his appearance in the bedroom's full-length mirror, just once, on the way out the door. A quick check of his diamond-bezeled Rolex confirmed that he was ahead of schedule. As a matter of fact, Vincent had a full hour to get to Jennifer's condominium. He locked the front door and activated the sophisticated electronic burglar alarm, all in one fluid movement. A bright red light next to the doorbell verified that the alarm's electronic sensors—stealthily positioned in and around the palatial residence—were armed and ready. In terms of computer language, Vincent Panachi's house was on-line.

Vincent Panachi resided in a very posh, upper class, area of Ft. Lauderdale known as Las Olas Isles. Each and every Isle was just as the name implies—a small island. Very rich, small islands. They were home to many wealthy people; some so wealthy that the Florida house was nothing more than a winter retreat from the bleak cold of the Northern United States. The seasonal residents did provide an advantage for Vincent's lifestyle though, because they kept to their own business. No snoops; no coffee-cup-clap-trappers hell-bent on determining who is doing what to whom. For the most part, wealthy people minded their own business, which suited Vincent Panachi to the tee. As far as they were concerned, he was nothing more than a wealthy, trust-fund baby, probably no different than their own son who was spending the winter at a ski resort somewhere. Las Olas Isles was just perfect for someone involved with a New Jersey crime family.

The double car garage door at Vincent's house silently raised, its electric opener gently guiding the five hinged panels up the well-oiled runners. Vincent watched through the Mercedes Benz's rear view mirror until he was satisfied that he had ample clearance to back the automobile out. His hand slid the gear shifter into reverse and the 500SL backed down the slight incline that was the driveway to his house. Vincent stopped at the bottom of the small hill, where the concrete driveway met the blacktop road. He reached above the passenger's sun visor and pushed a button on the cigarette pack sized remote control, then sat in the middle of the road while he watched the garage door close.

Vincent lived on Navarro Isle, and the tiny island had but one road, so traffic was not something he had to be overly concerned with. The road ran dead center of the full length of the island, which was a little over a mile long, and was lined by houses on either side. A small bridge located on the south end connected the island to exclusive Las Olas Boulevard. To the west of the island was the Navarro River; to the east, another canal paralleled the island until it widened into a small bay where it met Las Olas Boulevard. Vincent Panachi's home overlooked this bay. His was the first house on the island, and what a house it was—over four thousand square feet, Polynesian in design, with two hundred twenty feet of waterfront. In addition, the house came with a rather scandalous reputation. The original builder was one of the bent-nose-boys from New York City, whom was gunned down, mob style, in his own front yard. Vincent's front yard. Several years and several owners later, a very famous former football player for the New York Jets resided there. Now, Vincent Panachi lived there . . . and the ownership of the huge home had gone full circle—back to the crime families of the northeast.

The flashing red "No Service" light on his mobile phone changed to a steady green just as Vincent pulled away from the house. He stopped the Mercedes on the middle of the bridge then glanced over his left shoulder at his house. The outside security lights were on and they illuminated the full length of the dock. Vincent sat there for a few minutes and looked admiringly at his beautiful home.

Vincent turned east onto Las Olas Boulevard and headed towards the beach. The Isles of Las Olas—Hendrick's, Venice, Coconut, and Palm, to name a few—passed by while the luxury automobile approached the Las Olas Bridge. The concrete and steel structure provided passage across the Intracoastal Waterway, and when Vincent crossed it he saw boat after boat traversing the water highway. Ft. Lauderdale's nightlife had awakened.

Immediately after crossing the Las Olas Bridge, one enters another world better known as The Strip. Here, anything and everything goes. Las Olas Boulevard meets Highway A1A at the Atlantic Ocean, and Vincent turned north along the beach. To his right lay a white ribbon of beach that stretched as far as the eye could see. On the left side of the four-lane highway were countless bars, souvenir shops, restaurants, and hotels, their neon lights casting a spectrum of colors across the crowded sidewalk. The police maintained crowd control with officers on horseback and bicycles, of all things. However, when one saw the snarling traffic jams, bumper-to-bumper for miles while cars cruised up and down the strip, their modes of transportation seemed logical. As always, Vincent was mesmerized by all the activity. He watched the crowd as much as he did the car ahead of him until finally, the seemingly unending row of colorful lights ended.

Once highway A1A curved inland a couple of blocks, it became just like any other roadway, and between Sunrise Boulevard and Oakland Park Boulevard it did just that. Suddenly, the world seemed to return to some sort of order as the strip grew more distant in Vincent's rear view mirror. He still had several miles to go before he reached Jennifer's condominium, and during the drive he found his mind returning to thoughts of business. The trip up north had gone smoothly, and the Quill was in business. Vincent was noted for paying particular attention to details, so when Anthony Vitale had asked him to compliment Slick Nick on the job he did with his party, Vincent took it to heart. What Anthony Vitale wanted, Vincent would deliver . . . even if he did detest Slick Nick.

Vincent glanced down at his mobile phone long enough to punch in the telephone number for Slick Nick's restaurant. As soon as he heard the connection, Vincent picked up the handset and placed it against his ear. *RING! RING! RING!* Slick Nick answered the phone after the third ring.

"Yeah," Slick Nick snapped, his voice short of breath. Even though it was Slick Nick's private number, Vincent still found it to be a rude greeting.

"Nick, it's Vincent." There was a long pause. "Nick, are you there?"

"Yeah, I'm here. How are you, Vincent?"

If Vincent's telephone had sight as well as sound he would have seen Slick Nick in a state of near panic. The weasel had no idea why Vincent would be calling him, and of course his first thoughts were riddled with guilt. Vincent detected a cadence in Slick Nick's voice, but shrugged it off to the surprise he must have felt from receiving a call from Vincent.

"I'm fine, Nick. Just got back into town from seeing the old man. The reason I called is to pass along his compliments on the way you handled his party. His exact words were, 'A hell of a job.' Congratulations are in order."

Vincent had no idea why, but he was certain that he heard a sigh of relief through the telephone's receiver. On the other end of the phone line, Slick Nick was having trouble breathing. The combination of the coke and stress had momentarily caught him off guard.

Finally, after what seemed like hours to Slick Nick, he replied, "Wha . . . it was nothin'. You tell Mr. Vitale that I'll do it for him, again . . . anytime he likes."

"Fair enough," Vincent remarked, "I'll tell him."

An uneasy moment of silence passed over the phone connection before Slick Nick queried, "Anything else, Vincent?"

"That's all. Guess I'll say good-bye."

"Good-bye, Vincent."

Vincent pushed the *End* button on his mobile phone then replaced the handset onto its cradle. He pondered Slick Nick's strange tone of voice for a couple of minutes, but eventually came to the conclusion that it was nothing more than the mutual disrespect that they harbored for one another. Vincent's mind moved onto more pleasurable thoughts . . . like Jennifer Swords.

Visions of Jennifer's exquisite body flipped through his mind like a series of erotica flash cards. The intoxicating scent of her perfume was still so vivid in Vincent's mind that the remarkable detail of the memory even surprised him. Without thinking, his foot braked for the approaching red light. It wasn't until the automobile had stopped that he realized he was passing through Lauderdale-by-the-Sea, the last township before he reached Jennifer's condominium. The freedom flight in his mind had almost caused him to forget the champagne.

Vincent turned right at the light then drove toward the beach for one block. A landmark liquor store that had been in business since the late forties sat on the northeast corner. Vincent maneuvered the 500SL into an angled parking space, one that still showed a quarter's worth—fifteen minutes—of paid parking time left on the meter. The neon sign overhead the storefront window hummed when it changed colors from all red to all blue. Vincent walked into the liquor store and stopped at the checkout counter. Unlike the majority of the other liquor stores in the Ft. Lauderdale area, this one was not part of a huge, corporate chain. Instead of a supermarket-sized retail store manned by identical yuppies, all desperately trying to climb the same corporate ladder together, Vincent found a well taken care of, attractive, mature woman. Her eyes were pure . . . clean . . . white, and her smile radiant. There was no mistaking that this woman had been something special in her time.

"Where is your champagne, please?" Vincent asked.

Her eyes cast a glance towards the rear of the store, and Vincent's followed.

"Can I help you find anything special?" she queried.

Vincent must have appeared indecisive, because he was just replacing two bottles of Moet Chandon Brut Imperial when she appeared. That particular champagne was his fine wine of choice, but he had second thoughts about purchasing it that night. It had not taken him long to sense Jennifer's enjoyment of the best.

Vincent turned toward the attractive woman and replied, "Yes. Do you carry Dom Perignon champagne?"

She caught his eyes and held them in a stare before she responded, "Of course. They even sell that in the drug stores here in Liquordale."

Vincent laughed at her humorous remark while he thought that she must have pegged him as an out of towner from his accent.

"I keep it up front . . . behind the counter. Follow me."

Vincent did as she asked, and followed her to the front of the store. She sidestepped behind the counter while Vincent stopped directly across from her, the sales counter between them.

Vincent's curiosity got the best of him. He had always worked towards projecting an image of not being a tourist. Therefore, he wondered what he had done that might have prompted that informative statement from her. She was bent over, he assumed getting the champagne, and all that was visible was her back and the top of her head.

"I guess you think I'm a tourist because of my accent, right?" Vincent asked.

She didn't bother to raise her head as she casually replied, "Nope." Before he could ask her another question, she beat him to the draw. "How many bottles would you like?"

"Two, please."

The clinking sound of glass hitting glass was heard then she rose up. Two bottles of Dom Perignon champagne were firmly grasped in her hands. She gently set them down on the counter and smiled at Vincent. She cast her eyes again, just as she had done earlier.

"New Jersey license plate on your Mercedes," she said.

"Pretty clever," Vincent remarked as he smiled.

She merely shrugged her shoulders like it was nothing, but then quickly added, "I may be old, but I'm visual . . . very visual. Not much gets past me."

Vincent chuckled and decided to banter with her for a couple of minutes while he paid for the fine wine.

"That will be one hundred ninety dollars and seventy six cents, please."

"What else can you tell about me?" Vincent queried while he fished the money from his bankroll.

Her eyes looked down while she counted the money, but that did not stop her quick mind from thinking two thoughts at the same time.

"Plenty," she replied while her hands flipped through the twenty-dollar bills.

"Such as?" Vincent asked.

Her fingers played across the keys of the cash register like lightening before the drawer slid out. The experienced, wise, mature woman counted out Vincent's change without looking down.

"I've been in this town for a long, long time, and I've seen it all, at one time or another." She began bagging the champagne as she added, "And what I see in you is a young man falling hopelessly in love. Whatever kind of hold she has got on you, cost is no object. Think about it." Before Vincent could think of a clever reply, she beat him to the draw, again. "Look out there," she said as she pointed towards his car. Vincent's eyes followed her extended arm. She said, "I watched you maneuver your ninety thousand dollar car into a parking space that saved you a quarter on the meter . . . yet you didn't blink an eye to drop a couple of hundred bucks for two bottles of champagne . . . all in the pursuit of the game."

She slid the bag towards Vincent, and he grabbed it with both hands.

"Damned good. Maybe you have a crystal ball underneath that counter or something," he replied.

"No, I had that kind of power over men myself, at one time. I know exactly how the game is played . . . and I wish you luck," she laughed.

"Thank you," Vincent replied as he walked from the store.

Minutes later and a mile down the road Vincent realized that what she had said was true. He was falling hopelessly in love.

CHAPTER TWELVE

S everal high-rise condominiums and seaside restaurants slid past the automobile's windows before Vincent reached Jennifer's building; their close proximity to one another was such that it completely obstructed one's view of the Atlantic Ocean from highway A1A. As Vincent drove north along A1A, he leaned his head forward of the steering wheel and looked up at the huge concrete structures. Apartments were stacked one on top of the other as high as the zoning regulations would allow, and for the most part, the buildings were fully occupied. The monstrosities served as testimony to man's never-ending desire to live by the seashore.

Just ahead, Jennifer's condominium building loomed twenty stories high, rendering it virtually impossible to miss. The Mercedes decelerated to a little over five miles per hour before Vincent made a right hand turn into the entranceway of Jennifer's building. This time, however, Vincent did not follow the circular drive that led to the front entrance. Instead, the Mercedes 500SL stopped at the uniformed guard's gatehouse. The driver's side window silently lowered at the same moment the guard slid back the tiny house's glass door. Vincent turned towards him as the pudgy, middle-aged man stepped down from the wooden stool where he had been seated. The guard's hand grabbed a clipboard that appeared to have been casually flung onto the desktop as testimony to how boring the security job was. Nevertheless, the uniformed guard performed his assigned duty.

"Visiting someone?"

"Yes, I am. Vincent Panachi to see Jennifer Swords." Vincent replied as he flashed the man a confident smile.

The security guard flipped the top page on the clipboard with his left thumb. Meanwhile, his right index finger tracked down a list of names until he stopped midway down the page. Vincent watched the man read his name—literally, because the man's lips moved as he read. The security guard kept his finger firmly pressed against the resident's roster, careful to mark his spot.

"Yes, sir, Miss Swords has already called down." His eyes glanced back at the clipboard for a couple of seconds, then he added, "I see here I'm supposed to give you a guest parking sticker." Before Vincent had time to ask a question, the security guard reached across the tiny guardhouse and grabbed a bright-red sticker. When the pudgy man turned back, he instructed Vincent, "Sir, just peel this here label off then stick it to the inside of your windshield. This is so you can park your automobile overnight."

Without thinking, Vincent's eyes shot up and met the guard's. The two men held a momentary stare before the condominium's uniformed security man allowed a broad smile to form across his face. He recognized a sure thing, and of course it didn't take a rocket scientist to figure out that Vincent was in for an entertaining evening. The security guard was much too discreet to make an off-color remark. Vincent broke free of the stare and directed his attention to the sticker in his hand.

"I'll do that. Thank you," Vincent said.

"Just follow the ramp up to the second level. You can park in the rear, closest to the ocean. Have a nice evening, sir," the security guard replied nodding his head in acknowledgment.

This time, it was Vincent who nodded.

Vincent tapped the Mercedes' accelerator. At the same time, his right index finger applied pressure to the electric window's switch, which sent the pane of glass sliding silently up. Seconds later, the automobile began a series of tight turns as it steadily climbed from the ground level to the second floor parking garage. Vincent's good sense of direction helped lead him to the rear of the garage, because like all parking garages, every space and floor looked identical. He found an empty space all the way in the back, against the wall, marked *GUEST* in bold yellow letters.

Vincent stood at the doorway to the elevator with the two bottles of champagne in his hands. Lit numbers above the doorway alerted him as to the location of the elevator, and he could see that the push of the button had summoned it from the penthouse level. Vincent watched as the lighted numbers counted down, just as most people who are waiting for an elevator do. The countdown was somewhat hypnotizing. 16-15-14 . . . 7-6-5-4-3. The sound of a chime rang at the exact moment the number 2 illuminated then the elevator door opened. Perhaps it was anticipation, but the ride to the 19th floor seemed quicker than when he had watched the numbers count backwards. At any rate, the elevator delivered Vincent to the desired floor within a couple of minutes.

Vincent stood in front of the door to Jennifer's condominium and rang the doorbell. The faint sounds of ringing chimes vibrated through the outer door and released a flock of butterflies in his stomach. Here was a man who was accustomed to living life on the edge, yet the mere anticipation of seeing Jennifer Swords twisted his stomach into a knot. The sudden emotion took Vincent by surprise while he strained to suppress any outward expression of the feeling he was experiencing. His facial expression remained cool, calm, and collected.

Suddenly, without the sound of numerous dead bolts unlocking, the door opened.

"Hi, Vincent. I'm so glad you came. Please, come in," Jennifer said smiling.

Vincent returned the smile as he walked through the doorway, a bottle of Dom Perignon in either hand. He leaned forward and kissed Jennifer lightly on her lips. However, when he tried to withdraw, Jennifer wrapped her arms around his neck and held him tight while her tongue found its way into his mouth. The ensuing passionate kiss lasted close to a minute, during which time Vincent felt a heated rush all the way through his body to his loins. When Jennifer finally withdrew, both their lips glistened with moisture. She kept her arms around Vincent's neck while they looked into one another's eyes. They remained silent while a mutual message of passion and desire was telepathically transmitted between their souls.

"With a greeting like that, this champagne is going to boil if I hold it in my hands much longer," Vincent quipped breaking the silence.

Without breaking her hold on him, Jennifer tilted her head back in a hearty laugh. Her hair shook while she laughed and its sheen reflected the dimly lit lights of the chandelier above the dining room table. It was then that Vincent noticed the elegantly set table. Jennifer removed her arms from around his neck and allowed her slender fingers to slide down the sleeves of his soft sweater until her hands were over his.

"Well, I guess we better chill these on ice. Follow me." With that, she turned and walked toward the kitchen.

The dining room was not separated from the living room, but the china cabinet, chandelier, and mirrored wall gave it an appearance of being so. The table was set with fine china, the plates rimmed with pink-colored trim and twenty-four carat gold. Heavy antique sterling silver silverware adorned the place settings on either side of the china. A silver champagne bucket sat in the center of the table along with two crystal candleholders, their ten-inch, pink candles ablaze. Tiny inch-high flames danced to-and-fro when Vincent and Jennifer passed alongside the dining room table. The two place settings were beautiful.

A second champagne bucket was in the kitchen, and that one was three quarters full of ice. Vincent gently shoved one bottle of Dom Perignon into the waiting ice then placed the other one flat on its side in the freezer. He turned toward Jennifer.

"Shall we?"

"Oh, yes. You know how I love good champagne," she gushed while his eyes led hers in the direction of the champagne bucket.

The scene from the liquor store quickly flashed through Vincent's mind when he smiled and replied, "Yes, I do."

With the expertise of a five-star restaurant captain, Vincent carefully removed the cork from the bottle. Unlike 99.9 percent of champagne drinkers, Vincent was schooled in the correct manner of opening a bottle of effervescent fine wine, and it was something that Jennifer took notice of, mostly because she herself had not seen it done that way. Gently, but firmly, Vincent grasped the cork with one hand and slowly turned the bottle with the other. He was particularly careful to keep his thumb on top of the cork in order to prevent it from flying off the bottle. The result was a "hiss" rather than a "pop." Vincent removed the cork and a small cloud of gas chased it from the bottle's mouth. All of a sudden, hundreds of tiny bubbles raced one another to the surface in testimony that it was indeed a good bottle of fine champagne. Meanwhile, Jennifer placed two long-stemmed flute glasses on the counter beside the bucket. Vincent smiled as he filled them to the brim, then handed one to her.

"A toast," he said raising his glass.

"Salute, Amor, y Dinero!" She followed.

"Health, Love, and Money!" He translated as they clinked their glasses together.

Jennifer looked at him while she took a sip from her champagne glass.

"That was beautiful, Vincent."

It included everything that was important to her, as well, but she would have rearranged the order of importance, placing "money" before all else. Jennifer's philosophy was that money would serve as a lubricant for the other two. Of course, she did not share that preference of order with Vincent. It did, however, remind her of just what her objective was for that particular evening.

Jennifer took Vincent by his free hand.

"Would you like to see the rest of the condo?"

"Of course . . . from what I've seen it is beautiful."

She led him from the kitchen, through the dining room into the living room. A pale-pink colored, crushed leather sofa lined the wall. A rather large and quite colorful painting of a seascape was centered along the same wall. End tables and lamps sat on either end of the sofa, and the lamps' bases were clear glass filled with small seashells. Vincent held Jennifer's hand tight in his while she slowly guided him through the beautifully decorated room. He gave her hand a slight tug and she turned around. Vincent complimented her taste in décor and she thanked him. When she turned back around, she gave his hand a firm squeeze. A narrow hallway led to the bathrooms and bedrooms. What could have been a guest bedroom had been decorated as a den/study, and a bathroom was directly across the hall from that.

As they walked from the room, hand in hand towards the bedroom, Vincent said, "You've really done a nice job with this. Did you do it yourself?"

"Yes, I did. Thank you," Jennifer smiled a broad smile for there was nothing she enjoyed more than attention and compliments.

Jennifer gave his hand a firm squeeze, again. Ten more feet down the dimly lit hallway was the doorway to the condo's master bedroom. Jennifer's bedroom. Just the thought of her exquisite, nude body sent an involuntary shudder through his body. What he was not aware of though was that Jennifer was experiencing the exact same emotions. Perhaps it was because they both were excited that neither of them noticed the sudden dampness shared in their palms.

The master bedroom had a combination of qualities that delighted the senses, yet appealed to the mind. A king-sized bed was against one wall while an entertainment center lined the opposite wall. A forty-inch television monitor and a small stereo filled the cabinet. Indeed, it was an unusual display for a bedroom. However, as if Jennifer had read Vincent's thoughts, she purred, "I like to spend a lot of time lounging in bed. That's why I put his unit in here, rather than the living room."

Vincent smiled and nodded in acknowledgment that he understood, he himself often watched television from bed. The bedroom was rather spacious, due in part to its void of bulky dressers. Of course, Jennifer had not bothered to show Vincent the inside of the numerous closets, but if she had, he would have known for certain that she was not lacking in clothing. On the contrary, Jennifer Swords was a clotheshorse, extraordinaire.

Vincent turned to Jennifer and commented, "You're bedroom is absolutely gorgeous." He paused while he took a sip from the champagne glass, and Jennifer did the same. Vincent added, "And so are you."

Jennifer extended her free hand as if she was going to affectionately touch his cheek, but instead, she took his champagne glass. She turned around in silence, not saying a word as she set the two flute glasses down on her make-up table. When she turned back, she took two steps forward and wrapped her arms around Vincent's neck. Her lips pressed against his, softly at first, but harder and harder as the passionate kiss intensified. While Jennifer's tongue intertwined with Vincent's he wrapped his arms around her and pulled her body close to his. Jennifer's breasts pressed against Vincent's chest and he could feel the heat of her passion through the flimsy, silk fabric. Much to Vincent's pleasure, the cool material did little to conceal her excited hardened nipples. His right hand slowly followed the curvature of her spine to the small of her back. Vincent did not apply undue pressure, but nevertheless, Jennifer firmly pressed herself against him. She rose up onto her toes and shifted her weight onto her left leg while her right foot rose slightly higher than her other. The resultant shift of weight flexed the muscles on the left side of her buttocks and accentuated the roundness of her rump. Almost as if gravity had guided his movement, Vincent ever so slowly allowed his hand to slide down from the small of her back until it stopped by itself. His hand rested on the full roundness of her bottom while the flimsiness of the dress' smooth material did little to conceal the fact that Jennifer had on G-string panties. Instinctively, Vincent pulled her hips closer to him, so close in fact that her love mound pressed against the hardness of his manhood. Jennifer broke free from the kiss, yet maintained the firm grasp she had around his neck. Vincent felt the moisture of her lips and tongue as she kissed and moaned her way to his ear. Gently, Jennifer nibbled at his ear while she whispered in his ear, "Make love to me . . . please." Vincent rolled his head to the right and downward until their lips met, once again. Jennifer's partially opened mouth met Vincent's puckered lips as their tongues darted in and out of one another's mouths. Her arms clung to his neck, even tighter than before, while his right hand slid up the length of Jennifer's spine. The muscles in her back rippled and formed an indentation down the center where her spine was. It also formed an inch space where the zipper was pulled taut from either side all the way from its top to the small of her back. Vincent's roaming hand found the top of the dress' zipper without difficulty, despite the fact that it was hidden beneath a fabric flap. The quality construction of designer's dress was evident when a slight tug from Vincent's fingers sent the zipper effortlessly down the center of Jennifer's sexy back. His fingertips gently guided the zipper all the way to the roundness of her bottom. Jennifer let out a barely audible sigh, but the passionate force of her tongue in his mouth confirmed that she had emitted it. Jennifer released the tight hold she had around Vincent's neck and allowed her arms to fall to her side. The dress fell from her shoulders and exposed her melon-sized breasts with nipples thrust out a half-inch. Jennifer outstretched her thumbs and slid them in the sides of her fallen dress. She wriggled her hips while she gently applied downward pressure with her thumbs until the flimsy silk dress fell to the floor. Without looking down, Jennifer raised one leg at a time and stepped free from the pile of material gathered about her ankles. Vincent's eyes moved slowly down her body, taking in her golden bronze tanned skin inch by inch. It was then that he noticed only the skimpy G-string separated Jennifer from being completely nude. The view of her exquisite body made his manhood rock hard, and he told her so. Jennifer purred, "Let me see," her eyes half closed and her mouth partially open. Jennifer's hands found their way to his belt buckle then expertly unhooked it. Within a series of quick moves Jennifer had the front of Vincent's trousers open and her hand wrapped around his throbbing member. Slowly but deliberately, she guided him backward toward the king-sized bed. Once they reached the side of the bed, she released the compromising hold she held on him and placed that same hand on the center of his chest, then gently pushed. Vincent fell back onto the bed. Jennifer undressed him in stages, beginning with his shoes and working her way up until he was lying there naked. Her voice took on a deeper than usual tone when she instructed him, "Don't move . . . please." Vincent did as she asked. Meanwhile, Jennifer stood at the side of the bed, by Vincent's feet, and peeled off her tiny underwear. Vincent was watching her every move, and when she stood up he noticed her shaven love mound. Jennifer shook her head in a movement that tossed her long, blond mane of hair to one side while she moved onto the bed. Jennifer's muscular legs straddled Vincent's. She placed one hand on his chest to steady her, then maneuvered her hips into position. When her knees were astride Vincent's waist, she leaned slightly forward. Wisps of Jennifer's blond hair fell about his face, yet it did not prevent him from seeing her reach behind with her free hand. A split second later, Vincent knew for certain where her hand was headed; she grasped his throbbing manhood in her hand and guided it inside her. Vincent was by no means a virgin, yet he had never quite experienced the feeling that her clean shaven lips brought as she impaled herself on his manhood. Jennifer pushed hard, harder than before, then suddenly gasped as her vagina engulfed his love tool. Jennifer did not utter a word, but instead, pressed down hard against Vincent's chest. She developed a rhythm of her own as she slid up and down, in and out, on Vincent's manhood. Her rhythm began to sway her body from side to side, and her ample breasts bounced seductively, their nipples hard and erect. Vincent grabbed one in each hand while he gently massaged their pointed tips. Jennifer's moans grew louder and more frequent while her strokes become longer. She shifted her weight several times during grinding movements that sent them both into another world. Finally, her strokes became more deliberate, faster and faster, followed by moans that turned to screams of ecstasy. Suddenly, she dug her fingernails into Vincent's chest. She screamed and her body began quivering in an uncontrollable, rapturous orgasm. Jennifer's sudden, involuntary muscle contractions squeezed Vincent's manhood until the applied pressure sent him into an uncontrollable orgasm, as well. Jennifer's hands found his and her fingers found their way between his. While holding his hands, she let out a long sigh then guided Vincent's hands over his head. Jennifer's body followed, her heaving breasts laid upon his chest. Vincent was still inside her, and before she said a word he felt a second muscle contraction. She squeezed his fingers tightly and let out a slight moan. Seconds later, as she lay on top of Vincent, spent of all her energy, she kissed his neck several times while she whispered, "Oh, Vincent . . . that felt so wonderful."

"Yes, it did. You were wonderful," Vincent replied.

An hour had passed since Vincent's arrival at Jennifer's condominium, and of that hour, forty-five minutes had been spent having animal-like sex. It was far too early in their relationship to be *really* making love, yet Jennifer was experiencing feelings that she never had before. The delectable smell of dinner wafted throughout the condo and seemed to remind both of them at the same time that they had not eaten. However, it was Vincent who spoke up first.

"The evening's order seems to have been turned around." He squeezed her fingers when he added, "And, I loved it."

Jennifer's face was partially stuffed into the pillow, and her voice somewhat muffled when she agreed, "So did I."

Jennifer was the first from the bed. She grabbed the two champagne glasses from atop the make-up counter and padded off toward the kitchen. Vincent watched her melon-sized breasts bounce with the rhythm of her walk as she left the bedroom, then he sat up. By the time she returned, he had untangled his clothes and dressed. Jennifer handed him a flute glass full of sparkling Dom Perignon champagne. She took a sip from her glass before she placed it on the make-up counter.

"I guess you won't be surprised when I tell you that dinner is ready."

Vincent laughed, kissed her on the cheek and responded, "No, I won't." He winked at her as he started for the bedroom door. Her hand trailed off of his and he walked towards the doorway. Finally, Vincent called over his shoulder, "Don't be long, okay?"

While Jennifer got dressed, she attempted to analyze the emotions she was experiencing. Quite honestly, the feelings were frightening to her, because it was something that could not be defined in terms of black and white. For the first time in her life, Jennifer had to deal with a feeling that would have been more grey than definitive in color. Jennifer had never loved anyone . . . except herself. Now, all of a sudden, with her sights set on Vincent Panachi and the secure wealth he represented, Jennifer Swords had shooting pangs through her stomach and mind. Not only was it an extraneous feeling, but worse, it was an emotion that was very difficult to control. It was also something that Jennifer Swords had never figured on—Jennifer was falling in love with Vincent Panachi.

CHAPTER THIRTEEN

T he Quill was old enough to be Vincent's father, and then some. Like most elderly, the Quill had a habit of retiring early and rising early. Of course, after sleeping for nearly eighteen hours, the elderly man felt as well rested as he ever had. He awakened before the sun rose, and also before Jennifer and Vincent arose.

Jennifer and Vincent were still fast asleep in one another's arms. Their appetites for hunger and for sex had been well taken care of. Jennifer's dinner had been exquisite, despite the fact that the meal had been served over an hour later than planned. Her expert cooking had been washed down with the finest of champagne while the tiny flames of the table's candles cast a seductive light about the dining room. Jennifer and Vincent had talked and laughed throughout the entire meal, and conversation with Vincent had come so easily and naturally to her that it was frightful. In addition, it seemed to heighten her awareness of the emotional confusion she was experiencing. After dinner and a bottle of champagne later, Jennifer and Vincent had ended up in the bedroom, once again.

The Quill had long since stopped dreaming of beautiful, naked women. As a matter of fact, sex was something he never even thought about. Perhaps it was his age that influenced his lack of sexual desire; or then again, perhaps the thoughts had been voluntarily driven from his mind during his two-decade stay at the federal penitentiary he jokingly referred to as "Hotel Hell." At any rate the incarceration may have quelled his sexual desires, but it also had its upside. The Quill had remained perfectly sober during those enduring years behind bars, and the result was that his mind was razor sharp. Two decades of sobriety will do that to a man, and had, in this case.

On the other hand, the Quill was getting his rocks off too. For him, the satisfaction was not found through sexual gratification, but instead, through his powerful intellect. Now, while Jennifer and Vincent slept after their exhausting night of sex, the Quill was wide-awake and utilizing his brilliant mind to reproduce currency, in particular, twenty-dollar bills. Perfect resemblances of currency in circulation.

A cup of coffee sat next to the Quill's makeshift office, an eighteen by twenty-foot bedroom in the rear of the expansive, country club home. The equipment had been tediously placed about the room by Vincent's local boys while the Quill had directed their every move. With one exception, the sophisticated equipment lined a single wall of the bedroom. The additional piece of equipment, a computerized digital cutter, was situated in the adjoining bedroom along with several large folding tables identical to those used in a school's cafeteria. Perhaps the set up was somewhat makeshift, but then again, not too many print shops come together within a twenty-four hour period. All things considered, the operation was downright spellbinding, and the Quill's creative genius was spellbound by the high tech operation.

Just like in the days of old, the Quill wore a printer's apron, although these days it was completely unnecessary. Unlike the offset printing press—a printing process in which the inked impression is first made on a rubber covered roller, then transferred to paper—the modern, computerized equipment kept the mess completely clean, especially during the creative stages. The Quill took a sip from his coffee while he reviewed the process in his mind. The computer had warmed up and was ready to receive commands from its operator.

The Quill studied the computer's keyboard while he outlined the program, then he lightly placed his fingers on the concave, plastic keys. Instantly, the high-resolution screen and video color card came to life. To the Quill, the technology was a dream come true. He spent a couple of hours familiarizing himself with the computer and he found the sophisticated piece of equipment extremely user friendly. The first phase of the operation was spent scanning real money. Real money. The high-speed computer utilized an art program to clean up the scanned images, then that image was sent to the color printer. The result was astounding. However, the Quill was a perfectionist. Therefore, he sharpened the computer's image until the image was so perfect that no one could possibly tell the difference from the scanned image and the original. Of course, every step along the way had its purpose, and this one was not the bill per se, but the reserve seal and the serial numbers. The serial numbers were computer generated with the computerized typesetter. Finally, just before the first rays of sunlight penetrated the cracks in the room's closed blinds, the Quill began the second phase of the operation. The computer's program was tweaked to its highest rate of efficiency, then fifteen copies were produced on a sheet. Fifteen copies of flawless serial numbers and reserve seals, perfectly placed on what was to become twenty dollar bills. When the first copy came out, the Quill set down his cup of coffee and grabbed it with both hands. Slowly, methodically, he critiqued his own handiwork. First, it was a quick scan with his naked eye, just as any normal person would look at a bill. Afterwards though, the Quill took a magnifying glass and scrutinized the printed seals and numbers. His right hand held the magnifying glass steady while his left hand slowly moved the sheet beneath it right to left. Each and every one was meticulously inspected. Suddenly, the Quill laid the paper down and exclaimed, "Damn . . . I've done it." The reserve seals and serial numbers had always been considered the hardest to reproduce. Offset printing presses tended to smudge the ink in and around these, and clarity became the name of the game. The Quill had hit upon a computer formula that reproduced them as good as or better than the Treasury Department. Of course, when one takes into consideration the fact that the Bureau of Engraving and Printing's systems are far outdated and antiquated, it is not inconceivable that the computer could far surpass their mechanical presses.

The Quill got up from his seat and moved to the digital color copier. His hand shook slightly as he loaded the sheet with the fifteen copies into the machine, but the trembling was not from fear—it was excitement. The preparation took a couple of minutes, during which the copier's green-lighted switch seemed to goad him. Finally, the proper adjustments were made and the print switch depressed.

The high speed, high-resolution copier made a split-second whirring sound before the sheet literally shot out of the side of the huge machine into a plastic tray. Carefully, the Quill picked it up by the edges. Printed on the paper were fifteen flawless resemblances of the front of a twenty-dollar bill. The fronts of the bills were printed in black over the reserve seals and the serial numbers. The Quill was still in the experimental stages of the operation, so utilizing the information gathered from the computer's video color card, he adjusted the darkness of the black. The Quill flipped the paper with the fifteen fronts and reloaded it into the color copier. The computer's green-lighted switch beckoned him, once again, and the Quill depressed the switch. A rush of excitement surged through his body when the sheet exited the machine. The Quill picked it up then recycled it through the machine, again, except this time the color copier's toner was changed to a light green. The lighter color green was run on top of the already printed, much darker black. The rerun did the trick, and the bills came out perfect. As far as the images went, the fronts and backs were impeccable.

The Quill could hardly contain his enthusiasm as he examined the bill. The magnifying glass slowly swept across each individual bill while he scrutinized his handiwork. The process took five minutes. If there was a problem with the bills, he wanted to discover it now; not after production was at full speed. It was amazing, but as hard as he tried he just could not find fault with the resemblances. They were perfect, at least at this stage of the process, but it was not over yet. A final adjustment was made to the machine before the sheet was rerun, one last time. This time, tiny streaks of red and blue were scattered about the twenty-dollar bills like the tiny threads they resembled. The Quill's heart rate actually increased as the sheet exited the machine into the tray. With the same enthusiasm known by a research scientist on the verge of a major breakthrough, the Quill grabbed the piece of paper and headed towards the adjoining bedroom.

The computerized digital cutter was accurate to the millimeter. The Quill had already preset the size of a twenty-dollar bill in the computer's memory, and with the simple push of a button the sophisticated, highly accurate cutter precisely subdivided the paper into fifteen, twenty-dollar bill sized pieces. No errors; no over or undersized margins; only perfect replicas of the real thing. The Quill carefully gathered the pieces and laid them upon one of the tables. Atop another table were two plastic trays with a quarter of an inch of the nastiest looking fluid in them that one could possibly imagine. In reality, the fluid was a mixture of green, black, and yellow inks. The ink dyed the paper and gave the new money not such a new look. As a matter of fact, it was virtually impossible for the average person to even tell the difference between the original and the resemblance. The Quill withdrew a pair of surgical gloves from a box and slipped his aged hands into them. One at a time, he submerged the bills in the ink wash. It only took a second before the bills were thoroughly soaked. The Quill removed them as quickly as possible and laid them on top of one of the tables. The transformation took place right before his very eyes—what had been mere paper just minutes before was now a twenty-dollar bill. "Damn," he said out loud, "I really am an artist." The experiment was considered an unequivocal success, and in the Quill's mind, he had discovered the secret formula that would yield riches. He also mused that he had some long, tiresome days ahead of him. That particular thought, in retrospect, may have been the understatement of his life.

*   *   *

The smell of freshly brewed coffee wafted through the air and awakened Agent Murray's somnolent senses the very instant he opened the front door to the surveillance condominium overlooking Shylock's and Pegleg's. His men had already helped themselves to a morning cup, and for them that was precisely what it was—a morning cup. Those particular cups of coffee were just a continuation of the many they had already consumed throughout the night. Mark Murray stepped into the kitchen and poured himself a full cup. The rattling sound of the cup meeting the saucer drew a response from the other agents sitting in the condominium's living room.

"Nice to see you—join us, Murray," One of the agents called out.

Agent Murray laughed as he exited the kitchen and joined them in the living room, his coffee in hand. In sharp contrast to Agent Murray's neatly pressed clothes, the other men's clothes were crumpled and wrinkled—all the telltale signs of pulling an all night surveillance post.

The sun was barely above the horizon, yet for these men the sunrise marked the end of their day rather than the beginning of a new one. The night before had been the first night the Organized Crime Task Force had placed Vincent Panachi's house under round-the-clock surveillance. Agent Murray had ordered the surveillance, and that order had been based on a tip from Slick Nick. Apparently, according to Slick Nick, the Vitale crime family had hit it big on an upset football game. Betting had been unusually high and there was a lot of action with the bookmakers. Furthermore, at the direction of the Old Man, the bookies had set a different point-spread than Las Vegas had posted on the two favorite teams. As a matter of fact Slick Nick himself, through one of his restaurant employees, had got down with a bet. Of course, Slick Nick had known the inside track as to whom the bookmakers operated for, and therefore had not wanted his name associated with the sizeable bet, just in case he won. Well, he, just like ninety percent of the other bettors, lost. The Vitale crime family had won though. Big time!

The orange fireball rose fast over the open Atlantic Ocean and provided a backdrop for the bank of cameras that lined the condominium's wall of sliding glass doors. As usual, all cameras were aimed at Shylock's and Pegleg's, their diverse lenses already adjusted. Agent Murray surveyed the room and the agents in it.

"You gentlemen don't look any worse the wear, all things considered," the agent began the conversation.

The agents, all of whom got along with Agent Murray very well, responded with a sardonic grin on their faces. One of them spoke up.

"Bullshit stakeout, Murray. Didn't see shit all night," he said.

"What do you mean 'all night?'" Agent Murray queried.

"We're talking round-the-clock here, Mark," another agent spoke up.

"There is not really much to tell you. The subject's house was under surveillance all night long. His house, Murray . . . not him. The Mercedes pulled out of the island at approximately nine p.m., stopped on the bridge before Las Olas Boulevard for a couple of minutes then turned east towards the beach," the first agent clarified.

Silence filled the room for a few seconds while Agent Murray patiently waited for a continuation of the story, but no one spoke.

"And?" Mark Murray finally asked.

"Look, boss, the bastard never came back. We did not follow him, and he never came back to the house," the second agent remarked.

Murray rubbed his chin for a moment while he pondered their statement.

"All night, right?"

"All night," both agents answered at the same time.

"We would have followed him, but your orders were to watch the house . . . not him. The house didn't move, nor did anybody in it," the first agent added.

Before Murray could comment on the statement, the other agent piped up. "Maybe your informant gave you some bad information." There was a slight pause, for dramatics, before he added, "Maybe you should put his nuts in a vise and see if his memory gets any better." Agent Murray allowed a smile to form across his face, but his mind was elsewhere. Suddenly, Agent Murray developed a severe case of heartburn, but the worst part of the pain was the fact that this was the type of heartburn that a Rolaids could not take care of. This pain was a direct result of the surge of jealousy that shot through Agent Murray's body like a junkie's hotshot. He hid his feelings from the other agents, just as he did his assumption. He had figured out where Vincent Panachi had been all night long—with Jennifer Swords.

Agent Murray saved face the best he could by directing the conversation towards another angle of their surveillance when he asked, "So, how about the shots this past weekend? Did we get any incriminating pictures of Vincent Panachi?"

A third agent answered the question, because he was the one who had developed the surveillance pictures.

"No Panachi. No Scarab Thunder, either."

Agent Murray placed his fingertips together and held his hands chest high in front of him. Methodically, he pushed tip against tip while he contemplated the information. He knew for a fact that Vincent Panachi was a regular on the waterways during the weekends. If the Scarab had not been spotted Saturday or Sunday there was a reason why, and he wanted to know that reason. Immediately his thoughts turned to Slick Nick, and for a moment he pondered the thought that perhaps the restaurateur had intentionally misinformed him to throw him off. He wondered if, in fact, Slick Nick had told Vincent Panachi of their little agreement.

Suddenly, without premonition, Agent Murray announced to the other agents, "Perhaps I will put his nuts in a vise . . . just to see if he sings a different tune."

*　　*　　*

It was a few minutes past 9 a.m. when Agent Murray's dark-blue Ford sedan pulled into Slick Nick's driveway. Of course, the official-looking sedan had looked out of place at the restaurant, but nothing like it did in the posh Lighthouse Point neighborhood. BMWs, Porsches and Mercedes were the norm; not average, bland-looking automobiles like the Ford Crown Victoria. Agent Murray was not concerned with impressing anyone. While it was against his own set of cardinal rules to ever be seen at a confidential informant's residence, that particular morning he was seething. Mark Murray had not been an agent for the Organized Crime Task Force as long as Slick Nick had been a street punk, but nevertheless, he had been around long enough to have witnessed other agents being led astray by their so called 'rock-solid' informants.

Agent Murray pulled the sedan up to the garage door; so close that there was no way that Slick Nick could get his automobile around Murray's should he try something cute—like leaving while Mark was at the front door. Agent Murray had learned one thing about doorbells years ago the hard way—when the front doorbell is ringing, the person inside knows precisely where you are. That's the idea, unless you're an agent for the Organized Crime Task Force paying an unannounced visit to your unreliable snitch.

Agent Murray rang the doorbell then stepped back five feet from the front door. From that vantage point both the garage door and the side door that led to the swimming pool were within his field of view. Several minutes passed without a sign of life, so Murray pressed the doorbell switch again. This time he stayed close to the door until he heard the sound of ringing chimes from deep within the house. A few more uneventful minutes went by before the familiar sound of a deadbolt being unlocked resounded through the heavy, wooden, front door. Seconds later, the door opened.

It is human nature to look somewhat disheveled the first thing in the morning. However, when Slick Nick opened the front door to his house he looked like the wrath of Gods had styled his knotted hair. His eyes were half open and sunken into deep, dark circles. In general, Slick Nick looked terrible. It only took a split second for those bloodshot eyes to shoot wide open once his dulled senses recognized Agent Murray at his door. Slick Nick could not control the instantaneous look of fear in his eyes . . . or was it guilt that he had involuntarily shown?

Well, that was precisely the question in which Agent Murray intended to find the answer. Before Slick Nick opened his mouth, Agent Murray quickly stuck his right foot against the bottom of the door. Perhaps Slick Nick's next move was more out of the raw fear rather than logical thought, but at any rate, the frightened restaurateur leaned his weight against the door while he cowered behind it. However, his applied force was no match for Agent Murray. Besides, the agent had an advantage over Slick Nick—he was emotionally high-strung with anger, whereas Nick's senses were dulled by sleep, or the lack of.

The force from the opening front door flung Slick Nick backward into the foyer, and Agent Murray followed. When Mark was clearly inside the house, he slammed the door shut behind him. The sound reverberated throughout the tile-floored entranceway, but was soon overpowered by Agent Murray's boisterous voice.

"All right, you little piece of shit . . . I want the straight facts . . . and if you choose to lie to me, again, I'll personally see to it that you fry in the chair. Do I make myself perfectly clear?" Agent Murray screamed.

Slick Nick was visibly shaken when his voice reached a high pitched whine. "Mr. Murray, I've told you the truth, already . . . what is the matter?"

Agent Murray was well trained in the use of high-pressure techniques to obtain the truth. Fear was the primary motivator and it usually worked very well, particularly when the party in question was facing murder-one charges. Mark

Murray was relentless in his pursuit. He took two steps forward so that he was standing directly in front of the frightened restaurateur.

"You sent me on a wild goose chase, Nick. My men sat outside Vincent Panachi's house all night last night . . . for nothing. They're pissed at me, and I'm pissed at you. Now, I want to know the truth."

Slick Nick just stood there shaking while he stalled for time to think. While his mind replayed the weekend and the day before, Nick inadvertently blurted some of his thoughts out loud.

"Damn, I spoke with Vincent just last night . . ."

"When did you hear from Panachi?" Agent Murray inquired while interrupting Nick's train of thought.

Slick Nick recognized Murray's more civil tone of voice and relaxed a bit. He gathered his composure.

"He called me last night . . . at the restaurant. All he said was that the old man wanted to convey his thanks for the party at the restaurant. That's all."

Mark pondered Slick Nick's response for a few seconds.

"Was he at home when he called you?"

"No, I don't think so. I remember there were a couple of clicks across the phone connection, like he was being switched from one circuit to another. You know, a mobile phone," Nick replied.

Agent Murray nodded his head. Perhaps Slick Nick had been truthful with him, because Vincent was observed leaving his house. Agent Murray pressed him further.

"What about this mysterious 'big payoff' you told me about? We watched his house all night . . . and I can't tell!"

"How the hell would I know? Maybe they delivered the money some place else. Shit, Murray, he doesn't tell me those things," Slick Nick screeched.

Agent Murray realized he had squeezed Slick Nick just about as much as he possibly could. The man was not stable to begin with, and all that this interrogation would accomplish would be to totally reduce him to shambles. Therefore, Mark decided to play good-cop, bad-cop with his snitch. Gently, he placed a hand on Slick Nick's shoulder.

"It was just a simple misunderstanding, Nick. Not to worry. You're still in good shape."

Slick Nick did not know what to say, and consequently, said nothing in reply.

Agent Murray stepped backward toward the front door while keeping his eye on Slick Nick. His hand searched behind his back until he found the doorknob, then turned it. Agent Murray opened the door while he kept watching Nick. Agent Murray never even said good-bye. Instead he silently turned and walked away while Slick Nick closed and locked the door behind him. Slick Nick watched from the side window as the sedan backed out of the driveway.

The agent for the Organized Crime Task Force slowly accelerated the somewhat out of place vehicle down the posh, residential street while his mind was carefully reviewing the conversation that had just taken place with his confidential informant. Methodically, he played back the scene, step-by-step. Suddenly, something that Slick Nick had said made an impact on his reflection. Agent Murray's finely honed mind replayed the restaurateur's screeching voice when he had said, *"How the hell would I know? Maybe they delivered the money some place else. Shit, Murray, he doesn't tell me those things."* For a couple of seconds, Mark Murray was steering the Ford sedan by instinct only, because his calculating mind was miles away. Those few seconds spent in afterthought changed the course of his investigation. It was as if a bolt of lightening had struck him. The idea flashed in his head just that quickly. "Why didn't I see it before?" he asked himself out loud.

Agent Murray figured it out. Slick Nick had provided him with a vast wealth of general knowledge pertaining to the inner workings of the Vitale crime family, but apparently he was not privy to the knowledge of the daily routines. If Agent Murray were to successfully build a case against Vincent Panachi and the Vitale crime family, then it was imperative that he knew something about the daily workings of the family members, in particular Panachi. Mark knew that if he were able to get a strangle hold on Vincent, that the rest of the crime family would follow. His mind toyed with the idea while his instincts turned the sedan to the left, then stopped at the stop sign. His hands held the steering wheel in the ten and two o'clock positions, and he sat frozen at the wheel, his mind miles and miles away, deep in thought.

Without a moment's hesitation, as if he had been worried that the thought might escape him if he did not record it immediately, Agent Murray grabbed his micro-recorder and dictated a short message: "Pertaining to the Vitale investigation; secure a court order for a phone tap and a pen-register for one Jennifer Swords." The phone tap would record the actual conversation while the pen-register would decipher and record all incoming and outgoing telephone numbers.

Agent Murray smiled at his ingenious plan. That morning he had killed two birds with one stone, as the saying goes. Not only could he better monitor Vincent Panachi's daily activities, but now he would also know precisely what Jennifer Swords was doing with her social life. As he accelerated away from the stop sign, Mark felt a sudden, brief, pain in his heart. Of course, the sharp spasm that he experienced had become more than familiar to him over the months. Just the thought of knowing who and when Jennifer was enjoying sex with sent her STILETTO plunging deep into his heart, once again.

CHAPTER FOURTEEN

A t the very same moment Agent Murray turned the dark-blue sedan south onto Federal Highway, Vincent Panachi was exiting the garage at Jennifer's condominium. The layered parking levels prevented the brightness of the morning sun from shining directly onto the automobile, and consequently, Vincent's eyes were adjusted to the somewhat dim lighting. When he drove the Mercedes from underneath the protection of the garage into the sunlight the pain was excruciating. Without looking—not that he could have seen anyway due to his temporary blindness—Vincent reached into the glove box with his right hand and found his Ray Ban sunglasses. A quick movement flung open the temples, and he carefully placed the sunglasses on his face. The relief was instantaneous.

Vincent turned the luxury automobile north onto Highway A1A. The time was 9:30 a.m., which accounted for the smooth flow of traffic along the beach front roadway. If Vincent had left Jennifer's a few minutes before 9 a.m., no doubt he would have been swept into a sea of commuters, all scrambling to make it to work on time. Vincent had not planned his departure time accordingly. It had just worked out that way. "Perhaps it is an omen for the way the rest of the day will unfold," he silently speculated. The optimistic thought placed a smile on his face, and that smile remained there for quite a while. Vincent Panachi was happy. Very happy, as a matter of fact. Everything was going extremely well for the Vitale crime family, and the same held true for Vincent's personal life.

The sky was robin's egg-blue and cloudless. All in all, it was one of those dazzlingly beautiful days that made South Florida the winter playground for the rich and famous. Tourists had already begun flocking to the beach in droves, despite the fact that it was only mid-morning. Go-fasts streaked up-and-down the shoreline, their drivers craning their necks to check the babes at the many hotels along the beach. Another gorgeous winter day spent in fantasyland—Ft. Lauderdale, Florida.

Highway A1A intersected with Atlantic Boulevard, and Vincent turned the luxury automobile left at the light. The roadway took him up and over the bridge that spanned the Intracoastal Waterway before it headed west towards the Everglades. It was also the most direct route to the city of Coral Springs, and the Quill. Once he had crossed the bridge, the scenery quickly changed from the beach environment to strip center shopping areas. Vincent's mind returned to business just as quickly. Instinctively, his right hand reached over and lowered the volume of the blaring stereo. He had a lot of grown-up things to do that day, and the ride to Coral Springs provided him with the time to think; to organize a game plan. In retrospect, however, Vincent Panachi had not prepared himself for what that day had brought.

The shopping centers gave way to exotic car dealerships, which, in turn, gave the real estate back to the shopping centers. Businesses leapfrogged one another until eventually Atlantic Boulevard became residential. Another ten minutes passed before Vincent turned into the manicured subdivision of the Coral Springs Country Club. The Mercedes 500SL looked every bit the part of belonging there as it cruised past the palatial homes, and less than a minute later Vincent turned into the driveway of his rented house. That house, just like every other house in the posh neighborhood, looked as if there was not a sign of life inside. Everything was quiet, as it should have been. Vincent smiled, for he knew that even if one of his nosy neighbors were watching him through a crack in their drapes, he also looked every bit the part of belonging there. Although Jennifer could have been a little more attentive to not creasing his slacks when she had undressed him the erotic evening before, who in their right mind would have complained? He certainly had not. Instead, Vincent had utilized a trick that he had learned long ago from a flight attendant he had been dating at the time. He hung the slacks over a hanger, and hung the hanger on the far end of the guest bathroom's shower rod. The hot water faucet was turned to its fullest flow and hottest temperature selection. Once the water began steaming, he turned on the shower and closed the bathroom door behind him as he left the room. PRESTO! Ten minutes later, he had had freshly ironed slacks. Had one of the neighbors been watching, they would have seen a young executive, well dressed in a pair of expensive slacks and an alpaca sweater. "Damn yuppie," would have been more the expected reaction than, "He doesn't look as if he belongs in this neighborhood." If nothing else, Vincent was a detail man, and image was an important factor in making it all come together.

Vincent used his key to unlock the door. While arriving unannounced may have somewhat startled the Quill, there was no way that Vincent could have risked having one of the neighbors see him standing at the front door waiting for it to open. Vincent entered the house and walked towards the two bedrooms where the Quill had set up the print shop. The repetitive sounds from the high-speed machinery set a pulsating rhythm, and the computerized digital cutter's methodical strikes blended nicely with the regular recurrence of its beat. Before Vincent reached the rooms, he already knew that the counterfeit operation was in full swing. He smiled.

It was only natural for Vincent to have some preconceived notions about how the counterfeit currency was to be produced. But, as he soon learned, thinking about it and actually watching the action were worlds apart. He entered the nearest bedroom, the one that housed the manufacturing equipment, and his mouth hung open. The sophisticated machinery was literally spitting out sheets of twenty-dollar bills faster than he could count them. Vincent watched the process with a look of wonder and amazement on his face; thousands-upon—thousands of dollars were stacked-and-racked alongside the huge machine. With all of the things he had seen during his lifetime, he had never seen anything quite so mesmerizing. Vincent stood in the doorway for a minute before he moved towards the other bedroom.

The makeshift print shop had been slow getting started, yet the Quill had it up to full running speed long before Vincent's arrival. The result of his exceptional creative talent lay on the farthest table inside the room, next to the digital cutter. It wasn't until Vincent entered that particular room that the Quill became aware of his presence in the house. The elderly man was hunched over the cutter, busy removing a stack of freshly cut bills from the computerized piece of machinery. There was no way that the Quill could have heard Vincent's approach over the clanging and whirring of the machines, yet he turned towards him anyway. Now, it was the Quill's mouth that hung open as the sight of Vincent startled him. Without thinking the elderly gentleman blurted out the first thought that came into his mind.

"Jeez, Vito . . . you scared the hell out of me."

Vincent caught the slip of the name, but obviously, the Quill hadn't. Vincent held up his hands, palms outwards toward the Quill, then reassured him.

"Relax . . . everything is all right . . . and it's Vincent . . . Vito was my father."

The two men held one another's eyes for several seconds while a smile slowly formed across the elderly man's face. It was an expression formed from the admiration that the Quill had felt for Vincent's father. He had truly loved the man, and it gave him great pleasure to finally be involved in a project that the two of them had pursued decades ago, especially since Vito's son was playing a vital part in the operation. Perhaps in the old man's eyes this was his way of making up for the many years he had missed his best friend, Vito Panachi.

The Quill extended his hand to shake with Vincent. Instinctively, Vincent looked down at the elderly man's hand, and the Quill's eyes followed. Before Vincent made any comment, the Quill realized that his hand was still gloved. The Quill remarked, "Excuse me," as he peeled off the snug fitting rubber glove.

He further explained, "After you wear these things hours on end, you forget that you even have them on."

Vincent accepted his hand and the two men shook hands.

"I understand, my friend."

The Quill maintained a firm grip on Vincent's hand while he led him in the direction of the computerized digital cutter. Currency was lying atop the long, cafeteria-type tables in different stages of completion. On a table beside the digital cutter, however, were rows-upon-rows of neatly stacked twenty-dollar bills. The Quill relinquished the grasp he had maintained on Vincent's hand then motioned towards the stacks of money with a wave.

"Voila!" he exclaimed, his hand motioning to-and-fro in dramatic fashion.

Vincent stood next to the table and looked down in awe at the stacks of twenties. Not that they looked to be a large sum of money, and certainly Vincent had seen his share of large dollars in his days, but the currency looked so *real*. Vincent turned towards the Quill.

"May I pick one up?"

"Of course . . . but make certain that any of them you touch, you keep," the elderly gentleman answered. Vincent picked four bills from the top of a stack just as the printer added, "No fingerprints on these. They're sterile." Vincent did not bother to look up.

"I understand."

The two men stood in silence for over five minutes while Vincent examined the freshly made twenties. Front and back; front against another's back; two backs, side-by-side. Finally, Vincent looked up at the Quill. A smile formed across his face.

"These are flawless. I cannot tell the difference from a real one."

The Quill laughed while he patted the much younger man on the shoulder.

"Well, just remember that the government has to make them, too. These are the new, improved models."

Vincent and the Quill shared a good laugh.

"Let's go out to the living room where we can talk," Vincent suggested.

The two men walked towards the doorway, the Quill's arm around Vincent's shoulder while Vincent held the four, twenty-dollar bills in his hand.

The Quill motioned for the younger man to sit while he chose to stand. Vincent assumed it was because of the messy printer's apron that the Quill had on, but he did not ask. Actually it was the Quill who began the conversation, simple, direct, and to the point.

"Is everything okay?" the Quill asked.

Vincent looked up at the elderly gentleman and smiled.

"You know, that is precisely the question I was going to ask you. However," Vincent held the bills up so that they were at eye level, "I see that everything is going along rather smoothly."

The Quill's face flushed red, for the compliment actually embarrassed him. He averted his eyes away from Vincent's.

"Thank you."

Quickly, Vincent's mind figured out exactly why he had reacted that way—it was a carry over from the two decades the Quill had struggled for daily survival in prison. Prison—a living hell where words such as "Please," and "Thank you," are virtually unheard of. Instead, the prevalent language is straight from the inner-city streets where lower-classed individuals favor the universal term, "Mudda-fucka," as a noun, verb, adjective, and adverb.

Vincent changed the subject to much happier memories for the Quill.

"I will be seeing Capo Pelligi this afternoon. I'm certain that he would really like to see a few of these." Vincent waved the bills in a dramatic fashion, as if he were trying to entice a used car dealer to accept his final offer while he asked, "May I?"

"Certainly. There are approximately forty-thousand dollars worth finished. You are welcome to those."

"Thank you, Mr. Quill. This will give Capo Pelligi something to take back with him. No doubt, Anthony Vitale will enjoy seeing the finished product."

The two men engaged in some casual small talk that lasted close to fifteen minutes before it became apparent that the Quill was distracted by some of the bills that were in mid process. Vincent took the hint, and after placing the forty-thousand dollars in a briefcase the Quill had there, he excused himself.

"Thank you for your time. I know the Capo will appreciate this surprise."

Vincent patted the side of the closed case for emphasis then shook hands with the elderly gentleman.

The ride out of the posh neighborhood had been as uneventful as the ride in, and within ten minutes the Mercedes was headed south bound on Interstate 95 toward the Broward Boulevard exit. Vincent Panachi was en route to pick up nearly one million dollars in cash—the Vitale crime family's take on the football game.

*　　*　　*

Anthony Vitale was comfortably seated in the library of his palatial mansion. A roaring fire warmed the marble hearth in front of the fireplace while pieces of seasoned oak crackled in the licking flames. The room's vaulted, wood ceiling kept the room temperature cooler than the elderly gentleman preferred, and therefore, it was not uncommon to see smoke rising from the mansion's chimney at all hours of the night and day.

Anthony Vitale had not maintained his control over the crime family throughout the years by engaging the family's members in half-baked schemes and ideas. Each undertaking was carefully planned down to the minutest detail. It was the hours spent in his favorite room, the library, that conceived the elaborate plans the crime family undertook.

It was here that the decision was made to alter the Las Vegas point spread, and it was also in the library that the old man decided it would be best for Vincent to curtail his activities as bagman until the operation with the Colombians was completed. At his order, Capo Pelligi was dispatched to pick up the one million dollars in football gambling proceeds. Vincent was to be relieved of his responsibility to physically move the dollars from Florida to New Jersey, at least until the counterfeiting operation was completed. That courier assignment was now in the hands of Capo Pelligi.

While Anthony Vitale watched a flurry of tiny snowflakes whisk past the library's Palladian window, Capo Pelligi was observing the same snow storm from a different location—New York's John Fitzgerald Kennedy Airport (JFK). The wind howled at a steady twenty knots that sent the chill factor below zero degrees Fahrenheit. The stocky Italian stood close to the large, plate glass window in the lobby of JFK's Butler Aviation. His warm breath fogged the ice-cold glass before condensation caused several droplets of water to streak down the pane. Without thinking, Capo Pelligi rubbed his hands together for warmth.

Outside sat Learjet N30TP. The captain was seated in the business jet's cockpit while the co-pilot was inside the building updating their flight plan. Learjet N30TP had filed an instrument flight plan from the air with Washington, D.C. Flight Service while en route to Newark, New Jersey from Ft. Lauderdale, Florida. When the crew had been dispatched earlier that morning, they had been informed that their ultimate destination was to be Ft. Lauderdale, with a passenger pick up at Newark and JFK Airports. However, at the time of their departure from Florida, it had been uncertain how many persons would be accompanying the charter customer, Capo Pelligi, on the return flight. Once they had departed Newark inbound to JFK, that information had become available. Now, the co-pilot was busy updating the flight plan to reflect six souls onboard—two crew, Capo Pelligi, and three additional passengers. While the co-pilot handled the formalities, the captain kept the business jet's cabin temperature at a comfortable seventy degrees. Not quite as warm as their destination, but considerably warmer than New York's frigid temperature. The monotonous thumping sound of the ground power unit's diesel engine reverberated off the lobby's window, its thick, black electrical cord draped to the aircraft's external power plug. Capo Pelligi checked his wristwatch for the time, just as he had less than ten minutes earlier.

When he looked up, he noticed the dark blue van with the yellow rotating beacon approaching the building. It was the vehicle he had been patiently waiting for—Butler Aviation's courtesy van. Aboard the van were the Capo's guests, Señior Calerro and his two associates. Capo Pelligi had known all along precisely how many and the names of the persons who would be onboard the Learjet, but it was just his nature not to divulge any information to anyone outside the family. Whether it made any difference or not, it made the aged Capo feel better, so that's how it was done, even though the Colombian nationals were the same individuals that he had met at "the meet" in Atlantic City and Ft. Lauderdale. Period. After Anthony Vitale had assigned Capo Pelligi to pick up the gambling proceeds, the Capo had placed a call to Señior Calerro at his mountainside villa. Although it was somewhat of a short notice, Señior Calerro readily agreed to meet the Capo, mostly because Capo Pelligi had suggested that this would be a perfect opportunity for the head of the Colombian drug cartel to see a sample of the counterfeit money, not to mention meeting Vincent Panachi. Señior Calerro and his two associates caught Avianca's non-stop flight from Cali, Colombia to New York, New York, which had departed less than twelve hours after that phone call. Capo Pelligi was there to meet them. So was Learjet N30TP.

The courtesy van pulled beneath an awning that extended over Butler's entranceway, then stopped. The wind was whipping, and snowflakes swirled around the vehicle. Suddenly, the van's side door opened and three well-dressed men made a quick exit into the lobby. Señior Calerro was the second of the three men. Capo Pelligi watched while the men dusted the un-melted snowflakes from their expensive overcoats and waited until they had finished before he approached them. Capo Pelligi walked directly towards Señior Calerro, their eyes holding one another's steady gaze. Señior Calerro smiled, and the Capo returned a toothy grin. Capo Pelligi extended both arms in front of him, which left the Colombian uncertain as to whether the Italian wanted to shake his hand or hug him Italian style. Out of instinct, Señior Calerro extended his right arm in an offer to shake hands. Capo Pelligi accepted that offer and grabbed the Colombian's hand with both of his. Salutations were exchanged between the Capo and the three Colombians.

Just then, the co-pilot appeared from around the corner where the pilot's lounge was located. He noticed the group of four men standing together talking.

"Mr. Pelligi, are these your guests?" the co-pilot asked.

"Yes. These gentlemen are the rest of our passengers. We are all here."

"Very good. We were just issued an engine start time, so if you gentlemen are ready, so are we."

Capo Pelligi looked back towards his guests.

"I'm certain that you gentlemen are ready for some warmer weather, aren't you?" Capo Pelligi asked.

"Certainly, my friend," Señior Calerro laughed.

The other two Colombians both replied, "Sí," at precisely the same time.

"Well, let's do it," the co-pilot said.

The five men exited the warmth of the building and walked through the shivery, blowing snow towards the awaiting business jet. As they walked around the front of the aircraft, the first officer noted the captain was speaking into his headset. The co-pilot opened the Learjet's split door, and the passengers entered the aircraft one at a time. Before the last passenger had entered, a lineman appeared from inside the Butler building, and immediately began pulling the chocks from beneath the sleek jet's wheels. Seconds later, the cabin door was secured while the captain gave the lineman visual hand signals to spool up the GPU's electrical output. The mere touch of the captain's forefinger on the engine's start button began the turbine turning, and two seconds later it was lit. The captain repeated the same start up procedure for the jet's number two engine then he signaled the lineman, once again, with a hand signal. The lineman disconnected the GPU's black electrical cord and secured the jet's external power plug cover. Learjet N30TP was now self-contained and ready for flight.

The captain signaled the co-pilot with a nod of his head. Without further conversation, the co-pilot keyed his microphone and transmitted.

"Clearance delivery, this is November 30 Tango Papa at Butler, and we're instruments to Ft. Lauderdale, Florida."

With the speed that would have made any New Yorker proud, the controller barked, "Roger, 30 Tango Papa. Standby. Clearance is on request," which meant the computer was busy shuffling the instrument flights outbound and fitting Learjet N30TP into an appropriate slot for the trip south bound.

The computer, as well as JFK's controllers, did an outstanding job . . . all things considered. Learjet N30TP was airborne within thirteen minutes of their initial call.

*   *   *

At the very same moment that Learjet N30TP reported, "30 Tango Papa is vacating one-zero-thousand for flight level four-five-zero," Vincent turned his Mercedes 500SL off of Las Olas Boulevard onto one of the islands forming the posh neighborhood of Las Olas Isles. It wasn't his island, but it was damned close. As a matter of fact, the house that Vincent was going to was often referred to as the "golf course" among those family members knowledgeable of its existence. Why? Because, as Vincent had often pointed out, the house was but a nine-iron shot from Panachi's Navarro Isle home. Unfortunately for the Organized Crime Task Force, they had no knowledge of the existence of the drop house, and consequently had spent the entire night the night before maintaining a constant vigil on the wrong location. In theory, Agent Mark Murray had been one hundred percent correct in his assumption that Tuesday night would be the night the gambling proceeds would be delivered to the Vitale crime family. Agent Murray had been involved in the underground world of bookmaking long enough to know that Tuesdays were always straighten-up days, whereby the winners and losers saw their appropriate bookmaker and either collected or paid up. The winners were never chased down, naturally, but the losers could expect visitors by Thursdays if they had not surfaced. Over the course of approximately eight hours during Tuesday night, one million dollars in gambling proceeds had been delivered to the drop house.

Vincent wheeled the luxury car into the driveway and got out. The house and yard were fenced in with a high, wooden fence that assured the privacy of those inside. Aside from that, tall bushy palm trees lined the outside perimeter of the fence. From the street, the property gave the appearance of a jungle-like paradise. A slatted door provided a gateway onto the grounds and beside that was a push-button, electronic sensor coded door opener. Vincent Panachi punched in the appropriate numbers as fast as one would dial their own phone number, and the gate's dead-bolt lock withdrew with a buzzing sound. Vincent entered and closed the gate behind him. Once again, the lock was heard as the metal cylinder slipped back into its housing.

When Vincent had rented the home a little over a year ago, the grounds inside the fence were immaculate. Now, one year later, the lack of a professional landscaper was evident. Weeds had pushed their way into the well-groomed flowerbeds, and the edges of the manicured lawn overgrew the concrete pathway that led to the house. The ground's appearance did not bother Vincent though, because no one but the bookies ever came to the house. Even Vincent very seldom visited—only on Wednesdays.

Two crime family members lived at the house full-time, and it was their job to collect and protect the money until Vincent could fly it out. When Vincent reached the front door, he pushed the doorbell and waited. One minute later, a burly Italian wielding an Uzi machine pistol answered the door.

"Vincent . . . come in," he said.

Vincent smiled as he entered the foyer and affectionately patted the soldier on the cheek.

"Shoot anybody with that thing this week?" Vincent quipped.

"Not yet, boss," the stocky Italian returned the smile and replied.

The crime family soldier stepped aside to allow Vincent to pass by, into the living room.

"Everything okay?" Vincent queried.

The man grunted as he showed Vincent his discolored fingertips.

"Jeez, boss. We really hit it big this week. Just look at the ink stains on my fingers . . . must have counted well over a million dollars."

Vincent laughed. "Don't you just hate that when that happens?"

The comment drew another grunt from the soldier as he closed the front door. Before the man was able to say something in reply, a loud, ear-piercing squawk resounded throughout the living room. **SQUAWK! SQUAWK!** The sound of Vincent's voice had alerted a large macaw of his presence in the house. As Vincent walked towards the tiled living room, he and the tropical parrot eyed one another; the macaw perched on a wooden dowel in an oversized brass cage. The parrot had brilliant plumage that blended bright colors together as his feathers lengthened towards its long tail. Its head cocked to one side, then the other, as he maintained visual contact with the approaching human being. Suddenly, the macaw threw back his powerful, curved bill and spoke the intelligible words, ***"AWK . . . BIG MONEY . . . BIG MONEY . . . AWK!"*** Vincent turned so that he could face the gun carrying man behind him. A smile was on Vincent's face.

"Someday, I'm going to get that bird to tell me which one of you taught him to say that . . . then there will be hell to pay."

The soldier laughed. "That's a crime family parrot. You'll never get a statement out of him," the soldier said.

The two men shared a hearty laugh together, and it was that roaring sound of laughter that summoned the other occupant of the house from one of the two bedrooms.

Gino was also full-blooded Italian, but his build was smaller framed than the other occupant of the drop house. What he lacked in size, however, he made up in smarts. Gino was clearly the brains of the two. Gino sauntered into the living room and met Vincent next to the brass birdcage, his right arm extended in an offer to shake hands. Vincent accepted the outstretched arm, and the two men shook hands.

"Hello, Vincent," Gino said.

Vincent smiled as he nodded his head.

"Good morning to you. Everything on track, Gino?"

The designated head of the drop house smiled. "Never been better. Jeez, what a bonanza that game was." Gino tossed a casual glance over his shoulder towards his housemate, and Vincent's eyes followed. Meanwhile, he added, "We were up nearly all night long counting money. Big take this week . . . over a million. You've got one hundred and three, ten thousand dollar packages . . . $1,030,000."

"Yeah, it filled two American Tourister suitcases," the other man piped in.

Vincent made eye contact with each of the two men, individually, when he complimented them.

"Outstanding job . . . thank you," Vincent said.

Gino smiled, but the other man averted his eyes from Vincent's while he mumbled, "Thank you, boss."

Gino motioned towards the bedroom with a sweeping motion of his right arm.

"Would you like to take a look at it before we load it in your car?" Gino asked.

"You bet. There is nothing like the sight of a million dollars in cash to get the blood flowing," Vincent replied as he started walking towards the back of the beautiful house.

The three men were walking towards the bedroom and had entered into a short hallway when the macaw squawked, once again, ***"AWK . . . BIG MONEY . . . BIG MONEY . . . AWK!"***

"Shoot that fucking thing, will ya'?" Vincent said as the laughter carried them into the bedroom.

On the floor, sitting straight up next to the bed, were two American Tourister suitcases. They looked like any other piece of tourist's luggage. But, inside these were a cool million in cash. Vincent stared at the two pieces and pondered that thought for a second or two.

"Let's have a look," Vincent suggested.

The gun-toting soldier acknowledged Vincent's order with a grunt then laid the Uzi down on top of the bed. He grabbed the handle of the suitcase nearest to him and flung the heavy case up onto the king-sized mattress. The weight of the cash-filled case creased the bedspread while it sunk a half-inch into the bed. His large fingers fumbled with the two silver latches before they finally popped open with a snap. The suitcase halved, hinged along the bottom by a set of silver hinges, and he flipped the top portion over onto the bedspread. The inside of the large suitcase was neatly packed . . . no, more like stuffed . . . with bills.

"I doubt very seriously if you could get another dollar into that case," Vincent commented.

"It's as full as I could get it," Gino agreed.

"We'll make this quick and painless, as usual. Just let me confirm the number of packets you guys have here and we'll close it up," Vincent said to the two men.

"Fair enough," Gino replied.

It was not that the two soldiers were not trusted; it was just the way that it was done. It had actually been the old man himself who had insisted collections were handled in this manner. "That way," as he had pointed out, "you guys will watch one another a little more closely . . . makes it that much harder to skim off the top." Anthony Vitale was pretty sharp, and it was this method that kept him informed, almost to the penny, of what it cost to throw his annual birthday bash in Ft. Lauderdale. Quite sharp, indeed.

Vincent spent a half-hour carefully counting the contents of the opened suitcase, and when he was finished his figures agreed with Gino's. Gino's housemate closed the case and tossed the second one onto the top of the mattress. The bedspread formed a whole new pattern of wrinkles as the heavy case settled into the king-sized bed. He opened the second case just as he had the first, and once again, Vincent saw a suitcase filled to capacity. Gino handed him his figures, and Vincent went to work counting the ten thousand dollar packages. A half-hour later, the two figures concurred with one another and Vincent ordered the suitcase closed. At this point, in the eyes of the crime family, the responsibility for the cash now became Vincent's. Should anything happen to these gambling proceeds between now and the time he turned the two suitcases over to Capo Pelligi, it would be Vincent who must answer for it. The two men at the drop house had been relieved of their responsibilities.

Vincent spent another hour with the men at the house. Social chit-chat. Their duties were strictly gambling proceeds collections, and they had no idea of what else the Vitale crime family was into. Therefore, the last thing in the world Vincent would have brought up was the Quill and the counterfeiting operation. Little did the men know that during the course of the day, an elderly man holed up in a palatial home in the city of Coral Springs would produce nearly as much money as they had collected during the previous evening.

Finally, Vincent looked at his watch.

"Time to roll," he said.

Gino stood first.

"Put the bags in Vincent's trunk, okay?" Gino ordered his associate.

"Sure thing," the burly man said.

He stood, then slowly ambled toward the bedroom.

"I may want to store some currency here . . . perhaps in the back bedroom, or something. It may be here for awhile," Vincent said to Gino.

Gino smiled as he affectionately slapped Vincent across the back and replied, "Well that's okay, because I plan to be here for awhile."

Vincent laughed and offered his hand to shake. Gino accepted Vincent's hand and the two men shook hands. Gino walked him to the front door and laughed.

"I'll take care of your bird for you . . . until next week, then."

Vincent smiled. With a wave of his hand he called over his shoulder, "Ciao . . . until next week."

The burly Italian was waiting at the gate with the two suitcases full of money, and within minutes the American Touristers were loaded into the trunk of the Mercedes.

"Good-bye," Vincent said as he opened the driver's door.

By the time he slid behind the steering wheel, the gate had closed and the man was gone. Once again, the house was quiet. Vincent started the automobile's engine and glanced crossways to check for oncoming traffic before he backed into the roadway. When he did so, he noticed the briefcase full of counterfeit twenties that lay on the passenger's seat beside him. Instinctively, Vincent reached over and patted the case.

Moments later, the Mercedes turned east onto Las Olas Boulevard, towards the ocean. Vincent Panachi was en route to Marriott's Harbour Beach Hotel.

*   *   *

Approximately thirty minutes before Vincent had departed the drop house known as the "golf course," a pearl-colored, stretch limousine had entered Walker's Cay Jet Center through a fenced security gate. The DaBryan built, wide-bodied limo was the same one that Anthony Vitale had expressed to be his favorite. Even the chauffeur had been the same; by request, of course. The tips the chauffeur had received from the Newark group in the past had made a lasting impression on the young man, and therefore, he had made certain that he was in position when the Learjet arrived. As a matter of fact, the chartered limo had arrived ahead of schedule, and had waited on the Jet Center's blacktop tarmac.

The chauffeur had stopped the stretch limo where he was able to maintain a vigilant watch on the landing traffic, and there had been quite a few aircraft that day. However, the majority of them had been airliners or light twin-engine aircraft. No business jets. The driver maintained a constant vigil on the active runway for nearly twenty minutes before he spotted the familiar sleek fuselage of the Learjet as it was touching down on the end of runway 9L. The chauffeur watched the business jet decelerate down the lengthy concrete runway, then gently turn onto a taxiway that led to Walker's Cay Jet Center. He smiled. His tip had arrived, and his wait was over.

After the jet turned onto the ramp, trails of scorching hot exhaust rose from the approaching aircraft's two whining turbine engines and distorted the view rearward of the jet. Slowly, the business jet taxied toward the small terminal building. The chauffeur turned the key and started the limousine's large motor, then adjusted the air conditioner to its coolest setting. The cold air blew through the vents, and its temperature was in direct contrast to the heat waves that hovered inches above the ramp's asphalt surface. Suddenly, the sleek jet stopped. Even with the windows tightly closed, the pitch of the whining jet engines were deafening until the pilot killed the flame inside the turbines. The driver placed the transmission into drive and inched his way forward towards the gleaming jet. He stopped ten feet from the Lear's cabin door, the stretch limousine angled between the aircraft's elongated, tapered nose and the left wing's tip tank. Seconds later, the door to the business jet and the limousine's door opened simultaneously. It was as if the movements had been rehearsed.

The co-pilot was the first to exit the aircraft, followed by Capo Pelligi. The fireplug built Italian had to twist his shoulders somewhat as he stepped through the Lear's narrow doorway. Señior Calerro was next to exit, then his two associates. Finally, the captain of the flight exited the aircraft. Capo Pelligi shook the captain's hand, thanked him, then slipped him a fat envelope—ample payment, in cash, of course, for the cost of the charter and a little something extra for the crew. That little something extra totaled one thousand dollars—five hundred apiece. With tips such as that it was no wonder that the chartered flight had departed on schedule, in spite of JFK's inclement weather. The captain and the co-pilot both thanked him several times while the Capo watched Señior Calerro and his associates climb into the luxurious passenger compartment of the limousine. Finally, it was Capo Pelligi's turn.

"Good afternoon, Mr. Pelligi. It's always a pleasure to see you, sir," the chauffeur politely said.

"And it's nice to see you again, young man. Take us to the Harbour Beach," Capo Pelligi said flashing the driver a smile.

"Any luggage, sir?"

The Capo was seated now, and he looked up at the chauffeur when he remarked, "On the return trip. Let's go."

"As you wish," the driver said nodding his head before he gently closed the door.

Within minutes, the limousine passed through the fenced gate at Walker's Cay Jet Center, once again.

A northbound turn onto Federal Highway led them to the 17th Street Causeway, which, in turn, became Highway A1A. The Marriott Harbour Beach Hotel is two miles from the 17th Street Causeway Bridge and located on the beach, as the name implies. The four men were more than familiar with the hotel, as it had been the site for one of their previous meets.

The limousine pulled around the circular drive and stopped directly in front of the hotel's double-door entranceway. The bell captain recognized the pearl-colored stretch limo, and even though it was a local charter vehicle he associated it with the big tippers from New Jersey, the same guys who always took the expensive suite on the top floor. That was a very astute observation on the bell captain's part, which was precisely the case. Capo Pelligi had reserved the William P. Marriott suite, as usual.

The bell captain, along with one of his underlings, opened the vehicle's rear doors.

"Good day, gentlemen," he said as the four men piled out of the limousine. "Will you be checking in?" the bell captain asked.

"Yes . . . we have the William Marriott Suite, I believe. If you'd have the front desk prepare the paperwork, I'm certain the concierge would be more than happy to check us in upstairs," Capo Pelligi answered as the spokesman for the party. The bell captain was nodding his head in acknowledgement, but was unable to speak before the Capo continued, "Here is five thousand dollars to be applied to our account."

Capo Pelligi handed the young man an envelope an inch thick with hundred dollar bills, then pulled a horse choker sized money roll from his right-front trouser pocket. With the finesse of someone who had obviously done this a great number of times, the Capo peeled off two, one hundred dollar bills from the roll. He folded the bills lengthwise before he handed them to the bell captain along with the instructions, "A Mercedes 500SL will be arriving within the hour with my luggage. See that it gets to my suite, posthaste." The stocky Italian tossed a glance towards the other bellman and said, "And see that he gets one of the 'Franklins.'"

"Yes, sir!" the bell captain replied as he tucked the two bills into his pocket. "Now, let's get you and your party upstairs . . . if you'll follow me, please."

The bell captain walked towards the hotel lobby, and the Colombians followed.

Capo Pelligi turned to the chauffeur and said, "I left an envelope for you on the seat. Thank you. Be here at nine a.m., tomorrow morning. Back to the airport."

"Nine a.m., sir . . . and thank you," the chauffeur nodded his head as his right hand rose to his forehead, forming a salute.

Capo Pelligi disappeared into the hotel lobby, along with the others.

*　　*　　*

Vincent sat at the intersection of Las Olas Boulevard and Highway A1A, patiently waiting for the red light to turn green. Traffic along the beachfront highway was thick with tourists. Even so, Vincent eyed an opening in the flow and went for it. His foot lay on the accelerator pedal while his hands deftly maneuvered the luxury automobile between a Porsche and a BMW. The BMW blew its horn, but to no avail. Driving in Ft. Lauderdale during the height of tourist season could best be compared to driving in Manhattan. That is to say that traffic such as this was no place for the weak and faint at heart. Vincent dared not avert his eyes from the Porsche's rear bumper, which was only a car length away. He was all too familiar with the stop and go traffic along the beach.

The line of traffic moved at a slow but steady pace until they caught a red light, then another. Vincent looked at his watch. He was on schedule, as usual. Punctuality was one of his strong suits. The Marriott was just ahead, on the left.

Vincent turned left at the light and entered the Marriott's manicured grounds. Flowers lined the blacktop driveway as it serpentined up the knoll. Atop the elevation, Vincent saw small sand dunes covered with sea oats that bordered a white sandy beach. The ocean was calm, and the seascape quite serene. Unequivocally, it was an absolutely gorgeous day in South Florida.

The flower-lined driveway made an abrupt ninety-degree turn to the left then paralleled the luxurious hotel. Vincent continued onwards, and it led him to the hotel's plush reception area. The Mercedes 500SL looked the part as he passed several other expensive automobiles parked curbside. Vincent wheeled the car into the first available space, an opening in the line of valet parked cars that put him directly in front of the bell stand.

The bell captain was standing behind a waist-high booth, less than five feet from Vincent. Without thinking, his white-gloved right hand reached out and slapped the other recipient of Capo Pelligi's generosity. The younger bellman looked toward his supervisor first before he followed the direction of his stare.

"That's the car . . . the luggage for the suite," the bell captain said with a gush of excitement.

The younger bellman, who had never received a hundred dollar tip before, was quick to the draw. Before the words had finished leaving his boss' mouth, he was off the stool and moving toward the Mercedes. He called over his shoulder,

"Let's do it." The two men were at the luxury car within seconds after it stopped. The bellmen were excited.

Vincent was serene as usual, even though he had over a million dollars in cash in the trunk and another forty-thousand in counterfeit money in a briefcase lying on the seat beside him. Vincent was a pro. Out of habit more than anything else, Vincent checked his appearance in the rear view mirror. He swept his right hand across his hair then checked it, again.

Suddenly, there was a light knock on the driver's side window. *TAP-TAP*. Vincent turned his head to find the bell captain standing a couple of feet from the driver's door. Instinctively, Vincent's finger lay upon the electronic window's switch and engaged it. The window's tiny motor emitted a whirring sound as the pane of tinted glass disappeared into the door. The bell captain was all smiles.

"Checking in, sir?"

"No . . . however, I do have my business associate's luggage, and he asked that I bring it to his suite. Could you assist me with that?" Vincent replied with an exuberant smile.

Vincent glanced in his rear view mirror for only a split-second and noticed another bellman was standing behind the car, next to the trunk.

"But, of course. As a matter of fact, we've been expecting you. Mr. Pelligi advised us that a Mercedes would be delivering his luggage."

"Oh, he did, did he?" Vincent really smiled this time.

The bell captain smelt another big tip. His smile grew even larger than before.

"Yes, sir. Now, if you will pop your trunk latch, we will be more than happy to assist you in any way we can."

Vincent's right hand had already opened the glove box door. His index finger searched for the trunk release button, yet his eyes never left the bellman.

"Thank you."

The Mercedes' trunk lid popped open.

By the time Vincent unfastened his seat belt and got out of the car, the luggage had already been unloaded from the Mercedes' trunk. The bell captain quickly disappeared behind the automobile to assist the younger bellman wrestling with the cumbersome cases, and they placed them at the curb. The bell captain retrieved one of the pull carts used to move large amounts of luggage to and from the rooms to the valet area, and the two heavy American Touristers were loaded onto it. Vincent watched from the driver's side while the bags were loaded, then reached back inside the Mercedes and grabbed the briefcase.

The bell captain caught Vincent's eye as he raised his head from retrieving the briefcase.

"Just leave the keys in it, sir. I'll have it moved, right away." It was spoken with the tone of a suggestion, yet implied that it was not open for discussion. "Hotel policy, you understand," was the standard pat answer for any disagreements concerning the parking arrangements.

Before Vincent could reply one way or another other, the bell captain reached for a shiny, silver whistle that dangled from a gold braided cord hung chest high on his left side. He blew it, and the piercing shrill sound summoned a valet parker within seconds. The bell captain ordered him to put the Mercedes up front where they could keep an eye on it. In the same breath, it seemed, the bell captain turned his head slightly and addressed Vincent. "If you will follow me, sir, I will show you to Mr. Pelligi's suite.

Vincent nodded his head. Simultaneously, he motioned with his free hand. "After you," he said.

The bell captain had already begun moving the luggage when Vincent reached into his pocket and peeled a fifty-dollar bill from his roll. He nonchalantly handed the folded bill to the young bellman as he walked past him. The bellman tucked it into his pocket without looking, as he had been taught to do, and thanked Vincent. Of course, as soon as Vincent Panachi was out of sight, the bellman pulled the bill from his pocket and checked its denomination. Had Vincent heard him, he would have heard the exclamation, "All right . . . a fifty!" But, he hadn't.

The bell captain engaged Vincent in the customary small talk all bellman do—"Are you enjoying Ft. Lauderdale? Will you require anything special while you're staying with us?"

Vincent answered the rehearsed questions, not bothering to inform the hotel employee that he was a local. Once again, it was the New Jersey tag on the Mercedes that threw people off track. The small talk only lasted a few minutes before the elevator's chime announced that they had arrived at the hotel's top floor. The bell captain steadied the two pieces of luggage with a practiced hold as he rolled the stand and its upright bags across the elevator's open door frame. Vincent followed the bell captain as he turned right. The William P. Marriott Suite was at the end of the plushily carpeted corridor.

The bell captain stood to the side of the door and waited while Vincent knocked. Unlike the hotel's standard rooms, the suite had a brass knocker on the door. Vincent tapped it twice then waited. Suddenly, the door opened. Capo Pelligi stood in the doorway, his massive, thick, fire-plug built body nearly filling the opening.

"Vincent," he said, in a thickly accented voice, "I've missed you . . . come in . . . come in."

Vincent walked through the door and the bell captain followed. The Capo knew what was in the two American Touristers. Nevertheless he acted as casual as if the cases contained nothing more than ordinary clothing when he instructed the bell captain, "Just put those in the bedroom."

"Yes, sir," the hotel employee said as he wheeled the cart thorough the luxury suite's living room.

Capo Pelligi had a firm grasp on Vincent's free arm, just above the elbow, and guided him in the direction of the living room. Vincent held the briefcase in his opposite hand.

"Come, Vincent, there are some men I want to introduce you to."

Señior Calerro and his two associates stood as Capo Pelligi and Vincent entered the room. It was obvious to Vincent that the men were Colombian, as he had certainly seen his share of Colombians in and around Miami, Florida. Yet these men had more of an international flair about them. Vincent noticed their distinctive style, but, in particular, it was one distinguished looking gentleman that really caught his eye. Something about him was more debonair than his companions, but Vincent wasn't certain of what separated him from the other two. Whatever, the passing thought lasted only a few seconds before Capo Pelligi introduced the gentleman.

"Vincent Panachi, say, 'hello' to Señior Calerro."

"Hello," Vincent said as he extended his hand to shake.

"Buenas tardes, Señior Panachi," the distinguished looking gentleman replied. He accepted Vincent's outstretched hand and the two men shook hands.

"Call me Vincent, please."

The elderly man switched to nearly flawless English.

"If you wish, Vincent." He motioned towards the other two gentlemen with his free hand and said, "My associates. I will not bother to introduce you because their English is very limited, to say the least."

Señior Calerro's associates must have understood what he said, though, because they courteously nodded their heads towards Vincent, who, in turn, nodded back. The introductions were completed just before the bell captain appeared from the bedroom. Instinctively, Vincent reached into his pocket and quickly found another fifty-dollar bill. However, just as he was pulling it from his pocket to give to the bell captain, Capo Pelligi placed his ham hock-sized hand on Vincent's wrist and stopped him. The Capo already had a hundred-dollar bill neatly folded in his other hand. He handed it to the bell captain.

"Check on us in about an hour, or so. We'll probably need some ice by then," the Capo instructed.

The bell captain pocketed the crisp bill and exclaimed, "Yes, sir." Vincent was surprised the hotel employee hadn't clicked his heels and saluted before he left the suite. There was no doubt that the Franklin had elated him. The bell captain gently closed the door behind him without making a sound.

Vincent's facial expression concealed the fact that he was surprised to find the Colombians in the suite. Not that it mattered; it was just unexpected. His face had always been his sword during any negotiations, and therefore, Vincent had made a conscientious effort to show no outward emotion towards their presence. Instead, Vincent quickly looked about the suite and ascertained that something up and coming was taking place. Several sterling silver champagne buckets sat atop the dining room table, the necks of Dom Perignon champagne bottles protruding upwards through crushed ice. One bottle had already been opened. A cheese and fresh fruit platter was neatly placed in the center of the table, and, as of yet, had not been touched. From the looks of things, Capo Pelligi knew precisely what he was doing. The thought reminded Vincent of the briefcase he held in his hand—the briefcase filled with counterfeit money—and he wished he knew what the Capo was doing.

Capo Pelligi motioned to the Colombians with his hands.

"Please, sit down. Relax," the Capo casually said.

Vincent remained standing, as did the Capo. The Colombians resumed their seats, as well as the firm grasp they had previously held on their champagne glasses. The men were silent for several seconds.

"Mr. Pelligi, could I speak with you for a moment, please?" Vincent asked as he cast a glance toward the bedroom.

The seasoned Capo was quick on the uptake. He did not hesitate in the slightest, as if the suggestion had been a rehearsed cue, or something.

"Certainly, Vincent. It would be my pleasure." He turned toward the seated Colombian and politely said, "If you gentlemen will excuse us, we will be right back."

Simultaneously, the three men nodded their heads in acknowledgement. The Capo nodded to Vincent, who led the way to the bedroom.

Capo Pelligi followed Vincent into the plush bedroom then closed the door behind him. Vincent waited beside the king-sized bed, where the two American Touristers full of cash had been placed. He casually tossed the briefcase onto the bed, beside the luggage. Capo Pelligi watched as it plopped onto the quilted bedspread. Vincent and the Capo had dealt with one another many times through the years, and neither had a problem with being candid. Vincent turned the case slightly then placed his thumbs across both latches. Simultaneously, he moved them outwards and the latches popped open. Vincent shifted his attention to Capo Pelligi.

"I hope I have done the right thing by bringing this."

With that, Vincent flipped open the top of the briefcase so that the forty-thousand dollars in counterfeit money lay exposed. The Capo was awestruck. His movements almost qualified as slow motion pantomime when he plucked one of the twenties from the top of a stack then examined it closely. A minute of silence passed.

"It's unbelievable . . . these are beautiful."

"Are you going to show them to the Colombians?" Vincent queried.

The Capo excitedly waved the bill back and forth as if he were proudly displaying it to Vincent. A large grin formed across his face.

"Fuckin'-A' I'm gonna' show 'em. I invited them down here in hopes of seeing some samples. But these . . . they are going to love these."

The Capo held the bill up to the light and scrutinized it as if it were an afterthought.

"The Quill is a fuckin' genius, huh kid!"

Vincent had heard the Capo's coarse expletives many times before, so his language did not offend him in the least.

"Yes, he is," Vincent nodded his head and agreed.

The Capo reached over and closed the briefcase, then snatched it from the bed. He smiled at Vincent.

"They are really going to like this . . . and you, Panachi. You done good."

The compliment was followed by an affectionate pat on the cheek.

"Thank you," Vincent replied.

As if their next move had been telepathically discussed between them, the two men left the bedroom without further discussion.

When Vincent and Capo Pelligi reentered the suite's living room, the three men were talking among themselves. Rapid fire Spanish filled the room, but the conversation ceased when they saw the two Italians. Señior Calerro stood while his associates remained seated. The Capo crossed the room and stopped directly in front of the head of the Colombian drug cartel, the briefcase at his side. Capo Pelligi motioned to Vincent with his eyes and the quick look summoned the younger man to his side. Now, they both stood before the Colombians.

"Señior Calerro," the Capo started, "I am pleased to inform you that Vincent has brought you a present . . . a wonderful present." As the Capo handed Señior Calerro the closed briefcase he added, "A token of 'good faith' from our family to yours. I think you will enjoy working with Vincent."

Señior Calerro grasped the briefcase along its sides and smiled. Capo Pelligi removed his grip from the handle and returned the smile. The other two Colombians looked somewhat dumfounded over the exchange. Vincent just smiled he knew that they would like what they saw. Señior Calerro pivoted his body so that he could set the briefcase down on the coffee table. One of his cohorts surmised his intentions and cleared the small table of their champagne glasses. Señior Calerro gently laid the briefcase on top of the table.

Señior Calerro resumed his seat and turned the case accordingly so that he could open the latches, much the same as Vincent had just done in the bedroom. Vincent hovered unobtrusively nearby and remained silent. A nervous pang wrenched his stomach while he anxiously awaited the opening of the case. *POP* . . . *POP*. The Colombian slid his hands along the side of the case until his forefingers and thumbs were positioned where he could raise the top half. The other two Colombians leaned forward in their seats and watched Señior Calerro's every move. He opened the case and stared in silence at the eight stacks of twenties. To them, forty-thousand dollars was lunch money. However, it was not the amount that held the three men in wonderment—it was the quality.

Señior Calerro lifted a stack of bills from the case and peeled several twenties from the top. His associates did not make a sound when he handed them a couple of bills, apiece. The three Colombians closely examined the twenties in the following manner: toward the light; toward sunlight; front-to—back; back-to-front; side-to-side; and, last but not least, they scratched the paper to see if the printed fibers would come off.

"That's right, Señior Calerro, they're counterfeits," Capo Pelligi confidently replied.

The head of the Colombian drug cartel did not bother to acknowledge the remark; he was so engrossed with the currency. Neither did his associates, as they were deeply absorbed in their individual examinations. It was a couple of seconds later before Señior Calerro made a comment in his native tongue.

"Magnifico," he said.

"Perfecto," the gentleman seated to his left added.

"Ellos estan son sin defecto," the gentleman to his right said.

Even with Vincent's limited Spanish, he had figured out the first two words— magnificent and perfect—but the lengthy phrase had thrown him. As if Señior Calerro had read his mind, he looked up and translated.

"My friend says, 'They are flawless!' I agree."

That was the beginning of a long afternoon spent at the Marriott Harbour Beach Hotel. The bell captain had returned on the hour, as requested, and that request had been updated by the hour. Bottles-upon-bottles of Dom Perignon champagne had been shuttled to the suite throughout that afternoon, during which, Vincent and Señior Calerro became close friends and business associates. Finally, the meet was well into the evening, and it became apparent to Vincent that he would not make his prearranged date with Jennifer. Not a problem . . . business came first, always.

Vincent excused himself and went to the suite's bedroom to place a call to Jennifer. At the time it seemed harmless enough. After all, all he was doing was canceling a dinner date. It's not as if he were going to conduct family business over the telephone. Vincent knew the cardinal rules, and abided by them. It was those simple rules that maintained their anonymity.

Vincent sat upon the bed and dialed Jennifer's number. She picked up the telephone on the second ring, and Vincent explained that he had been delayed on some unexpected business matters . . . people in from out of town . . . they would rain check the dinner until the following evening. By his account, the entire conversation lasted less than three minutes.

By the digital counter on the Organized Crime Task Force's recorder, the first phone call recorded on their newly acquired phone tap ran three minutes, twenty seven seconds, to be exact. Jennifer Swords' home phone was now wired for sound.

* * *

Agent Mark Murray was relaxing at home. A half-full can of Budweiser beer sat beside two empties on the small table beside his reclining chair. A telephone was next to the beer cans, and the television's remote control was beside that. Mark was comfortably relaxing for a change, and the television was tuned to HBO. The eight o'clock movie was half over when the telephone rang.

Without removing his eyes from the screen, Mark's right hand found the remote control and turned the television's volume down. He was much too engrossed in the movie to have hit the mute button, thereby silencing the idiot box altogether. Instinctively, his hand grabbed the telephone's handset and he placed it against his ear.

"Hello," Agent Murray answered.

The voice that came through the receiver was immediately recognized as the agent in charge of electronic eavesdropping, or, as it was jokingly referred to within the agency, "Pest Control."

"Murray, put that beer down and listen to this . . ."

Agent Murray interrupted the caller in mid-sentence.

"Fuck off, Jackson. What? Have you got my place wired, too? Got me on video?"

The professional eavesdropper laughed.

"Murray, your life is not interesting enough for me to bug."

Agent Murray returned the laugh.

"True."

"Well, I have some news for you . . . listen up," Jackson remarked.

The agent in charge of 'pest control' played the recorded conversation between Vincent Panachi and Jennifer Swords, and the recorder's magnetic tape had captured their voices perfectly. The very second that Mark heard Jennifer's voice answer the phone, his right hand hit the remote control's mute button. The room was void of any noises outside of Jennifer's voice. A second later, he heard Vincent's voice. Mark listened intensely while he hung on to every word of the three and a half minute conversation.

"God damn, Jackson, that was great. Did the pen register decipher the incoming number?"

Jackson was proud of himself, and his enthusiasm was evident in his voice.

"Marriott . . . Panachi called from the Harbour Beach Hotel."

Murray thought for a couple of seconds.

"Room number?"

"No can do, my friend. However, I knew you would ask that question, so I took the liberty of checking with the hotel's manager. He doesn't want any problems . . . he was more than happy to tell me that the only check-in he has had from New Jersey, today, was for the William P. Marriott Suite. Does the name Pelligi mean anything to you?"

Agent Murray bolted upright in his recliner as his thoughts ran a mile-a-minute. Suddenly, as if he had no control over his mouth, he blurted the name, "Capo Pelligi . . . one of the biggest with Vitale crime family." The connection was silent for thirty seconds while Murray thought. When he spoke again, he said, "Get the surveillance team over there, right away. I want to know Panachi's every move. Got it, Jackson?"

Jackson's voice was excited when he replied, "I'll take care of it. Bye."

"Good-bye," Agent Murray said and laid the handset back onto the phone cradle.

While his hand was in the vicinity, he hit the remote control's mute button. Suddenly, the room filled with sounds of the eight o'clock movie.

CHAPTER FIFTEEN

T he next morning was as beautiful as the previous one had been; the sky a robin's egg-blue and cloudless. Although it was just a few minutes past 8 a.m., Capo Pelligi had already been awake for over an hour. Of course, it had taken quite a few persistent rings from the hotel's wake-up call service to awaken him. The multitudinous bottles of Dom Perignon champagne they had consumed the night before had left him with somewhat of a hangover. However, the disagreeable after effects of the excessive alcohol consumption was nothing compared to what one feels from an evening spent with cheap booze. That feeling, at least from the Capo's personal experiences, was best described as a hang-around, as opposed to a hangover. For the most part whisky left him bedridden for a full day, and a full day wasted was a luxury the Capo could not afford. Today he had to do Vincent's job, and physically move the gambling proceeds from Ft. Lauderdale to Newark. It had literally been years since the Capo had performed bagman duties, but, just as he had assured the Shark, *"You's never forget how it's done."* Capo Pelligi recalled the smile on the old man's face when he told him that. That thought brought a smile to the Capo's face, as well, while he enjoyed breakfast on the suite's veranda, alfresco.

Downstairs, the pearl-colored, stretch limousine slowly maneuvered around the hotel's circular driveway while the chauffeur took visual parking instructions from the bell captain. Both men had reported for duty earlier than usual, but that had been okay with them. As a rule, they did not usually receive hundred dollar tips. Capo Pelligi had already established himself as a high-roller and a sure big tipper. Although Capo Pelligi was not scheduled to be downstairs for another forty-five minutes, already the limo's driver and the hotel employees could feel the Franklins in their pockets. After a series of waving arm directions, the DaBryan built limousine stopped directly in front of the lobby entrance, precisely the spot where Vincent's Mercedes had been parked the night before.

The bell captain had not been on duty when Vincent left, but the note thumbtacked to the edge of the chest-high bellman's booth informed him that the Mercedes had pulled out a few minutes before midnight. A small notation on the bottom of the paper suggested that the driver appeared to be slightly intoxicated. Coincidentally, almost the exact same observation was noted from two separate vantage points by individuals of the Organized Crime Task Force's surveillance team. The only difference in the notations were that the agents had filled in the driver's name—Vincent Panachi.

A single car with two agents had followed Vincent when he pulled away from the Marriott, and when they compared their notes afterwards, each set of surveillance personnel had come to the same conclusions—Panachi was bombed. At any rate, they had followed him home, and, with the exception of bouncing the right front tire off of the curb once on Las Olas Boulevard, he had made it home safely. Vincent Panachi was indeed drunk, and was still fast asleep when the Capo checked out of the Harbour Beach Hotel.

At precisely 9:02 a.m., Capo Pelligi and the three Colombians exited the front lobby entrance. The bell captain held the door for the gentlemen while the chauffeur moved toward the trunk of the limousine. The four men walked through the door, then the luggage cart followed with the two American Touristers intact. Señior Calerro carried the briefcase containing the forty thousand in counterfeit twenties. Señior Calerro did not share the knowledge of what was contained in the two, large suitcases, but the representatives of the Colombian drug cartel were not stupid. They knew . . . and they knew enough not to ask. Business was business, and if the Vitale crime family had been able to combine their business with the current business at hand—the counterfeit project—then more power to them. Had Señior Calerro been aware that he and his associates had been photographed no less than twenty-five times while getting into the waiting limousine he may have had a different opinion. The thrust of the picture taking, however, had been concentrated on Capo Pelligi, whom the opportunity to photograph was considered a windfall for the agents of the Organized Crime Task Force. In particular, it was Agent Mark Murray who had been left dumbfounded with this sudden unexpected stroke of good luck.

The limousine pulled away from the hotel at 9:18 a.m. with two surveillance vehicles in tow, unbeknownst to the limousine's driver, of course. Had the chauffeur been aware of their presence, perhaps he could have made an attempt to lose the tails. Instead, the agents simply followed from a safe distance, remaining three-to-four car lengths behind the limo in the bumper-to-bumper traffic along Highway A1A.

Twenty minutes later, the limousine took the expressway fork for the entrance way to the Ft. Lauderdale International Airport. Needless to say, the agents' radios were crackling with a flurry of conversation between the two trailing vehicles. The surveillance operation had come together so quickly the night before that no one was really quite certain just how far the pursuit was authorized to go. The agents queried one another across the airwaves until the decision was made. They decided by unanimous agreement to let Agent Murray make the judgment call, just as they told him, via the radio.

"Christ, Murray, the limo's pulled into the International Airport. Anything we do there is going to be on the five o'clock news. You're gonna have to put your name on this one . . . make the call."

Agent Murray did not hesitate a single minute before he issued the orders.

"Stick with Pelligi. If he gets out of the limo, follow him. I want to know what he has in those two suitcases."

The agent in the pursuing vehicle protested. "But we don't have probable cause, do we?"

"Just do it . . . I'll take the heat on this one," Mark barked back.

The agent in the automobile looked at his partner and shrugged his shoulders as he keyed the mic.

"You've got it . . . by your orders." The radio fell silent for approximately thirty seconds before the same agent broadcast to the other trailing vehicle, "Did you get that?"

"Got it," the voice of the second vehicle's driver answered.

The expressway that had allowed for high-speed travel just minutes before slowed to less than five-miles-per-hour and became bumper-to-bumper with traffic. The limousine, as well as the two automobiles belonging to the Organized Crime Task Force, merged into the scores of cars racing against the clock to match a flight schedule. The length of the elongated limousine prevented it from strategically maneuvering around vehicles that had stopped to drop off departing passengers and their luggage. A combination of lane switching and the assorted use of curse words finally placed the pursuing agents in their desired position—directly behind the DaBryan built, pearl-colored limousine. The three vehicles inched their way through the snarling traffic as the procession of anxious travelers searched for their appropriate terminal. First, the domestic airlines passed by the automobiles' windows; Delta, American, and U.S. Air. The four-lane roadway curved to the left and joined the domestic terminal with the airport's international terminal. Midway along the concourse, in between Bahamas Air and Aero Mexico, the limousine slid from the snail's pace procession and pulled curb side. The turn happened so quickly that it was impossible for the first following vehicle to do anything but drive past the limo. The second, however, did stall long enough to find a curbside space behind the limousine, and pulled into it. Meanwhile, the first vehicle found a space curbside, twenty-five yards ahead of the limo. By the time they had parked the vehicle the chauffeur was already out of the limo and had walked around to the curb side passenger's door. The limousine's rear door opened, and Señior Calerro and his two associates exited the vehicle.

Suddenly, the two vehicle's radios were buzzing with activity. The agents waited to see what was going to happen with the Capo. They had their orders, and those orders had been very specific—*"Stick with Pelligi . . . I want to know what he has in those two suitcases."* The agents carefully monitored the situation and evaluated their next move. The second car radioed the first.

"Ah, we've got three foreign nationals here, and the chauffeur . . . all out of the vehicle. No Pelligi . . . no luggage. Just a minute . . . one of the foreigners is carrying a briefcase. That's it. Nothing more . . . Advise."

An agent in the first vehicle radioed back. "We wait. Our orders are for Pelligi and the cases. Nothing more."

There was a pause across the airways that lasted several seconds before the acknowledgement came through.

"Roger that."

The two cars full of Organized Crime Task Force agents patiently waited until the three Colombians entered the International Concourse and the chauffeur got back inside the limousine. The suspect, one Capo Pelligi who hailed from Newark, New Jersey, remained seated in the rear of the luxurious limousine when it pulled away from the curb and merged into the traffic. The tails picked up the elongated vehicle once again, as it began moving.

The procession of vehicles crawled along with the flow of the departing automobiles. An occasional shuttle bus, or two, from the various car rental agencies merged into the flow but none impeded the agents' views. They maintained constant surveillance on the limousine while the airport terminal grew more distant in their rear view mirrors. Ahead, the four-lane roadway split. Two lanes exited the airport while two circled the airdrome's perimeter, and the limousine followed the northbound perimeter road. Naturally, traffic along this roadway was considerably less. The agents fell back and spaced two cars between themselves and their subject. Nevertheless, the limousine remained in full view as they began their wide circle of the airdrome's boundary. The limo passed several cargo forwarder operations and a huge plant which provided pre-packaged in-flight meals for the various airlines serving the Ft. Lauderdale airport. Ahead, Fixed Base Operators, as those operations servicing general aviation aircraft are known, filled the north side of the field; South Florida Aircraft, Red's Aviation, Walker's Cay Terminal, just to name a few.

Suddenly, the stretch limo flashed its left turn signal and braked. Two vehicles driving in the opposite direction passed while the limousine waited, during which time the agents of the Organized Crime Task Force closed the gap between themselves and their subject. A single car remained between Capo Pelligi and the agents. The traffic cleared and the limousine turned into the Jet Center.

The agents operating the radios stepped on one another, meaning that both had tried to broadcast at precisely the same moment. The end result was unintelligible. The limo passed through the security gates and drove toward a row of business jets. The second car excitedly attempted to contact the first car.

"State your intentions . . . state your intentions . . . ," the agent quickly broadcast.

A split second later, the first car responded.

"We're going in. Block the gate . . . nobody passes . . . in or out."

By the end of the short transmission, the first car had already passed through the security gate at Walker's Cay Jet Center and was headed toward the row of business jets.

"Roger . . . we've got the gate."

Instinctively, the driver of the first car quickly glanced in the rear view mirror and saw the second car enter a low speed power slide. The second car stopped sideways directly in the middle of the security gate, making it impossible for anyone to enter or exit.

The limousine had turned the corner of the small terminal building seconds before the second car entered the slide, and they were not cognizant of the fact that they had been boxed in. The first car slowed its pursuit, the idea being that the agents wanted to arrive when the driver was out from behind the steering wheel. The corner of the fixed base operation building was inching closer, and without thinking, the driver wiped his clammy palms on his trouser legs. His partner lightly slapped him on the arm to get his attention. When he looked over at his partner, he recognized the inquisitive look on the man's face. A nod of his head was the acknowledgement that was necessary. His partner keyed the mic that was already in his right hand and said, "It's a go . . . it's a go."

By the time the agent dropped the microphone, the tires were squealing. The smell of burning rubber followed the screeching sound of the tires as the vehicle shot around the corner of the building. The limousine was dead ahead, less than fifty yards away, as the agents of the Organized Crime Task Force screamed toward their objective. Just as the driver had calculated, the limousine's chauffeur was out of the automobile and was in the process of opening the rear passenger's door.

The hood of the elongated car was parked diagonally between the Learjet's wing and tail. The agents could read the aircraft's registration number as they rapidly approached the limousine—*N30TP*. Two well-dressed pilots stood alongside the sleek jet, patiently waiting the arrival of their charter customer. The last thing they had expected was a confrontation at their aircraft.

The agents for the Organized Crime Task Force stopped their vehicle mere feet from the rear of the limo. The driver literally slammed the automatic transmission into park, his right hand on the shifter and the other on the door handle. The sedan rocked from the sudden braking, and both agents jumped out. Neither felt that it was necessary to draw their weapons, yet out of habit, the driver placed his right hand on his, but kept it holstered. His partner withdrew his shield.

The chauffeur's facial expression registered the shock he must have felt; his eyes opened wide and his mouth hung open. The agent closest to him placed a finger over his own mouth and signaled the surprised driver to remain quiet, which the chauffeur did. Big tips, or not, this was clearly something he did not want to get involved in. Within seconds, the agent who had driven the sedan replaced the chauffeur's hand on the limousine door with his own. *CLICK*. The rear passenger's door to the beautiful limousine flew open and the agent for the Organized Crime Task Force stuck his head inside the vehicle.

"Greetings, Mr. Pelligi. My name is Agent Torrezze with the Organized Crime Task Force, and my partner and I are here to help you with your luggage."

Before the surprised Capo could respond, the second agent was heard ordering the chauffeur.

"Pop the trunk . . . now."

Capo Pelligi remained calm, but his wrinkled forehead revealed his true inner feelings—Capo Pelligi was concerned. The agents opened one of the large suitcases and saw that it was full of cash—lots of cash. The second one was full, as well.

The agents addressed the crew of the Learjet first when they informed them that their charter customer would not be leaving with them. Afterwards, the agent who had driven the vehicle invited Capo Pelligi to join them on a tour to downtown Ft. Lauderdale. The Capo responded to their cordial invitation with six words—"I want to call my lawyer."

*　　*　　*

Vincent awakened slowly that morning. With the seemingly endless bottles of champagne they had consumed the night before combined with his early morning departure, it was no wonder that he felt tired.

A crystal clock hung on the kitchen wall with its hands positioned a few minutes past eleven o'clock. Vincent busied himself brewing a fresh pot of coffee while the bright sunlight streamed through the kitchen window's Levelor blinds and cast shadowy figurines across the terra-cotta tile floor.

Fifteen minutes later, the aroma of hazelnut coffee wafted through the air and awakened his liquor-dulled senses. Vincent steadied himself with both hands while he leaned over the counter to check the status of the brewing coffee. There was no mistaking the fact that he had way too much to drink the night before. Vincent felt the trembling in his wrists as his hands pressed against the kitchen counter. He checked the coffeepot. What had been a steady stream of rich, dark coffee before had become dripping drops. The coffee was done, finally. Vincent grasped the pot by its black, plastic handle and poured himself a full cup of wake-up.

A set of sliding glass doors led from the kitchen to the pool-side patio area where a table with seating for four provided the setting for Vincent's daily ritual of morning coffee alfresco. Vincent sat in his usual seat, facing the water. The air was still and the canal was completely void of ripples. The smooth water had a mirror-like finish that reflected images of the large sailboats moored across the canal. Vincent's Scarab sat motionless at the dock, its lines hanging limp. The tranquil morning had all the makings for an extremely peaceful day . . . until the telephone rang.

Vincent answered the portable telephone after the second ring.

"Good morning," he said.

The voice on the other end was not as cheerful, but it wasn't the tone that threw Vincent off. It was the caller, Anthony Vitale. The old man never called. Never. The surprise shot a surge of adrenaline through Vincent's system that awakened him more than an entire pot of coffee would have. Instinctively, Vincent bolted upright in his seat and listened. The old man's message was brief.

"Vincent, go to an outside line and give me a call . . . immediately."

Vincent swallowed hard as he found the words to reply.

"Right away. Bye."

Anthony Vitale did not respond, but merely replaced the telephone on its cradle. The long distance connection was broken within seconds, long before a trace could have identified the caller's origin. Vincent pushed the *end* button on his portable phone and laid it beside the cup of coffee. He drained the cup in one long gulp.

Vincent was dressed and out of the house in less than fifteen minutes. It seemed to him that he had driven the two miles to the pay phone by instinct alone, because he certainly did not remember the drive. His mind had been preoccupied trying to second-guess what had prompted the head of the Vitale crime family to call him. After all, wasn't Capo Pelligi in town?

Vincent stood at the pay telephone, one of two housed next to a couple of soft drink machines at a Citgo service station. He was reminded of his terrible hangover when he fumbled with the quarters while depositing them into the phone's coin deposit slot. The Crown Royal sack full of quarters spread across a small piece of metal protruding from underneath the telephone booth. Ordinarily, Vincent could have dialed the number strictly from memory. However, that particular morning he had to reference his phone directory, just to make certain that it was indeed the correct number he had dialed. The familiar, computerized voice came through the telephone's earpiece.

"Please deposit two dollars and forty-five cents for the next three minutes."

Vincent quickly rammed the change through the phone's opening as he had countless other times. The telephone company's computer registered the correct deposit and even credited him with the extra five cents. Vincent shook his head in disgust as he listened to the recording, because he knew from experience that

that was just another come-on. If you talked under the three minutes, you received no refund; if you talked beyond the three minutes, you owed another forty-five cents. "Whatever," he mumbled out loud, but there was no one present to hear. As usual, the touch of Vincent's fingertips had put him in touch with a modest home located along the outskirts of Newark. The phone clicked twice while Vincent's call was call-forwarded to Anthony Vitale's mansion. Without thinking, Vincent drew a deep breath as the connection rang.

As if it had not been strange enough that the old man had called, it had really been out of his normal patterns when Anthony Vitale personally answered the ringing telephone.

"Vincent?" he queried.

"Yes, it's me," Vincent answered.

The elderly man did not beat around the bush. The direct approach had always been his style. Anthony's voice was calm.

"There have been some complications down your way."

There were several seconds of silence across the telephone line, and whether or not the old man had done it purposely for dramatics, it had certainly had that effect. That was definitely not what Vincent wanted to hear. However, whatever had happened, he would have to deal with it.

"Oh?" Vincent queried.

"I just received word from our Consiglio," Anthony continued, "and it seems that Capo Pelligi was stopped at the Learjet by the Organized Crime Task Force."

Vincent's reaction was involuntary.

"Holy shit," he exclaimed.

The old man's voice was composed and void of emotion.

"How bad is it, Vincent? How much?"

Vincent did not hesitate when he answered, because to do so would have shown weakness and the old man despised weakness even more than losing money.

"Over a million dollars," Vincent said.

There was another moment of silence before the old man spoke, again. His voice was soft and reassuring.

"So be it. Everything will be fine. The Consiglio departed by private jet over an hour ago and should be in Ft. Lauderdale by one p.m. He will handle this fiasco."

"Should I meet him when he arrives?" Vincent asked.

Anthony's response was lightning quick when he replied.

"No . . . absolutely not. I want you to shut down our gambling operations and lay low until we get to the bottom of this. Close the golf course and shut down the bookies. Something is not right here, and I intend to find out what it is."

"Yes, sir," Vincent said.

Vincent's heart rate had the rhythm of a jungle drum while he held the telephone's receiver against his ear. Suddenly, as if nothing out of the ordinary had happened, the head of the Vitale crime family asked, "And is my favorite nephew still seeing the blond?"

"Yes, sir. Everything seems to be going along quite well, thank you."

"I'm happy for you, Vincent. Why don't you take her away for a few days . . . maybe a few weeks . . . until we sort this thing out?"

Vincent knew it was more than a suggestion. The old man knew more about what had happened than he was saying, and he was telling Vincent to get lost until the dust settled. Message received.

"That sounds like a wonderful idea. Thank you."

Anthony Vitale smiled and Vincent could sense the warmth in his voice.

"Very well, then. You have a good time and call me in a couple of weeks. I'll let you know how everything turned out. Not to worry . . . our Consiglio is the best there is."

Vincent returned the warmth through the telephone.

"Good-bye," he said.

The old man said the same then hung up.

Vincent stood next to the phone and thought about the call. The Shark had been around a great number of years, and certainly knew more about the business than Vincent ever would. Somehow, someway, he was sending Vincent a message . . . and that message was not to be anywhere close to the problem. The Shark had his own ideas about how to solve problems such as this, and Vincent could only surmise what that solution would entail—the problem would sleep with the fishes.

Vincent was still deep in thought when the pay telephone rang. Without thinking, Vincent picked up the receiver.

"Please deposit one dollar and fifteen cents for the past four minutes," the computer said.

Vincent reached for the bag full of quarters and shoved a handful into the slot. Seconds later, the computer thanked him. He hung the receiver in its cradle and looked at the phone with disgust. Ma Bell had taken him for ten cents, this time.

CHAPTER SIXTEEN

A gent Mark Murray sat in his office at the downtown headquarters for the Organized Crime Task Force and leaned back in his chair while he observed the two men seated across the desk from him. One of the well-dressed gentlemen did not wear a tie, and his thick, bulldog-like neck filled the unbuttoned opening in his expensive, silk shirt. That man was Capo Pelligi. The gentleman seated beside him was impeccably dressed in what appeared to be a custom tailored suit costing upwards of two thousand dollars, at least by Murray's estimation.

When he had first entered the office, Agent Murray stood and offered his hand to shake, but Capo Pelligi had remained seated. Not by choice, you understand, because his right wrist was handcuffed to the heavy wooden chair. The well-dressed gentleman accepted Agent Murray's offer, firmly grasped his hand, and then introduced himself.

"My name is Salvatore Santori, and I am legal counsel for this gentleman seated here."

His arm made a slow, elegant sweep in the direction of Capo Pelligi. Agent Murray introduced himself.

"Please, have a seat," Agent Murray motioned to the seat.

The seat he had motioned towards was the only empty chair in the cramped office. Instinctively, Salvatore Santori swept the creases in his trousers downward as he sat.

"Thank you," the Consiglio said while he systematically adjusted one shirt cuff at a time until they were perfectly matched, one inch below the suit jacket's sleeves.

Agent Murray watched while his thoughts confirmed that this guy was smooth; Smooth and confident. The Consiglio for the Vitale crime family was reputed to be the best mouthpiece dirty-money could buy.

Mr. Santori had arrived in the Ft. Lauderdale area between 1 and 2 p.m., and his chartered jet had landed at Ft. Lauderdale's Executive Airport rather than Ft. Lauderdale International. A fifteen-minute taxi ride had placed him in downtown Ft. Lauderdale where it had dropped him off in front of the Broward Boulevard headquarters for the Organized Crime Task Force. An elevator badly in need of repair had shuttled him to the building's third floor where a second-career security guard with a huge handled gun had shown him to Agent Murray's office. Just before he had entered the office, Mr. Santori checked the time on his expensive wristwatch. He knew from experience that Anthony Vitale would ask him what time he had arrived, and what time he had departed.

"Christ, Anthony," he had told the head of the crime family once before—jokingly, of course—"you'd think I work by the hour. What do you care how long it takes to spring your men?"

Anthony had calmly explained, "Because these task force agents react like poker players. Like gamblers, they will divulge their positions by the amount of time it takes them to make a decision on whether to pass or play. In other words, if they stall too long, they're bluffing."

Those words played through Salvatore's mind as he slid the diamond studded cuff linked sleeves over his watch.

Agent Mark Murray and Consiglio Salvatore Santori exchanged pleasantries for approximately five minutes before the business at hand begun, and, just as Murray expected, the legal counselor came out of the first round swinging. The mouthpiece's voice was controlled and confident.

The Consiglio had always practiced the adage that the best defense is a good offense and, with that in mind, he leaned forward in his chair and went into attack mode.

"Agent Murray," he scowled, "you are illegally detaining my client."

Mark Murray stalled for time as he addressed the accusation with a question.

"I am?" he queried, his eyebrows raised far enough to wrinkle his forehead.

The Consiglio was far more adept at controlling a line of questioning than any agent had ever hoped to be. After all, it was he who was an accomplished attorney, not the field agent he was speaking with. The Consiglio regained control over the conversation.

"Is my client under arrest?"

Agent Murray stared directly at the Capo and hesitated before he answered.

"No, he is not."

The attorney leaned back in his chair as he continued the line of questioning.

"Then you are holding him illegally . . . against his will?"

Agent Murray shifted his glaring stare to the legal counsel for the crime family. He pondered the question before he answered, mainly because he did not want to box himself in for a potential harassment suit.

197

"Well, counselor, your client was found in possession of over a million dollars in cash. What does he have to say about that?"

"My client has nothing whatsoever to say about that. Why? Because from a legal standpoint, you have violated my client's constitutional rights pertaining to search-and-seizure. Regardless of what you found in his possession, you had no probable cause, and therefore, your search was unconstitutional."

The agent squirmed somewhat in his seat.

"We had probable cause."

The counselor verbally leapt on him like a tiger on its prey.

"What? How?"

"Suspicious circumstances," Agent Murray countered.

The seasoned attorney scoffed.

"Not enough . . . what else have you based these outrageous accusations on?"

The agent fiddled with something on his desk top.

"Counselor, perhaps your client would like to take a stab at explaining the circumstances that gave rise to his having possession of these monies."

The Consiglio waved his hand as if he were dismissing a child.

"You are backpedaling, Agent Murray. This is ground we have already covered. Now, I ask you, again, what have you based these outrageous accusations upon?"

Agent Murray did not particularly like the way the line of questioning was headed. Unfortunately, he spoke before he thought.

"We had reliable information from a confidential informant."

The expression on Capo Pelligi's face alerted the agent to the fact that he had made a serious error in judgment the very second after he had spoken. Capo Pelligi looked towards the Consiglio, only to find the legal counsel looking at him. Their eyes met and they telepathically exchanged identical thoughts—"A fucking 'Rat' in the Vitale crime family!" The attorney averted his eyes and redirected his attention to the matter at hand.

"Do you intend to bring charges against my client?" The Consiglio asked.

Agent Murray breathed a sigh of relief, because this turn in the line of questioning was somewhat of a detour from the direct attack approach he had been under.

"That will be left up to the District Attorney. However, you may consider the money confiscated under the Remission and Forfeiture statures."

The legal counsel considered his options while he pondered the situation. A minute passed before either of the men spoke.

"Since the confiscation matter falls under civil and not criminal jurisdiction, perhaps we could come to some sort of agreement," the Consiglio suggested.

Now, the attorney was talking language that the agent understood . . . making a deal.

"What did you have in mind?"

The Consiglio was more accustomed to having to plea bargain with ruthless New Jersey prosecutors over murder-one charges. Having to convince some under-funded government agency to accept one million dollars should not be that impossible of a task, he assured himself. The well-dressed attorney leaned forward in his seat and placed his hands together, fingertips against one another. His mouth curled at the edges as if he were smirking about some unknown fact pertinent to this conversation that he, and only he, knew. It was nothing more than court room dramatics.

"Let's supposed that your agency kept the million dollars, and that my client agreed not to drag you into a lengthy, very costly court battle over ownership of the money . . . would that not warrant a reprieve from any and all criminal prosecution pertaining to this matter?"

Agent Murray leaned back in his chair and looked at the ceiling. He held this pose for two minutes while he supposedly was contemplating the offer. Had the truth been known, which was precisely what the Consiglio had surmised, they never had any intentions of referring this matter to the D.A.'s office. It was Agent Murray's position that their investigation could not survive the publicity that the U.S. Prosecutor's office would place on an arrest such as this. No, he would have to be patient. Capo Pelligi was a fine head to mount, but he was not the head that Agent Mark Murray wanted the most. This had become personal, and he wouldn't be happy until it was Vincent Panachi squirming in his office. After the two minutes passed, the agent leaned forward in his chair and placed his palms on top of the desk, flat out. Slowly, he pressed his weight against his hands until he stood. Agent Murray walked from behind his desk toward the two chairs. Capo Pelligi watched the man's every move while the agent inched his way closer to him. Murray's right hand disappeared into his trouser pocket, and he kept it there until he was standing directly in front of the Capo's chair. At the same moment Agent Murray spoke, his hand withdrew from the pocket. He had a small key firmly grasped between his thumb and forefinger. He turned his head toward the attorney.

"I think we can work that out. Now, get this piece of shit out of my office before I change my mind."

Agent Murray turned his head again facing toward the Capo and leaned forward a little. His eyes squinted as he focused the key on the small opening in the handcuffs. The tiny key found its mark and the cuffs dropped open after one quick turn. The Consiglio turned to his client.

"You're a free man . . . let's go," he said.

The Capo never even said good-bye, but then again, neither did Agent Murray.

Capo Pelligi exited through the building's Broward Boulevard entranceway, which was considerably different from what the two crime family members were accustomed to. The driver saw the pair and immediately brought the taxi to a halt, curb side. Capo Pelligi was closest to the vehicle and opened the passenger's door. The Capo entered the taxi and slid across the vinyl-covered seat until he was beside the far window. Salvatore Santori followed. The Jamaican taxi driver spoke so quickly that his words sounded like jabber.

"Where to, mon?"

"Ft. Lauderdale Executive Airport . . . Banyan terminal," the Consiglio replied.

Capo Pelligi faced Salvatore Santori and began speaking, but, in an afterthought, he stopped in mid-sentence and directed the taxi driver, "I need to use a pay phone . . . stop at the first pay phone you see."

The Jamaican did not verbally respond, but he acknowledged the order by nodding his head. The taxi weaved to-and-fro through the downtown area traffic until, finally, the driver pulled off the boulevard into a self-service gas station. A bank of three telephones sat on top of a concrete pedestal, none of which were in use. The Capo opened the rear door and called over his shoulder as he exited the vehicle, "I'll just be a couple of minutes. I want to give Vincent a call and fill him in on what's happened."

Capo Pelligi dialed Panachi's home telephone number from memory, but reached a recording. It took him a couple of seconds to recall Vincent's mobile number, but he was able to remember it. Quickly, the Capo deposited another twenty-five cents and dialed the number. Five-seconds and two rings later, Vincent Panachi's voice sounded through the telephone's ear piece.

"Hello."

The Capo identified himself, sort of.

"I'm certain that I do not have to tell you who this is," the Capo said.

"No, that won't be necessary."

"We've had a little situation come up, here . . . ,"

Vincent interrupted the Capo when he informed him, "Yes, I've heard . . . the old man called."

Several seconds of silence passed across the connection while both parties composed their next questions. Capo Pelligi kept the wording as brief as possible while still getting the subject matter across.

"The golf course?" the Capo asked.

Vincent knew that the Capo was referring to the drop house, and fortunately, he had already been by there and confirmed that all was well. At least for now . . . Vincent silently assured himself. Out loud, in response to Capo's question, Vincent answered, "the course is in good condition, but the fairways will be closed indefinitely for observation. It is possible that the grass has some sort of bugs."

Capo Pelligi nodded his head in agreement as if Vincent were standing beside him. The Capo was silently talking to himself, as well, and those thoughts were that the golf course was in good condition only because the 'fucking-rat' did not know about it. Methodically, he made a mental note of that fact. Eventually, there would be enough of these mental notes to pin down who had snitched. Capo Pelligi drew an audible breath.

"I understand . . . and the Quill?"

"The Quill's health is very good. The doctor has diagnosed that he is completely immune from the disease. Apparently, it was not contagious enough to spread rapidly from person-to-person."

The Capo pressed for more information.

"You've seen him?" he asked.

"As a matter of fact, I just left him. He was busy . . . very busy," Vincent replied.

Capo Pelligi nodded his head, again, while he held the phone's receiver to his ear. Tiny beads of perspiration formed above his busy eyebrows, yet they went unnoticed. His mind was whirling with thoughts. Seconds later, he asked, "And you?"

Vincent let out a short laugh.

"By order of the old man, I'm taking a well deserved vacation. Couple of weeks . . . maybe more."

"Alone?" the Capo asked.

Vincent laughed, again, before he answered, "Taking a friend . . . a blond friend."

This time it was the Capo who laughed.

"Have a good time . . . bye."

The phone clicked, and the connection was broken.

Capo Pelligi walked back to the taxi and got in. The driver quickly maneuvered the vehicle through the gas station and onto Broward Boulevard with a screech of the sedan's tires. The rapid acceleration had been for naught, though. Within minutes, the taxi was deadlocked in traffic.

*　*　*

South Florida's traffic is horrid, and it really doesn't matter which city one is in—Ft. Lauderdale, Pompano Beach, Deerfield Beach, Lighthouse Point, or Boca Raton—because traffic wise, they are one in the same. Vincent sat deadlocked in bumper-to-bumper traffic, just like every other day during the season. Capo Pelligi and the Consiglio were gridlocked in traffic, also. However, they were in Ft. Lauderdale while Vincent was miles north, in Boca Raton.

Vincent had spent the better part of the afternoon cleaning up loose ends, and now that he had the Quill out of the way it was but a short jaunt from Coral Springs to Boca Raton, in particular, Slick Nick's restaurant. Slick Nick didn't have any dealings with the gambling operation run by the Vitale crime family, but he was in Vincent's territory, and therefore, Vincent wanted to alert him to the fact that he would be out of town for a few weeks. Under the circumstances, Vincent felt that a face-to-face conversation would be best.

The traffic moved along at a snail's pace, but it was steady. Finally, Vincent reached his turn off and wheeled the Mercedes up to the front door of Slick Nick's restaurant. It was 3:30 p.m. and Vincent figured his timing was perfect. The only persons that would normally be there would have been Slick Nick and the Maitre d'.

"Hello, Nick," Vincent called out.

Slick Nick recognized the voice, and turned towards the direction of the sound so quickly that he almost pinched a nerve in his neck. The color drained from Nick's face.

"Vincent?" he queried, but he already knew who the voice belonged to.

Vincent walked towards Slick Nick, who was standing next to his office door, and Vincent's face became visible.

"How are you?" Vincent asked as he extended his hand to shake.

Instinctively, Slick Nick met Vincent's hand with his, and the two men shook hands.

"Things are fine, Vincent. Thanks for asking, but I'm sure you didn't come all the way up here just to ask me that."

Vincent noticed that the restaurateur's hand was clammy, and his mannerisms nervous.

"No, I didn't. Can we talk for a minute?" Vincent asked.

Slick Nick swallowed hard, but the vertical movement of his Adam's apple went unnoticed by Vincent. That was ironic, because Slick Nick felt as if he had a tennis ball stuck in his throat. Slick Nick had a lack of nerves, yet he recovered very well when he stepped to one side and made a sweeping motion with his right arm.

"Let's talk in my office," Nick suggested.

"Certainly," Vincent simply replied.

Slick Nick sat down behind his desk and Vincent seated himself in a chair across from him. It was no secret that the two men did not care for one another. In addition, there was the subject of Jennifer Swords . . . a sure winner to make the tempers flare. Fortunately the two men made a concerted effort to avoid that particular subject, and maintained their mental and emotional composure.

After a few minutes of social chitchat, Vincent got to the purpose of his visit. He leaned forward in the chair and uncrossed his legs.

"Nick, the family has had some problems. Capo Pelligi got picked up with a million-plus-dollars in his possession. That's too much cash to convince someone that you found it in the back of a taxi, if you get my drift."

Slick Nick's pulse was beating as fast as if he had done a line of ninety-percent pure cocaine.

"Yeah," Nick agreed, with a desert-dry mouth, "I see what you mean."

"Well, as a result of that fuck-up, we have shut down the gambling operation until the dust settles. As a matter of fact, I'll be taking a vacation for a few weeks . . . that's the reason I stopped by. I wanted to let you know that I will be unavailable . . . so stay out of trouble, okay?"

Slick Nick thought he was going to have a heart attack in his office right then and there. His mind rolled from the possibilities. He wondered if it were possible that Vincent already knew that it was he who had squealed the information about the money? Was Vincent there only to set him up for a hit? Nick fought to maintain his composure.

"Do you have any idea how this happened?" Nick queried.

Vincent shook his head.

"Not yet, but I assure you Capo Pelligi will leave no stone unturned until he finds out who was responsible for this. He is pissed-off, big time."

Nick's heart registered fear and palpitated, accordingly.

An uncomfortable moment of silence followed then Vincent casually glanced at his watch.

"Jeez, it's already 3:50. Nick, I've got to get going before I get caught in the rush-hour traffic. You know the old saying, 'I've got places to be and people to do.'"

Slick Nick managed a laugh, although he wasn't feeling too humorous. In addition, the 'people to do' part reminded him, once again, of Vincent and Jennifer. If only he had Vincent's cash, she would be with him . . . or so he believed in his twisted mind. Vincent stood, and Slick Nick started to stand. Vincent held his hands out, palms facing Nick.

"Keep your seat . . . I'll show myself out." Vincent walked out of the office and called out over his shoulder, "Good-bye, Nick."

Vincent maneuvered the Mercedes back into the flow of traffic and headed south along Interstate 95. Without thinking, he checked the small circular clock on the dashboard—it was 4 p.m. The thought really hadn't crossed his mind while he was conversing with Slick Nick, but now that he had noticed that it was late in the afternoon, he wondered where the Maitre d' might have been. It was not like him to be late for work. All he could think of was that Slick Nick must be furious with him for his tardiness.

The southbound traffic flowed steadily through Ft. Lauderdale's northern neighboring cities, but slowed to a stop-and-go pace just after Vincent reached the Ft. Lauderdale city limit. Ironically, the Mercedes stopped halfway between Cypress Creek Boulevard and Commercial Boulevard. Ft. Lauderdale's Executive Airport was one mile to the west. Vincent was inching along the freeway when suddenly a gleaming Learjet roared directly overhead. The sleek business jet climbed like a homesick angel while its throaty turbine engines thundered. It was a safe guess that no one else on the freeway but Vincent knew whom was onboard that particular aircraft. At least he thought he had known. Vincent had only been partially correct in his assumption because Capo Pelligi was the sole passenger aboard the chartered jet. It seemed that his would-be traveling companion, Consiglio Salvatore Santori, had remained behind at the orders of Anthony Vitale.

Vincent was not privy to that communiqué, and quite frankly did not need to know. Furthermore, he did not want to know. After all, the head of the crime family had already given him a suggestion, as Anthony Vitale would have referred to it, and Vincent had understood the underlying meaning. The Shark did not have to spell it out for Vincent, because he already knew—the less knowledge he had of the impending plans to deal with this breach of security, the better off he would be. There had been no arguments from Vincent. While he may not have been completely aware of the comings and goings of the Consiglio, there was one thing that Vincent was definitely certain of—the old man, indirectly, of course, was busy laying a whole bunch of 'rat traps' in-and-around Ft. Lauderdale. Nobody, NO-FUCKING-BUDDY, ratted out the Vitale crime family and lived to brag about it.

The thunderous noise of the Learjet lessened to the point that the decrescendo allowed Vincent to think clearly, once again, out loud. "Whatever happens," he said with no one to hear "I'm outta' here!" Vincent Panachi was en route to the Beach Side Travel Agency to pick up two airline tickets, one for himself and the other for Jennifer Swords. He had always been a good listener. Oh yes, sweet Jennifer . . . pleasurable thoughts filled his head all the way to the Oakland Park Boulevard exit, his exit.

* * *

The life of a restaurateur had made Slick Nick nocturnal, and 4 p.m. was like the morning to him. So far, his morning had not gone very well.

Slick Nick sat at his desk, his fingers repeatedly running through his hair while he pondered his situation. It could no longer accurately be described as a dilemma, because a dilemma would have inferred that he had a choice between evenly balanced alternatives. Unfortunately, that time had passed for Slick Nick, and he knew it. Fear had started an emotional forest fire that led his mind through a series of changes, and the recklessness resulting from those thoughts resulted in the birth of a desperado. With nothing to lose, Slick Nick's twisted mind brought him full circle; so far, in fact, that his visions were filled with wonderful delusions of grandeur. He had formulated the plan weeks before, but now it was time to put it into action. The restaurateur's psychotic state of mind fed the flames of that emotional forest fire until he had thoroughly convinced himself that he was infallible. He knew that he and Jennifer were really one in the same—all that really mattered to either one of them was the money. With money, she would be happy with him, and he knew it. He believed it. He also knew how to get his hands on a couple-of-million dollars . . . quickly. With that much cash Jennifer would become his, and they would run away together. He was certain of it . . . so certain that he was willing to literally bet his life on it.

Slick Nick stopped stroking his hair, which he had been doing unconsciously for over fifteen minutes. That alone independently marked the fact that Slick Nick had found an inner peace with regards to his problems. Without thinking, Nick's hand found the small mirror in the top drawer of the desk. A golden tooter lay beside it, and he grasped the straw-shaped object and the mirror in the same movement. The vial of ninety-percent pure cocaine was in the right front pocket of his tuxedo's trousers. He used his American Express Platinum card to form a small pile on the mirror then subdivided that into two equal lines. *WHIFF* . . . *WHIFF*. The lines disappeared.

Seconds later a fire burned in his brain, yet its flames felt entirely different than those emotional flames he had endured just moments before. The coke high overrode any questions of doubt he may have harbored and made him feel infallible. Slick Nick was incapable of error . . . just ask him . . . he would tell you. A combination of the marching-powder fueling his psychotic state of mind with his delusions of grandeur made Slick Nick feel bulletproof, and that was precisely what he had better be if Vincent ever found out what he was scheming. Like all coke-heads, Slick Nick found it difficult, if not impossible, to implement his plan. It was so much simpler to just sit back and enjoy the coke-fire buzzing in his brain. This time, however, he really had to get going. What he needed was an ally.

Slick Nick thumbed through his Rolodex file searching for Darlene's phone number. It took only a minute to find it, and he quickly pressed the appropriate numbers on the telephone. The hairdresser's receptionist answered the phone after the second ring. Slick Nick's voice was as familiar to the receptionist as hers was to him, when he asked to speak with the popular hairdresser. "Certainly," she said then added, "I'll get her for you, now." Darlene was on the phone within a minute.

"Nick, dah-ling, how are you?" she queried.

Nick's brain was too geared up to engage in small talk.

"I'm fine . . . but I need you to do me a real favor, okay?" Before the hairdresser could answer one way or the other, Nick spoke, again. "I need to talk to Jennifer Swords . . . it's important. I want you to tell me when she is coming into the salon next."

There was only the slightest hesitation before the hairdresser answered.

"Nick, dah-ling, she is here, now."

A surge of adrenaline shot through Slick Nick's veins and his heart raced. His mouth became desert-dry, yet he was able to speak intelligibly.

"Keep her there. Whatever you do, don't let her leave. I'm coming over there, right away."

"She's sitting in my chair, right where she will be when you get here."

Nick did not thank her, nor did he find the time to say, "Good-bye." He just dropped the phone as if it had been on fire. It was his mind that was on fire.

*   *   *

Jennifer Swords tilted her head forward, far enough so that Darlene could get the round brush between her hair and the nape of her neck. The roaring sound from the hair dryer filled her ears while long, methodical strokes of the brush followed rushes of warm air on her head. Every few seconds the warm feeling would disappear, yet the roar remained. During those short intervals Jennifer envisioned the hairdresser brushing and drying her long hair. She leaned forward, slightly further than before, and relished the sensual delight of the brush's bristles as they gently scratched her back during the down stroke. The combination of the hot air and the mini back massage relaxed her.

It's not like Jennifer had been any great ball of nerves when she arrived at the exclusive hair salon two hours earlier. On the contrary, she exuded charm and happiness. Things really had begun going her way, and it appeared that her perseverance was getting ready to pay off. That arrogantly impudent observation's purpose was to inspire confidence. Vincent Panachi had called her earlier that day and suggested, at the spur of the moment, that the two of them go away for a little vacation.

"I would love that, Vincent," she had cooed through the telephone. "How long should I pack for . . . a couple of days?"

"Better make it a couple of weeks. By the way, are you a gambler?"

Jennifer's devious, money hungry mind had immediately reflected that she had spent over half of her divorce settlement gambling on snaring financial security, but obviously, she was not going to divulge her thoughts to Vincent. Jennifer had pushed the thoughts to the back of her mind and had reentered the conversation.

"Oh, Vincent, that's always been too expensive for me . . . but I'd love to try," she had told him.

To her knowledge, gambling was one of the most expensive vacations one could take. She recalled how the girls at the elite country clubs had spoken about their gambling trips, and how they had been so nonchalant about their husbands losing ten, maybe twenty-thousand dollars at a whack. Mere 'street cake' to them. "Lunch money," as one of the particularly filthy-rich wives had described the gambling loss. Jennifer also had no problem remembering how envious she had been. "Never, again," she mumbled under her breath as she gaily concluded that she had found her own financial security blanket—Vincent Panachi.

"Pardon, me?" Vincent had asked, having barely heard her unintelligible speech.

"Oh nothing . . . I was just thinking how excited I am . . . that's all." Jennifer had smoothly recovered. Quickly, she had added, "I've always wanted to learn. Will you teach me?"

Vincent laughed when he had replied, "Of course. It would be my pleasure."

She wanted to throw a well placed mental spear foremost in his thoughts before she had let him off the phone, so Jennifer had casually said, "I'll make you a deal . . . if you'll make my days special at the tables, I will make your nights special in the bedroom. Is it a deal?"

Vincent had paused several seconds before he answered, for dramatics sake, as if he had really had to consider her offer.

"How could I possibly turn down an offer such as that?"

"I had hoped that you wouldn't," Jennifer had laughed.

"Deal," he had said.

Travel plans were discussed, and before they had even hung up their respective telephones, Vincent felt the heat and the familiar rush into his loins. It was settled—Vincent Panachi and Jennifer Swords were going to the Bahamas.

Darlene moved toward the top and sides of Jennifer's hair, and Jennifer luxuriated in the soft touch of the professional stylist. Although the two women had gossiped quite a bit during the coloring and trimming of Jennifer's blond hair, the past fifteen minutes had been spent in silence, with the exception of the relaxing sound of the blow dryer. The warm air made a whistling sound as the blower powered it through the brush's bristles. She felt the brush move toward her forehead, and Jennifer closed her eyes. It felt wonderful.

Days spent at the beauty parlor or on a massage table were what Jennifer Swords was made for. She was certain of it, because nothing could feel that good unless she was meant to do it all the time. Somehow . . . someway . . . she knew the rest of her life would be spent in the lap of luxury. She replayed those thoughts over and over while the warm air carried her away to her dream world.

Without warning, the relaxing sound stopped, as did the flow of warm air. Instinctively, Jennifer half opened her eyes and focused. For a split-second, she could not believe her own eyes; they shot wide open in disbelief. She was seeing what she previously couldn't believe. Standing before her was none other than Slick Nick.

Jennifer could not hide the surprise in her expression. She did, however recover rather quickly when she said, "Hello, Nick. I have to tell you that you are the last person I would have expected to run into here."

Slick Nick made an effort to keep the conversation light when he agreed, "You're one hundred percent correct there, Jennifer, but I'm not here for my looks."

Jennifer had always been able to manipulate Slick Nick, and immediately took control of the conversation when she pressed, "What are you doing here, Nick?"

"I need to talk to you . . . in private."

The hairdresser had not spoken a word, because the last thing she wanted to do was show favoritism. Jennifer looked up at Darlene and asked, "Are we finished?"

The hairdresser nodded her head and began removing the cotton smock. The tension in the air was so thick that it could have been cut with a knife. It was obvious to Jennifer that this was not a chance happening—that the hairdresser had fed Slick Nick information about her whereabouts—and it was equally as obvious to the hairdresser that Jennifer had figured that out. Slick Nick merely smiled and said, "Let's talk in my car. I'm parked just outside."

Darlene lifted the smock then Jennifer stood. Slick Nick made a sweeping motion with his left hand in the direction of the salon's front door, and Jennifer led the way. Nick followed in silence.

Just as Slick Nick stated, his automobile was parked in front of the building. Jennifer Swords knew the Mercedes Benz all too well and immediately recognized it. It was unlike Slick Nick to actually open the door for her, but he was right there when she reached for the handle. She slid onto the leather seat while he walked around the front of the car and entered from the driver's side. Jennifer leaned her head against the windowpane and shifted slightly in the seat so that she could sit sideways and talk. Jennifer remained passive while she patiently waited for Slick Nick to speak. Nick appeared to be somewhat nervous, and his eyes were slightly bloodshot. He looked tired. Even so, his red and irritated eyes showed sincerity when he turned to Jennifer and said, "This is probably the most important conversation of your life, because the outcome will affect you for the rest of your life."

Slick Nick paused for a couple of seconds, and afterwards Jennifer interjected, "Pretty heavy words, Nick."

"But, true," he smiled when he answered. An uncomfortable moment of silence fell between them, almost as if Slick Nick had to mentally review what he was going to say. Finally, he drew in a deep breath and said, "I have a proposition for you . . ."

"A what?" Jennifer interrupted him.

"A proposition," he was undeterred by her question.

"Okay, I'm listening," Jennifer said as she tossed her hair with a shake of her head.

Nick reached over and placed his hand on top of hers before he spoke. His eyes were sincere when he said, "Jennifer, we are one in the same. You want security, and so do I. I know you think that you can find it in Vincent Panachi, but you don't know him like I do. He's a cock-hound, and eventually, he will toss you aside, just as he had done the other women in his past. Although your future looks bright now, and you're having a lot of fun, you have no financial security. His money and lifestyle are not the type that you can take to court and receive alimony. As a matter of fact, marrying him would be the worst mistake of your life. Wives learn too much, and consequently, they would never let you go."

"Who is 'they?'" She asked,

"The Vitale crime family . . . as if you didn't know."

Jennifer sat in silence for a couple of seconds while Slick Nick let the statement sink in. Afterwards, he continued, "We are both in the same financial predicament—my future security is no more secure than your own."

"So . . . what's your proposition?" Jennifer queried.

Slick Nick took a deep breath and exhaled, slowly.

"Jennifer, I have always loved you. I want to be with you. We can run away together and all of this will be behind us, forever."

Jennifer always placed money first and foremost in her thoughts, and this time was no different.

"How? With what? You just told me that your financial situation was not forever."

"No, I told you that OUR financial situation was not forever, but we can fix that," he corrected her.

"How?" she asked, her interest perked.

"I have it from very high sources in the Vitale crime family that Vincent is going to have two and a half million dollars in cash in his possession very soon. I intend to take it, and you, and leave the country forever."

Jennifer looked at him for several seconds with a look of disbelief. He could tell that he had her undivided attention, and that her wheels were turning. Slick Nick moved in for the kill.

"Vincent will never give you that money . . . but, I will. All you have to do is tell me when he has it in his house, and I'll take care of the rest. Half for you, half for me. Of course, with all that money, I'm sure that you would want to go with me when I leave the country. The South Pacific, maybe."

Jennifer's greed overrode any feelings of love that she may have had. After all, she could learn to love, but she doubted very seriously if she could gather together one million and two hundred fifty thousand dollars. To say that she was tempted would be the understatement of the decade. Her mind played at the possibilities, then she asked what she thought was a pertinent question.

"What about repercussions? Don't you think Vincent will come after you?"

"I seriously doubt it . . . the whole bunch of them will be in jail, soon," Slick Nick smirked.

Jennifer sat in silence for several minutes while she thought about his proposal. Finally, after what seemed like hours, she leaned toward Slick Nick and kissed him on the cheek. Her hand was already on the door's handle when she said, "Call me in two weeks . . . we'll work it out, somehow."

Slick Nick remained speechless while she opened the Mercedes' door and got out. When he started the car, though, he let out a whoop. Soon he would have it all—Jennifer Swords, the money, and a future. Slick Nick reached into the glove box and brought out a small vial of coke. A celebration toot was in order.

*   *   *

Vincent sat in the small strip center office of the Beach Side Travel Agency. The tinted plate glass window on the storefront shaded the office's occupants from the blinding afternoon sun that blazed down upon the westward exposure. Virginia, a lovely middle-aged woman who always handled Vincent's travel needs with the utmost of professionalism, sat across from Vincent and meticulously outlined his airline tickets and hotel accommodations. Her desk was piled high with file folders and brochures, and in Vincent's opinion, there was no finer travel agent anywhere.

Her explanation took the better part of fifteen minutes, but as usual, it was an enjoyable quarter of an hour. Time well spent, the travel agent outlined a marvelous trip for Vincent and Jennifer. Vincent paid the bill and received travel vouchers in return, thereby bypassing the problems with the United States Customs Service for taking more than ten thousand dollars in cash out of the country. Now, everything was paid for, and what he took in cash was spending money. An equitable arrangement for all parties involved—with the exception of the Customs Service, of course. However, Vincent Panachi could have cared less about them.

Vincent thanked Virginia and departed the office. Shylock's was nearby, so he decided to stop in for a quick one. The drink would allow him time to visit a few minutes with his friend, Tony. Unbeknownst to Vincent, it also gave the valet parking surveillance team one more opportunity to photograph him.

Just before he pulled into the semi circular entrance his mobile telephone rang. Vincent answered it on the second ring.

"Hello," he said.

"Vincent, this is Sal . . . just wanted to make certain you have your travel arrangements set. Do you?" the elderly man asked in a gruff voice.

Vincent was taken aback by the surprise call, but he recovered his composure quickly, and replied, "As a matter of fact, we'll be departing for the Bahamas in just under three hours. Is everything okay?"

The Consiglio, who had just finished reading a report from a prominent South Florida private investigator casually remarked, "I've had to call in the exterminators. It seems that I have rats in my house."

Message received.

Vincent thanked him, and the two men broke the connection.

*   *   *

Three hours and twenty minutes later, Vincent Panachi and Jennifer Swords were seated in the first-class section of a Delta Airlines' jet winging its way east toward Nassau, New Providence, Bahamas. Less than an hour later, it arrived.

CHAPTER SEVENTEEN

F riday mornings were always hectic for the Organized Crime Task Force. The surveillance teams scrambled to secure enough film for the upcoming weekend as they were cognizant of the crowd Shylock's and Pegleg's would draw. No doubt, the go-fast boats would be rafted one off another until they reached eight-to-ten deep. The agents carefully loaded the bank of cameras that lined the wall of sliding glass panes and overlooked the drinking establishments. They were gearing up for the weekend flotilla of "Lauderdale's Players."

The roof and parking lot of the Denny's restaurant could be seen from the condominium, as well. An agent loading a camera that housed the 300 mm lens slowly guided the elongated optical spyglass north of Shylock's. It took a small adjustment to fully focus on the parking and roof top area of the Denny's restaurant. Then suddenly, his boss' sedan filled the viewfinder. He called over his shoulder, "Yeah, Murray's there, all right."

Agent Mark Murray's dark-blue Ford Crown Victoria sedan was easily identified among the other patrons' cars. The agent peering into the camera's lens added, "He'll be up here, soon."

One of the other agents on duty said, as he continued refilling the cameras with film, "Load and lock."

The split-second the words escaped his lips, the sound of a camera-back snapping into place was heard.

Agent Murray and the agent in charge of electronic eavesdropping were seated in a booth alongside the restaurant's glass front. The meeting was not by chance, yet it had been organized with little to no notice. As a matter of fact, Agent Jackson had called the meeting only an hour before.

A half-full pot of coffee sat between the two men, and the ashtray contained two cigarette butts. Jackson busied himself with smoking a third, despite the early morning hour. A trail of smoke wafted into Murray's eyes causing him to frantically wave his right hand in front of his face to disperse the irritating cloud. His left hand held a report that Agent Jackson had given him.

"Christ, Jackson," he exclaimed, "I don't particularly care if you want to slowly kill yourself, but spare me . . . if you don't mind."

Agent Jackson merely smiled while he exhaled a slow trickle of smoke through his nostrils. The two streams became one, inches from his face.

Mark Murray read the report in silence, his eyes scanning back and forth across the pages. Agents in general are not the paperwork type. Never have been; never will be. Certainly, Agent Murray was no different. He did, however, take particular interest in the report delivered to him that morning as it was a transcript of the telephone conversation between Vincent Panachi and Jennifer Swords. Without looking, his right hand found the finger hold on the coffee cup and he raised the piping hot cup to his lips. Instinctively, he cooled the rim by blowing on it before he placed it against his lips. Even so, the jet-black liquid was hot when he drank it. His hands trembled slightly when he got to the line, ". . . *I'll make your nights special in the bedroom. Deal?*"

Quickly, his eyes shot to the far left margin and double-checked whom the speaker had been—JENNIFER SWORDS. Her name was boldly typed in the one-inch margin beside the line. A sudden, brief, sharp spasm twisted Murray's stomach. The pain became familiar. The thought of her legs wrapped around Vincent Panachi sent Jennifer's STILETTO sinking deep into his heart, again.

Agent Mark Murray gathered his composure, just as he always had, and Jackson was none the wiser. Calmly, Murray laid the report on the table and said, "It looks like our pigeon has flown the coup." He paused for a few seconds before he queried, "You don't think Panachi's been tipped off, do you?"

Agent Jackson took a long pull off his cigarette then tamped the glowing red-hot tip flat in the ashtray. He dropped the butt alongside the other two then said, "There is no way, Murray. He's just gone off with the broad to get laid for a couple of weeks . . . he'll be back."

Mark nodded his head in agreement, but remained silent. Jackson's answer to the question had twisted the handle of the stiletto and the pang was felt deep within Murray's heart. Finally, he replied, "Yeah, I guess you're right."

Agent Murray took another sip of his coffee; then another; followed by yet another. His mind was miles away in thought. Without being aware that he had done so, Murray mumbled, "I'm gonna get that fucking Panachi."

Jackson made out the words and he remarked, "Sure you are . . . sure you are, buddy."

Mark did not respond to the comment. His mind was still miles away, deep in thought. However, at that moment, one could have placed an exact number on the miles. Agent Murray's thoughts were on Nassau, Jennifer and Vincent, and what they were doing that very moment.

* * *

The warm crystalline waters of the Bahamas glistened from the rising sun and tall palm trees cast shadows across the beach in front of the Crystal Palace Resort and Casino. The ocean was calm and the air still. Overall, one would be hard pressed to find a more tranquil setting than what is commonly referred to as the Bahamian Riviera.

In contrast, the nights are filled with all the action one can handle. Dazzling discos; restaurants with cuisine fit for an emperor; Las Vegas-style extravaganzas; and of course, a glittering casino featuring everything from blackjack, roulette, and slots. It was the casino that had attracted Vincent Panachi to the Bahamian Island this trip.

After settling into their luxurious suite, Jennifer and Vincent went directly to the casino and had a run at the blackjack tables. They shifted from table-to-table until they found a croupier who dealt the cards they liked. Vincent patiently taught Jennifer how to play. At the same time, he concentrated on his own game, and that concentration paid off handsomely.

The pit boss noticed Vincent's generous betting and the copious rack of chips neatly stacked before him. Vincent did not hesitate to order a rack of blacks, which equated to ten thousand dollars worth of one hundred dollar chips. He purchased green colored twenty-five dollar chips for Jennifer, and she conservatively placed her bets one chip at a time. Vincent, on the other hand, covered the rest of the playing field by placing a black chip bet in each of the eight remaining openings on the blackjack table. Consequently, every hand the croupier dealt, Vincent and Jennifer wagered eight hundred and twenty five dollars against the house. Over a period of hours, a considerable dollar figure changed hands between the croupier and Vincent, with Vincent finally emerging as the winner. Vincent was a big winner that night.

It was the pit boss' job to recognize players, and he watched Vincent's wagering with a keen eye. Unbeknownst to Vincent, the pit boss slipped away from his station and stopped by the hotel's front desk. "Yes, here it is," the beautiful front desk clerk said as she pulled up Vincent's check-in information on her computer. "He is booked in a suite for two weeks," she informed the casino pit boss.

The pit boss had not shown the slightest bit of indecision when he whipped out a comp form from the breast pocket of his tuxedo jacket. His hands quickly scratched out the appropriate endorsement while he said, "Mr. Panachi's expenses will be covered by the house. Please forward his room and meal charges to me personally."

The clerk took the endorsed comp form and filed it along with the others. Her hands made a lightening quick entry into the computer and it was done. Vincent Panachi's stay at the Crystal Palace Resort and Casino had been comped by the casino's management. This sort of thing was the norm for the casino when a high stakes gambler was identified. They did not build those multi-million dollar hotel conglomerates by paying off winners. They knew, just as all astute gamblers know, that the odds are in favor of the house, and that eventually the cards would turn. The pit boss did the correct thing. Vincent may have won big that particular evening, but if he were to stay and play throughout a two-week period, there were no doubts that the hotel would emerge as the financial victor. In essence, that's what pit bosses are there for. In addition, it was their job to promote the hotel's public relations. Keep the customers happy, and they will keep coming back.

When Vincent tired of playing and decided it was time to cash out, the pit boss saw his opportunity to promote that goodwill. It was the pit boss, himself, who delivered the empty chip rack to Vincent, then helped him stack his ten thousand dollar winnings. The pit boss causally mentioned, "Congratulations on your win . . . and to show our appreciation for your playing with us, the casino has comped your suite and meals during your stay, Mr. Panachi."

"Thank you. Thank you very much," Vincent replied while he offered his hand to shake.

"It is our pleasure . . . and I hope to see you at the tables, again . . . soon," the pit boss replied as he received Vincent's hand and shook it while he made a slight waving motion with his other.

It was the sophisticated approach of letting Vincent know that the casino expected him to play on a daily basis to offset their expenses incurred by comping his stay. Whether he won or lost was a gamble that they both risked. However, they both were aware that the odds favored the house. That's why they call it gambling.

Jennifer watched very closely when Vincent generously tipped the croupier five black chips. Afterwards, Vincent turned toward Jennifer and winked when he asked, "Could you carry one of these, please?"

Without waiting for her response, he shoved a rack of black chips in her direction. Jennifer grabbed the foot-long rack of chips and smiled when she quipped, "Shopping money?"

Vincent stood with the other rack in his hands. He leaned over and gently kissed her on the cheek, then said, "Why not? Let's roll."

Jennifer stood then followed him toward the casino's cashier. Her thoughts had been on the money. "Ten thousand in one night," she pondered. "Not bad."

Later that night Jennifer remained true to her word, and both she and Vincent enjoyed two very satisfying orgasms. Jennifer's undulating orgasms squeezed every drop of semen from Vincent's throbbing manhood while her legs mimicked the movement of her quivering lips. Jennifer flung her trembling legs tightly around Vincent's back, squeezed hard and screamed during the tremulous throes of her self-satisfying orgasms. Afterward, Jennifer and Vincent were spent. They fell asleep in one another's arms within a matter of minutes.

The following morning the sun warmed the crystalline waters of the Bahamas and also came into view through a one-inch opening in the bedroom's drapes, shining a beam of light directly into Vincent's eyes. The irritating glare disturbed his sleep and awakened him. Vincent tossed the covers aside with a sweep of his right arm then glanced at the sleeping beauty beside him. Jennifer Swords was still fast asleep.

Vincent walked softly when he crossed the suite's bedroom, careful not to make any noise that might disturb Jennifer's sound sleep. He closed the bathroom door before he turned on the light, and was careful not to bang the toilet seat against the porcelain tank when he lifted it. Vincent had not made a sound. However, there was little that he could have done to muffle the waterfall-like reverberating noise he made when he relieved himself. Most things in life are negotiable; the need to take that morning piss is not one of them. The hollow sound was deadened by the flush of the toilet.

Vincent simultaneously turned off the bathroom light while he opened the door. He checked the bed and saw that Jennifer was still asleep. The stream of sunlight that had awakened him just moments before shone across his side of the bed. Jennifer had pulled the covers half over her head, far enough so that her eyes were covered. Her mane of blond hair laid across the pillow and spread in every imaginable direction. She was sound asleep.

Vincent dressed in silence, quietly slipping into a pair of white Bermuda shorts and a navy-blue Polo shirt. A cotton belt covered with fish designs and a pair of beige boat shoes completed the ensemble. Vincent was careful not to disturb the mound of change lying atop the bedroom's walnut dresser. Carefully, he found his money clip and silently slid it into the right front pocket of his shorts. The telephone number that he needed had been committed to memory. Fortunately, it was a number he never had the need to use. Nevertheless, just as every professional player has done, Vincent memorized and recited the emergency number on almost a daily basis. In case of emergency, the telephone number was a secure line with which the Vitale crime family members could access the Consiglio. A database. Under the circumstances, Vincent felt that staying in touch with the family's legal counsel was a prudent thing to do.

The suite was conveniently located by the bank of elevators and within seconds the push of the button summoned one. Vincent pressed the button for the lobby and the elevator's door hissed while it closed. A minute later, the car arrived at the lobby level. Vincent had scoped out the lobby the night before and knew precisely where the public telephones were located. He turned right as he exited the elevator and followed a corridor that eventually led to the swimming pool area. In Vincent's case it was not the pool area that interested him. He stopped twenty feet from the end of the well-lit hallway, in front of the last telephone in a bank of six. The telephones were empty, with the exception of an elderly lady garbed in a straw hat and one piece bathing suit. Vincent glanced over at her and smiled, even though the woman failed to notice him. She was much too preoccupied with the telling of her story to have been concerned with whom may be standing next to her. The woman's arms were flinging in every direction as she enthusiastically dramatized the story with her hands. "A coffee-cup clacker," Vincent offhandedly remarked to himself. He turned his back to the woman and punched a lengthy series of numbers into the touch-tone telephone, one of which was an AT&T International Calling Card number. Direct billing is the only civilized means available to someone who wants to place an overseas call from the island nation of the Bahamas. That number—the AT&T International Calling Card—had been designated, "For emergency use, only," by the gentleman who had issued it to him some time ago. Both the credit card number and the number he dialed had been issued to him by the crime family's Consiglio, and the legal counsel had assured him that both were secure numbers. "Well, I'll be fucked if they're not," Vincent mused to himself. The ringing of the overseas number interrupted his thoughts. The telephone's satellite technology never ceased to amaze Vincent, within seconds he was connected to a telephone inside a home in a posh subdivision on the outskirts of Newark, New Jersey, U.S.A.

*   *   *

The Consiglio answered the telephone after the second irritating ring. Instinctively, he glanced at his expensive wristwatch while he crossed the room towards the phone. "God damn it," he grumbled, "it's a little early for the shit to start hitting the fan."

When his right hand removed the receiver from the cradle and gently placed it against his ear, his voice was much more controlled than his initial emotions. "Hello," he said in a dignified tone.

The voice was one of a seasoned professional, and although it had been nothing more than a single word greeting, the legal counsel evoked a resonance and demeanor worthy of any federal courtroom.

"It's Vito," Vincent said, using his father's name rather than his own.

The Consiglio knew who was on the line, just as he had known Vito Panachi very well. The legal counsel remarked, "You always were sharp . . . I knew that you would know to call."

Vincent barely had time to acknowledge, "Yes, sir," before the Consiglio interrupted him by adding, "God damn new fangled mobile phones. Mark my words . . . they will end up being the death of us all. All the 'heat' needs is a simple scanner and your conversations are public property. Stay off that God damn thing, Vito."

"That's why I waited to call you on a secure land line, Sal," Vincent smiled.

"Smart boy, Vito. Smart boy," he complimented Vincent.

A couple of seconds of silence fell across the connection, which is not uncommon during a satellite connected overseas call. Finally, Vincent queried, "So how extensive are the rats? Have they infiltrated your entire house, or are they only in the basement?"

What he was really asking was whether or not the informant had reached all the way to the top of the crime organization, or had it merely been street level members that had been exposed. Unfortunately, the answer was not the one that Vincent hoped for.

The Consiglio let out an audible sigh before he informed Vincent, "It does not look good. Of course, our investigation is in its early stages, but the private investigator I hired was able to spread a little cash around and get to the bottom of what has happened so far."

If one considered forty thousand dollars as "a little cash," then more power to them. For Anthony Vitale it had been insurance.

"Pay whatever it takes . . . no matter what the figure is . . . I want to know what the hell is going on down there," the head of the crime family had instructed the Consiglio upon his departure to Florida.

Nothing ventured; nothing gained. The investigator had easily found someone intimately connected with the investigation that was willing and able to spill the beans. The professional investigator listened to the information given to him in confidence while he chronologically outlined and typed the events. That report had been given to Anthony Vitale immediately upon the Consiglio's arrival back in New Jersey.

"Does the old man know the details yet?" Vincent asked.

The legal counsel coughed before he answered, "Oh yeah . . . he's got the report, and is probably reading it as we speak. You know he's an early riser anyway. In the meantime, let me fill you in. God damn, Vito, you're a fuckin' star, for Christ's sake." Even before the Consiglio began, that statement in itself sent a shiver down Vincent Panachi's spine. Of course, that was nothing compared to the rest of the report.

Vincent listened to the family's legal counsel while he gave Vincent the *Reader's Digest* version of what had taken place. Vincent's concentration level was at its highest, and he totally fixed his attention upon the matter at hand. As a matter of fact, he had absolutely no idea whatsoever if the sunburned tourist who had been standing next to him just minutes before was even still there or not. Furthermore, he didn't give a damn. It would not have mattered anyway, because Vincent was not doing any of the talking. He just stood there at the public phones, his mouth hanging in awe, while the Consiglio continued. It was this conversation that enlightened Vincent Panachi to the fact that he was the target of an Organized Crime Task Force probe. Needless to say, the news did not make him happy.

It was amazing how many thoughts were going through Vincent's mind while he was listening to the Consiglio reveal the highlights of the private investigator's findings. Naturally, the thought first and foremost was his concern for Anthony Vitale.

Vincent listened without interruption. Suddenly, the Consiglio paused then asked a question.

"Vito, just who in the hell is this Agent Mark Murray?" the legal counsel queried.

Before Vincent could tell him that he had no idea, the Consiglio fired off another question.

"Have you ever had a run in with this prick?" he added.

Vincent was dumbfounded, just as the Consiglio had been, because it was as obvious to Vincent as it had been to the legal counsel, once he had heard the contents of the investigator's report, that this investigation was fueled by a personal vendetta between Agent Mark Murray and the Vitale crime family's very own Vincent Panachi.

Vincent could not help but wonder what the head of the crime family thought about this cluster fuck, and it was ironic that Vincent chose those particular words to describe the scenario during his moment of wonderment. Unbeknownst to him, Anthony summarized the private investigator's report with the exact same words.

"What a cluster fuck!" He exclaimed.

Vincent stood with the telephone firmly pressed against his ear while he listened. That moment, however, his thoughts were far removed from the tropical paradise he was calling from. His imagination went into overdrive, creating a mental image of the old man reading the report the Consiglio had given him. The picture he conceived in his mind was not very far from what was really happening.

*   *   *

Typical of the New Jersey winters, another low pressure system swept in during the early morning hours, and the gloomy weather blanketed the entire state with a shroud of gray. The temperature fell below the freezing point, yet it had not begun to sleet or snow as of daylight. Nevertheless, Anthony Vitale's butler anticipated his boss' first order of the day and consequently had built a fire in the library's marble fireplace long before the head of the crime family awakened. When Anthony Vitale entered his favorite room in the palatial mansion, the roaring fire had already warmed the library to a comfortable seventy-two degrees. He was certain of it, because he checked the small thermometer that sat on top of his large mahogany desk.

A breathtaking view of the estate's forest-like grounds could be seen from the desk, but the dismal, gray-colored sky made it an uninteresting view to the elderly gentleman. Instead, he stared at the fire and marveled at the rising, yellowish flames that licked the top of the polished-stone fireplace.

Outside frost formed on the hardwoods that paralleled the estate's cobblestone driveway, and although he couldn't see it from the mansion Anthony imagined frost clinging to the entranceway's iron gates. The huge oak tree in the center of the driveway only served to cast a darker shade of gray across the circular drive, and made the outside world appear that much colder to the old man.

Of course, the library's dark mahogany paneling did not make the room look any warmer, but the fireplace made up for that. Anthony Vitale was quite warm, and quite satisfied. That was until he read the report the Consiglio had given him.

The six-page report compiled by the private investigator lay on the center of his desktop. Anthony picked it up, along with a cup of coffee that sat alongside it, and carefully read the report. His eyes moved quickly across the page, sometimes coming back and slowly rereading the same paragraph. It was a slow, tedious means of reading, but he had discovered that this system allowed him to digest the material in its entirety. For him, it was a format that worked. The head of the crime family read and reread the investigator's report one page at a time until he had practically memorized its contents. The Consiglio had been correct in his analysis when he stated, "We've got some problems down in Florida. Fortunately, they have not gotten beyond Florida . . . yet. We have got to nip this thing in the bud . . . or, it could very well get out of hand and become the downfall of us all."

Anthony Vitale laid the report down on top of his desk. He leaned back in his reclining chair and swiveled it so that he could better face the twelve-foot Palladian windows. The view of the manicured grounds had always been his favorite view while he pondered a particular situation, and that was precisely what this had become—a situation. As the head of one of the nation's most formidable crime families, he had been under investigation a countless number of times. For some strange reason, however, this time he had to agree with his legal counsel and the private investigator's opinions that the investigation seemed to have targeted his nephew, Vincent Panachi. Anthony Vitale found it odd that the Organized Crime Task Force would be more interested in Vincent than himself, particularly in light of the fact that their snitch had outlined, in nauseating detail, the complete chain of command of the Vitale crime organization, at least in as much detail as the rat had known. Anthony Vitale clasped his hands together and placed them behind his head while he thought out his counterattack plan. Outside, a sudden gust of wind stirred the trees.

The plan was simple—if you remove the motivating factor, the problem maker will lose his motivation. In this particular case, the motivating factor was Vincent Panachi. If he were to take an early retirement, at least until the dust settled, perhaps this Agent Murray would simply go away. But, there was no way that the head of the crime family could leave something as important as that to chance. No, he needed to insure the family's position, and Anthony had an answer for that, as well—if you remove their star witness, they have no case. The snitch had to die, for two reasons: one, to squash the Organized Crime Task Force's investigation; and the second . . . well, that reason was quite obvious—according to organized crime law, snitches and rats must die.

Anthony Vitale leaned forward and pressed a button on his intercom. The butler's voice answered from the kitchen, "Yes, sir?"

"Send Capo Pelligi in, please."

"Right away, Mr. Vitale."

Anthony pushed the report aside. He had made his decision, and now he would give that assignment to the Capo. Certainly, after what he had been through with the scene at the Learjet, Capo Pelligi would enjoy this assignment. He would definitely take pleasure in eliminating Slick Nick.

This action would take care of the snitch. However, there was still the matter of the Quill and his project. Anthony Vitale made a commitment, and it was a commitment that had been made in the name of the Vitale crime family. Just like his father before him, the Vitale's word was their bond. Therefore, after careful consideration, the head of the crime family made the decision to discontinue all operations within Vincent Panachi's territory, with the exception of the counterfeiting operation. For Anthony Vitale, it was more than the money—his family's reputation was on the line. The Vitale crime family MUST deliver at all costs.

There was a knock at the library's door that sounded more like thumps through the solid mahogany. Anthony swiveled his chair toward the doorway and away from the windows. "Enter," he called out during the turn.

Capo Pelligi entered the library and stopped just inside the doorway. He nodded his head, in respect, as he said, "Don Vitale."

"Come in . . . sit with me," the head of the crime family said as he motioned with his right hand.

* * *

When Vincent hung up the telephone, he glanced to his right and noticed that the woman who had been standing beside him earlier was nowhere in sight. Once he checked the time on his watch, however, it was no wonder. He had been on the phone for thirty-seven minutes, and that conversation left him with plenty to think about.

Vincent followed the corridor to its end where suddenly the lobby's plush carpeting turned into concrete and stone surrounding the pool. Already there were scores of tourists comfortably laid out on vinyl mats placed atop wooden lounge chairs. Vincent walked a slow paced lap around the pool. The smell of suntan oil filled the still morning air while bikini clad beauties stretched out on their chairs. These were the women that lived for their suntans. For the most part they were absolutely stunning. Nevertheless, Vincent was totally oblivious to their gorgeousness. His thoughts blocked out everything else but the conversation he had just had with the Consiglio. That thirty-some-odd minute conversation had changed his life . . . just like that.

Vincent pondered his situation for ten minutes, during which he walked several additional laps around the swimming pool. He always had been cool, calm, and collected, and Vincent had no intentions of handling this misfortune in any other manner. There were, however, some unanswered questions in his mind. He had been taught long ago, by Anthony Vitale himself, that patience was a virtue. As the elderly gentleman had once told him, "If you are patient, and do not make hasty or snap decisions, somehow, someway, the answers or persons that you seek will invariably expose themselves."

Those words of wisdom had been of use to Vincent a vast number of times during his reign as the head of the Vitale crime family's South Florida operations, and furthermore, the Shark's philosophy had been right on more often than not.

While Vincent walked around the pool area, he came to one definite conclusion—the counterfeiting operation must be completed. His thoughts had been analogically alike with Anthony Vitale's at least with reference to the Quill's operation. Vincent reasoned that the gambling could go away; the loan-sharking could go; for that matter, Vincent himself could go; but, at all costs, the crime family's reputation must remain intact. The counterfeiting operation would continue, Vincent decided and he would discuss his feelings about this with the head of the crime family the first chance he got. For the time being, he reminded himself that there was nothing that could be done but to be patient. If Vincent knew Anthony Vitale as well as he thought he did—and Vincent did—he knew that the hit had already been ordered. That would take care of half the problem; the other half could wait. After all, Vincent was on vacation.

Vincent reentered the hotel lobby and casually walked towards the bank of elevators. He greeted several fellow tourists with a, "Good morning," along the way.

An elevator car sat waiting, its doors wide open, and Vincent entered without breaking his stride. He had the car to himself, and a simple push of the desired floor's button sped him to the hotel's top floor. The suite was footsteps away after the elevator's polished doors slid open. Vincent inserted the credit card sized key into the suite's electronic lock and opened the door. As soon as he opened the door, the steady rhythmic beat of island-style music filled his ears. The sounds were coming form the bedroom. There was no mistaking that Jennifer was awake.

Jennifer had woken up shortly after Vincent left to place his call. Her morning started considerably slower than her travel companion's and consequently, she had the opportunity to just lie in bed and think for ten to fifteen minutes. As she lay in bed with her head comfortably propped up by two feather pillows, Jennifer reveled in the thoughts of how her plans were coming together. She pondered her past, compared it to her present, and then considered her future. Here she was, a relatively unattractive girl from New Jersey, who through the miracles of cosmetic surgery had become a shapely, attractive woman. She had come a long way from the blasé winters of New Jersey to the white-sandy beaches of sunny Nassau, and now, through the jealously and cocaine induced state of insanity that Slick Nick had succumbed to, it appeared that she had found her way to financial security, as well. Jennifer Swords was quite full of herself as she lay in the luxurious suite and contemplated her life. She had come to one very important conclusion during that quarter of an hour of pleasurable thoughts, and that was that she must keep Vincent Panachi completely and totally mesmerized with her . . . at least until she found out the information that Slick Nick requested. Jennifer had one sure-fire way of doing that, and her past conquests served as testimony—sex. She would hold him as long as necessary with her sexual magnetism.

"Good morning," Vincent called out from the suite's living room.

Jennifer was seated at the small cosmetic counter in the bathroom, carefully applying her daytime make-up. With the exception of a small thong-style bikini bottom, she was naked. Her melon-sized breasts bounced in rhythm with the strikes from her elbow as she carefully applied waterproof mascara to her already dark eyelashes. The movement hardened her nipples and made them jut forward nearly a half-inch. She returned Vincent's greeting then added, "I'm in the bathroom getting ready."

By the time she finished the sentence, she heard Vincent enter the bedroom. Jennifer put the mascara away then quickly checked her make-up. Her face had been perfectly applied. The only thing missing was her lipstick, but that had not been forgotten. Jennifer purposely omitted that from her morning make up ritual, and she did it for premeditated reasons. After all, when an act is planned beforehand the only applicable description is "premeditated," and that was precisely what Jennifer had done. While she had lain in the bed she decided to give Vincent the best blow-job he had ever had in his life, bar none. And coming from Jennifer that was no idle threat; she considered that sexual act her specialty. She was certain that once she applied a lip lock on Vincent, she would have his undivided attention throughout the entire day. The night would take care of itself . . . she would see to that.

Jennifer stood and checked her hair in the mirror. A quick sweep of her hand brushed the lengthy mane forward over one shoulder, and she left it that way, sexily draped over her right breast. Jennifer leaned against the doorframe and stuck her head through the doorway. She saw that Vincent had sat down on the edge of the bed. Jennifer said, "Hi," and he turned his head towards her.

"Hi. How are you this morning?" Vincent replied.

By the time he had finished his question, Jennifer had walked through the bathroom doorway, her bare breasts seductively jutting forward. Vincent watched as she walked towards him, her voluptuous bosom bouncing with the rhythm of her stride while her bare feet padded across the thick piled carpet. Vincent felt his manhood involuntarily rise. Just the sight of her made him rock hard. She waited until she stood just inches away from him before she answered, "Feeling wonderful, Vincent."

Jennifer placed both of her hands on Vincent's chest and leaned her weight forward. As Vincent fell backwards, her left nipple brushed his face.

"I have something special that's gonna make you feel wonderful, too," Jennifer said.

"What might that be?" Vincent said playing along.

By now Jennifer had slid her hands from his chest to his belt buckle and had begun unfastening it. She looked up and met his eyes. Slowly, Jennifer licked her lips then said, "I'm going to suck your balls dry."

If there had been an appropriate savoir-faire remark for that situation, Vincent had been unable to think of it. Anyway, within seconds of her comment, any debonair remark that he may have considered would have been overpowered by the sounds of his pleasurable moans. All Vincent could see was the back of Jennifer's head with her blond hair flung across his stomach and chest. There was no mistaking where her mouth was, and what she was doing with it.

After what seemed like forever, Vincent shuddered in the throes of an unbelievable orgasm. The second that Jennifer felt him about to peak, she gently massaged his balls with her fingers while her lips made long, slippery strokes up and down his throbbing shaft. To him, it felt like an explosion within his mind; to her, she hadn't missed a drop of his love juices. She knew from experience . . . it had been a good one. There was no doubt in her mind that she now had Vincent's undivided attention . . . or so she thought.

Jennifer would have been surprised at what his real thoughts had been at that particular moment. While it was true that she had given him the best blow-job he ever had, there was a question that remained unanswered, and that question burned in his mind since the Consiglio posed it to him. The legal counsel raised an excellent question when he asked, *"Who in the hell is this Agent Mark Murray? Have you ever had a run in with this prick?"*

Vincent found those questions to be very pertinent, particularly since he had just been informed that he was the target of an investigation instigated by this agent.

Vincent ran his fingers through Jennifer's hair and guided her face towards his. He complimented her with, "Honey, that was the magnificent."

Jennifer smiled. It was a confident smile, because SHE was certain it had been his greatest.

* * *

Even though a great number of years had passed since the Quill had enjoyed a steamy, sexual interlude such as Vincent had just experienced, he did not mind. To the Quill, watching sheet-after-sheet of brand new twenties roll hot off the press was better than sex. The operation was in full swing, and it was all the computerized digital cutter could do just to keep up with the sophisticated machine's mass production. The Quill side stepped to the far end of the whirring machine and scooped up a two-inch thick stack of fresh bills to be cut.

"Damn, they're perfect," he complimented himself out loud while he quickly glanced over them. Quickly, he carried the stack to the other bedroom where the resounding blows from the digital cutter was heard rhythmically whacking away at another two-inch thick stack of money, one sheet at a time.

*   *   *

The sun was setting over the northern hemisphere when Learjet N30TP was sequenced onto the final approach course for Ft. Lauderdale's runway 9L. The captain glanced over at the co-pilot and commanded, "Approach flaps."

The co-pilot did not verbally acknowledge the command, but the increased pressure on the control yoke confirmed to the captain that ten-degrees of flap had been extended. The experienced captain re-trimmed the aircraft while he visually checked the flap indicator gauge. Even though the crew had illuminated the "Fasten Seat Belts" and "No Smoking" signs five minutes earlier, the co-pilot still checked the passengers. He craned his neck as he turned his upper body as far as he could to the left, then called out, "Check your belts for landing, please. We'll be on the ground in a couple of minutes."

The "couple of minutes" part was not negotiable with the controllers because the Learjet was following a Delta Airlines' 727 on a two mile final. Just then, Approach Control called Learjet N30TP.

"Lear 30 Tango Papa's two miles from the outer marker and cleared for the approach. Maintain twenty-two-hundred feet until reaching Snape (the coordinate name for the 9L outer marker), and contact the tower on 119.3. Good day."

Instinctively, the co-pilot repeated the instructions back to the controller then wished him a good day as well.

In the passenger's cabin Capo Pelligi and two unidentified guests were aboard the business jet. The flight crew had flown Capo Pelligi a number of times, but they had never seen the two other men. Mr. Pelligi had not introduced them for a reason. The two men were professional hit men who never failed. They were like robots once they received their orders, and this time their orders had been received directly from the man himself—Anthony Vitale. There would be no acceptable excuses; the Shark made it very clear that he wanted blood. Slick Nick's blood. As a matter of fact, Anthony Vitale's voice had been so soft when he ordered the contract that Capo Pelligi had to strain to understand him. But that was a message in itself, for the quieter the head of the crime family got was directly related to how upset he was. Anthony Vitale was pissed . . . and Slick Nick was history.

The co-pilot's estimated flight time was right on the money. Learjet N30TP landed safely and rolled to the high-speed turn off. Walker's Cay Terminal sat just across the taxiway. Capo Pelligi and the two unidentified passengers were met by a limousine that whisked them away before the business jet's turbine engines had stopped spinning. To the two professional pilots, that sort of behavior was nothing they hadn't seen before. After all, this was Ft. Lauderdale, Florida.

CHAPTER EIGHTEEN

During the following week, Jennifer and Vincent romped on the beach, and in general led a carefree lifestyle. The evenings were spent gambling in the hotel's magnificent casino, followed by love-making with a frequency that Vincent had never experienced. One morning after a particularly wild night spent in the sack, Vincent recalled remarking to himself that Jennifer had an insatiable appetite for sex. His comment actually had been more graphic, "The woman knows more tricks than a monkey knows on six feet of grapevine." The comment made him chuckle, and even though he had laughed quietly, Jennifer had heard him. She questioned him while she leaned against the opposite side of the closed bathroom door. Vincent still had the smile on his face when he answered, "Just feeling happy, sweetheart."

"Me too," she replied.

Vincent and Jennifer had been in the islands for just one week, yet Jennifer was certain that she had Vincent preciously where she wanted him, and thoughts of his money and her ultimate plan never left her mind.

Vincent had experienced high-pressure situations, and he had learned from them. He knew that there was little to nothing that he could do about the task force's investigation, but he was certain that Anthony Vitale was taking care of the situation. He did not know how, but he was convinced that he would find out soon enough. In the meantime he followed the advice that he had given to a number of his underlings when he said out loud, "Live every day to its fullest, because you can never be certain if it will be your last."

Before Vincent had left Ft. Lauderdale he had tied up all loose ends concerning the family's businesses, which included making certain that the Quill's operation was kept fully supplied. There was nothing left for him to do except to enjoy the sun, surf, and Jennifer's expert love-making. It was a tough life, but someone had to do it!

Vincent's boys had been instructed to wait exactly one week to make their delivery to the expansive home in the Coral Springs Coral Club subdivision. It was not unusual for delivery and service trucks to be seen entering the upper-middle class neighborhood, but it would have been out of the ordinary to have seen one entering after business hours. With that in mind, the boys decided to make the Quill's delivery just like any other delivery service—smack in the middle of the day!

Their coordinated timing was like a sophisticated military operation when, at precisely 1 p.m., the white cargo van turned into the driveway of the rented house. Metallic service-oriented signs hung midway along the van's paneled sides and served as a decoy. The very second the van entered the driveway, the garage door electronically began to open and the driver waited less than a minute for the opener to complete its job. The masquerade had worked perfectly, and the van eased its way into the two-car garage.

The elderly gentleman standing in the open doorway gave hand signals to direct the driver into the garage as far as possible. The Quill stood just inside the laundry room, leaning through the doorway. His upper body was somewhat twisted causing his right shoulder to press against the doorjamb while his left arm rested crosswise against his chest. His left index finger lightly rested on the electronic garage door opener's switch. Once the Quill was sure that the vehicle had ample clearance, he depressed the small, doorbell-like button and the elongated, screw-like machine mechanically lowered the heavy, wooden garage door. The two occupants of the cargo van waited until they were certain that the garage door had fully closed before they exited the vehicle. It had been some time since they had initially met the elderly gentleman and helped move the equipment into the house.

"Come in, gentlemen. Come in," the Quill said as he stood in the doorway and motioned for them to enter.

"Mr. Quill," the driver said as he nodded his head in the gesture of salutation.

His partner remained speechless, but did nod his head as he walked past the Quill.

"We'll make this quick and simple. You boys should be out of here in twenty minutes, or so," the Quill advised.

"No problem . . . just show us where you would like the stuff placed," the driver called out over his shoulder.

Instinctively, the Quill pointed towards one of the back bedrooms with his right hand, but the finger-pointed direction was to no avail. The two men were several feet ahead with their backs to him.

"Just put it all in that last bedroom. You'll see other boxes in there . . . just like the ones you have," the Quill said.

The numerous boxes that contained reams of paper lined one wall of the back bedroom. So far, the Quill had already used nearly one-hundred-and-fifty reams of the 75/25 paper. Twenty-five boxes were neatly stacked into two columns that resembled decorative cardboard pillars. One-hundred-and-twenty-five boxes formed a perfect twelve-by-twelve foot square that started flush against the far corner along the same wall. The remaining six boxes stood against the end of the cardboard square to begin a new column. There was a method to the way the Quill had arranged the boxes. The decorative pillar boxes contained unprinted paper and the boxes in the twelve by twelve square were full of flawless twenties. Finished products. Done. History. Sterile. Ready for delivery.

The driver stuck his head in the door of the bedroom and noted the arrangement of the boxes. Vincent had not selected the driver for this assignment because the driver was stupid. On the contrary, the streetwise driver surmised the Quill's unique filing system.

"How about if we put them along this side wall, next to the small column you have there?" the driver suggested.

The Quill and the two men exchanged knowing glances, but none of them spoke the obvious truth. It was much better that way, or so the rules of the street had taught them.

"Good idea . . . that would be just perfect," the Quill replied.

The driver tapped his partner on the shoulder and motioned towards the garage with his eyes.

"Done," he said to the Quill.

The two delivery men worked methodically until all of the boxes in the van were unloaded. Although Vincent's crew had nothing to do with the everyday routine on the production end, they were doing an outstanding job of stocking the provisions necessary to keep the Quill on schedule. The one hundred twenty-five boxes packed with twenty dollar bills was evidence of their team effort.

The Quill was pleased. The driver and his co-worker had the van unloaded and its contents neatly stacked in the designated bedroom within exactly twenty-one minutes. He stood in the doorway of the makeshift printing shop and surveyed the materials. A smile formed across his face as he affectionately patted the driver on the shoulder.

"Good job. See you next week?" the elderly gentleman queried.

The van's driver winked at him and smiled.

"Same time, next week." The driver turned to his partner and said, "Let's hit the highway."

Once again, the Quill operated the garage door's electronic opener from the laundry room's doorway. The elderly gentleman watched as the van backed out of the driveway and waited until the vehicle had completely turned around before he depressed the button again. The electric opener made a whirring sound as the heavy door began lowering. The entire delivery process had taken less than half-an-hour. Aside from sleeping, that was the longest break the legendary counterfeiter had taken all week. Already, there was in excess of ten million dollars lined along that bedroom wall. The Quill chuckled at the thought then closed the laundry room door. "Time to go back to work!" he exclaimed out loud, but no one was there to hear.

*　　*　　*

By the time Slick Nick performed one last check of the restaurant's rear doors, it was 2:45 a.m. The late nights spent closing had been a drag, but he had little choice now that the Maitre d' was gone. Nick would have had questions from the staff if he had brought somebody new into the restaurant. Questions that he really did not care to deal with. So far, the Maitre d's disappearance had been covered up well by Slick Nick and by Agent Murray. There had not been a single word in any of the newspapers about the Maitre d's mutilated body. As far as Nick knew, the Vitale crime family did not know a thing. After all, hadn't Vincent come to see him a little over a week ago? And, he hadn't said anything strange, or made any weird comments, had he? "No," Slick Nick answered out loud to his inquisitive thoughts, even though he was the only person in the restaurant.

The building's lights had been dimmed, just as they were each night after the restaurant closed. Nick stood in the center of the restaurant and took one last look around. The place was nice, but he was going to enjoy that cool million in cash even more. For now, he was destined to operate the restaurant. Soon, all of this would be nothing more than a memory; he would have the cash . . . and Jennifer. He would have it all, just like he always should have had. "Yeah," he commented out loud as he looked down at his black tuxedo, "Maybe I'll trade this in for a handmade, silk, flowered shirt when we reach paradise." He laughed at himself. He felt good. Nick had snorted a monster line of cocaine not even a half-an-hour before, and his brain was still buzzing.

Slick Nick twirled a round brass key ring around his index finger as he walked towards the restaurant's front door. His fingers were bent at the knuckles, and the single key on the ring barely cleared them with every brisk whirl. He continued to twirl the key until he opened one of the double glass doors and stepped through. He inserted the key into the door's deadbolt, turned it, and then listened for the click to confirm that the doors were locked. He smiled. It was another day gone and one day closer to his goal.

Slick Nick slowly walked towards his Mercedes, noticing that several cars were still parked in the restaurant's lot. Many patrons routinely left their automobiles parked in that lot overnight, so that in itself was not unusual. Some patrons had too much to drink; some continued to party and choose to car-pool, and some had gotten lucky at the restaurant's small and elegant bar. So, it was not uncommon to see the two Lincoln Continentals parked near his car.

Nick thrust his right hand into his trouser pocket and fished for the Mercedes' keys. Seconds later, while attempting to position it right side up, the key reflected the parking lot's lamp light. One of the two men seated in the Lincoln parked closest to Nick's Mercedes saw the key's reflection. The bright lights had been used to the men's advantage when they had parked beneath them earlier that night. Rather than illuminating the interior of the automobile, the glaring lights shown down upon the Lincoln's roof and cast a dark shadow inside the car, which made the men nearly invisible. The sparkle from the car key woke the driver's sluggish senses and he immediately swung his right hand in the direction of the passenger's seat. His un-aimed swing found the second man's rib cage.

"Come to life . . . it looks like our boy is on his way out." The driver said.

The second man did not say anything, but the rustling sound of his clothing rubbing against the Lincoln's leather seats alerted the driver that his partner had reacted. Like a pair of jaguars stealthily awaiting their prey, the two men patiently waited, shrouded by the cloak of darkness the Lincoln provided. They knew that it was only a matter of time. So did Capo Pelligi, who was calmly observing from the other Lincoln Continental parked nearby.

From his vantage point, the Capo was of the opinion that Slick Nick did not stand a chance in hell of escaping with his life. As the Capo knew, staging hits can be precariously dangerous, and he recalled having been overly dependant upon circumstances and chances that one could not possibly control. Now, as the Capo looked on, he could not help but admire the ingenuity of the new generation of shooters. Slick Nick definitely had problems; big problems.

When Slick Nick got within ten feet of his automobile, the man seated on the passenger's side of the Lincoln opened his door. He had already placed a small piece of electrical tape over the door's courtesy light switch that prevented the Lincoln's interior lights from illuminating when the door opened. The man silently slid out of the car with cat-like practiced movements while gently pushing the heavy metal door closed. The click of the latch was barely audible. Slick Nick had not heard a sound. The man crouched as he made his way toward the front of the Lincoln, his stocky body hidden behind the fender. The man patiently waited in the crouched position while he counted-off seconds to himself. He knew from experience that if he allowed his target one-second-per-step, the timing would be such that he would catch the restaurateur while he was concentrating on unlocking the automobile's door. The man seated behind the steering wheel utilized this technique also. Although the two men were silently counting-off the seconds to themselves, they were in perfect synchronization. Practice makes perfect, and these two men had operated as a team many times before. ONE THOUSAND ONE; ONE THOUSAND TWO; ONE THOUSAND THREE; ONE THOUSAND FOUR . . . the count-off continued until they simultaneously reached ONE THOUSAND TEN. It did not matter how many times the two had worked together, at least when it came to the adrenaline rush. Each hit had been an adrenaline rush, and this job was no different. The man who was crouched beside the front fender reached into the right pocket of his windbreaker and gingerly placed his hand on a 200,000 volt stun gun. The use of a stun gun was a technique that the Capo had admiringly referred to as, "new generation ingenuity." The man's right hand easily found the molded finger grips on the non-lethal devise, and he grasped it firmly in his hand.

The stun gun is based upon electronic pulse technology. The relatively small device emits an electrical shock that renders the recipient powerless, usually in the neighborhood of 90,000 volts. The shooters, however, had a pair of Z-Force Stun Guns capable of delivering a shocking 200,000 volts—a delivery equivalent to that of a well-placed, pissed-off, mule-kick that *WILL* bring down the biggest man on the planet Earth. What made this new generation technology so fascinating to the Capo was the fact that all of this could be accomplished without leaving a mark on the target. In the old days, he would have had to smack the living hell out of someone with a blackjack to achieve the same affect. With the stun guns, however, only their nervous system was affected. In essence, the shooters hit hard from the inside out.

The shooter crept around the front of the Lincoln, his body hugging the chrome bumper and grill. The driver watched the front-quarter panel, fully aware of his partner's movements, even though he was unable to see him. At the same moment, Slick Nick was somewhat hunched over attempting to get the key into the car's lock. He had his back toward the Lincoln Continental.

Suddenly, the driver's eyes registered a blurring movement that quickly swept across his field of vision from right to left. It was his partner making his move. The man moved with the speed and stealth of a wild cat in the jungle—one foot ahead of the other; swift movements only on the balls of his feet. The driver instinctively placed his right thumb and forefinger on the automobile's ignition key. He was ready and waiting for the moment when he would turn that key.

The unforeseen approach was over before Nick could have possibly done anything to prevent it. The attacker withdrew the stun gun from his windbreaker pocket. His thumb lightly rested on the stun gun's side-mounted trigger button, but his hand clutched the device with a death-like grip. His arm was bent at the elbow, forming a ninety degree angle. The stun gun was positioned with the two prongs facing forward and angling slightly inward, similar to a snake's fangs. The shooter carefully positioned the device at eye level, then, after only a split second, placed the metal fangs against the back of Slick Nick's neck. The very instant that the prongs made contact with Nick's flesh, the shooter depressed the stun gun's trigger. With the unexpected suddenness of a lightning flash, 200,000 volts of electricity discharged directly into the restaurateur's neck. Nick bolted upright, his fists tightly clenched while he grasped the door key with an involuntary, deathlike grip. The shock had not killed Slick Nick, but one could not tell by appearance only. His knees had buckled from underneath him and his face had taken on a glazed, wide-eyed stare that accentuated the fear and surprise he felt. One second was all it took; but that one second spent with 200,000 volts running through his body must have seemed like an eternity.

Slick Nick's frazzled nervous system temporarily shut down, and he crumpled onto the asphalt parking lot like a limp dishrag. The shooter carefully guided his fall, careful not to let the restaurateur hit his head and spill any blood. These men were professionals and they were not about to leave any clues at the scene of the abduction.

Even before Slick Nick's body had gone limp from the electric shock, the Lincoln Continental's motor turned over. With split second timing, the driver threw the gears into drive. The four-door sedan leapt forward and screeched to an abrupt halt directly next to the restaurateur's limp body. The shooter grabbed the left-rear passenger's door handle and swung it open while his other hand supported Slick Nick's dishrag-like body. Simultaneously, the driver slammed the transmission into park while his left hand pulled hard on the door handle. He leaned his weight on the door and flung it open. Less than a second later, the driver was out of the vehicle and standing beside his partner. Neither man spoke. They knew from experience what had to be done. Each of the men grabbed Nick by an arm then carefully guided his limp body onto the Lincoln's back seat. Nick was just beginning to stir, yet his senses remained pretty much lethargic. He posed no physical threat, but the men could not risk the possibility of him screaming for help. There had been no question in the men's mind as to what body part to tape first. Quickly, the shooter followed the restaurateur's body through the Lincoln's rear door while his partner closed the car door behind him. Slick Nick was lying prone on the back seat with the shooter on top of him. Meanwhile, the driver hurriedly slid behind the steering wheel. His movements were orderly and methodical as his left hand pulled the door closed and his right dropped the gear selector into drive. The driver heard the distinct sound of duct tape being torn as he punched the accelerator. The rapid acceleration caused the shooter in the rear of the car to lose his balance, yet he was still able to find his mark with the duct tape. His fingers firmly grasped a four-inch piece of duct tape that was stretched taut as he placed it over Slick Nick's mouth. The restaurateur grunted in protest but his noises were to no avail; already the shooter had begun tightly wrapping Nick's wrists together with a three-foot length of the tape. Nick squirmed and wriggled, but his writhing movements were in vain. The shooter had heard many a tough guy beg, so Nick's muffled squeals did absolutely nothing. Instead, the shooter reached up and whacked him hard on the back of the head. The slap momentarily sedated Slick Nick, but it had been more out of fear than physical pain. The shooter took advantage of the restaurateur's listless movement by rapidly taping his ankles together. The coup de grace was a double strength length of tape that connected his ankles with the wrists, rendering Slick Nick completely immobile. The shooter leaned up and admired his handiwork—the Vitale crime family's snitch looked like a trussed chicken. Suddenly a pair of headlights flashed across the shooter's face from the rear of the vehicle. Instinctively, the professional checked them and confirmed to the driver, "Capo Pelligi is right behind us."

"Good," the driver replied.

Slick Nick had heard them and began squirming and wriggling. Once he had heard the Capo's name, the restaurateur understood what was going down.

The driver pulled out of the restaurant's parking lot onto the busy, four-lane highway and Capo Pelligi followed, clinging to the rear bumper as the two identical Lincoln Continentals headed west along the roadway.

Inside the first luxury automobile, Nick's body was beginning to ache from the uncomfortable position he was trussed-up in, and there was a dull, steady pain in his rib cage where the barrel of his .38 caliber revolver had wedged itself between two of his chest's arched bones. The restaurateur's eyes were wide-open and bulging from fear. The shooter's hand pressed against Nick's head and prevented him from lifting it, as if he could have. Even so, by the frequency of the street lights they passed, he was able to discern that the automobile was traveling west. They were headed away from the beach . . . away from civilization. If Slick Nick had been in a position to raise his head high enough to see the roadway, he would have recognized the area. This was the same route that he had driven during that early morning when he had murdered the Maitre d'. This time, unfortunately for Slick Nick, it was he who was being taken for a ride.

The Capo had positioned his Lincoln directly behind the kidnap vehicle so that his vehicle would serve as a buffer between any unnecessarily curious persons, particularly if those persons happened to be in pursuit of the lead Lincoln. After what that snitching prick had put him through with the million dollars at the airport, he would not have missed this moment for anything.

The two Lincolns traveled west until they reached Highway 441 then turned north. There were fewer street lights the farther north they drove. After a seemingly lengthy period of time, the lead vehicle switched on its left turn signal, then turned west onto Highway 27. The Capo followed. The rural roadway was completely void of street lights. After they had made that turn, there was not doubt in Slick Nick's mind where the men were taking him.

The headlights of the Lincoln in the lead illuminated the dark roadway, its dual beams on high. Tall stalks of sugar cane flanked the two-lane highway, and a green sign with white reflectors read *BELLE GLADE 6*. A couple of days earlier the shooters had carefully scoped out a sugar cane field that would suit their purpose, and the driver had taken his navigational bearing from that same mileage sign.

Instinctively, the driver reset the Lincoln's odometer as the vehicle passed the road sign. When they traveled two-point-three miles farther, the driver braked hard then turned left. The pitching and bucking of the Lincoln's chassis confirmed that they were indeed on the pothole-filled dirt road they had previously chosen.

Slick Nick had begun whimpering during those last few miles, but soon his weak whining sounds changed to audible grunts when the Lincoln hit the dirt road. The restaurateur's pistol barrel was painfully jabbing him in the ribs with each and every bump.

Capo Pelligi's Lincoln bounced and bucked just as much as the one in front of him. His headlights alternated between shining down on dark, rich, fertile dirt and scanning the bushy, tall, sugarcane stalks. Nevertheless, he remained right on their taillights.

They continued along the dirt road for a half mile until suddenly, the lead Lincoln's brake lights shown bright in the Capo's eyes. The Capo also braked.

By the time the Capo got out of his car and walked over to the lead car, the shooters had already removed Slick Nick. They had placed him on his knees beside the sugar cane, his wrists and ankles still bound to one another with duct tape. Slick Nick's eyes widened, and what little color had remained in his face immediately drained at the sight of the Capo. The fireplug-built Italian walked in front of Nick in an affectedly self-important manner and stopped. The shooters stood on either side of Slick Nick, each supporting him by an elbow. The Capo glanced from side-to-side, making eye contact with each of his soldiers before he calmly addressed Slick Nick.

"You're a real piece of shit, Slick. Do you know that?" the Capo said as he leaned over Nick.

Nick's eyes were lowered when he let out a muted grunt.

Capo Pelligi's hand moved as fast as lightning, as he grasped Slick Nick by the hair. The Capo snapped Nick's head back while viciously ripping the duct tape from his mouth. "You were pretty cocksure of yourself, weren't you?" Capo Pelligi screamed into Nick's face. Slick Nick began mumbling unintelligibly, but that did not deter the Capo from verbally laying into him. Capo Pelligi reminded Nick, "Save your tears, you no good lying cock sucker. You cost the family at least one million dollars . . . and there is no telling how much information you gave them." The Capo paused for a few seconds to regain his composure; he was getting wound up. Slick Nick mumbled something in his defense, but this act of innocence only served to infuriate the Capo even more He was enraged. Capo Pelligi's free hand swung hard from Nick's blind side and slapped him hard on the cheek. "Shut-up!" he exclaimed. Suddenly, the Capo's voice lowered and his demeanor appeared calm. Capo Pelligi spoke softly, "Slick Nick, you have been unmasked . . . you turned informer on the family . . . and now you will pay." The Capo released Nick's hair, and then addressed the two shooters. "Give me five minutes to get out of the area before you give this piece of shit a Colombian necktie."

* * *

Late the following afternoon Agent Mark Murray sat at his desk while he methodically worked his way through a stack of backlogged paperwork. He hated paperwork, and his procrastination to do it served as evidence of his strong dislike. As a matter of fact, he hated the office in general.

His third floor office was cramped, and the furnishings fell somewhere in between old and antique. Nevertheless, it had never bothered him before. "What the hell?" he had always quipped to his cohorts, "I'm never here anyway," he would add, and, at the time that had pretty much been the case. Agent Murray spent as little time as possible in the office.

The past week had been a different story. Spirits had been jubilant. After all, it was not every week that an operation netted the Organized Crime Task Force one million dollars in cash. Overnight, Agent Murray had become a living legend around the Broward Boulevard headquarters of the Organized Crime Task Force. Not bad for someone who had rarely been seen in the office.

Agent Murray had even received a number of congratulatory phone calls, which the switchboard operator had found particularly amusing. She had been conditioned to say, "Agent Murray is not in the office at this time. May I take a message, please?" And, she had caught herself saying it a few times during the first part of the week, even though Murray had been in his office. Now, she had it down to a science by simply put the calls directly through to his extension. It was for that reason that Agent Murray was caught off guard when the phone on his desk rang.

"Agent Murray," he answered the telephone with the handset cradled against his right ear.

"Detective Polk here . . . Earnest Polk with the Palm Beach County Sheriff's Department."

The name had not registered with Agent Murray right away, but the reference to the Sheriff's Department sparked his memory banks. Now that Agent Murray had placed the voice, his mind quickly matched a face to go with it. When Agent Murray responded, he visualized the heavyset man as he remembered him, dressed in an ill-fitting, polyester suit.

"Detective Polk . . . what a pleasant surprise. What can I do for you?" the agent queried.

"Well, it's a good thing that my secretary hung on to your card. Otherwise, I'm not certain I'd remembered your name. Hell, I forgot the other feller's already . . . you know, your boss," the detective replied.

"Yes, sir," the agent patiently appeased him before he asked, again, "How may I help you?"

"I believe it's me that's gonna help you, partner," the detective chuckled.

The comment was unexpected, yet Murray played into him, "How so?"

"Hell's bells, you boys must be missing another one of them Mafiosos down there in Lauderdale . . . 'cause we found us another one, earlier this afternoon."

"What makes you think he was Mafia?" Agent Murray asked as he sat up in his chair and leaned his weight on his elbows.

"Well, you see, we don't get too many tuxedo-dressed corpses left around these parts. And another thing . . . this weren't no ordinary killing. Them boy's ain't to be fucked around with, if you get my drift. Why, they carved this feller's neck from one side to the other then pulled his tongue out through the slit. The damn thing was just hanging there like some sort of cheap-ass necktie! Imagine that."

"Columbian necktie . . ." Murray thought out loud.

"I beg your pardon."

"That's known as a Colombian necktie . . . and your assumption is more than likely correct. That's usually a signal from the bent-nose boys that they have caught a snitch in their organization. Sort of a message to others who might be considering the same thing," replied Agent Murray.

"Shit fire! Well, there was something else that I thought may interest you, seeing as you and your partner come all the way out here to see that other tuxedoed feller," the detective said.

"Yes?" Murray prodded him.

"We found us a .38 caliber revolver on the deceased's body, which, by the way was not too far from where we found that other feller's body. Now, my thinking is that maybe this is the weapon that shot that feller twice from point-blank range. Remember?"

That question was the understatement of the year. This had become the most important investigation of Agent Murray's career, for professional, as well as personal reasons. Hell yes he remembered! That phone call, and at that moment, was when the reality of the situation struck him, and a lump the size of a golf ball quickly formed in his throat.

Agent Mark Murray knew long before he drove out to Belle Glade and the Palm Beach County Coroner's Office that he was going to find Slick Nick there.

CHAPTER NINETEEN

S lick Nick's body had been found just after 1 p.m. by several migrant workers who had been laboring in a sugar cane field nearby. They discovered the body and phoned it in to the Palm Beach Sheriff's Department. The phone call pertaining to the gruesome discovery was immediately transferred to the Detective's Division, and Detective Polk's partner, Detective Jack Farmer, was the duty officer that fielded the call. He took down the pertinent information then called over his shoulder to his partner, "Polk, got another suit murdered in the fields . . . just outside of town." Detective Polk placed his flattened palms on top of his desk and pushed hard to raise himself from the seat. They had just returned from lunch, and Polk's massive stomach was quite full from the barbecued pork plate he had consumed.

They drove in Detective Polk's unmarked sedan to the site where the body had been discovered. Several workers were gathered near the site, but none of them had gotten close to the body since it had been reported. Once Detectives Polk and Farmer stood next to the body, it was obvious why. The body had been exposed to the blazing Florida sun for a half day, and the stench had become overwhelming. The two detectives could smell the decomposing corpse long before they saw it, causing Detective Farmer to gag several times, nearly vomiting. Fortunately he had regained his facial color and composure after just a few minutes while Detective Polk had been totally unaffected. Polk had even gone so far as to have cracked a couple of tasteless jokes about his partner's face being very close to the same color purple as Slick Nick's.

Slick Nick's body was a mess. The humidity and heat was torrid from the still breeze in the sugar cane fields. Consequently, Slick Nick's body was quite bloated by the time the detectives found it. The slit throat had allowed so much blood to escape his body that the corpse had turned a mauve shade of purple, and, as Detective Farmer could testify to, the smell had been rancid.

Detective Polk surveyed the murder scene for nearly an hour before he called in Dr. Kramer, the coroner for Palm Beach County. The short, elderly gentleman arrived on the scene within the half-hour, dressed in his usual lime-green surgical garb. The coroner took one look at the puffed-up corpse then bee-lined it back to his hearse. Within minutes he returned with a black, plastic body bag, its reinforced zipper running six feet in length, ample enough to handle Slick Nick's height.

It took the combined efforts of both of the detectives and the coroner to load the swollen corpse into the body bag, during which there had been a few minutes when the other two had questioned whether or not Detective Farmer was going to make it. It was quite apparent to them that he did not find the task enjoyable. Nevertheless he had held up his end, and Nick's body was placed in the rear compartment of the county's hearse.

Up until that point no one outside the group at the murder scene had been privy to the knowledge of what had happened out there in the sugar cane field. That exclusivity was short-lived. As with all government agencies, there had been a small mountain of paperwork to be filled out, particularly because of the nature of their find. Murders are high profile, whether they happen in the city or the country.

The coroner had his share of paperwork, especially in light of the mandatory autopsy when a murder victim is found. The detectives would also have quite a stack to fill out themselves. Not only were they already swamped with their own share of the bureaucratic bullshit paperwork, but now they had to do something else that neither of them found pleasurable—they had to report the incident to their superior officer, "by the most expedient means available to the officer in the field." Detective Polk still recalled his instructor interpolating the meaning of that sentence when he had told the academy's graduating class, "For those of you who don't know what the word 'expedient' means, just put the news out over the Motorola;" his terminology for the police-band radios found in all of the department's vehicles.

When one is surrounded by thousands of acres of nothing but sugar cane, the most expedient means is the Motorola. The detectives broadcast the news of what had taken place over the unmarked sedan's police band radio, and their superiors received the transmission at the Sheriff's Department's headquarters building located in Palm Beach. However, they had not been the only one monitoring that particular frequency.

* * *

Ft. Lauderdale's premier newspaper is the *Sun Sentinel*, and its offices are located along the New River; a mainstream waterway that flows through the center of Ft. Lauderdale's high-rise business district.

Inside that multi-story office building are many different divisions, all cooperatively working towards the same goal—to produce a daily newspaper that is both interesting and informative. Like all daily newspapers, the *Sun Sentinel* is filled with ninety-percent bad news, ten-percent good news. Unfortunately, that formula is what sells newspapers. It is as if people revel in the misfortune of others. Perhaps it is their only means to bolster their own morale. Nevertheless, business is business, and that formula has sold newspapers since the conception of the publishing industry.

One of the divisions of the *Sun Sentinel* does nothing but monitor the police band radios in hopes of picking up a breaking story. Ms. Phyllis Lloyd, a ravishing beauty in her early forties, was the investigative reporter who headed up that department. She was renowned as being an outstanding investigator and interviewer within an industry widely known as being cutthroat. Ms. Lloyd had worked her way up through the newspaper's different departments— advertisements; feature articles; useful information; editorials; and finally, where she had found her niche; recent news. Ms. Phyllis, as she was called around her office, had an uncanny knack for sniffing out headline-making stories. Perhaps it was due in part to her alluring appearance, but somehow, Ms. Lloyd had earned her reputation by her ability to extract some juicy tidbit of information from the person she was interviewing.

That afternoon, the police channels had been broadcasting the usual expected radio transmission such as traffic accidents and home burglaries, but nothing near the sort of thing that Ms. Phyllis could have sunk her investigative teeth into. That was until the communiqué between the detectives and their superior had been intercepted by the *Sun Sentinel*'s monitoring room. Within minutes after that conversation had been intercepted, Ms. Phyllis Lloyd listened to a tape recording of the conversation. She had a nervous habit of tapping a pencil on her thigh while her analytical mind carefully broke up the whole of the conversation into its parts to find out their nature. In this instance, the investigative reporter had focused on the words, "murder victim dressed in a black tuxedo . . ." Without realizing it, she had begun furiously tapping away with the pencil against her right thigh while she listened. The tape had her undivided attention, and eventually she looked down and realized that she had slid into her unconscious habit. She had recently made a concerted effort to cease the tapping altogether, but at least she had stopped the annoying habit of repeatedly banging her pencil on the desk. Her thigh was silent, much to the joy of her co-workers. That unruly habit had never failed to subconsciously scrutinize a potential story and had sniffed out many a headline maker. She had learned to trust her intuition. Seeing that pencil had confirmed it—there was a story to be told in the Belle Glade murder.

Ms. Phyllis ran her hunch by her editor, and he gave her his blessing. "Go for it," he said. The editor knew from experience that if anyone was able to find a story there, she could. He recalled that she had worked closely with the Palm

Beach County Coroner on other stories in the past, and had maintained a good working relationship with him.

It was late in the afternoon when Ms. Phyllis departed her downtown Ft. Lauderdale office and set out for Belle Glade.

The rush hour traffic was thick along Interstate 95. Ms. Phyllis did not mind because it gave her ample time to think and to call the coroner who had already agreed to meet with her. By the time she reached the exit for Highway 27, Ms. Phyllis had already prepared several intriguing questions for the coroner; one of which dealt with any and all connections that this tuxedo-clad corpse might have had with the last and only other tuxedo-clad corpse they had found.

Agent Mark Murray had departed Ft. Lauderdale an hour prior to Ms. Phyllis and fortunately had found Highway 441 free from traffic, so he drove that route. He also utilized the travel time to think about the possibilities, and there had been a lot for him to ponder. The Vitale crime family investigation had turned into the largest investigation the task force had ever undertaken, and it had been spearheaded by Agent Murray and his very informative snitch. Slick Nick's information had opened opportunities that investigators dreamed of, and that dream was very close to becoming a reality. Or was it? The question burnt in Mark's mind. During the drive to Belle Glade, out of frustration, he slammed the steering wheel several times with his hand. The agent knew that his investigation would go to shit if that was Slick Nick's body lying on the morgue's marble table. Up until this point, everything had been perfect. One by one, he had planned to take them all down, but without Slick Nick's testimony that would not be possible. Then he feared the worst. Without his informant's guidance, he may not be able to successfully build a case against his number one target, Vincent Panachi. Agent Murray slammed the steering wheel, again. "Fuck!" he exclaimed. He was obsessed with the idea of ruining Vincent; so much so that he could not see that it was distorting his own quality of life. Between the undying torch that he carried for Jennifer Swords and his obsession with getting Vincent Panachi, the man had really gone mad. As if those monomaniacal thoughts had not been enough while Agent Murray drove towards the Palm Beach County Coroner's office, he also had to deal with the added pleasure of the horrible conclusion that Slick Nick was dead. For some strange reason, he had known it was him. He felt it . . . long before he saw him. That premonition had remained foremost in Agent Murray's thoughts during the remainder of the drive and it added to his unsound mind.

Dusk had fallen over the township of Belle Glade by the time Ms. Phyllis Lloyd reached the coroner's office. She had been there before and recognized the bland, unmarked sedans driven by the detectives. There was also a late model Volvo parked in the lot; Dr. Kramer's, she presumed. A fourth automobile, a Ford Crown Victoria, was parked diagonally across a bright yellow space marker, positioned in such a way that it took up two parking spaces. The sedan gave the appearance of someone who had parked in a hurry. Actually, properly parking the vehicle had been the last thing on Agent Murray's mind when he had whipped it into the lot, a half-hour earlier. Ms. Lloyd parked her car two spaces over, next to his.

When she entered the building, Dr. Kramer and Mark Murray were standing in the lobby talking. Dr. Kramer's face immediately lit up at the sight of the attractive woman. He knew that he was too old for her, yet it never hurt to dream. He always considered her to be extremely attractive. She had that look; the type of stunning beauty that everyone took notice of whenever she entered a room. Although she was past forty, Ms. Phyllis Lloyd was very well preserved. There was no doubt that she still possessed that special magic gorgeous women seem to have. The coroner felt it before just as he felt it now. Mark also found her alluring beauty quite mesmerizing.

The coroner smiled as he extended his hand to Ms. Lloyd. Her movements were graceful as she accepted his right hand with both of hers, her right lightly clasped in the traditional handshake fashion while her left covered his. She mirrored his smile as their eyes held a momentary stare.

"It's good to see you, again, Ms. Lloyd," Dr. Kramer said as he broke the gaze.

"And you, too," she replied. The two were still posed in their greeting handshake as she continued, "Just look at you . . . why, you look wonderful."

Dr. Kramer felt his face flush, and although he couldn't see it, he was absolutely certain that his cheeks were glowing red. He realized that it had been many years since he had looked wonderful, but regardless of whether he had looked it or not, she certainly made him feel that he did.

"You're sweet," he responded, "I see you haven't lost that touch," They both giggled like teenagers as she gently slid her hands away from his.

Ms. Lloyd held her smile.

"Thank you." After a few seconds she added, "Aren't you going to introduce me to this handsome gentleman?"

Dr. Kramer had momentarily been lost in his thoughts, but the question quickly returned his mental presence. He motioned toward the man standing beside him.

"Ms. Phyllis Lloyd, say, 'Hello' to Mr. Mark Murray."

The agent extended his right hand to shake and corrected the doctor.

"Mark, please."

She accepted his offered hand.

"Phyllis . . . nice to meet you."

"Likewise," Mark replied.

"Mark, is an agent for the Organized Crime Task Force, and," the coroner added as he turned toward Agent Murray, "Ms. Lloyd is an investigative reporter for Ft. Lauderdale's *Sun Sentinel* newspaper."

They looked at one another and simultaneously commented, "How interesting." That broke the ice, and they burst out laughing at themselves.

"So, what brings you out here to the big city?" Mark queried.

"The tuxedo murder, of course," she replied flashing him her irresistible smile.

It was that type of provocative, presumptuous statement that had earned Ms. Lloyd the reputation of an outstanding interviewer. Her investigative mind had already put together the mysteriously clad body with the presence of the handsome gentleman from the Organized Crime Task Force. As a matter of fact, she recalled the automobile outside that had been hastily parked. There was no doubt in her mind that there was a story hidden here, and she intended to find it.

The statement caught Agent Murray off guard. Up until this point he had managed to keep an airtight seal on the investigation of the Vitale crime family. Now, standing before him was the God damn newspaper. His mind whirled as he searched for the proper response, but so much had happened so quickly there just really was not one. Just as soon as he had seen Slick Nick laid out on that marble slab, he knew it was over. He had lost his star, and only, witness. Now, the investigation was in shambles. But wait . . . perhaps fate had dealt him a loaded hand. The newspaper; Vincent Panachi; the crime family's dealings in South Florida; the execution of Slick Nick, his confidential informant. Yes, he assured himself. "Perhaps your being here is a blessing in disguise." Mark said to Ms. Lloyd.

"I beg your pardon?" she replied.

Agent Murray took her by the elbow and led her to a small sofa against the wall. Along the way he said, "Let me tell you a most interesting story."

"Yes, please do," Ms. Lloyd flashed him an alluring smile, "I would like that very much."

The two talked for nearly an hour while Mark outlined the entire investigation from beginning to end, during which Ms. Lloyd scribbled notes at a furious pace. She had driven out to Belle Glade in hopes of uncovering a story, but what she had discovered had all the potential of becoming a headline maker.

Dr. Kramer had not begun the autopsy and the body was still in its original condition with its tongue grossly protruding from the slit throat. Nevertheless, the seasoned reporter insisted that she wanted to see the tuxedo clad corpse, and now that it had been officially identified by Agent Mark Murray as Slick Nick, the coroner had removed the John Doe tag from its right big toe. The murder victim now had a name for the newspaper.

Dr. Kramer escorted Ms. Lloyd back to the lab. She slipped her arm through his as they walked down the corridor that led to the rear of the building while Mark trailed behind. Once they reached the doorway, the coroner abruptly stopped. He turned to the beautiful woman, a serious look on his face, and asked, "Are you certain that you want to do this? I mean . . . well, it's pretty gruesome."

Ms. Lloyd squeezed his arm in a feign attempt to show that she was totally comfortable with viewing the murder victim. In reality, she was scared shitless.

Writing about it and actually living it are two vastly different worlds. But, if she was going to write a feature story filled with morbid details about the gangland-style killing, then she needed to feel that initial shock.

"Yes, I'm certain . . . I'll be all right," she said with an air of confidence.

"She'll be okay, Dr. Kramer," Mark added. "Just open the door so we can get this over with."

The coroner did just that, and the three of them entered the chilly laboratory. Once again, Ms. Lloyd clung to the doctor's arm and held onto it until he reached out to pull back the sheet that covered Slick Nick's grotesque corpse. Suddenly, Ms. Lloyd involuntarily let out a bloodcurdling scream. She turned, as if to run away, but her legs had already gone limp. Phyllis fell directly into Mark's arms.

Mark caught the beautiful woman's fall just before she hit the floor. He supported her weight in his arms, and her head rested against his chest. He looked down at her and noticed the beads of perspiration that had formed across her forehead. Her eyelids were closed and her breathing labored, but he knew that she would be all right. Instinctively, he stroked her beautiful hair and assured her, "You'll be okay in a few minutes, just take deep breaths." She merely moaned.

The initial shock had been something she had never felt before and she had fainted. However, the human mind can react with little or no conscious perception on the part of the individual. In spite of the fact that she had fainted, Ms. Lloyd's subconscious mental activity still mainstreamed, "Feature story . . . feature story," over and over like a distant voice calling from within her mind. She was unconscious for less than five seconds, yet it seemed like five hours to her. Ms. Lloyd slowly opened her eyes and oriented herself, then looked up. Her eyes met with Mark's concerned look. Suddenly, a smile formed across her face and she assured him, "I'm fine . . . thank you."

His stare relaxed and his expression changed to one of relief. He returned the smile and said, "I'm glad. I was worried about you for a couple of seconds . . . you're certain that you're all right?"

Her arms reached up to his while he held her at the elbows.

"Yes . . . yes, thank you, again."

Ms. Lloyd took a few minutes to reflect upon her thoughts and now that she had regained her composure, she was certain that the "Tuxedo Murders," were going to make one hell of a feature story. It was quite evident to her though that she should refrain from disclosing some of the particularly gruesome details.

Phyllis spent another hour at the coroner's office, but did not venture to the rear of the building or the laboratory. Most definitely, the one look had been quite enough. The experience left her with a good feeling that she had made a friend, as well as a valuable contact, within the Organized Crime Task Force. In retrospect, it was only a matter of time before that definitive description changed from "valuable" to "invaluable."

After bidding the gentlemen farewell, Ms. Phyllis Lloyd got into her car and left Belle Glade via Highway 27. She was a mile away, perhaps two, before the cellular telephone came on-line, the green light on the handset replacing the red, no-service light. Her right hand ripped it from its cradle a split-second after her long, acrylic fingernails had tapped out the telephone number for her editor's private line. Immediately, she pushed the send button with her thumbnail then placed the mobile phone's handset against her ear. Seconds later she said in an excited, almost breathless voice, "Smitty, don't talk . . . just listen. Hold the right hand column on tomorrow's front page, and hook me into the Dictaphone. I'm going to dictate the morning's headline feature story . . ."

By 3 a.m. the first paper was off the press. An interoffice courier ran the armful of papers he was carrying throughout the multi-story headquarters for the *Sun Sentinel*. As per the instructions he had received earlier that evening, the courier delivered several copies to the offices of Ms. Lloyd and her editor.

Ms. Lloyd had passed the stage of feeling exhausted hours before, and was staying awake by pumping herself full of strong, black coffee. Once her feature story had been transcribed and the editor had read it, Smitty had shown as much enthusiasm towards the story as his investigative reporter when she had phoned it in. Consequently, he had placed the feature story on the front page of the morning's paper.

Now, Ms. Phyllis Lloyd picked up the copy that had been casually tossed onto her desk by her editor. She looked up and met his stare. He was smiling while he held a copy in his hand. "Pretty good work, kid-o," he complimented her.

"Thank you," she replied. The investigative reporter looked down at the paper and read the bold printed headlines:

NORTHEAST CRIME FAMILY HAS SOUTH FLORIDA STRONGHOLD

CHAPTER TWENTY

F t. Lauderdale plays host to many of the world's rich and famous, so the *Sun Sentinel* is also distributed nationally and internationally, mostly by prepaid subscription. The newspaper's publisher had worked out a deal with Federal Express so that they would pick up parcels of newspapers as they rolled off the press in the early morning hours. It was an equitable arrangement that allowed the overnight carrier guaranteed freight while the newspaper received overnight delivery to faraway destinations. Consequently, the *Sun Sentinel*'s on time subscription delivery track record rivaled that of the *Wall Street Journal*.

That morning deliveries were made on schedule to two pertinent destinations: Newark, New Jersey and Nassau, Bahamas.

* * *

NASSAU, NEW PROVIDENCE, BAHAMAS . . . 9:15 A.M.

Vincent was taking an early morning stroll along the Crystal Palace Resort and Casino's lagoon-like swimming pool. The ten days he and Jennifer had spent at the hotel had relaxed him beyond belief, so much so that he now considered 9:15 a.m. to be early morning. There was no doubt in his mind that he could easily adjust to this lifestyle. The days and nights had been pleasurable. He had found his Eden. The only connection that he had maintained with the real world had been through the hotel's very small combination newsstand and gift shop which received foreign newspapers on a daily basis. The *Wall Street Journal* and the *Sun Sentinel* were two of the foreign papers it sold.

Vincent continued his slow-paced walk around the pool until he reached the concrete walkway that serpentined its way through a flora-lined path and led back to the hotel's lobby entrance. When he reached the glass door, he opened it and was immediately surrounded by a burst of cold air as it rushed through the opening and clashed with the morning's tropical heat. An automatic door closer hissed while it prevented the metal-framed pane of glass from slamming shut. The carpeted corridor led him past a bank of six public telephones, but they held no interest for Vincent. Actually, he had not placed a call to the states in well over a week, and as Vincent walked past the telephones he recalled that the last had been when he had spoken with the Consiglio the morning after their arrival in Nassau.

The hotel's combination newsstand and gift shop was located between the bank of public telephones and the elevators—a well thought out store front location because the hotel guests must walk past the small shop either on their way to the public telephones or the swimming pool area. One way or the other, most guests ended up purchasing something during their stay at the luxurious hotel. There were always a few diehard budget travelers that resisted the temptation to enter the store, but on the other hand, that loss of revenue had always been made up by opulent guests such as Vincent Panachi. Vincent had purchased a morning newspaper from the small shop every day since their arrival, and while doing so, had picked out a number of small trinkets for Jennifer. If one refers to a pair of four hundred and eighty-five dollar, 18K gold, starfish earrings as a trinket, well . . . what can be said? Vincent had showered Jennifer with surprise gifts on a daily basis, all purchased during the pursuit of the morning paper.

Vincent pulled the shop's glass door open and entered. The young woman seated behind the cash register flashed him a radiant smile, the whiteness of her perfect teeth sharply contrasting against her ebony skin.

"Good morning, Mr. Panachi," she greeted him.

"And good morning to you, young lady," he replied through a smile. "Are the stateside newspapers in yet?"

"Yeah, and there has been a run on them this morning," the woman remarked as she slid off the padded stool. She bent over and retrieved a copy from underneath the cash register while Vincent watched, then handed him the newspaper. It was the same stateside newspaper that he had purchased every morning, Ft. Lauderdale's *Sun Sentinel*. "I saved you one before they all sold out," the clerk said.

"Thank you, sweetheart," Vincent replied as he smiled and winked at the young Bahamian beauty. He folded the newspaper and stuck it underneath his right arm. "Get anything new in since yesterday?" he queried.

"Yes!" she gushed. She hurried from behind the counter and led Vincent by the arm towards the jewelry cabinet. Excitedly, she informed him, "You have just got to see these new earrings. They are so cool . . ."

Ten minutes and three hundred dollars later, Vincent walked out of the retail store, a small box neatly gift wrapped in colorful foil in his right hand and the newspaper folded underneath his arm. The elevators were a mere twenty feet away. The newspaper could wait until he got to the suite, and therefore, he kept it folded while he waited for a set of polished elevator doors to open. Seconds later the single ring of a bell announced the availability of an elevator car. Vincent stepped inside along with several other hotel guests. The elevator made five stops along the way to the hotel's top floor, where the suite was located. Once it arrived the bell announced his arrival with a now familiar ring, just as it had the previous stops. Vincent exited the elevator and turned right. Their suite was only footsteps away.

Once he was inside the suite he called out, "Are you almost ready?"

Jennifer had gotten up when he had left to get the paper. That had become her morning ritual, because it allowed her enough time to apply her make-up while Vincent was away. She had made a point of always looking fresh when he returned. Jennifer had fully applied her daytime make-up.

"Yes," she called back, then added, "I'm in the bedroom."

Vincent still had the foil covered box in his right hand and the newspaper underneath his arm when he entered the suite's bedroom. Jennifer was seated on the edge of the bed, casually dressed in a pair of neatly pressed cotton shorts with a matching blouse. Her hair was pulled back into a ponytail that gathered at the nape of her neck.

"Hi," he said, and smiled.

She looked at the smile on his face, but her peripheral vision could not help but notice the small, gift wrapped box that he was holding in his hand. She returned the smile.

"Hi," she replied while she silently pondered what was inside of the box. Knowing Vincent, it could have been anything. But, by gauging the size and shape of the box, she determined that it contained a pair of earrings. Another pair of earrings, as he had already given her several. In defense of his own generosity and free spending, Vincent had rationalized his behavior by reminding himself that the purchases had been made with found money. Since the casino management had generously offered to comp the expenses for his room and meals, it left him with a sizeable credit from the Beach Side Travel Agency's prepaid voucher that he had presented to the front desk clerk when they had checked-in. Six hundred dollars per night times fourteen nights. Paid in full. After all, it was only money. He leaned over and kissed Jennifer lightly on the cheek as he handed her the colorful foil wrapped box.

"For me?" she gushed.

"Of course. It's just a little trinket. Nothing big," Vincent replied. With that, he placed the folded newspaper on top of the bedspread then cupped her hands in his. "Go ahead. Open it," he instructed her.

Jennifer peeled away the wrapping paper and gently lifted the lid from the small box. Inside, sitting on top of a padding of cotton, were a pair of beautiful, solid 18K gold, conch shell shaped earrings. Jennifer drew in a deep breath as she lifted them from the cotton padding. "Oh Vincent, they are so beautiful!" she exclaimed. He had thought so, as well.

"Yes they are, and they will be much more beautiful on you. Try them on," he suggested.

Jennifer leaned over and kissed him before she stood up. "Okay," she called over her shoulder as she walked towards the bureau against the bedroom's far wall. Vincent watched as she sashayed across the room, her hips swinging in an ostentatious manner. He shook his head and smiled.

While Jennifer busied herself with her new earrings, Vincent grabbed the folded newspaper and slid toward the head of the bed. Two pillows were already stacked one on top of the other, and he gave them a couple of quick punches to fluff them up. Vincent nonchalantly kicked off his boat shoes and leaned back against the fluffy pillows. He could not have been more relaxed . . . until he unfolded the *Sun Sentinel*. Vincent's eyes quickly scanned the headlines, but what he read came as such a shock that it really did not register properly in his mind. He slowly re-read the dark, bold printed headline on the front page of the morning paper: *NORTHEAST CRIME FAMILY HAS SOUTH FLORIDA STRONGHOLD.* Vincent Panachi, a high ranking member of an organized crime family and who was renowned to be serene and composed, at all times, let out an audible gasp while he re-read the newspaper's heading.

Jennifer had already put the earrings on, and had turned around at the very same instant that Vincent gasped. She mistook the sound as an approval of the way the jewelry looked on her, and asked for more reassurance from Vincent. She stood at the foot of the king-sized bed and turned her head from side to side when she queried, "Don't they look wonderful on me?"

Vincent barely shifted his eyes from the article he was reading when he peered over the top of the outstretched newspaper. "Gorgeous," he complimented her, but even she could tell that his remark had been made halfheartedly. She thrust her bottom lip out in a dramatic expression of her disapproval at being ignored. Jennifer needed attention. At that moment, there was nothing short of setting herself on fire that she could have done to distract Vincent from reading the front page of the *Sun Sentinel*. Her childish ploy went unnoticed by Vincent. He was too enthralled in Ms. Phyllis Lloyd's feature article.

The article broke down the Vitale crime family into divisions before it further speculated on what criminal activities those particular divisions handled. Agent Mark Murray had not missed a trick when he had unsparingly given the investigative reporter a verbal review of the Organized Crime Task Force's entire file on the Vitale crime family investigation. Naturally, Vincent was named in the article as the family's South Florida representative. It even went so far as to speculate that Vincent answered directly to Anthony Vitale, the reputed head of the northeast-based crime family, and only to Anthony Vitale.

Vincent finished the article then went back and re-read a few of the hotter paragraphs; in particular, the paragraphs that dealt directly with the family's South Florida involvement. Ms. Lloyd had thrust the Belle Glade murders to the forefront of the feature article and had labeled them, "The Tuxedo Murders." That had helped with the favorable results of the article—favorable for the publisher—and had helped to launch the additional feature stories in editions yet to come. Ms. Lloyd had used the tuxedo murders as her vanguard by characterizing the violent murders as a particular trait of the Vitale crime family. While that may not have been true, it had served as a vehicle that sold a lot of newspapers, and that particular edition had sold out.

Jennifer was not going to compete with a newspaper for Vincent's attention and it was her intention to let him know. On her hands and knees she got on top of the king-sized bed then slowly crawled towards Vincent, who was still hidden behind the outstretched newspaper. Suddenly, she took the end of her lengthy ponytail and pulled it through her cupped hand until the end resembled a man's shaving brush then lightly swept it across the back of Vincent's hand. The newspaper made a rustling sound when he wrinkled the front section. When he instinctively looked in the direction from which he had felt the tickle, Jennifer's face was there, smiling at him, just inches away from where the newspaper had been.

"Can't that wait?" she queried as her eyes met his. Vincent smiled, then folded the paper and laid it on top of one of the pillows beside him.

"Well, I suppose," he joked.

Jennifer swung one leg over Vincent's mid-section then placed her hands on either side of his head, just above his shoulders. Slowly, she lowered herself on top of him as their lips met in a passionate, sensual kiss. Vincent wrapped his arms around her back as their tongues met one another's. Jennifer's eyes were closed, lost in the intense emotional excitement of the moment. Vincent's were, too . . . well, one was closed, anyway. The other was looking at his wrist watch. He could certainly afford to spend a little time with Jennifer, but not too long. He knew for certain that he must call the Consiglio at the emergency only number, very soon.

*   *   *

NEWARK, NEW JERSEY . . . 9:15 A.M.

The Consiglio was the sole passenger in the elongated, Cadillac limousine when it entered the palatial estate of Anthony Vitale. The chauffeur blew the horn twice before he sped past the mansion's sentry post. The two crime family soldiers posted on guard duty at the estate's huge, iron gates appeared less than happy with their assigned duties, and the Consiglio had noticed. No wonder; he had seen their warm, moist breath crystallize in the frigid, cold air. They, in turn, had witnessed the automobile's exhaust pipe spew a stream of cloud-like smoke that trailed the luxury vehicle while it wound its way along the curvy, cobblestone driveway. As soon as it was out of sight, one of the soldiers exclaimed to the other, "Let's close the fuckin' thing . . . I'm freezing my ass off!"

"Fuckin'-A, let's do it," his partner eagerly agreed.

By the time the two men had swung the heavy, iron gates closed, the Consiglio had already entered the mansion. Unfortunately, he did not bring good news with him. Carefully folded and tightly clasped in his gloved hands was a copy of that morning's *Sun Sentinel*.

The butler showed the Consiglio to the mansion's library where the head of the crime family was waiting. The butler announced the Consiglio through the library's closed door. One second later Anthony Vitale's voice called out, "Come in, please . . . come in."

"Thank you," the counselor said to the butler as he opened the heavy door and entered the room. The butler followed.

Anthony was seated on a leather-upholstered, reclining armchair, and a large, mahogany desk sat between him and the Consiglio. A roaring fire successfully warded off the cold with its blue and orange flames that licked the top of the marble fireplace. The Consiglio literally felt the winter's chill by merely looking through the library's twelve-foot high, Palladian windows. Outside, the sky was an obscure grey and the estate's grounds were covered with frost. The Consiglio slowly walked towards Anthony, but stopped when he reached the desk. He carefully laid the morning edition of the *Sun Sentinel* on top of the polished desk then systematically removed his gloves and coat and handed them to the butler. Anthony Vitale was an astute man. He knew that when the legal counsel had called earlier that morning that it meant trouble. The head of the crime family glanced past the Consiglio and dismissed the butler with a sweeping motion of his right hand. The servant complied by silently backing through the doorway, the Consiglio's overcoat and gloves draped across his outstretched arms. After the servant closed the library's solid mahogany door, Anthony queried, "Well, what has prompted this early morning visit?"

The Consiglio had represented the Vitale crime family for a great number of years and knew precisely how to handle the elderly gentleman. He swept the newspaper off the desk top and unfolded it so that the headlines faced up and could easily be read. The legal advisor did not answer right away, but instead walked towards Anthony with the newspaper in his hands. Anthony stood, but remained beside the reclining chair. When the counselor got within arm's reach, he handed the head of the crime family the copy of the *Sun Sentinel* and suggested, "Perhaps you should sit down while you read this. Take your time . . . read the entire article, then enlighten me as to what you would like done."

Anthony Vitale read the entire article then he depressed the button on the intercom and instructed the butler, "Find Capo Pelligi and get him here, right away."

By half past the hour, Capo Pelligi was seated beside the family's Consiglio.

Anthony Vitale's favorite chair was within good conversation range of the sofa where the Consiglio and Capo Pelligi were comfortably seated. The butler had thrown another log on the fire when he had shown the Capo in, and now, the fire was roaring. The seasoned oak crackled as blue and orange flames licked the fresh wood. Other than that, there was not a sound in the room.

Capo Pelligi was seated on the right end of the sofa, the one closest to the windows. His legs were crossed, right over left, and his right elbow rested on the sofa's armrest. The *Sun Sentinel* was outstretched as it had been for nearly ten minutes. The Capo was not a slow reader, it's just that he had re-read the entire feature article twice just to be certain he had gotten all there was to get out of it. It was not good, and he had been mentioned, by name, in the front page article more than once. Anthony Vitale was partially reclined, and the head of the crime family gently tapped his fingertips against the chair's overstuffed arms while he patiently waited for the Capo to finish the article. Capo Pelligi folded the newspaper and laid it beside him. Anthony looked over at him, as did the Consiglio.

"Well?" the head of the crime family queried.

"Don Vitale, we have never had anything like this happen before. I don't like it. I don't like it one bit. This Agent Mark Murray is on a rampage."

"This could very well be a personal vendetta this Agent Murray has launched, and its focal point appears to be aimed towards Vincent and our South Florida operations," the Consiglio interjected.

Anthony Vitale cranked the handle on the side of the chair and sat up straight while, at the same time, he swung it around so that he was facing the family's legal counsel. The head of the crime family stated, "Perhaps you have found the solution to the problem, counselor."

"What do you mean?" Capo Pelligi asked.

The Consiglio slid forward on the sofa until he was seated on the edge of the cushion, his upper-body weight supported by his elbows resting on his knees.

"If I read you correctly, Don Vitale, we should concentrate on this Agent Mark Murray," he answered.

"Precisely," Anthony said before quickly adding, "What do we know about this Agent Murray? Is there anything we can get on him to hold over his head? What reason, if any, would he have to go after Vincent? And, is this investigation really focused at my nephew, or is it the family he is after? Another thing, find out if he's on the take . . . and if not, could we put him on our payroll?"

"It could be possible to get the answers to those questions, but it is going to cost," the Consiglio countered.

"How much?" Capo Pelligi chimed in.

The Consiglio directed his answer towards the head of the crime family.

"It would probably be a safe guess to say somewhere in the neighborhood of fifty grand."

Anthony Vitale scratched his chin for a couple of seconds, as if he were deep in thought.

"What about the private investigator you used before? He seemed to be connected to someone in this investigation. Maybe that person would know something about this Agent Murray."

The Consiglio nodded his head while he agreed.

"My thoughts, precisely."

"What about Vincent? We haven't heard from him yet, have we?" Capo Pelligi queried.

"Not as yet, but not to worry. As soon as we are finished here, I'll man the emergency-only telephone. He'll be calling very soon, if he hasn't already tried," the Consiglio answered with a reassuring smile.

"I agree. Vincent is a smart one. He will know not to panic. He thinks levelheaded, just as his father did before him," Anthony chimed in smiling.

There were a few moments of silence in the library while all three men pondered the context of their meeting. Finally, Anthony slapped both palms down hard on top of the leather covered arms of the chair. The loud sound got the undivided attention of both men seated on the sofa, and they looked towards the head of the crime family. First, he ordered the Consiglio, "Take fifty thousand and get down to Florida as soon as you hear from Vincent. When he does call, tell him I want to speak with him tomorrow, in person, here at the mansion. And counselor, if we are lucky enough to get something from this fishing expedition, I want to know about it right away. I don't care if you must fly all night. Understood?"

"Yes, Don Vitale," he replied then added, "I'll leave right away."

The Consiglio stood at the same moment the Capo suggested, "I'll go with him to Florida."

Anthony calmly held up his hands, his palms facing outward toward Capo Pelligi, and said, "No. You stay here . . . you are much too hot to be showing your face around Ft. Lauderdale.

"Yes, Don Vitale," the Capo replied.

Anthony pushed himself up from his favorite chair.

"That concludes this morning's business, gentlemen." Again he reminded the Consiglio, "I want some answers, soon." The legal counsel nodded in acknowledgement.

Suddenly, as if it had been pre-planned, the library's solid mahogany door opened and the butler stood in the doorway. He said, "Your overcoat and gloves, sir. The limousine is waiting . . ."

*　　*　　*

FORT LAUDERDALE, FLORIDA . . . 9:15 A.M.

The weather in Ft. Lauderdale that morning was considerably different from that found in Newark. The sky was cloudless and azure in color. The Atlantic Ocean was calm and the color of a deep-blue, gem sapphire. From the Organized Crime Task Force's tenth story surveillance post, the sky and the sea became one when looking toward the horizon. The blended blues seemed to stretch to infinity.

Inside the penthouse condominium, Agent Mark Murray and four other agents for the task force were seated in the living room. The reflective film on the wall of the sliding glass doors prevented the blinding, morning sun from shining intensely into their eyes as they faced the east. Ten stories below, several boats passed alongside the condominium building while transiting the Intracoastal Waterway. Aside from that activity, the beach had already begun filling to capacity with veteran sun worshipers, their golden-bronzed tans serving as testimony to their dedication. Any other morning the guys would have had the surveillance cameras' powerful, telescopic lens trained on several of the bikini clad beauties, but not this particular one. Instead, each of the agents had his face buried in a copy of this morning's *Sun Sentinel*. Just about the only sound that was heard in the condo's living room was the rustling of the newspapers as the agents shifted in their seats or turned a page. Every few minutes one of the men would make a comment, and undoubtedly it was an obscene word or expression. At any rate, the agents of the task force were enjoying themselves, immensely. It was not as if they had made the big bust they had hoped for—not yet anyway—but, as they read the front page feature story, each of them imagined how that article was playing havoc within the Vitale crime family. To the agents it was all a game, and if that game had been tennis then the score would have been: ADVANTAGE—AGENTS. Or at least that would have been the way they would have scored it.

Ms. Phyllis Lloyd's portrayal of Agent Mark Murray had been exemplary, and probably had leaned more towards larger-than-life. Mark had taken, and was still taking, a lot of ribbing from his cohorts about the article, but he pointed out to the other agents present in the room, "This article has saved our investigation of the Vitale crime family. It is doubtful that Vincent Panachi will be able to survive this type of negative publicity. There is no doubt in my mind that the head of the family is not going to look favorably upon this notoriety."

"Yeah, I don't recon I'll be getting many shots of Panachi in his Scarab Thunder any time soon," one of the other agents remarked.

"Well, if you miss him and find you have the urge to see his face, you can always look in the file cabinet. There are plenty of good color pictures of him and the Scarab," another agent quipped.

A wave of laughter filled the living room and overpowered the barely audible remark, "Fuck off!" The laughter became louder.

Agent Murray had been one of those who had joined in on the laughter, although it is doubtful that he would have taken so much pleasure in the feature article had he known that this morning's *Sun Sentinel* had sparked another investigation—one initiated by the Vitale crime family.

*   *   *

CORAL SPRINGS, FLORIDA . . . 9:15 A.M.

The beautiful city of Coral Springs was enjoying the same cloudless sky as Ft. Lauderdale Beach, even though it was ten miles inland. However, that azure-colored sky had gone unnoticed by the Quill. The Quill had been holed up inside the Coral Springs Country Club residence for weeks. It seemed that days had turned into nights; nights had turned into days, until the Quill, himself, had lost track. The one thing that he was certain of though was that productivity could not have been any higher.

The Quill stood beside the rear bedroom's doorway, but out of the way of the two men who were busy loading and unloading the boxes. Quite frankly he welcomed the break when they had shown up thirty minutes earlier because he had begun working shortly after 3 a.m., and up until their arrival had worked straight through. His eyes had deep, dark circles around them, the telltale sign of his not getting enough sleep, but he did not care. Production was way ahead of schedule, and that was all he really cared about. Now, as he stood in the doorway and watched, Vincent's men were removing the first half of the Vitale crime family's commitment to the Columbians—twenty-five million dollars in perfect, counterfeit twenty dollar bills. The two men had its removal down to a science. A hand truck stacked high with boxes would go out of the bedroom to their van in the garage, and then a load of boxes filled with a fresh supply of 75/25 paper would come back in. All the Quill had to do was watch.

Needless to say, none of the three had seen the morning edition of the *Sun Sentinel*, but it would not have altered their plans even if they had. There had been no mention of this operation in the paper, and that was only because neither Slick Nick nor the Organized Crime Task Force had any knowledge of its existence. The two men whom Vincent had entrusted with this job were the most loyal under his command, and he had known, unequivocally, that when he had issued them the supply delivery schedules and given them the exact date for the counterfeit money pick-up, that his orders would be followed to the tee. They had been.

The Quill watched as they wheeled the last load of new money through the doorway, and he followed the two men to the garage. The elderly gentleman stood at the entrance way to the garage while Vincent's boys loaded the last of the boxes into the white van. At that moment, the front page feature article in that morning's *Sun Sentinel* could not have held a candle to the intense rush that the two men in the van were experiencing, and they had not even left the house yet.

It was a natural high that stayed with them for the entire eleven mile ride from the Quill's place in Coral Springs to the golf course house off of Las Olas Boulevard. It was not every day that someone gets to experience the excitement of driving across town with twenty-five million dollars in counterfeit money stashed behind their seat. Fortunately the trip was made without a hitch, and the Columbian's money was delivered safely to Gino.

As for the Quill, he was back at the grindstone by the time the two men arrived at the 'golf course.'

* * *

NASSAU, NEW PROVIDENCE, BAHAMAS . . . 11:10 A.M.

It had been nearly two hours since Vincent read the startling article in the *Sun Sentinel*, and quite frankly, rolling around on the bed while making-out with Jennifer had been the best thing he could have done during that time. Amazingly so, her soft caressing touch helped to ease his concerned state of mind and clarified his thinking, considerably. Reason had overwhelmed the momentary panic he had experienced, and now, logic prevailed in Vincent's mind.

Vincent lay on the king-sized bed with his arms clasped behind his head. Jennifer's head lay on his chest while he lovingly stroked the back of her head and ran his fingers through her ponytail. He had all the outward appearances of a totally relaxed man, yet inside, his mind was carefully contemplating his options. As far as he could tell, Agent Mark Murray had utilized the news media to force a game of interplay between the Vitale crime family and the Organized Crime Task Force. Otherwise, Vincent had reasoned during the past hour, Agent Murray would have had nothing to gain by revealing the full depth and scope of the Organized Crime Task Force's ongoing investigation. No, that would not have made any sense, whatsoever, he assured himself. However, what would have made sense to Vincent was closer to what had actually been in Agent Murray's mind when he had revealed everything to the newspaper's crack investigative reporter, and that was to rile the crime family enough to stir them up; to force them into a game of action and reaction. In Agent Murray's mind, the elimination of his confidential informant had all but killed the agency's investigation. At best, it was in troubled waters. However, if the bad publicity and resultant heat brought on from the newspaper articles could force the crime family to make some mistakes, maybe his case could be salvaged. The only missing link in the agent's deductive thinking had been his underestimation of Vincent Panachi's intelligence. He had failed to take into account Vincent's considerable street smarts. It was a fact that in order to survive in Vincent's world—a world filled with treachery fueled by an underground economy; one must have a natural aptitude for sniffing out those situations that are not as they appear. The feature article in today's paper had opened the door to a lot of unanswered questions, and if Vincent had figured it out in the time span of a couple of hours, then one could be self-assured that Anthony Vitale had figured out Agent Murray's angle, as well. Vincent was glad that he had taken the time to think things out, to mentally explore the possibilities, and he was ready to place a call to the Consiglio.

Vincent lightly tapped Jennifer on the shoulder.

"Sweetheart, I'm going to go downstairs for a little while." Jennifer tilted her head back and looked up at him. Before she could even speak, Vincent clarified, "I won't be gone long . . . fifteen or twenty minutes at the most."

The fingers that had been lightly scratching his chest, just seconds before, flattened out as she pressed herself up.

"Okay, I'll wait for you here," she said.

Vincent gave her ponytail a slight tug, in jest, before the same hand gently guided her by the back of her head until their lips met in a passionate kiss.

When their lips parted, Vincent eased from beneath her and rolled off the side of the bed. She did the same on the opposite side of the king-sized bed and instinctively Jennifer noticed the *Sun Sentinel* lying on top of the pillow. There was no way for her to know what an impact that newspaper was to have upon her life.

Vincent walked into the suite's living room, and Jennifer followed in his footsteps with her arms thrown across his shoulders and neck. They playfully walked that way until they finally reached the suite's entrance way. As they stood at the door, Vincent turned and gave her a peck on the cheek.

"See ya', soon," he said as his hand turned the doorknob.

"Bye," Jennifer called out as he walked through the doorway. As soon as the door closed, Vincent's thoughts returned to the matter at hand. Whatever the circumstances were, Vincent was certain that the family's legal counsel would have some answers and advise for him.

Vincent was able to summon an elevator within seconds after pushing the chrome button, and unlike his earlier ride, he was the only passenger. He was fortunate; the elevator made a nonstop descent from the hotel's tenth floor to the lobby level. As Vincent exited the elevator, he attributed the lack of guests packed into it to the late hour of the morning. It was too late for breakfast, too early for lunch, and a beautiful day outside. With that deductive reasoning, he turned right and headed towards the bank of public telephones. With any luck, he mused, the telephones would be empty, too. Luck was with him. As he proceeded past the combination newsstand and gift shop, he could see that the bank of six public telephones were completely unoccupied. Vincent slowly cruised past the empty telephones until he reached the last one. Past that, only twenty feet of the corridor remained between him and the glass door that restrained the torrid, tropical heat from entering the cool, air-conditioned area. Even though he had previously called the emergency telephone number only once before in his life, Vincent had no problem reciting the number out loud while he punched in the lengthy series of numbers. He held the receiver close to his ear and listened for the acoustical signal the touch-tone telephone made when it placed an overseas call via the telephone company's satellite system. Within seconds, the now familiar hollow sound was heard in the background, its deep-toned and echoing resonance broken only by the intermittent ringing of the overseas telephone. That telephone was in the Consiglio's residence.

It took three rings before the family's legal counsel answered the telephone. "Hello," he said.

Vincent recalled that the last time he had placed a call to the Consiglio it had been fairly early in the morning. Instinctively, he glanced at his wrist watch and saw that it would be afternoon in a little over a half-hour. A reasonable hour to call, he reassured himself.

"Good morning, sir . . . its Vito, again," Vincent replied.

"Good morning, Vito . . . I have been waiting for your call," the voice on the other end was filled with enthusiasm.

The statement caught Vincent somewhat by surprise when he blurted out, "You have?" before he took the time to logically think the statement through. However, as soon as the words had left his mouth, he understood the statement. The Consiglio had already seen the morning's edition of the *Sun Sentinel*.

His afterthought was immediately confirmed when the Consiglio replied, "Yes, we have already seen the newspaper."

There was a slight pause across the overseas connection, and neither of them had been quite certain if it was due to the satellite connection, or if one was waiting for the other to comment about the article. Vincent decided to break the silence when he queried, "'We' meaning you and Anthony?"

"That is correct with the exception of adding the Capo. He was present, as well," the Consiglio replied.

Vincent took a deep breath.

"And?"

The Consiglio laughed, probably to break the tension more than anything else. Certainly Vincent had not said anything amusing.

"Well, each of us has some traveling ahead of us, today. Me, I'm headed to Florida to handle a few things for Anthony. And you . . . well, as much as I hate to spoil your romantic holiday, Anthony wants to see you, posthaste."

Vincent swallowed hard, "Is he pissed about the article?"

The Consiglio allowed himself to laugh out loud, again, before he replied, "On the contrary. I believe it would be better described as concerned about you and your well being. He loves you, Vito, just as I do. Now, catch a flight into Kennedy, and I'll have the Capo come out in the limo and pick you up. What should I tell him . . . first thing in the morning?"

"Have him check the schedule . . . I'll be on the first flight in the morning that Delta has out of Ft. Lauderdale to JFK. I'll look for him curbside at the Delta baggage claim."

The family's legal counsel smiled, "Done deal. I've got to get going myself, now . . . take care, and more than likely I'll see you at the mansion, tomorrow."

The statement left Vincent a little confused, but whatever, he opted to just say, "Bye."

"Yes, good-bye, Vito."

The line went dead in Vincent's hand as the overseas connection was broken. Vincent replaced the telephone receiver in its cradle and calmly walked towards the hotel's front desk. He had a lot of arrangements to make in a very short period of time. Meanwhile, upstairs Jennifer had unfolded the copy of the *Sun Sentinel* and begun to read it.

Once Vincent had left the suite, Jennifer walked back into the bedroom. Since he had told her that he would be gone for fifteen or twenty minutes at the most, Jennifer decided to relax and wait for his return.

She plopped onto the bed and, without looking, reached to her side to fluff up the pillows and touched the newspaper lying on top of them. Naturally, with fifteen minutes to kill, Jennifer stuffed the pillows behind her back until she was sitting up, and opened the folded copy of the *Sun Sentinel*. Just as Vincent had experienced earlier that morning, the headline leapt out at her, and she let out an audible gasp. Her eyes quickly scanned the capitalized, bold-print headline. Jennifer Swords had never been noted as being a speed-reader, yet the way she whizzed through the feature article would have made Evelyn Woods proud. Jennifer was able to identify and retain the key subject matter. In her case, the obvious point of interest had been Vincent Panachi's name. Of course that had caught her eye first, but then, as she read the article further, the phrase, "The Tuxedo Murders" caught her attention. Next it was Anthony Vitale's name, shortly followed by Capo Pelligi's. Immediately, the names registered within her memory. Although she had not been properly introduced to Anthony Vitale, she had seen him at his annual landlubber party. It was also there that she had met Capo Pelligi, but, of course, he had been introduced as Mr. Pelligi. It was not until she read the paragraph that dealt with the Belle Glade murders that she read the name of one of the tuxedo murder victims, Slick Nick.

Jennifer could not believe her eyes. She backed up and re-read the entire paragraph. According to the article, Slick Nick's body had been discovered in a sugar cane field located on the outskirts of Belle Glade. The article did not expound the gruesome details of how he had been murdered, but it did state, "Execution-style killing."

Any normal person would have felt a chill run up their spine realizing that they had intimately known the person whom had been gruesomely murdered, however, Jennifer felt nothing. She quickly refolded the newspaper and replaced it and the pillows in precisely the same position they had been when Vincent had left the room. Jennifer got up from the bed and smoothed out the wrinkles on the bedspread. She casually checked her watch as she slipped her feet into a pair of flats and calculated that she had at least five minutes before Vincent would return.

She rechecked the newspaper's position one last time before she walked out of the bedroom into the living room. Jennifer opened the drapes and sat down on the sofa, just as if she had been there the entire time.

While Jennifer sat there, her thoughts were on Slick Nick. One would think that thoughts of the times they had spent together would have been first and foremost in her mind. WRONG! Jennifer Swords *was* reminiscent about Slick Nick. However, what she was recalling, in as much detail as she possibly could, was their last conversation that had taken place in his Mercedes in the parking lot at the hair salon. The same conversation where Slick Nick had revealed to her, in confidence, that Vincent was going to have two-and-a-half-million dollars in his possession, very soon.

She contemplated that information for a few moments before the idea flashed in her mind. Now that Nick was out of the picture, why should she settle for only half? If she had been willing to pass along information that would have netted her half, why not go for it all? Why not, indeed, she pondered. The more she thought about it, the better it sounded to her. Vincent had been with her the entire time since she had had the conversation with Slick Nick, so if Nick's information had been correct, Vincent had not taken possession of the cash yet. All she would need to do is get herself into his house, as a guest, for awhile. Suddenly, a large smile formed across Jennifer's face. "Thanks, Slick Nick!" she exclaimed out loud.

Jennifer wanted financial security badly enough to deprive herself of ever finding true happiness through love, which has too many variables to deal with. Greed knows but one desire, and Jennifer was full of desire. Now, desire had interjected a new variable that was totally foreign to her. As hard as it was for her to admit it to herself, Jennifer thought that she might be falling in love with Vincent Panachi.

Just then, the electronic lock on the suite's door clicked and the door knob turned. Jennifer looked towards the entranceway as Vincent entered the living room. Immediately, she jumped up from the sofa and ran across the room to him. She threw her arms around his neck and placed a kiss on his cheek. He embraced her and she clung to him, their cheeks pressed against one another's.

"You haven't been down at the earring store, again, have you?" she joked.

"No, I'm afraid not," Vincent half-whispered in her ear as he squeezed her tight.

"Good," Jennifer giggled.

Vincent slid his arms up to her shoulders then held her at arm's length. As he looked into her eyes, he said, "I'm afraid what I do have, though is not very good news."

Jennifer allowed a look of concern to shadow her gleeful expression.

She grasped his cheeks with her hands and stared into his eyes.

"Is everything all right? Are you okay?"

Vincent was touched by this display of concern for his well-being; however, he was quick to answer.

"Unfortunately, something has come up . . . and I'm afraid we're going to have to cut our vacation a little short."

Jennifer had already expected this, yet she never let on that she knew a thing.

"Vincent, I'm just grateful for the wonderful times we have had. Is that all that's worrying you?"

They looked into one another's eyes and held a momentary stare. It was Vincent who broke the trance-like moment.

"You really are something special, Miss Jennifer."

She just smiled and looked down. She did not say a word. There was nothing more that needed to be said. Jennifer knew that she had him. He was dangerously close to becoming fully entangled in her web.

By her calculations, either way it went she was a winner.

*　　*　　*

CALI, COLOMBIA, SOUTH AMERICA . . . 11:30 A.M.

At the same moment that Vincent and Jennifer were hugging in a hotel suite in Nassau, Bahamas, Anthony Vitale and Señior Calerro were engaged in an overseas phone call. The call had taken the head of the Columbian drug cartel by surprise. It was a rare occasion for two powerful men of their caliber to ever speak on the telephone, much less to one another. If normal procedures had been followed, the communiqué would have been handled by a designated upper-echelon Capo and his Colombian counterpart. Nevertheless, the head of the Colombian drug cartel had gathered his composure and had been quick to offer the head of the Vitale crime family several ingratiating compliments. When he had finished, Anthony Vitale had offered several ingratiating compliments to Señior Calerro, as well.

Once they had the formalities out of the way, it was time to get down to business. As it was the head of the Vitale crime family who initiated the call, it was customary for him to bring the order of business to the table. It was equally as customary for the recipient of the call to listen without interrupting. Otherwise, something as simple as that breach of etiquette could have been construed as an insult. Therefore, when Anthony Vitale began speaking, Señior Calerro listened carefully.

"I have a favor to ask of you and your organization, and if you will grant me this wish I will be in your debt."

Anthony paused for several seconds, during which the hallow sound of the satellite-relayed call filled the telephones' receivers. Señior Calerro waited several seconds before he spoke up, just to be absolutely certain that he would not interrupt Anthony Vitale. Once he was assured of that, Señior Calerro courteously interjected, "Of course we would be honored to help in any way . . . . please, if there is anything that we can do it would be our pleasure to offer our assistance, just as you and your organization have already done for us."

"Thank you, Señior Calerro. Now, please listen carefully . . . this is what I have in mind . . ."

Señior Calerro listened and the only times that he spoke were to clarify and coordinate the logistics involved in Anthony Vitale's plan. Finally, at the end of their conversation, the head of the Colombian drug cartel assured him, "The arrangements will be taken care of . . . you have my word of honor."

The two men talked for less than fifteen minutes, yet that particular conversation became the basis for a lifelong friendship. During that brief period of time, the two powerful men had seen in each other what they cherished even more than their millions of dollars—respect and honor.

CHAPTER TWENTY-ONE

S alvatore Santori was comfortably seated in the rear of the Learjet. As usual, he chose the right side of the leather-covered divan sofa, yet he could have had any seat he wished. The Consiglio was the solo passenger aboard the early morning flight from Ft. Lauderdale to New York's, JFK Airport.

They were a little over two hours into the flight, and it would be another half-hour before the sun rose. The passenger's compartment was dark, with the exception of the faint lights emitting from the cockpit's instrument panel. The Consiglio had been sitting in the dark for close to an hour while he pondered his trip to Florida.

Outside the aircraft, the starboard wing's position light cast an eerie greenness into the thick, dense clouds. Salvatore leaned forward in his seat and looked out the oval-shaped, porthole window. He watched as greenish cotton balls whisked past the aircraft's sleek, tapered wing. Salvatore found it to be quite an optical illusion, and had he not known better he would have sworn that it was the clouds that were moving, rather than the private jet. Whatever the case may have been, between the optical illusions outside the aircraft and the high-pitched, monotone whine that the two turbine engines emitted inside the aircraft, it had a most hypnotic effect on him. Suddenly, Salvatore was extremely tired. He turned his head away from the window and blinked hard twice in an attempt to shake the drowsiness from his eyes. Without thinking, his right hand automatically reached overhead for the air conditioning vent and adjusted it to its maximum flow. He aimed it directly toward his face and the cool air shocked his senses enough to awaken him.

A minute later, Salvatore reached overhead and adjusted the vent again, pushing it to the side so that the stream of cool air did not blow directly upon him. While his hand was up there, he pushed the tiny switch for the overhead reading lamp. The small light illuminated an area approximately three feet in diameter. The Consiglio reached inside of his jacket with the same hand and withdrew a gold cigarette case. He effortlessly opened the case with his thumb and forefinger. At that same moment, his left hand procured a matching lighter from his trouser pocket. Just as he withdrew a cigarette from the elegant case, the *NO SMOKING/FASTEN SEAT BELT* sign at the forward end of the passenger cabin illuminated. The Consiglio replaced his smoking paraphernalia just as quickly as he had withdrawn it. Seconds later the pitch of the engines changed from the high-pitched whine he had been listening to for hours, to nothing more than a mere whisper as the Learjet began its descent from its en-route cruising altitude of forty-one thousand feet. He heard, rather than felt, the catch on his seat belt when he buckled it across his waist. He knew from experience that the descent from cruising altitude would take in the neighborhood of twenty-five minutes. He decided to make good use of that time by re-reading the file lying beside him on the divan sofa. As legal counsel to Anthony Vitale, it was his professional responsibility to evaluate the situation and make a recommendation based on factual information, as opposed to speculation. Being the Consiglio, he was expected to know the facts backwards and forwards prior to calling a "meet" with the head of the crime family. Unfortunately, the information that Salvatore had received earlier from the private investigator in Ft. Lauderdale had opened up Pandora's Box, and in this case, any recommendation that he could make would be conjectural. There was simply no other way. What he intended to tell Anthony Vitale was based entirely upon theory; however, if his theory was even close to being correct, it was a chance the family could not take. Not now; not ever.

Salvatore Santori read the investigator's report, again, while the Learjet slid down a long slide at 480 knots across the ground. The fuel-sucking, turbine engines barely made a sound, and if it weren't for the occasional turbulence they encountered along the way, he could have sworn that he was sitting in a living room chair rather than a sleek jet torching its way through the early dawn sky.

Salvatore finished reading, closed the file folder and placed it beside him on the divan. He glanced at his expensive wrist watch and estimated their remaining flight time to Kennedy International at ten minutes. The aircraft was still in the clouds, but as he looked out of the window he saw that the sky was becoming lighter. Within moments, the sun would rise and bring a new day. The Consiglio reached overhead and turned off the reading lamp. In the same movement, he momentarily rubbed his eyelids with his thumb and forefinger.

Suddenly, the Learjet broke free from the overcast that blanketed the northeast United States, and the flame-colored ball was visible low on the horizon. The pitch of the turbine engines changed, and the aircraft banked several times. Minutes later, the legal counsel barely felt a thump as Learjet 30TP touched down at New York City's JFK Airport.

The private jet angled off the runway as it followed the high speed taxiway. It took two more turns before they reached the outer taxiway, then the captain guided the aircraft along that blue-lighted taxiway to the general aviation area. When he made another turn, Salvatore Santori looked through the porthole window and saw large, illuminated letters that stretched across the front of a huge aircraft hangar. *BUTLER AVIATION*. The Learjet taxied straight ahead, then made a sharp turn and braked in front of the fixed base operation's awning-covered entrance way. The captain cut the turbine engines' fuel supply and they immediately emitted a deep, throaty groan. Seconds later, the co-pilot opened the door. In the meantime, the Consiglio had gathered his belongings, which included the file folder lying beside him. He thanked the crew for a smooth flight as he stepped from the sleek jet into the chilly, New York dawn. As soon as he exited the aircraft, a limousine turned the corner of the building and headed towards the aircraft. It only took a second for Salvatore to identify the luxury automobile as belonging to Anthony Vitale, and he knew for a fact that only the head of the Vitale crime family utilized that particular vehicle. Therefore, as he watched the limo approach, he felt certain that Anthony would be inside the luxurious passenger's compartment. The limousine pulled alongside the Learjet's left wing and stopped. Suddenly, the right rear window lowered and an arm flung out. Salvatore walked towards the limo while Anthony motioned to him.

The chauffeur walked around the front of the elongated Cadillac, his gloved hand sweeping across the hood. His other hand was tucked into his front trouser pocket where it was warm. The warm leather covering his palm left marks where he had pressed it against the cold metal. As the chauffeur worked his way toward the rear of the vehicle, he kept a keen eye on the approaching Consiglio, and timed himself accordingly. The chauffeur reached the rear door at precisely the same instant that Salvatore Santori did. The chauffeur's hand moved so quickly the movement was nothing more than a blur to the Consiglio, then the passenger door swung wide-open. Salvatore smiled at the man, and the chauffeur nodded his head in acknowledgment. It was necessary for him to pivot his body in order to step into the limousine, and while Salvatore did so, he happened to glance back toward the sleek jet. He noticed that the turbine engines were still spinning and looked as if they would be for quite some time. Interesting, he thought. Once he was inside the compartment, the chauffeur closed the door behind him. Suddenly the cold chill outside was forgotten and was replaced by a comfortable seventy degree temperature. Seconds later, the driver's door slammed shut and the vehicle accelerated.

Anthony Vitale was seated on the rear seat. The collar of his cashmere coat was turned up in the back, and a maroon scarf was loosely wrapped once around his neck before it crisscrossed the overcoat at chest level. Salvatore looked over at him. The heavy outer coat's collar framed the elderly gentleman's head, while the dark scarf contrasted his pale skin. An expensive pair of soft leather gloves laid across his lap.

"Good morning, counselor," Anthony softly said.

The Consiglio managed a smile, even though he was trying to maintain a professional expression of grave concern. The legal counsel had laid the file folder between them on the seat when he had gotten in the limo, and now, instinctively placed his hand on top of the folder while his eyes met Anthony's and held them in a stare.

"Good morning, sir."

"Well, I see you took my request to heart and flew the information up here as soon as possible. Haven't had any sleep, have you?" the head of the crime family asked.

"No, sir, I haven't. But, to be perfectly honest with you, I couldn't have slept anyway . . . not until you had a chance to review this material. Besides, I had hoped to meet Vincent up here."

"That's why I tagged along to pick you up," Anthony said as his eyes shifted and glanced down at the closed folder. "Vincent's flight is scheduled to arrive within the half-hour. That should give us ample time to go over what you've got, beforehand . . . won't it?"

"For fifty-thousand dollars we got a look at the task force's files," the family's legal counsel announced. He handed the head of the crime family the file folder and continued, "And you bought yourself a look at his personal files. I believe you will find this information interesting, if not shocking."

Anthony accepted the file folder in his right hand. Even though the sun had risen, there was still not sufficient light for reading. The elderly man reached overhead and switched on one of the limousine's courtesy reading lights. A beam of light shown down on his lap. He centered the file folder in the illuminated circle and opened it. The first thing that he noticed was a color, glossy eight by ten photograph of a man standing alone. Anthony picked up the photograph with both hands and held it at an angle to reduce the glare. The head of the crime family studied the photograph for a couple of seconds.

"Agent Mark Murray?" he queried.

"Yes, that's him," the Consiglio nodded his head. "That is also him in the next photograph . . . but, see if you recognize who he is with."

Anthony laid the first photograph to the side then picked up the second. That particular photograph was not as sharp as the first. In comparison, the first had been shot during daylight hours under bright lights; the second looked to be some sort of surveillance-type photograph that had been taken at night with poor lighting. Nevertheless, the head of the crime family was able to make a positive identification of the photograph's subjects. He turned toward the Consiglio.

"That is the same woman that Vincent was with at my birthday party. Jennifer something another."

"Swords," the legal counsel added. "Jennifer Swords."

It was not necessary for the family's legal counsel to explain the ramifications of Jennifer Swords and Agent Murray knowing one another. Anthony squinted as he studied the photograph's details closer. The picture appeared to have been taken as the two of them were entering a motel room. The lit sign in the upper left hand corner of the picture was not entirely clear, but even so, the old man was able to discern the words *HOLIDAY INN.*

The renegade agent that the private investigator had gotten to had more than a desire for money—he also had a deep-seated dislike for Agent Mark Murray, and had taken it upon himself to open his own file on him some time ago. At the time the photographs of Mark with Jennifer had been taken, the renegade agent was gambling that Murray would attempt reconciliation with his estranged wife. If that had happened, it was his plan to send his estranged wife copies of the photographs. As things turned out, it didn't. However, he had always been a believer that everything happens for a reason, and in this particular case, it had happened to his benefit. When the private investigator had approached the renegade agent for the Organized Crime Task Force the day before, he had been exceptionally receptive to his offer, "Fifty thousand dollars for information on Agent Mark Murray? Have I got something for you . . . meet me in one hour," was all the resistance he had offered. At least that had been the story that the private investigator had told the Consiglio when he had turned over the file. More than likely, the renegade agent had gotten forty thousand, and the investigator had pocketed ten thousand. After all, it was his business.

There were several other photographs inside of the file folder; one was the photograph of Vincent and Jennifer together taken by the surveillance camera and agent photographing the valet parking area at Anthony Vitale's landlubber party. The head of the Vitale crime family slowly flipped through the pictures. Finally, he closed the folder and laid it on the seat between them. His left hand reached overhead and turned off the reading lamp. At the same time, he turned towards the family's legal counsel and asked, "Sal, what does it all mean?"

"All I can give you are possibilities . . . speculation," the Consiglio sighed.

"Please, share your thoughts with me . . ."

Salvatore shifted in his seat so that he was facing the elderly gentleman a bit better. Their eyes met one another's and held a momentary stare.

"Of course, this is nothing more than conjecture, but let me run a couple of scenarios by you . . . none of which are good."

Anthony never even flinched. He merely said, "Proceed."

That conversation lasted until it was time to pick up Vincent.

*   *   *

A beautiful flight attendant leaned over and lightly nudged Vincent on the shoulder. Over the years, her soft touch had awakened many weary travelers in an identical manner. Vincent had barely opened his eyes before she smiled and courteously informed him, "Excuse me, sir, but we'll be landing in approximately fifteen minutes. The captain has illuminated the fasten seat belt/no smoking sign. You'll need to raise your seat back and check your seat belt for landing, please."

Vincent managed a smile as he rubbed the sleep from his bleary eyes. His right hand groped about the side of the armrest until he felt the round button that controlled the seat's position. He depressed it, and the seat back slowly raised itself to its stanched upright position. Once the sleepiness had cleared from his groggy mind, he remembered that the cabin lights in the first class section of the L-1011 jet airliner had been dimmed shortly after their takeoff from Ft. Lauderdale. The more he thought about it, the more he realized that it had been a combination of the darkness and the soothing sounds of the airliner's huge turbine engines that had induced him into such a sound sleep. When he looked around it was obvious that the flight attendants had adjusted the cabin light's rheostat switch before they had awakened him, because now the first class cabin of the Delta Airlines' jet was well lit. The attractive flight attendants were scurrying about, delivering suit coats and overcoats to the other first class passengers. Judging from all the commotion in the cabin, it was apparent to Vincent that he had been the last person she had awakened. Even so, he felt as if he had just closed his eyes. In comparison to a full night's sleep, it had been nothing more than a mere catnap.

Vincent had been on the go since he had read the feature article in the *Sun Sentinel*. Nassau runs on island time, and henceforth it had not been easy getting off the island on such short notice. Vincent and Jennifer had departed the island that evening, and had arrived stateside around 9:00 p.m.

Vincent had offered to take Jennifer to dinner, and she had accepted. He had wanted the dinner to be something special, mainly because he was uncertain when he would see Jennifer again. At that particular moment, Vincent had been uncertain about most everything, with the exception of his feelings for Jennifer. The dinner had been special, and Vincent had been very careful to skirt around the issue of any imminent travel plans. Jennifer had known better than to ask. She knew; and for her it had meant that she would be just that much closer to achieving her own goals. She had wanted him to go.

After they left the restaurant, Jennifer returned to her condominium and Vincent went back to his house. A clock on the kitchen wall confirmed his late hour of his arrival—11:45 p.m. His eyelids were quite heavy, and he was certain that if he did not rest soon he would go totally out. Vincent decided to pour himself a shot-glass of whisky, and by midnight he had done just that. Afterwards, he opened the sliding glass doors so that the cool, night air might help to keep him awake. Vincent stepped onto the wooden deck then sat there in the dark while he sipped his drink. Lights from the palatial living room cast shadows of the patio furniture onto the dock. He had not been able to turn off his mind, and even the several strong pulls taken from the whisky glass did not prevent his thoughts from whirling through the past, present and future. A number of those stops were thoughts about Jennifer, during which he glanced at his watch several times. Due to the darkness, however, he was unable to note the hour. Vincent was certain that it was well past midnight, yet he reached for the portable telephone and dialed Jennifer's home number with complete disregard for the middle of the night hour. Fortunately Jennifer was still awake, and she answered the telephone after one ring. The two of them talked for over a half-hour before she said good night. Vincent jokingly corrected her when he had replied, "Morning . . . it's good morning."

That call may not have awakened Jennifer, but the same could not have been said for the Organized Crime Task Force's agent in charge of electronic eavesdropping. Agent Jackson had been startled when the tape recorder set to Jennifer's telephone number had automatically engaged itself and begun recording their conversation. Aside from that, the pen-register machine sitting next to the recorder had begun flashing the incoming telephone number. Even though his senses had been somewhat foggy, Agent Jackson had recognized the seven digit number right away. That telephone number belonged to Vincent Panachi's Las Olas Isles residence.

Vincent had made no mention of the fact that he was going out of town during the recorded conversation. Therefore, the agent was none the wiser to Vincent's impending travel arrangements. The only information that Agent Jackson could have passed along with any certainty would have been Vincent's whereabouts during the recorded conversation.

Vincent's reservation had been made under a fictitious name, and that flight was scheduled to depart Ft. Lauderdale for New York at 4:00 a.m. "The Early Bird," the cheerful sounding voice had labeled it when he had made the reservation. "Early bird, my ass," he had grumbled when the taxi let him off at 3:15 a.m. in front of the Delta curbside check-in.

Now, as he shook the sleep from his mind, that curbside stop seemed as if it had happened just minutes before. Of course, that would have been physically impossible, because the L-1011 airliner was in a descent profile somewhere between Washington, D.C. and New York City.

The flight attendant's approximation had been more or less correct. Twelve minutes after she had awakened Vincent, the huge passenger airline descended through the cloud deck. Suddenly, rays of sunlight struck the gleaming aircraft and shown through his window. Vincent looked out and saw the reddish-orange sun hanging just above the horizon. He watched it rise for a few seconds before the aircraft banked to the left, its huge, aluminum wing blocking the sun from view. He knew that the pilot was lining the aircraft up on its final approach to the runway. Instinctively, Vincent checked the security of his seat belt by giving the lap belt a firm tug. Seconds later, the L-1011's landing gear made a thumping sound when they locked into place. As Vincent gazed out the window at the rapidly approaching terrain, he imagined the first officer confirming the same to the captain. "Gear down and locked, sir. Three green."

"Roger," the captain would have acknowledged. In reality though, the captain had just acknowledged the tower's landing clearance.

"Delta six two four, cleared to land," had barked through the pilot's headset, complete with an unmistakable, New Yorker's accent. One minute later, the captain gently placed the three hundred thousand pound L-1011 onto a runway at the JFK International Airport.

Passenger deplaning was simple for Vincent because the only thing he had with him was a copy of yesterday's *Sun Sentinel*. He tucked the folded newspaper underneath his arm and made a beeline towards the aircraft's forward exit while the other passengers were busy retrieving their carry-on luggage. Vincent was the first passenger through the jet way corridor. He had been to the Kennedy airport a number of times, which allowed him to make his way to the Delta baggage claim area without hesitation.

When Vincent stepped from the warm building into the frigid cold of a New York winter's dawn, the bitter, artic temperature stung his face. Without thinking, Vincent turned up the collar on his knee-length, leather coat. His hand held the coat's collar closed, his arm tightly clutching the *Sun Sentinel* newspaper beneath it while he waited and closely watched the seemingly endless line of limousines and taxicabs parade past. Vincent wasn't certain of which of the family's limousines had been dispatched to pick him up. However, according to the conversation he previously had with the Consiglio, the Capo should be in that limo. Vincent reasoned that Capo Pelligi would certainly be able to identify him standing alongside the curb easier than he could discern one of the family's limousines from the countless number of limos jockeying for position. Vincent stood in front of the baggage claim sign and patiently waited, his hand constantly adjusting the neck of the coat to combat the biting cold.

A limousine quickly changed lanes and skidded to a stop directly in front of Vincent. Perhaps it had been because he had expected a different limousine rather than the one that had pulled up, but it took Vincent a couple of seconds before it registered that the limousine in front of him belonged to Anthony Vitale. It was still relatively dark on the baggage claim level, even though the sun had risen. An eight-lane overpass that separated the arrival and departure traffic from the passenger terminal shrouded the lower level with its mezzanine structure. The limousine was parked curbside, and the chauffeur had turned on its emergency flashers. Still, Vincent did not approach the vehicle, even though he was almost certain that it belonged to Anthony Vitale. The key word "almost" because when one is in a city of eight to ten million people, the chances of coincidentally running across an identical "anything" are pretty high. As if the old man had been reading Vincent's mind, he rolled down the rear window far enough to get his arm out, then waved. The cashmere coat was the second thing that looked familiar to Vincent.

He stepped off the curb towards the limousine, which placed him close enough to make out Anthony's face. Vincent smiled. At the same moment, the rear door of the limousine opened.

Vincent ducked his head as he stepped into the limo. If he had been surprised to see Anthony and the Consiglio, he did not show it. He took a seat on the rear-facing sofa. Vincent said, "Good morning, gentlemen," The *Sun Sentinel* was clutched in his left hand while he leaned forward to shake hands with his right.

Anthony Vitale was the first to shake Vincent's hand, and in a manner befitting of a concerned parent, remarked, "Vincent, your hand is freezing. What, I don't pay you enough money to afford a good pair of winter gloves?"

Vincent was speechless. He turned to the Consiglio who returned his dumbfounded look. Vincent was not sure, but from the Consiglio's expression it appeared that they were sharing the same thought—the Vitale crime family had just had a feature article written about it, confirming the fact that they are under investigation by the Organized Crime Task Force in Ft. Lauderdale, and the head of the family is worried about whether or not Vincent has a friggin' pair of winter gloves? Before either of them said a word, Anthony said, "Get yourself some gloves, Vincent."

Vincent smiled, shook the Consiglio's hand, then handed Anthony the Ft. Lauderdale newspaper and said, "What I'd rather do is make this all go away."

Anthony could see the grave concern on Vincent's face, and he leaned forward and affectionately patted Vincent on the knee.

"Not to worry, lad, everything will turn out okay," he said.

The Consiglio turned and faced the head of the crime family, because he had just spent a half-hour with the man, and this was news to him.

Anthony had already read the newspaper article in its entirety, and unbeknownst to the Consiglio, had made decisions and plans based upon that article, especially pertaining to Vincent and his future. What he had not been aware of when he had made those decisions was the connection between Vincent's girlfriend, Jennifer Swords, and Agent Mark Murray.

The limousine pulled away from the curb and immediately became snarled in the typical New York bumper-to-bumper traffic so innate to JFK International Airport. The head of the crime family calmly folded the newspaper and laid it on the seat. In the same motion, he grabbed the file folder the Consiglio had given him and placed it on top of the gloves on his lap. Anthony looked up at Vincent.

"I'm familiar with the newspaper article, but thank you for bringing it anyway. There is something else though that, quite frankly, has me more concerned than that." His fingers fumbled nervously at the file folder before he got a firm grip on it. Vincent knew better than to question the elderly gentleman. If it had something to do with him, Anthony would not hesitate to confront him with it. The head of the crime family handed Vincent the file folder then, when he was withdrawing his hand, reached overhead and switched on a reading lamp. Vincent looked down at the closed folder, then back up at Anthony Vitale. The expression on his face reflected the puzzlement he felt. Anthony suggested, "Counselor, why don't you fill Vincent in on what he has there."

"As you wish," the Consiglio courteously replied.

Vincent shifted his attention to the legal counselor. The Consiglio met his gaze and they held a momentary stare before the counselor said, "What you have in your hand was recently purchased from a renegade agent for the Organized Crime Task Force. This information came to me through a very thorough private investigator located in Ft. Lauderdale." The Consiglio made a waving motion towards the file as his eyes shifted down and looked at it. "Open it up . . . I think you will find the information inside poses some interesting possibilities."

Vincent opened the manila folder and found several photographs covering a two page, typewritten report. He carefully lifted the top photo from the stack and tilted it towards him. The overhead reading lamp did a sufficient job of lighting the subject's face, yet the low wattage bulb made the photograph appear somewhat grainy. Vincent clearly made out a face he was certain he had never laid eyes on before. His eyes shifted from the photograph back to the Consiglio, who was still looking at him. Vincent's confused expression said it all, and the legal counsel calmly explained, "The man in the picture is Agent Mark Murray of the Organized Crime Task Force, and he is the one responsible for the ongoing investigation into the Vitale crime family's affairs, as well as the feature article that ran in yesterday's *Sun Sentinel*."

Vincent clutched the photograph in his right hand and waved it as he queried, "So what is this guy's problem? Why, all of a sudden, is he after the family?"

"That's an interesting question, Vincent," the Consiglio's voice was calm. "The answer is I am of the opinion that it is not the family he is after . . . he is after you."

"Pardon me?" Vincent said as he lowered the photograph and sat upright.

The Consiglio shifted his eyes to the manila folder, and advised him, "Look at the next photograph, Vincent. Tell us if you can identify the persons in it."

Quickly, Vincent shuffled the top photograph to the side and grabbed the next one in the stack. The legal counsel and Anthony watched closely as Vincent maneuvered the eight-by-ten photo into the light. Seconds later, they could tell from Vincent's widening eyes that he had made Jennifer. His eyes shifted across the photograph while his mind absorbed every detail. If he had not been looking at it himself, he never would have believed it to be true. Jennifer Swords and Agent Mark Murray together; and it was apparent that their meeting was more than a mere acquaintance. Vincent winced as he made out the *HOLIDAY INN* sign in the upper left hand corner of the photograph. Vincent mumbled, "Jennifer Swords," out loud without being fully cognizant that he had done so. The initial shock had been such that he had unwittingly verbalized his thoughts aloud.

"Precisely," the Consiglio replied. His voice brought Vincent out of his momentary trance, and Vincent looked up at the legal counsel. The Consiglio, as well as Anthony, witnessed Vincent's facial expression of heartache.

"Do you know when this photograph was taken?" Vincent queried.

The legal counsel motioned with his hand toward the manila folder and said, "If I'm not mistaken, I believe that information is included in the investigator's typed report."

Vincent placed the photograph to the side and shuffled through the others until he came upon the two page report. He lifted and tilted it until it was centered in the reading lamp's circular beam of light. Vincent was a fairly quick reader, yet it took him several minutes to read the report in its entirety. He wanted to absorb every detail that it had to offer, and he did.

According to information supplied to the private investigator, which was henceforth given to the family's legal counsel, Jennifer Swords and Agent Mark Murray had been involved in a torrid, sexual relationship whereby they attempted to, as the renegade agent had so eloquently described it, "Fuck each other to death on many occasions." One's initial reaction to that sort of statement would be that the renegade agent was some sort of pervert to have maintained such an intimate surveillance on Agent Mark Murray, but in this case it only served as a prime example of the deep-seated hatred that the renegade agent felt towards Murray. Jennifer Swords meant nothing to the renegade agent. She just happened to have been in the wrong place at the right time, and now that information was in the hands of the Vitale crime family.

There was one other piece of information that Vincent had found particularly disturbing—the report divulged the fact that Jennifer Swords' home telephone had been tapped by the Organized Crime Task Force for quite some time. That little tidbit of information sent Vincent's mind into overdrive. Vincent laid the report down while he pondered the ramifications of Jennifer's home number having been monitored by the boys. It did not take him long to put together that their conversations were not all that had been monitored throughout the past weeks or months—his movements and whereabouts had been also known. The next thought that came into Vincent's mind was the phone call he had placed from the Marriott hotel suite to Jennifer's residence the evening he had met with the Colombians. Perhaps it had been a coincidence that Capo Pelligi had been busted at the Learjet, yet Vincent knew better. Besides, he did not believe in coincidence. The task force could never have been that lucky, even with Slick Nick's help. Unfortunately, the Capo's arrest had not been a chance happening, Vincent reasoned.

Vincent looked at Anthony first then shifted his gaze to the Consiglio. Slowly, carefully, he said, "I don't think she's an agent."

"I don't either," the Consiglio agreed. "However, it is quite obvious that there is a connection between Jennifer and this Agent Murray, and until we can establish what that connection is, you are in a very precarious position. In light of this new information, I would unequivocally classify you as the target of the task force's investigation. Capo Pelligi was lucky, but," the Consiglio turned toward the head of the crime family so that he could address him, "I cannot guarantee that I could work the same magic for Vincent. This Agent Murray is a loose cannon on deck, and as for Vincent's well being, he stands a good chance of becoming cannon fodder."

"I agree," Anthony said before he turned to Vincent and asked, "What about you?"

"It certainly sounds that way, doesn't it?" Vincent replied.

"I'm afraid so, Vincent," the Consiglio agreed.

Meanwhile, the sun had raised high enough to irradiate the interior of the limousine. Anthony reached overhead and switched off the reading lamp. The limousine was now moving along at a fairly rapid pace, despite the fact that they were still in heavy traffic. The three men became quiet for several minutes while they gazed out of their respective windows at the passing countryside, each momentarily lost in their own thoughts. Not surprisingly, their thoughts had been the same—for the safety and security of the family, Vincent Panachi had to take an early retirement. The limousine followed an interchange that placed them on another expressway. It had been quite some time since Vincent had driven from New York to New Jersey, yet he still recognized the expressway as the route to "The Garden State."

It was Anthony who broke the silence first when he said, "I'm glad that you are both here, because I have made a decision. If the truth be known, I actually made this decision yesterday morning, and by noon, I had implemented a plan." Anthony shifted his eyes to Vincent and looked intently at him when he continued, "It is important to me that you understand what a difficult decision this has been for me. My emotions were torn throughout the entire night as to whether I had made the right decision or not. However, after seeing the Consiglio's report this morning, I am now confident that I have made the correct choice."

Vincent just sat there and took it all in. He had no idea what to say, because he did not know what the head of the crime family had planned for him. Vincent had learned patience. He knew the elderly gentleman well enough to know that whatever plans Anthony had made would have been with Vincent's best interest at heart. Vincent replied, "I'm certain that you have, sir."

Anthony Vitale made no response, and he turned his head so that he was looking out the side window, once again. Vincent took the opportunity to glance over at the Consiglio with hopes that he might supply some sort of definitive insight into his destiny. Perhaps a knowing wink; or maybe a reassuring nod. Instead, the family's legal counsel arched his eyebrows and shrugged his shoulders in such a manner as to say, "I have no idea what he is talking about." Although the message had not been verbalized, Vincent understood what the Consiglio had meant. Salvatore Santori had represented the Vitale crime family as legal counsel for decades, and during that period of time he had come to know Anthony's mannerisms well. He and Vincent would wait it out together, he knew just as Vincent knew that Anthony Vitale would disclose his plans when *he* was ready, and not before.

The traffic thinned somewhat, and the warehouse districts that had lined either side of the expressway since the International Airport gave way to a forest of leafless, hardwood trees. Anthony continued to gaze listlessly out of the limousine's window, mesmerized by the passing scenery. At least that was what Vincent had thought. In reality, the elderly gentleman's razor-sharp mind was reviewing his plan. Vincent and the Consiglio will just have to wait until we reach the mansion, Anthony mused. For the immediate time being, Anthony Vitale was enjoying the ride.

On the other hand, Vincent's mind had not remained idle. Thoughts of Jennifer ran through his mind like a whirlwind. It was all just so hard for him to comprehend. He thought that he had known her so well; her wants and desires; her sexual cravings; her personality. Now, all of a sudden, Vincent was not certain that he knew her at all. What made matters even worse was that Anthony Vitale and the Consiglio shared that same feeling. It no longer mattered who or what Vincent perceived her to be. Somehow, someway, Vincent had to place her in a situation where she could show her true colors. He had to contrive a scheme so shrewd as to provide her with ample opportunity to outsmart herself; a plan where only she could make the choices that would affect the outcome. Then, and only then, could Vincent successfully convince Anthony and the Consiglio that it was never her intention to do him any harm; that her knowing Agent Mark Murray was nothing more than a coincidence. Vincent pondered those thoughts, quietly formulating a plan as the limousine's speedometer clicked off the miles en route to Anthony Vitale's mansion.

Who knows what was going through the Consiglio's mind during the ride, but whatever it was had kept him quiet during the remainder of the trip. Neither Anthony nor Vincent spoke. Everyone seemed to be content in their own little world until the limousine slowed to enter through the estate's huge iron gates. The silent time had been spent productively. By the time they had reached the estate, Vincent had hit upon a plan, and Anthony had also thoroughly thought his plan through.

The chauffeur pulled to the gate and blew the Cadillac's dual horn twice. The blaring trumpets startled the limousine's passengers. Outside in the blustering cold, two armed guards wrestled with the heavy gate as they slowly swung it open. Seconds later, the limousine accelerated, and Anthony quipped, "Welcome to my humble abode."

"Thank you," Vincent smiled.

CHAPTER TWENTY-TWO

T he library in the mansion had always been Vincent's favorite room, just as it was Anthony's. Vincent was more familiar with that room than any other room in the palatial estate, and justifiably so, because Vincent had met with the head of the crime family in that very same room countless times prior to this occasion. Their meets had occurred with such frequency through the years that Vincent had many opportunities to witness the changing of the seasons. Every year he had watched as the estate's hardwoods evolved from an impenetrable forest of green foliage to a woodland of leafless trees, then go full circle back to flourishing sprouts and blossoming flora. The library's twelve-foot windows placed at one's disposal magnificent views of the mansions' swimming pool area and its manicured grounds. That particular afternoon, however, the view through those windows held nothing of interest to the four men inside the library. The usual breathtaking view seen through those massive panes of tempered glass was somewhat depressing to Vincent. The sky was grey with dark, angry-looking, stratus clouds that brushed the tree tops with dramatic sweeps of grey. The overcast made the woodland appear lifeless.

Inside the mansion, the ambiance was anything but lifeless in the library. A roaring fire filled the marble fireplace and warmed the mahogany-paneled room while crystal snifters filled with expensive, aged brandy warmed the inner organs of Anthony Vitale, Capo Pelligi, Salvatore Santori, and Vincent Panachi. This particular meeting was like none other that Vincent had attended. It wasn't the people present that made it any different; nor was it the location; it was Anthony Vitale's demeanor. Several times during the morning and again earlier that afternoon, the head of the crime family had begun to say something to Vincent, but suddenly stopped. It was as if there had been something troubling on his mind, yet he just could not bring himself to divulge it. Vincent knew the elderly gentleman well, yet he could not recall the last time he had seen Anthony drink brandy. Champagne, yes; brandy, no. Vincent just went with the flow. He knew that Anthony would share whatever was on his mind when he was ready. Enjoy the moment, Vincent reminded himself.

Patience had always been one of Vincent Panachi's strong suits. It was a good quality, because the later in the afternoon it got, the more the meet became a bull-shit session rather than a meeting of the minds. Perhaps it was due to the quantity of brandy that had been consumed throughout the afternoon. Whatever the case may have been, Anthony Vitale was, without a doubt, tipsy by the time evening arrived. By the time sunlight had given way to total darkness, everyone was a little drunk.

Maybe that had been what the head of the crime family had waited for—that precise, euphoric moment one pleasurably experiences while caught somewhere between being mildly sedated and totally inebriated. If so, Anthony Vitale's timing was impeccable. All three gentlemen had reached that familiar, alcohol-induced state of mind where they were feeling healthy, happy and prosperous. Anthony, on the other hand, had not allowed himself to reach that euphoric plateau, and wouldn't; not until he had spoken with Vincent.

Anthony was seated on his favorite reclining chair throughout the entire meet, but suddenly, he stood. The head of the crime family clutched a snifter of brandy in one hand while he delicately wrapped the fingers on his other hand around an expensive, Cuban cigar. Capo Pelligi and the Consiglio were seated beside one another on the sofa, and they were engaged in their own conversation. Vincent was seated on the far end of the sofa, closest to the windows. He wasn't really a part of the conversation that was taking place next to him, but he did courteously listen and face their direction. Anthony Vitale stood then walked toward the windows. He caught Vincent's eye along the way, and Vincent returned the elderly gentleman's gaze. A second later, Anthony cocked his head to one side in a motion meant to signal Vincent to join him at the windows. Instinctively, Vincent nodded his head in acknowledgement. The Consiglio and Capo Pelligi were so engrossed in their own conversation that Vincent decided against interrupting them. Instead, he just quietly stood up and walked toward the windows. The two men seated were none the wiser, or perhaps they just had not cared.

Anthony stood at the twelve-foot high panes of glass and faced the outdoors. It had been described as, ". . . facing the outdoors," rather than ". . . looking out the window," because the glare from the library's lights prevented either of them from being able to see outside. Nevertheless, Anthony faced the manicured grounds as if he were taking it all in. Vincent joined him at the window and glanced in the same direction that the crime boss was staring. The only thing visible was a reflection of the two of them standing there. That was symbolic, Anthony Vitale was not just staring at a reflection of the two of them standing there together; he was reflecting upon the many years the two had spent together. To Anthony, Vincent was like his own son.

Anthony swirled his brandy glass until the dark-colored liquor rotated fast enough to produce an eddy in the center. He watched the tiny whirlpool for a few seconds before he made it a point to direct Vincent's attention to it. Anthony positioned the crystal glass in such a manner that allowed Vincent to easily look into it, and Vincent did so. Vincent had absolutely no idea what the elderly gentleman had found so fascinating about a vortex in the center of a snifter of brandy, yet the head of the crime family fixated upon the whirlpool as if he were on drugs. On the contrary, Anthony's keen mind had never been sharper. Anthony always had a stratagem, and he had previously planned to utilize the brandy snifter as a visual aid while making his point. He gave the glass another quick swirl, then turned to Vincent and causally remarked, "You know Vincent, sometimes life is just like this glass of brandy."

"How so?" Vincent asked while glancing into the glass.

"Well, just a few moments ago, the brandy in this glass resembled a calm sea. Smooth sailing." The elderly gentleman continued to stare down at the snifter and continued, "However, as soon as I began swirling the snifter, that smooth surface quickly became a whirlpool, and, as you know, whirlpools suck down anything and everything in their vortex. Not smooth sailing."

Anthony looked up at Vincent. Vincent looked up also, and met Anthony's stare. While they looked into one another's eyes, Vincent saw that the elderly gentleman's were watery. The head of the crime family said, "Vincent, imagine you being at the center of this whirlpool." Anthony gave the brandy snifter another quick swirl for dramatics' sake, and the dark-colored liquor whirled around the sloping edges of the crystal glass. Instinctively, Vincent looked down into the glass. Vincent was still not certain what point the elderly gentleman was trying to make, however, he had begun to get an idea. After all, it did not take a rocket scientist to understand the whirlpool effect that the *Sun Sentinel*'s feature article would have upon the Vitale crime family; in particular, to Vincent Panachi.

"Not a very good position to be in, would you say?" Vincent remarked.

"No, I'm afraid not," Anthony said as he looked up at Vincent. The elderly gentleman paused for a moment, while the vortex in the brandy glass lost its velocity and the expensive liquor's surface became smooth, once again.

Anthony Vitale twirled the cigar in his fingers several times before he stuck the hand-rolled, Cuban smoke in his mouth. His left hand fished about his trouser pocket for his lighter, which he found with little trouble. Two flicks of the lighter's switch ignited its butane, and the head of the family held the one-inch flame to the cigar's end while he puffed and rotated it with his teeth. Within seconds, the cigar's tip was glowing red. Anthony extinguished the lighter's flame and exhaled a huge cloud of smoke. Vincent involuntarily coughed twice before saying, "Excuse me."

"Don't like these damned things, do you?" Anthony asked as he removed the cigar from his mouth and grunted several quick laughs. He then quickly answered his own question by quipping, "Good . . . damn things will kill you." The head of the crime family took several more draws from the cigar. Each time he did, Vincent watched how the glowing red tip reflected brightly on the pane of glass. The reflection had caught Anthony's eye, as well, but to no surprise. He had made certain that the brightness was noticeable. That cigar had also been pre-planned theatrics. Anthony Vitale took a deep-breathed draw from the cigar—deep enough that assured a glowing red tip for several seconds afterwards—then removed the cigar from his mouth and held it at eye level so that Vincent could observe the flame-colored, glowing tip. "The tip of this cigar looks pretty hot, doesn't it?" Anthony observed. Vincent was looking at it and was about to answer his obvious question when Anthony continued, "You know it's a funny thing. If I just leave this cigar alone, the fire will go out and the cigar will remain intact. On the other hand, if I continue to draw off of it, that tiny red tip will sooner or later consume the entire thing. There will be nothing left to smoke. See?" The elderly gentleman pointed at what had been a flame-colored tip, just seconds earlier. It had nearly extinguished itself before Anthony stuck the cigar in his mouth, again, and took another deep draw from it. As before, the tip immediately became red-hot. Anthony withdrew the cigar from his mouth and held it lengthwise in front of Vincent's face. He said, "Imagine that you are the tip of this cigar, and that the rest of it is the family." He paused for several seconds before he continued to allow ample time for the symbolism to sink in. Anthony looked at Vincent with a very serious expression of concern on his face and commented, "Vincent, you have been like a son to me . . . and now, just like the tip of this cigar, you are red-hot." That sentence brought all of the elderly gentleman's theatrics into scope for Vincent. The head of the crime family had cleverly conveyed what he may have missed had he used only words. The whirlpool effect and the glowing cigar tip had punctuated his point, and now it was extremely clear to Vincent.

The head of the crime family took a pull from the snifter of brandy before he continued. His forehead wrinkled as he scrunched his eyebrows together. Together, they formed a pained expression. Even so, Anthony's outward calm hid his greatest fear—the fear that something would happen to Vincent; something out of his control; and out of reach of his considerable connections. Anthony looked in to Vincent's eyes and said, "Your father saved my life . . . and I owe it to Vito to save your life. The thought of any harm coming your way is more than I could bear. Furthermore, if the same thing were to happen to you that happened to the Quill, there would be little to nothing I could do to protect you." The elderly gentleman motioned toward the sofa, his fingers gently clutching the half-full brandy snifter, and added, "Our legal counsel has already told me, in so many words, that it is *you* the Organized Crime Task Force is after. At first, I had trouble believing that theory . . . but, now, with these pictures of this agent and your girlfriend together? Not good, Vincent . . . not good at all." Anthony Vitale paused long enough to take a sip from his drink. The cigar had long since gone out, yet he continued to clutch it tightly between his fingers.

"I agree, sir," Vincent interjected during this silent moment.

It seemed that the head of the crime family could not withdraw the snifter from his lips quick enough before he replied, "I should damn well hope so, Vincent. After all, the Quill spent the better part of two decades in the joint, and I could not . . . will not stand to see that happen to you. Therefore, I have made some arrangements to ensure your continued safety. How far along is the Quill with our counterfeit project?"

The question was such a rapid departure from the subject they had been discussing that it caught Vincent off guard. He paused for several seconds while he calculated precisely how far along the Quill was in production. "Over half completed," Vincent replied.

"And how much longer before he has met our goals?" Anthony queried.

"Two weeks, on the outside," Vincent estimated after he pondered the question for a moment. "He is moving right along."

"Good . . . that will work," the head of the crime family replied.

Anthony walked across the room and placed the unlit cigar in the ashtray sitting on the desk then returned. He affectionately placed his arm around Vincent and exclaimed, "I hope you realize how much I love you, my boy . . . and, it is only because of my love for you that I am going to say what I am about to say." Anthony squeezed Vincent's shoulders with his arm, and Vincent turned his head so that he could look into the elderly gentleman's eyes. Just as he had suspected, they were indeed watery. Anthony's voice was low and calm when he said, "I want you to take an early retirement from the family. Things in Florida have just gotten too hot for you to stick around. Now, as a retirement present from me to you, I am going to give you the remaining 10 million dollars of the proceeds from the counterfeiting operation. Don't worry about the Quill . . . I'll take care of him on this end. I want you to just disappear . . . leave everything behind . . . boat, car, house, whatever, and disappear."

Vincent was flabbergasted, and his expression reflected it. Anthony's words had hit him like a freight train, and his jaw involuntarily dropped in astonishment. His thoughts had been so preoccupied with his discovery of Jennifer's connection to Agent Mark Murray that he had not really given thought to what might become of him and his role within the crime family. To leave everything behind . . . everything? "What about Jennifer Swords?" Vincent queried.

"What about her?" the head of the family tossed back at him. Both men were silent for a moment then Anthony Vitale asked, "Are you in love with her, Vincent?"

Vincent Panachi swallowed hard, because up until this point in their relationship, he had not been placed in a situation where it was necessary to answer that question to anyone . . . including himself.

"Yes, I believe I am . . . at least I thought I was before I saw these photos," he replied.

"Well, what do you have in mind?" the elderly gentleman asked.

Vincent took a deep breath.

"I have formulated a plan, and with your permission, I would like to implement it. Should she do the right thing, then it will redeem her from any and all doubts that these photographs have raised."

Anthony removed his arm from around Vincent and rubbed his forehead for a couple of seconds. Finally, he looked at Vincent and said, "Very well, I will listen to your plan. However, first you must listen to mine. Listen carefully, Vincent, for you only have two weeks remaining. After that . . . no more Vincent Panachi."

Anthony Vitale's voice got even lower until it was just above a whisper. His mouth was inches from Vincent's left ear, and Vincent listened intently without interrupting. It was obvious to Vincent that the conversation was not meant to be shared with the others present in the library, but that was not unusual. As Vincent listened it amazed him that one, fifteen minute conversation between Anthony Vitale and Señior Calerro could chart out the course that another man's life would take, and in this case, that is precisely what that conversation had done for Vincent Panachi. On the other hand, the conversation that followed between Vincent and Anthony did exactly the same thing for Jennifer Swords . . . she just did not know it yet.

By the time Vincent and Anthony finished trading plans with one another the elderly gentleman's snifter had been emptied and refilled, twice. Much to Vincent's surprise, the head of the crime family had not invited either of the other two men in the library to join their conversation. Perhaps Anthony had viewed this time spent with his favorite nephew as quality time. The occasions where just the two of them could sit and talk for hours on end had been so few and far between. Whatever the case may have been, the head of the crime family did, however, find the time to meet individually with Salvatore Santori and Capo Pelligi later that same evening after Vincent had gone to bed. Anthony apprised the men of his plan, and had gotten a nod of approval from the family's legal counsel. By early morning, everyone was up to running speed on Anthony's plan. Vincent's plan, however, had remained confidential between Anthony and Vincent. Vincent had requested that it remain confidential, and Anthony had not hesitated to grant him that wish. After all, Anthony's main concerns were seeing Vincent happy, healthy, prosperous, and of course, free to enjoy life.

* * *

FORT LAUDERDALE, FLORIDA . . .
FIFTEEN HOURS LATER . . .

Vincent stood at the Hertz rental car counter and impatiently tapped his fingers on top of the counter. Although patience had always been one of his more admirable qualities, after standing in a seemingly endless line of tourists unable to make up their minds, Vincent had reached his limit for calm endurance. Finally, after having waited over forty minutes, he reached the service counter where an extremely attractive, and highly efficient, young lady immediately began preparing his rental contract.

Vincent nervously glanced at his watch and looked at the time, just as he had done every five minutes during the past half-hour. It was 4:18 p.m., and he had an important meeting to attend at precisely 5:00 p.m. This meeting was so important that Anthony Vitale had repeated the time and place to Vincent at least ten times during their ride from his mansion to JFK International Airport. Vincent had even caught himself repeating it over and over during the Delta flight into Ft. Lauderdale's International Airport. Obviously, the thought had crossed his mind, once again, as he stood waiting for the young lady to finish. A moment later, she slid a contract in front of Vincent and said, "Mr. Panachi, if you'll just sign here and initial in the two squares, we'll have you on your way in a few minutes." The Hertz representative's cheerful promise had been truthful. By the time Vincent was finished tucking away his copies of the rental agreement, the Lincoln Continental he had rented pulled beneath the rental office's awning. Vincent thanked the young lady and made his way through the huddled masses awaiting their turn to rent an automobile. As he exited the building he glanced back and shook his head in amazement. A young man in a neatly pressed khaki shirt held the driver's door open for Vincent, eager to help him with the luggage he did not have. Nevertheless, Vincent peeled off a five-spot and pressed it in the young man's palm.

"Thank you, sir!" the younger man exclaimed as he closed the Lincoln's door.

The interior of the car was cool and smelled of fresh, northern pines. Vincent recognized the car wash scent.

Traffic exiting the airport area moved along at a fairly good pace and, within a matter of minutes Vincent was on I-595, westbound. He followed the multi-lane superhighway west until he reached the cloverleaf interchange then exited onto Interstate 95, northbound. He glanced at his watch again—4:34 p.m. Vincent deftly maneuvered the Lincoln Continental to the far left lane, despite the fact that it had a two person minimum overhanging sign. Already, the arterial boulevards of Ft. Lauderdale were beginning to dump their rush hour traffic onto the expressway. Vincent had lived the good life in South Florida for a number of years, and he knew that it was only a matter of time before I-95 would become a stop-and-go parking lot. He also knew that if he were to get caught up in that mess, there would be absolutely no way he would make his five o'clock meeting at the Ft. Lauderdale Executive Airport. As an afterthought, he depressed the Lincoln's accelerator another quarter of an inch.

Just as he had suspected, the traffic continued to thicken, although it had not yet reached the far left hand lane which he was still cruising in. The one thing that no one is capable of stopping is the expiration of time, although Vincent certainly wished that it were possible. It was 4:45 p.m., and he had just past the Sunrise Boulevard interchange. He had two more exits and approximately five miles to go before he would reach Commercial Boulevard, the exit for Executive Airport. Instinctively, Vincent glanced down at the speedometer and read the numbers 72 on the digital instrument. He could not have gone any faster even if he had wanted to. The five o'clock rush hour traffic had merged itself onto the freeway and had slowly shifted into the two center lanes. The Lincoln Continental was boxed in the two person minimum lane, but it was boxed in at 72 miles per hour.

The sign that denoted the Oakland Park Boulevard exit sped past the Lincoln, and Vincent began working his way toward the far right hand side lane. That was a two mile feat, but he managed to accomplish it with a minimum use of profanity. It was 4:54 p.m. when the Lincoln Continental exited onto Commercial Boulevard.

The drivers of the Indianapolis Brickyard 400 would have certainly been proud of the way Vincent Panachi zigzagged through the rush hour traffic along Commercial Boulevard toward the Executive Airport. In particular, his destination was hangar number twenty-four. Vincent slowed the vehicle when he saw the sign that read *EXECUTIVE AIRPORT—SOUTH ENTRANCE*. He turned right and followed the roadway as it curved along the airport's perimeter. Vincent passed several fixed base operators and scores of private aircraft before he saw a row of dark-green hangars that fit the description Anthony Vitale had given him. He slowed the Lincoln to five miles per hour as he searched the huge, aluminum structures for the number twenty-four. Six buildings later, he found it—a professionally displayed sign with black, bold letters over a white background that read *HANGAR 24*. Vincent pulled into one of the four available parking spaces then got out of the car. It was a very nondescript building. A concrete walkway lined with small azalea bushes and mulch ran from the hangar's parking lot area to a single door entrance into the building. Vincent followed that pathway to the door then entered. A small reception area with a single desk was just inside the doorway, and behind the desk was a beautiful, young woman of Spanish descent. She was obviously not accustomed to very much walk-in traffic, because Vincent's sudden appearance startled her.

"May I help you?" she asked.

"Yes, please." Vincent flashed her a confident smile, "I have an appointment to meet with a Mr. Lazarro. Is he available?"

"And your name, sir?"

"Vincent Panachi . . . I believe he is expecting me," Vincent answered.

"Yes, I believe he is. Just a moment, please. I'll be right back," the dark-haired, dark-eyed, olive-skinned beauty said as she stood. Her English was slightly accented by her native dialect, but her grammar had been impeccable. Vincent watched as she disappeared down a corridor in the direction of the rear of the building. Five minutes later, she reappeared and informed him, "Mr. Panachi, Mr. Lazarro will see you now. Just follow the corridor until you reach the last office on the left." She smiled as she sat down, again, behind the desk, and Vincent smiled back. She was a stunning beauty, and as Vincent walked down the corridor he thought about her radiant smile. She was far too special to be only Mr. Lazarro's personal receptionist. It would not be until months later that Vincent heard of Mr. Lazarro's marriage to the Spanish beauty.

The last door on the left was cracked open several inches and Vincent gently pushed on it. The heavy, wooden door swung effortlessly on its well-oiled hinges, and Vincent entered the office. Mr. Lazarro's office was designer decorated and resembled an apartment more than an office, although it did have an enormous, solid teak desk among its creature comforts. A championship-sized billiard table, constructed from the same expensive, yellowish-brown hard-wood, filled one side of the room. A mirror-lined wet bar was recessed into the far wall. Across from the billiard table was a matching leather sofa and chair, casually arranged nearby the desk in such a manner that allowed for intimate, informal conversations. It was there, seated on that leather-covered chair, that Vincent Panachi first laid eyes on Mr. Lazarro.

Mr. Lazarro looked Colombian . . . and he was. He had straight, dark hair that had been meticulously pulled back into a ponytail and clasped at the nape of his neck. His facial features were sculptured with a strong jaw line that tapered to a lantern jaw. His eyes were dark as coal and looked as though they could penetrate deep into a man's soul. He smiled as he stood. Vincent noticed that he was not very tall, but that he was in topnotch physical condition. There was no mistaking that the man would be a formidable adversary, if provoked. Vincent surmised that this was a man who took good care of himself, and had the wherewithal to do so. Although Vincent had not known it at the time, his assumption had been right on target. Mr. Lazarro was not only the Colombian drug cartel's Miami representative; he was also Señior Calerro's nephew.

Mr. Lazarro walked around the sofa and crossed the plush-carpeted office. He extended his hand and met Vincent at the doorway where the two men shook hands.

"Carlos Lazarro," the Colombian introduced himself.

"Vincent Panachi," the Italian cordially replied.

"You're just in time for cocktail hour," Mr. Lazarro stated as he released Vincent's hand and made a sweeping motion toward the wet bar. "May I pour you something? A whisky, perhaps?"

"I thought you'd never ask." Vincent remarked as he smiled at his host.

Carlos burst out in laughter while he led the way to the mirror-lined bar. He stopped midway and turned toward Vincent and commented, "I can see that we are going to get along very well."

"I certainly hope so," Vincent replied.

Carlos placed a hand on Vincent's shoulder and said, "Not to worry, my friend, my uncle has thoroughly briefed me. He tells me that you are a very competent man." The compliment only served to confuse Vincent, because he had no idea whom Mr. Lazarro's uncle was, and Anthony Vitale had made no mention of that fact.

Vincent concealed his momentary state of confusion and attempted to clarify Carlos' statement.

"I'm sorry, have I met your uncle?"

Carlos smiled when he replied, "But of course. My uncle is Señior Calerro, and he has given me . . . let me see, what were his exact words, 'Carte Blanche' to help you and your family. Incidentally, I have read the *Sun Sentinel* article. I have to say, Vincent, you are a star!" The Colombian slapped him hard on the shoulder in jest then added, "Let me get you that drink. What's your pleasure?"

"Crown Royal, please. Straight up."

"One Crown Royal coming up," Carlos remarked as he headed to the bar. A moment later, he gently placed a rocks glass three quarters full in Vincent's hand. Carlos held an identical drink in his own hand and lifted it to eye level when he proposed a toast. "To our meeting," he said.

Vincent duplicated his movements and they touched their crystal glasses together. *CLINK*. A moment later, the Colombian suggested, "Let's sit down over here." He pointed his drink across the office, in the direction of the sofa and chair then added, "We have a lot of details to go over. Please, ask all the questions you would like, because there will not be another opportunity. I am leaving in the morning for Cali, Colombia to report back to my uncle. The next time we meet will be two weeks from today."

Vincent already knew the basic plan—he had gotten that from Anthony Vitale—but, this meeting was about details. Paying attention to details is what separates the professionals from the amateurs, and Vincent already knew that these men were professionals.

Vincent and Carlos sat on the sofa. Carlos leaned back and casually rested an arm on top of the sofa while he crossed his legs. He looked relaxed, and he was. Vincent took a sip from his drink and patiently waited for the Colombian to speak. Seconds later, Carlos Lazarro began by saying, "First I will give you the overall plan, then we'll go back and cover it step-by-step. Fair enough?"

"Sounds good," Vincent replied.

Carlos shifted in his seat so that he could better face Vincent when he spoke. He looked Vincent in the eye, and Vincent saw that the Colombian's dark eyes were glistening from excitement. Señior Calerro's nephew said, "First things first . . . the aircraft is in this hangar. Now here's the plan . . ."

Señior Calerro's plan encompassed many intricate details. However, the complexity of having so many elaborately arranged elements most certainly left a window of opportunity for screw-ups. The two men recapped their respective responsibilities a final time before they bid one another farewell. When Carlos suggested that they run through the plan one last time, he placed emphasis on the words, ". . . final time," because when the two of them met again, there would be no turning back. At that point in time, Anthony Vitale and Señior Calerro's plan would have passed the point of no return for Vincent. Vincent Panachi and Carlos Lazarro talked for nearly two hours. Afterwards, each man had a clear cut perspective of the master plan.

Carlos walked Vincent to the front of the building, where the two men shook hands in the small reception area before Vincent left. As Vincent walked through the doorway he glanced at his watch. It was 7:30 p.m. "Interesting," he remarked out loud as he walked toward his rented automobile. The remark had been made in reference to the fact that the beautiful, young lady was still there, despite the hour.

Vincent only wished that his life was so trouble free that he could drive down the highway and idly contemplate whether or not Carlos Lazarro was making-it with his personal receptionist, but alas, that was far from the truth. The meeting with Carlos had taken care of Anthony's plan, yet Vincent still had to coordinate his own plan—the plan that centered around Jennifer Swords. Just the thought of her confused his emotions, once again. On one hand, he worshiped the ground that she walked on; on the other, he was no longer certain of who she was, or what she wanted from him. If he somehow had more time to delve into her soul, he felt certain that he could answer those questions. But, he didn't. Vincent Panachi had two weeks to tie up all the loose ends in his life. Two weeks, period. Vincent loved her and hoped that her choice would be the right one, but, if not, it was better that her true character and moral strength be exposed now. There would not be a second chance; Vincent Panachi would no longer exist.

Vincent's thoughts preoccupied his mind so much that he driven eight miles before he snapped out of his self-imposed trance. Immediately, he recognized Sample Road and the sign that read WELCOME TO THE CITY OF CORAL SPRINGS. Even though he had no conscious knowledge of doing so, intuition had steered the Lincoln toward the Quill's house.

It was dark by the time Vincent reached the posh community of Coral Springs Country Club. He made a left turn off of Sample Road and entered the exclusive subdivision. Unlike the previous times he had driven through the posh neighborhood during the midday hour, the palatial homes looked full of life. As a matter of fact, each house had several rooms lighted. It was far and away different from the lifelessness he had previously witnessed during the daylight hours.

Vincent used the cloak of darkness to his advantage when he pulled the Lincoln into the Quill's driveway, and walked directly to the house's front door. Had it been daylight Vincent would have used his key to enter the house. However, the last time he had done that he had surprised the Quill while he was working in the rear of the house. Vincent's unexpected appearance had startled the elderly man so that he had almost suffered cardiac arrest. This time Vincent chose to ring the doorbell. The electronic sensor sent a signal that rang the harmonically tuned bells inside the house. **DING-DONG**. Vincent waited for a minute before he depressed the lighted switch, once again. **DING-DONG**. The harmonious tones resounded throughout the house, and Vincent was certain that the Quill had to have heard them. The sounds of deadbolt tumblers unlocking were heard through the heavy, wooden front door, and then it opened.

The Quill's hair was mussed and his clothes rumpled. His eyes were sunken deep into dark circles. In general, the Quill had the appearance of someone who had not had a decent night's sleep in several weeks. The Quill had averaged no more than four hours of sleep per day for weeks, and the mass production of counterfeit, twenty dollar bills reflected his continued efforts. The Quill was way ahead of schedule, and loving it.

The sight of Vincent standing outside the doorway was unexpected, yet the elderly man quickly recovered from the surprise.

"Vincent," the Quill smiled and said, "What a pleasant surprise. Come in, please."

Vincent stepped through the doorway into the foyer where he and the Quill shook hands.

"It's good to see you, Mr. Quill. Is everything okay? Is the project on track?" Vincent asked.

The elderly gentleman slipped his hand free from Vincent's, then playfully slapped Vincent on his upper arm and remarked, "Better than okay, and well ahead of schedule."

"Outstanding work, my friend. Outstanding," Vincent smiled and complimented the seasoned counterfeiter.

"Let's sit down for a while," the Quill suggested. The elderly man turned and walked into the living room, and Vincent followed. They both sat down on the sofa; the Quill with his hands politely folded and resting on his lap, Vincent with his legs crossed and one arm flung over the top of the sofa. Both of them were experiencing different thoughts as they silently sat there, each waiting for the other to begin the conversation. The Quill did not particularly like surprise visits, and was wondering what had brought Vincent all the way out there. Vincent, on the other hand, was wondering if the Quill had any knowledge of the article that had run in the *Sun Sentinel*. Finally, it was the Quill who broke the silence when he asked Vincent, "So, what brings you out here on a Tuesday night?"

Vincent had a particular reason, but he wanted the elderly gentleman to relax a little before he discussed business. Vincent replied, "Well, I just returned from Anthony's mansion, and he asked me to personally extend his well-wishes. I told him that you were doing one hell of a job on this project, and he asked me to remind you that he will take care of your time and efforts, personally."

The Quill blushed somewhat before he replied, "Please tell him, 'Thank you,' for me."

"I would be more than happy to do that for you, however, you can tell him yourself, hopefully in a little over two weeks," Vincent remarked.

"He will be in Ft. Lauderdale?" the Quill asked.

"On the contrary, you will be in New Jersey. It seems that a couple of things have arisen whereupon it has become necessary to speed up our delivery schedule. Can you have everything completed in thirteen days?"

The Quill shifted in his seat and turned toward Vincent. A large smile was on his face, he already knew how far ahead of schedule he was on the project. The Quill replied, "I can have my end ready in ten days. Complete."

Vincent returned the man's smile and remarked, "Fantastic work, Quill. Fantastic. I take it the boys have kept you well supplied during my absence?"

"Yes, they have, as a matter of fact. They are a very efficient pair of workers," the Quill answered.

"They are my best," Vincent added.

There was a moment of silence between the two men then Vincent said, "As you're ahead of schedule, Quill, there is one other thing I need from you. I have already discussed this with Anthony, and he has given it his nod of approval."

"What can I do for you, Vincent?"

"Quill, I need an additional two million dollars in counterfeit twenties, and I would like for them all to have the same serial numbers. Can you handle that request?"

The Quill pondered that question for a moment while he calculated the production time necessary to produce that amount. If Vincent had requested different serial numbers, it would have been physically impossible for him to produce that amount is such a short period of time. However, without the need to change the serial numbers—the most time consuming, tedious portion of the entire project—the production stages were, for the most part, automated. The Quill looked Vincent in the eye and replied, "For you and Anthony, of course. There is something I would like to point out, though, which I am certain that you two have already considered. Even though I can guarantee the quality, the bills will be worthless in a matter of days if you use the same serial number. They will be on the hot sheet within a week of turning up, no matter where that happens."

"Yes, we did discuss that," Vincent flashed the elderly, seasoned counterfeiter a confident smile and continued, "Not to worry, Quill, I know what I'm doing."

"There has never been a question of that."

"There are a couple of small favors I would like to ask of you," Vincent added.

"Yes?"

Vincent withdrew a sealed envelope from the lightweight sports jacket he was wearing and laid it on the coffee table.

"I would like this two million placed in two, large, American Tourister suitcases rather than the boxes we are packing the Colombians' twenties in." Vincent's eyes shifted toward the sealed envelope sitting on the coffee table and the Quill's followed. Vincent added, "Please place that envelope in one of the suitcases, somewhere in between the layers of cash; somewhere where it will not be readily visible when the case is first opened." Vincent paused for a few seconds to allow time for the instructions to sink in.

"Whatever you would like done is the way it will be," the Quill replied after a moment of silence. "No problems here."

Vincent reached over and affectionately patted the elderly gentleman on the knee.

"Anthony told me you were a gem, and he was right."

The Quill blushed, once again.

"Now, let's discuss taking delivery of the balance of the boxes . . . ," Vincent continued.

Vincent and the Quill continued to talk for another half-hour before Vincent casually glanced at his watch. It was 8:25 p.m. Vincent looked at the Quill.

"Quill, I've got to get going. I still have another stop to make. Are we clear on everything?"

"Everything will be handled just as you have requested; just have your boys here on schedule," the Quill nodded his head. "My end will be ready."

Vincent offered his hand to the Quill and the two men shook hands.

"Done deal," Vincent said.

"I agree," remarked the Quill.

The two men stood and the Quill walked Vincent to the door where they said their good-byes. Five minutes later, Vincent turned the rented Lincoln onto Sample Road and headed east, toward Interstate 95. Traffic moved along well on both roadways during that early evening hour, and Vincent was at the Broward Boulevard exit within twenty minutes. He exited onto the main thoroughfare and followed it through downtown Ft. Lauderdale. Just past Federal Highway, he turned onto Las Olas Boulevard. Five minutes later, he was at the Isles. Vincent passed his own island and continued until he had reached the Isle where the golf course was located, then wheeled in the driveway.

Vincent got out of the Lincoln and quickly punched the appropriate coded numbers into the gate's electronically operated deadbolt. The box emitted a ten second buzz and Vincent entered the fenced-in grounds. Inside the drop house Gino had been alerted of the entry, and met Vincent at the front door with an automatic pistol tightly clutched in his hand.

"Oh, it's you," he said.

"I can see it's a good thing, too," Vincent quipped.

"Welcome home, boss. Come in," Gino laughed.

"Thank you," Vincent replied. "I cannot stay long, but I do have something important to discuss with you; a plan that requires your expertise."

Gino and Vincent talked for fifteen minutes. Gino was sharp. He needed no reasons; asked no questions. He just got the job done, and he did whatever Vincent asked of him. Timing was everything in Vincent's plan, and he stressed that to his faithful employee. Gino had one thing to say, "Consider it done, boss."

It was five minutes after ten when Vincent pulled beneath the awning in front of the Hertz rental car agency. The employees had changed shifts since he had been there earlier, and there were no lines at the counter. The rental return was painless compared to when he had rented the car, and within minutes he was in a taxicab headed toward his home in Las Olas Isles.

Vincent found his house just as he had left it. The electric timer had cut lights on and off in different rooms of the house while he had been away, and now it was apparent that the timer was on the living room cycle. Vincent paid the taxi driver then let himself in through the front door. Immediately, he picked up the telephone and dialed Jennifer's home number. Vincent glanced at his watch between the first and second rings and saw that it was a quarter 'til eleven. Jennifer answered the phone after the third ring.

"Hello?" she said in a soft voice.

"Hi," Vincent replied.

"Oh, Vincent, how are you?" she gushed.

"Never been better," although, in reality, the very second he heard her voice, memories of the photograph flooded his mind.

"Good. It's so nice to hear from you . . . I missed you, today."

Jennifer had suspected that Vincent had gone out of town, and that the trip had something to do with the article in the *Sun Sentinel*, yet she made it a point not to share her suspicions with Vincent. Instead, she chose to portray the concerned lover.

"Did you get your business taken care of?" Jennifer was referring to the statement that Vincent had made in the hotel room.

"Yes, I did . . . and, I missed you, too."

Vincent was tired. The night before had been a very long night, and it had been followed by a long day today. He wanted to cut to the chase. His plan called for knowing Jennifer's every move, as well as the Organized Crime Task Force not knowing his. The only logical thing to do, without raising any suspicions from either Jennifer or the listening parties on her telephone, was to move her into his house. That was an integral part of his plan.

"Sweetheart, why don't you grab a few things and stay with me at my house?" Vincent suggested.

There were a few expected moments of silence across the phone line. Meanwhile, Jennifer could not believe her good fortune. That was precisely what she had needed in order to make her plan work, also. Imagine, the hen inviting the fox into the hen house for an extended stay. After a reasonable pause, as if she had to consider the commitment of staying at his house, Jennifer asked, "How many things?"

"Why don't you bring enough clothes so that you won't have to go back to your condo for a couple of weeks, or so. We'll play it by ear from there, okay?"

Jennifer balled her fist in excitement and under her breath said, "Yes!"

"I'll be over with my clothes within the hour," she said to Vincent.

"I'll be waiting . . . bye," then he hung up the phone. His plan was in motion. The rest was up to Jennifer Swords.

* * *

Across town, Agent Jackson had listened in on their conversation while the eight inch reel-to-reel recorder had recorded it. Within minutes, Agent Jackson had Agent Murray on the telephone.

"Wake up, Murray. It's Jackson," he said after Mark answered.

"I'm awake, and it's a good thing, too. Why are you calling me at this hour, Jackson?

"Because I thought you might be interested in hearing the latest surveillance conversation between Jennifer Swords and Vincent Panachi."

Mark Murray sat up in bed and muted the late night program he had been watching on the television.

"Okay, let's hear it," he said.

"It's hot news . . . standby."

A few seconds later, Agent Murray listened to the recorded conversation.

Agent Jackson had no idea what he had done, but the knowledge of Jennifer Swords moving into Vincent Panachi's home had caused Agent Mark Murray to experience the most restless night of his life. The rising sun the following morning found him in his kitchen drinking a glass of Alka-Seltzer; The night before had been one hell of a night.

CHAPTER TWENTY-THREE

T he following three days had proved to be very frustrating for the Organized Crime Task Force; in particular, Agent Murray. For three days and nights they had not had a single sighting of Panachi or Jennifer. It was as if they had holed up in Vincent's house and for an interminable period of time. At least it had appeared to be seemingly endless to those agents who had been assigned to surveillance duty on Panachi's Navarro Isle home. Their daily reports to Agent Murray had been exactly the same every day since they had assumed their surveillance position. DAY ONE: No significant movement; DAY TWO: No significant movement; DAY THREE: No significant movement. Now, it was Saturday, day four, and Agent Murray was absolutely certain that his ulcer was acting up. Taking swigs of Maalox had become a way of life during those past three days. It seemed that the familiar burning feeling in his stomach was due to the frustration felt over losing their edge on Vincent Panachi. Without the ability to track his whereabouts through Jennifer and her tapped telephone, it had become a tedious, man-power-exhaustive task to gather basically the same intelligence information. Agent Murray's superiors were not overly excited about his having tied up a substantial amount of their manpower on this investigation, and quite frankly, if it had not been for the million dollars the agents had seized from Capo Pelligi as a result of their surveillance efforts, the powers in charge would have remanded Agent Murray's surveillance orders.

It was not the agents' fault that their reports had been so mundane, and they most certainly were not guilty of having been derelict in their duties. The agents had maintained an around-the-clock vigil; they just had not seen anything worth reporting. In fact, that had been precisely what Vincent had wanted them to see—nothing. He did nothing; he went nowhere; he had not made a phone call in three days; and, he knew Jennifer's whereabouts the entire time, because she had been there beside him. Vincent also knew that this little hide-and-seek game was driving the task force crazy. Murray didn't have a clue that Vincent knew about Jennifer's phone being wired, and Vincent knew that Murray had either listened in on his call to Jennifer or had heard a recording of the conversation. With that in mind, Vincent had initiated his plan by causing somewhat of a diversion. In its simplest terms, there was no mistaking the fact that Vincent was hot, and after reading the feature article that had appeared on the front page of the *Sun Sentinel*, any astute person would have drawn precisely the same conclusion that the family's legal counsel had drawn—Vincent Panachi was the target, and therefore the person whom the Organized Crime Task Force would concentrate their considerable surveillance force upon. Vincent had not moved from his residence; but not because he was paranoid. Vincent and Jennifer had experienced a wonderful time inside his house during the past three days. They had slowly worked their way through two cases of Moet Chandon champagne, at least a dozen movies, and engaged in mad, passionate, lovemaking several times a day. While Vincent had kept Jennifer and the agents of the task force busy, Vincent's plan has been staged. The pertinent players had been busy during the past three days making the appropriate arrangements, as per Vincent Panachi's instructions; Vincent's boys had reloaded the Quill with supplies, and meanwhile had removed another one hundred and fifty-five boxes of perfectly printed, twenty dollar bills. The two men had driven the twelve-and-a-half million dollars to the golf course where Gino had unobtrusively stashed it alongside the other twenty-five million in counterfeit dollars. That back bedroom now had four hundred and sixty-five boxes full of money stashed in it. While the boys and Gino had been involved in the logistics of moving the dollars, Carlos Lazarro had flown to Cali, Colombia; met with his uncle, Señior Calerro; and flown back to Ft. Lauderdale, Florida. Although he had not communicated with Vincent, and wouldn't for ten more days, all was as it should be. The fact that there was no communication between the two said it all. Anthony Vitale and Vincent Panachi's plans had taken on lives of their own.

Saturday had provided the task force with a break in their monotonous surveillance routine when, shortly after 11 a.m., Vincent and Jennifer were spotted exiting his home through the rear, sliding glass doors. Within minutes they were in his Scarab Thunder, and the agent watching the rear of Panachi's house from across the canal reported that to the agents posted at the front entrance of the Navarro Isle home. It was redundant when the radio crackled, once again, "He's started the engines on the go-fast." The powerful, big-block, V-8, gas guzzlers made a thunderous roar that resounded up and down the relatively quiet canal between Navarro Isle and Hendrick's Isle. The chrome exhaust stacks coughed up gallons of sea water while the full racing cam equipped engines idled. Ten minutes later, peace and quiet returned to the canal, and the Scarab Thunder was gone.

Just as the agents assigned to the Navarro Isle location had anticipated, the Scarab thunder had gone to Shylock's, along with just about every other go-fast that had been on the water that morning. By the time the task force's surveillance team overlooking Shylock's and Pegleg's had reported sighting the Scarab Thunder, it was well past noon. The bar at Shylock's was packed—standing room only, three deep at the lower bar—just as it had been every Saturday afternoon, for years. Sport fish yachts were tied up along the elongated wooden dock that spanned the distance between the two waterfront bars, and beyond those nearly every make and model of big boy's dream toys had rafted off of the mega dollar yachts: Scarabs; Cigarettes; Aronows: Donzis; Apaches; and Sonics, just to name a few. At any rate, Vincent Panachi's Scarab would have been just another go-fast out for a weekend jaunt—at least as far as the Organized Crime Task Force was concerned—had it not belonged to him. However, ever since his Scarab had been sighted, ten of the twelve surveillance cameras housed in the tenth-floor condo were trained upon Vincent Panachi and his Scarab Thunder. Vincent Panachi could have cared less. As the agents peered down at them, it appeared that Jennifer did not have a care in the world either. It was precisely that sort of free-from-all-cares attitude that Vincent was displaying, combined with the fact that he was with Jennifer Swords that had Agent Mark Murray seething mad. As he watched them through one of the cameras' powerful lenses, he swore under his breath. Out loud he said, "I'll get you yet, Panachi."

Agent Murray just did not get it. There, ten stories below, was a South Florida representative for the Vitale crime family, and he was acting as if the *Sun Sentinel*'s front page feature article had not affected him one way or the other. Panachi's unconcerned behavior bordered flagrant arrogance. The whole purpose of the article had been to shatter Vincent's confidence and security, in hopes that he would panic and begin making mistakes; mistakes that the task force would be anxiously waiting to pounce on. Apparently, however, that single article had not achieved the desired result; Vincent was his usual cool, calm and collected self. It appeared that it was business as usual.

Mark Murray backed away from the tripod-mounted camera and rubbed his eyes. Perhaps it had been a combination of the bright sunlight and the strain of looking intently through the camera's tiny view-finder that had caused his temples to throb with every beat of his pulse. Whatever the cause may have been, Agent Murray had one hell of a midday headache. He pondered the annoying Panachi situation while he sat on the sofa and gently massaged his temples. An idea flashed into his mind. The *Sun Sentinel*'s feature article had been a sell-out for the newspaper publishing company. No doubt, the publisher would look favorably upon any follow up articles. Agent Murray reached for the telephone and dialed Ms. Phyllis Lloyd's direct line. Surprisingly for a middle of the day Saturday, the investigative reporter answered her private line after the second ring.

"Phyllis Lloyd," she said in her most professional tone. Her editor had agreed, without hesitation, to allow her to install a direct access phone line in her office. Her noteworthy reputation preceded her, and the private line enhanced her ability to obtain street-info. Agent Murray was not providing her with street level scuttlebutt. Her feature article on the Vitale crime family had been met with such great acceptance that it had the potential of becoming an award winning investigative report. She had a pad and pen ready to jot down any information; because one could never be certain what potentially lucrative tidbit of information a caller had to offer.

"Phyllis, Agent Murray speaking," he replied.

"Mark," she gushed. She immediately recognized his voice and instinctively placed the tip of the pen against the yellow, stick-on note pad. "How are you?"

"Doing fine . . . and yourself?"

"Fine, thank you," she replied. There was an awkward pause across the phone line.

"Are you busy this afternoon?" Mark queried.

Phyllis Lloyd had not achieved her reputation as a tough, investigative reporter by not being direct.

"Why Mark, are you asking me out on a date?"

Mark Murray's face flushed red and he could feel the heat on his skin. The direct question had caught him off guard, yet he recovered quickly.

"Now, that's a thought. However, what I really called about was to see if you would be interested in doing a follow up, feature article on the Vitale crime Family's South Florida activities . . . and, to ask you if you would join me for dinner, tonight?"

Phyllis giggled that infections laugh—the same contagious laugh that had swooped Dr. Kramer off his feet.

"Yes, to both questions. When and where?"

Agent Murray smiled as he visualized her radiant smile.

"Well, I have a special treat for you. How would you like to visit the surveillance outpost where Vincent Panachi is under surveillance, as we speak?"

"I would like that very much," the seasoned reporter quickly replied. "Just give me an address, and I'm on the way."

Agent Murray clutched his fist tight and made a single downswing with it. "Yes!" he silently congratulated himself.

"Are you familiar with the condominiums across the waterway from Shylock's?"

"Yes," she answered.

"Okay, can you meet me in the lobby of that condo building in, say, twenty minutes?" he asked.

"I can," Phyllis replied.

"Good, I'll see you downstairs in twenty minutes. I'm certain that you are going to thoroughly enjoy this," the agent remarked.

"I'm sure . . . I'll see you in twenty minutes. Bye," Ms. Lloyd replied.

The investigative reporter was accurate in her estimate; she arrived at the condo precisely nineteen-and-a-half minutes after Mark had hung up the telephone. Not bad timing from her downtown, river-front office, he had remarked to himself as he watched her walk toward the condo's lobby. Phyllis greeted Mark with an affectionate kiss on the cheek, and then they casually chitchatted during the elevator ride to the building's tenth floor—the penthouse.

The years spent as a first-rate, investigative reporter had given Phyllis access to many after the fact details, but, to date, she had never had the opportunity to be involved in an actual newsworthy story in the making. Now, as she stood in the living room of the task forces' surveillance condominium, Phyllis was in awe at the bank of cameras aimed towards the two waterfront drinking establishments. She, just like any other normal person, would never have guessed that they were there, or that they had been there for God knows how long. She turned to Agent Murray and asked, "Would you mind terribly if I looked through one of your cameras?"

"That's why you're here," Mark chuckled as he motioned toward the wall of sliding glass doors. "I wanted you to see organized crime at play."

Phyllis casually tossed her purse on the sofa as she walked toward the cameras. She selected the third one from the left; a thirty-five millimeter Nikon with a 200 mm lens attached. As she leaned forward and placed her right eye against the camera's view-finder, her thick, lustrous, brunette hair toppled across her face. She instinctively brushed it from her eye with a quick sweep of her right hand while her left rested ever so gently on the camera's tripod. The powerful lens had been trained directly upon Panachi's Scarab, and a crystal-clear close-up of Vincent Panachi and Jennifer Swords seated on the Scarab's rear seat filled the view-finder. At the same moment, Agent Murray was observing the same view, with the exception that his camera had a 600 mm lens attached. Consequently, the field of view was much narrower, but much more detailed. Jennifer filled his camera's view-finder.

"So, is that Vincent Panachi in the back of that speed boat?" Phyllis queried.

Agent Murray withdrew from the camera long enough to look in the direction of Phyllis Lloyd. She was glued to the camera, obviously intrigued by it all.

"That's him," Agent Murray replied as he turned his head back and looked into his camera.

"Who's the woman? Do you have any identification on her?"

There were a couple of seconds pause before Agent Murray answered her. He had been watching through the powerful lens when Jennifer Swords had turned to say something to Vincent. During which, the cloudless sky had allowed the sun to radiantly reflect off of her necklace. When she had turned back around, Mark made precise, minute adjustments to the super-powerful lens until the reflection had been fine tuned and fully focused. Murray felt the blood rush from his head, and his hands tingled while he looked through the view-finder. The necklace filled the lens as he read the familiar word, *STILETTO*. He winced at the thought that he had given Jennifer that necklace, and why he had chosen that particular word to be spelled in diamond chips. Even now, the pain still cut deep in his heart. Agent Murray answered Phyllis' question while he continued to look into the tripod-mounted camera.

"We have absolutely no idea who she is . . . ," Mark Murry's voice trailed off.

There was something in the way he had answered her question that made Phyllis turn her head and look at him. Agent Murray was standing steadfast at the camera, fixated by what he was watching. Phyllis Lloyd continued to stare at him for nearly fifteen seconds, during which, Mark was so preoccupied with the sight of Jennifer Swords that he was oblivious to the fact that he, himself, was being watched. The combination of women's intuition and Phyllis' basic inquisitiveness refused to let her accept the agent's statement at face value. Instinct told her that there was more to it than he had led her to believe. She made a mental note of it before she turned her head and, once again, looked through the camera with the 200 mm lens attached. She saw Vincent lean over and say something in Jennifer's ear before he stepped out of view. Seconds later, Jennifer disappeared from the field of view of both cameras. Within minutes, Jennifer and Vincent were engulfed by the crowd of party revelers that surrounded the lower bar at Shylocks.

There was not another sighting of Vincent Panachi until late that same afternoon when he and Jennifer fired up the Scarab's powerful engines and leisurely motored down the waterway towards the Las Olas Islands. That afternoon had not been fruitless for Mark Murray though; it had provided the agent with a comfortable, casual, unhurried atmosphere which he had utilized to his advantage. He showed Ms. Lloyd Panachi's surveillance file along with the countless number of photos that had been snapped over the months. By the time the Scarab Thunder motored out of sight of the surveillance cameras' telephoto lens, Ms. Lloyd had her next headline-making, feature article already written, in her mind. It was just a matter of getting it down on her word processor before the newspaper's Monday morning deadline.

Moments before Agent Murray and Phyllis Lloyd left the tenth-floor condo on their dinner date, the task force's Las Olas Isles' surveillance team reported, via radio, that the Scarab go-fast had returned to Panachi's Navarro Isle home. With the exception of noting that the house's lights had been turned on and off in several rooms throughout the night, their daily report had ended the same. DAY FOUR: No significant movement.

*   *   *

MONDAY . . . 6:30 A.M.

Urban areas, in general, abound with convenience stores; some of which are considered landmarks whereby entire communities shop there daily. Full service dry clean laundries are often located next door, making the one-stop-shop that more attractive to the busy consumer. Las Olas Boulevard has such a convenience store—the 7-11. Its location is such that a great number of people residing in the Las Olas Isles area stop there every morning to buy a newspaper, among other things. It is the only place where one may purchase a paper at six-thirty in the morning. The convenience store is located just over the Navarro River Bridge, and two blocks form Vincent Panachi's house.

The agents assigned to surveillance duty at Panachi's island home were six-and-a-half hours into their eight hour shift, and their bodies were screaming for more coffee. Strong, black coffee; the type brewed at the 7-11. Since the weekend, the agent in charge, Mark Murray, had ordered two man teams on around-the-clock shifts to watch Vincent Panachi's movements. However, with the exception of taking the Scarab to Shylock's on Sunday, there hadn't been any movement outside the house. Vincent's bizarre behavior had the surveillance agents, as well as Mark Murray, baffled. The topic of conversation that had kept the two agents awake during those six-and-a-half hours had been centered around speculation on what Panachi was up to. Finally, after hours of verbalizing every pensive, speculative thought that had come into their minds, they tossed a coin to determine which one would walk to the 7-11 for coffee and a morning newspaper.

The loser of the coin toss walked west along Las Olas Boulevard, across the pink bridge that spanned the Navarro River, then past the private hospital. The 7-11 was just beyond that building. It was a quarter-'til-seven when the agent entered the well-lighted store, and already the parking lot was filled to capacity. There was a line of customers four deep standing at the cash register. Most were dressed in casual jogging attire, and all held a large cup of coffee and a newspaper in their hands. It appeared that no matter what walk of life they were from, they all shared the exact same wants and needs the first thing in the morning. The agent followed two people to the rear of the store where the coffee pots were set up. Among the pots of different flavored coffees, he found what he was looking for—straight, black coffee enriched in caffeine. "High test" at its finest. The agent poured himself and his partner a large cup each and place a to-go cap on them. The line at the register had moved steadily, yet it was still four persons deep. He walked past the registers toward the front of the store. There were copies of that morning's *Sun Sentinel* stacked high in two, wooden display racks. The agent nonchalantly scooped up the top copy and folded it beneath his arm. It wasn't until he had stood in line at the register long enough to reach the countertop and set the two coffees down that he had an opportunity to sneak a peek at the morning's headlines. As he read the bold printed headline, his eyes widened and his eyebrows rose. A strange thought flashed through his mind—although they may have had to sit on surveillance duty night after night, it was obvious that they had not been the only ones working. Judging from the *Sun Sentinel*'s headlines, their superior had been putting in some long hours developing the public relations angle of the Panachi investigation. That morning's headline read: *ORGANIZED CRIME TASK FORCE CLOSING IN ON NORTHEAST CRIME FAMILY*. Below and to the right were the words: *FEATURE ARTICLE by Ms. PHYLLIS LLOYD*. The agent had a smirk on his face when the un-naturalized foreign resident working the cash register asked, "Will there be anything else, sir?"

The agent slid the two coffees to the center of the counter and asked, "Could you bag these, please?"

After that polite request left his mouth, the agent dropped his eyes back down to the opened newspaper. There was no mistaking that Agent Murray, through Ms. Phyllis Lloyd, was keeping the heat on the Vitale crime family; in particular, Vincent Panachi.

*   *   *

Across town in hangar number twenty-four at the Ft. Lauderdale Executive Airport, Carlos Lazarro entered the building. It was a mere coincidence that the hour was precisely 9:00 a.m. The Colombian drug cartel's Miami representative could not have been further from the conventional nine-to-fiver. However, his dazzling beautiful personal receptionist adhered more to the established hours customary to the business world. It was she who unlocked the office door every morning, precisely at 9 a.m., and did so for no other reason than appearance sake. That particular morning though, there had been a reason the two of them had arrived together. Carlos Lazarro, acting on direct orders from Señior Calerro, had their two most trusted airframe and powerplant (A&P) mechanics scheduled to go over the plane with a fine-toothed comb.

Inside the huge aluminum hangar, two Cessna 404 Titans had been carefully positioned at an angle to one another. Their polished fuselages gleamed from the powerful overhead lamps that shown down upon them, suspended high above, inside the hangar's structural steel ceiling. The two aircraft had been somewhat modified to accommodate the drug cartel's special needs, which included satellite navigation systems and internally installed, long-range fuel tanks that allowed for non-stop flights from Florida to a clandestine airstrip somewhere deep within the jungles of Colombia, South America. The Cessna 404s had a pair of 350 horsepower, fuel injected, turbo-supercharged engines hanging off those fuel-laden wings that made the aircraft capable of hauling a ton of cargo—more than ample load-lifting capability required to transport the cartel's expected shipment of fifty million dollars in counterfeit, twenty dollar bills and deliver it with pinpoint preciseness.

Carlos walked directly to the metal door at the end of the corridor and opened it. The hangar's massive sliding doors were secured from the inside by a huge padlock, which he opened. It took his entire body weight to crack the heavy doors a mere twelve inches. Instantaneously, sunlight streamed in and shot a beam of light across the hangar's painted-concrete floor. Carlos turned and walked back to his office. The A&P mechanics would be there soon, and barring no unforeseen disasters, both Titans would be in topnotch condition by the end of the working day.

Carlos sat down behind the solid-teak desk in his office and leaned back in his chair. His hands were clasped behind his head and his boots were propped on the edge of the desk top. It was the quiet part of the day, and he was taking advantage of the serene moment by pondering. His moment of contemplation was interrupted when his personal receptionist entered the office. She held a cup of coffee and the morning newspaper in her hands.

"Today's *Sun Sentinel* and coffee for his Highness," she quipped.

Carlos waved his hand at her jokingly and replied, "Just leave them on the desk top . . . you're excused." He looked up at her and smiled. She placed the cup of coffee on his desk, as ordered, but instead of laying the newspaper down beside it, she quickly rolled the paper up and swatted him with it across the ankles. Carlos reacted by quickly sitting up, but not quickly enough to prevent her from charging behind his desk. The Spanish beauty flashed him a radiant smile as she plopped onto his lap.

"Here's your paper, Squire." The dark-eyed beauty unrolled the newspaper before she placed it on the desk, then wrapped her arms around his neck and gave him a passionate long-lasting kiss. Afterwards she left, leaving Carlos to enjoy his morning ritual; a ritual that included a passionate kiss.

Carlos Lazarro repositioned the coffee cup within comfortable reach then slid the paper to the edge of the desk. He scooped up the *Sun Sentinel* in his right hand and angled it slightly so that he could read it more easily. When he glanced at it, the bold printed headline appeared to leap from the front page: *ORGANIZED CRIME TASK FORCE CLOSING IN ON NORTHEAST CRIME FAMILY*. Without looking, he grasped the coffee cup in his left hand and guided it to his lips. His eyes methodically scanned back and forth across each line while he rapidly read the feature article. For a Colombian national, his command of the English language was exceptional. Ms. Phyllis Lloyd's feature article portrayed Vincent Panachi as an active crime boss in the Vitale crime family, and continued to go so far as to imply that the Organized Crime Task Force was but a step away from shutting them down. Whatever the case may have been, the front page article in that morning's *Sun Sentinel* did not deter Carlos Lazarro from his mission. His end would be ready, on schedule.

*   *   *

The morning sun shown through the single window in agent Mark Murray's cramped, third floor office in the headquarters for the Organized Crime Task Force. Agent Murray could almost see Vincent Panachi's Navarro Isle home from his

308

office, and could see it from the big boss' fifth floor office. The ray of sunlight cut across half of his ancient wooden desk top at an angle where a copy of that morning's *Sun Sentinel* was stretched open. It was one morning that the contrast between the sunlight and his desk lamp went unnoticed, because Agent Murray was absolutely entranced with Ms. Phyllis Lloyd's feature article.

There was a light tap on his office door. Murray instinctively checked the time before he said, "Come in." 9:18 a.m., and Agent Murray's first appointment for that morning had been scheduled for 10:00 a.m., when he was due upstairs for the Monday morning strategy meeting held in the director of the task force's office. It was apparent that his director had decided to hold an ex parte meeting with Agent Murray. The field agent was surprised, perhaps even somewhat shocked, when he saw the big boss, Wade Jessup, enter through the doorway. It was an unwritten rule that the top floor brass did not go downstairs. It was beneath them . . . no pun intended. Murray saw that his boss had a copy of the *Sun Sentinel* in his hand. He also observed, with great relief, the usual Monday morning grump was smiling.

Agent Murray stood the moment he realized who had entered the tiny room. Wade Jessup crossed the office in four steps and extended his right hand across the desk.

"Good morning, Agent Murray," he said.

"Good morning, sir." Mark met his boss' hand with his own and the two men shook hands. "What can I do for you, this morning?"

His boss casually withdrew his hand and made a motion toward the two, wooden chairs situated across from Murray's desk. One was the uncomfortable chair where Capo Pelligi had been handcuffed.

"May I sit down?" his superior queried.

Mark's face flushed red.

"Excuse me . . . of course. I guess you caught me by surprise. It's not often that I see you down here."

Both men sat; Agent Jessup, then Agent Murray. The boss tossed a folded copy of that morning's *Sun Sentinel* on top of Murray's desk so that the bold-printed headline was face up.

"Well, it's not everyday that the newspaper gives us a write up like this one. God damn, Murray, what did you do to inspire this reporter?"

Agent Murray wasn't certain how to take the remark, and just remained silent with a dumbfounded expression on his face. His boss gave him a mischievous wink meant to suggest that perhaps Mark may have engaged in a little sexual interlude with Phyllis Lloyd. The truth of the matter was the Agent Murray had been the perfect gentleman during their dinner date, despite the fact that Phyllis Lloyd had become somewhat suggestive as the evening evolved. Agent Murray had much more of a burning desire to hang Vincent Panachi than he did to bed the attractive, investigative reporter. It was a chance he could not have afforded; she had already agreed to do the article. And, what an article she had written.

"I invited her to the surveillance condominium. Panachi was at Shylock's that day."

Agent Jessup leaned forward so that his index finger struck the newspaper directly on the headline. He tapped the words: *ORGANIZED CRIME TASK FORCE CLOSING IN ON NORTHEAST CRIME FAMILY* as he enthusiastically exclaimed, "Now *I* want him! I want you to come down hard on this Panachi character, and I want you to plan it for one week from tonight. Let's bring him in."

"On what charge?" Agent Murray queried.

His superior removed the finger from the newspaper and leaned back against the chair. He slowly crossed his legs as he looked at Mark Murray and gave him a knowing stare.

"That's what will take a week. Let me handle the routine paperwork. Don't worry . . . with this much publicity, you'll have a valid arrest warrant. Just set it up . . . one week from tonight—next Monday.

Agent Murray nodded his head in acknowledgement as he now completely understood why the strategy meeting had been held as an ex parte meeting. The Organized Crime Task Force was making preparations to railroad Vincent Panachi. Murray held his boss' stare and smiled.

"Count me in!"

*   *   *

The sky was cloudless and beautifully blue when Jennifer and Vincent woke up. While they lay in bed, he peered through the drapes and confirmed what the evenly spaced, multiple streams of sunlight that entered his easterly facing bedroom hours earlier had suggested—it was an absolutely gorgeous day. Vincent removed his hand from the slit and watched the heavy, linen drape fall until the opening closed. A quick check of the clock on the nightstand revealed the time to be 9:45 a.m.

Jennifer was lying on her side with two feather pillows fluffed beneath her head. Vincent turned toward her and propped himself up on one elbow. He gently swept a wisp of hair from her eyes.

"Good morning," he said. Jennifer smiled as she replied the same. Vincent suggested, "It's a beautiful day . . . let's take the Scarab down to Shylock's for lunch then we'll go for a ride. What do you think?"

Jennifer hugged both pillows as she rolled over onto her stomach, her mane of hair falling to one side as she looked at Vincent.

"Oh Vincent, I'd love to, but Mondays are the days set aside for my hair and nails. And, after missing two appointments while we were in Nassau, I just *have* to go today."

Vincent had not planned on that answer. Spending the entire afternoon with a hair stylist is just not something most men do. He had to do some quick thinking, because the last thing he needed was to have Jennifer out and about without his having any idea whom she might contact—very possibly no one; but on the other hand, perhaps Agent Mark Murray. Somehow, someway, he had to keep her occupied, and with him. Vincent reached over and casually ran his fingers through her hair. He complimented her.

"Are you trying to drive all the men crazy, or what? Your hair is beautiful. Can't you just take this one day off . . . . , please? It is such a nice day out. It would be a shame to spend such a gorgeous day inside."

Jennifer had to do some quick thinking also. Her plan had called for utilizing some of the time that she was supposedly at the hair salon to search through Vincent's house. She tilted her head down, as if she were pondering his invitation, while Vincent continued running his fingers through her thick hair. In reality she was considering the complications of her own plans. Jennifer knew that Vincent would not sit around the house if she did keep her appointment. After all, they had not left the house for days, with the exception of going boating. Surely, she reasoned, he would have to run some errands sooner or later. On the other hand, Jennifer contemplated maybe it would be better if she waited him out. Besides, now that she had made him aware of her regularly scheduled appointments it should be easier for her to get away the following Monday. That way Vincent would not suspect a thing, and it would allow her to carry out a much more thorough search for the money. If the cash was in the house she would find it, and she would find it by next week at the very latest. It was only a matter of time Jennifer reminded herself. Yes, she assured herself, next Monday would be better. Jennifer lifted her head and turned to face Vincent with her alluring eyes.

"It *is* a beautiful day . . . and we have been having so much fun together. I guess Darlene can live another week without seeing me. Let's go boating!"

"Alright, let's go!" Vincent enthusiastically replied.

Jennifer mistook his eagerness as inspired enthusiasm. However, more to the point, it had been an exclamation of relief.

Less than an hour later, Vincent Panachi's Scarab Thunder was moored dockside at Shylock's. Unlike the marine madhouse found there on the weekend, Monday was a very slow day for the dock hands, and there were only four other boats moored alongside the wooden dock.

Less than five minutes after Vincent and Jennifer had pulled away from his Navarro Isle dock, the Scarab's departure had been reported, via radio, to the surveillance team overlooking the two popular waterfront bars. They, in turn, had reported the arrival of the go-fast at Shylock's back to the field agents posted nearby Vincent's home, via the same discrete radio channel. Afterwards, the agents posted in the tenth floor condo trained three cameras with various sized lenses on to Vincent's Scarab. The first photographs taken were of Vincent helping Jennifer off of the boat and onto the dock. However, without further adjustments to the cameras' powerful telephoto lens, their movements quickly placed them outside of the three cameras' fields of view. The surveillance team was certain that they had not gone far. The agents moved without hesitation to the condominium's bedroom balcony and watched until Vincent and Jennifer had entered Shylock's. They knew that Vincent would sit at the lower bar.

Vincent and Jennifer chose two stools at the lower bar, and of course they had made certain beforehand that they were seated at Tony's station. There were less than a dozen people scattered about the lower bar, but the lunch crowd was beginning to trickle in through the front door. Fortunately most of the patrons were seated on the far end of the lower bar and in another bartender's section, which provided Tony with the opportunity to socialize with his customers. Naturally, he was always delighted to see Vincent seated at his bar, but that particular morning Tony was more than eager to speak with his friend, Vincent Panachi. He did, however, have the good sense to wait until Jennifer had excused herself to go to the ladies' room to freshen up her makeup.

Tony cast a quick glance over his shoulder and confirmed that Jennifer was indeed on her way to the ladies' room and out of earshot before he reached beneath the bar and grabbed a copy of that morning's *Sun Sentinel*. The bartender walked over to Vincent and stood across the bar from him before he causally tossed the newspaper on the bar. The *Sun Sentinel* landed directly in front of Vincent, face up and at an angle. The bold printed headline leapt off of the front page at Vincent: *ORGANIZED CRIME TASK FORCE CLOSING IN ON NORTHEAST CRIME FAMILY*. Despite Vincent's usual calm composure, he involuntarily swallowed hard as he quickly scooped up the paper and read the feature article.

"My friend, you are a fuckin' star!" Tony remarked.

Vincent paused from reading long enough to look up and comment, "So I am . . . and according to this article, I am nothing more than a fading star."

The bartender had seen many players come and go, but none that had maintained the staying power Vincent Panachi had demonstrated. Tony really wasn't certain if this was just another storm that would blow over within a matter of weeks. Nonetheless, he felt that it was his duty as a friend to offer a piece of noteworthy advice to Vincent.

"Just watch your ass, Vincent . . . watch your ass."

Little did he know just how far advanced Vincent's plans were to cover his ass.

"Thank you, my friend," Vincent replied.

He reached into his pocket and removed his money clip, then peeled a twenty dollar bill from it, folded the bill and placed it on the bar. Tony had witnessed this move a countless number of times. The bartender placed his hand on top of Vincent's and prevented him from pushing the tip toward the edge of the bar.

"This one's on me, pal," Tony remarked.

Vincent momentarily stared into his friend's eyes before he pocketed the bill.

"Thanks, again." Vincent said. He finished the article then folded the newspaper and handed it back to Tony. "Put that away before Jennifer returns, okay . . . and tell her I had to make a couple of phone calls, please. I'll be back in a few minutes."

Tony replaced the newspaper beneath the bar and replied, "Done deal," but Vincent had already begun walking toward a bank of pay telephones located between the two bars in the outside, patio dining area.

By the time Jennifer returned from the ladies' room, Vincent was on the telephone. His first call was placed to Carlos Lazarro. Vincent recognized the receptionist's, soft-spoken voice.

"Hangar 24 . . . how may I help you?" Vincent identified himself and asked to speak with Mr. Lazarro. "Certainly, Mr. Panachi . . . please hold while I transfer your call," she said.

"Thank you," Vincent replied as he looked over at Jennifer and waved.

Seconds later Carlos picked up the line.

"Vincent, how are you?" he asked.

"Everything is fine." Vincent replied. There was a short pause before Vincent asked, "I take it that you've seen this morning's paper?"

Carlos was cool, and his voice remained steady.

"Yeah, I read it . . . and I didn't see anything in there that we didn't already know."

"No problems then?" Vincent queried.

"Nothing will stop the plane from flying . . . at least on my end," the Colombian replied with a tone in his voice that was as cold as ice.

"Good . . . I like your attitude."

"It is business, Vincent, and business comes first . . . always."

However, due to the circumstances Vincent felt a change of plans was neccesary . . . something had to switch-it-up in the plan, if for no other reason than his personal peace of mind.

"That's what I like to hear. Now, can you handle the departure next Monday, rather than Tuesday?"

"What time of day, Monday?" the pitch of Carlos' voice did not change—as if the date change was insignificant to his operation.

"Early afternoon," Vincent responded.

"Done . . . I'll make the proper arrangements on the other end."

There were no questions asked as to why.

"So, I'll see you early Monday afternoon, then?" Vincent confirmed.

"We will be ready on our end, Vincent. I'll see you Monday. Until then, amigo . . ."

"Thanks, Carlos. Bye." They hung up their telephones at precisely the same moment.

Vincent stood at the pay telephone for a couple of minutes while he thought out the context of his next call. When he picked up the receiver, he dialed the telephone number for Beach Side Travel Agency. Vincent's usual travel agent answered the telephone on its second ring.

"Beach Side Travel," the middle aged woman's cheerful voice answered.

"Virginia, this is Vincent Panachi. How are you?"

"Oh, hello, Mr. Panachi . . . it's so nice to hear from you."

Vincent winced, because he was certain that she had seen not only this morning's article in the *Sun Sentinel,* but had read the previous feature article, as well. He knew that Virginia read the newspaper on a daily basis, yet it appeared that she had chosen not to bring up the subject, and if she didn't, Vincent wasn't going to.

"I need your services, again, Virginia."

"Where to, Mr. Panachi?"

"Rio de Janeiro, but the travel arrangements are not for me. Make the ticket out in the name of Ms. Jennifer Swords, first class, one way, departing Ft. Lauderdale next Monday night. Can you handle that?"

"Of course," she replied. "And will you be picking the ticket up, Mr. Panachi?"

"Could you just mail the ticket to my house, please?"

The mailing of the airline ticket as opposed to him picking it up at the travel agency had been what Vincent had pondered during those couple of minutes between calls. Vincent had always had what some refer to as a sixth sense, and that capacity—to discern the true nature of a situation—told him that there was a very strong possibility that the task force would begin following his every move. In retrospect, Vincent's intuitive thought could not have been closer to the truth, for now that Agent Murray's superiors had become involved in the Vitale crime family investigation, the manpower problem had evaporated. The agents could watch Vincent as much as they liked, yet they still would never have knowledge of the airline ticket he had just purchased. Vincent planned to utilize the safest, most sacred delivery service known to the free world—the United States Postal Service—as his courier. The professional travel agent replied, "Of course, Mr. Panachi. It will go out in tomorrow morning's mail. Anything else I can help you with, today?"

"You're the greatest, Virginia. That should take care of it. Thank you," Vincent replied with a smile.

"And thank you, Mr. Panachi," she courteously replied. "Bye now," she added before she hung up the phone.

Vincent exhaled a sigh of relief that she had not questioned him about the articles. He had always thought of her as a nice lady.

Vincent reached into his pocket and withdrew another quarter then deposited it into the pay telephone. He had one more quick call to make in order to finalize his plan. His index finger dialed the telephone number of the Las Olas Isle's golf course house faster than he could have dialed his own home phone number. The telephone rang four times before Gino finally answered.

"Speak to me," he said.

"Okay, I will," Vincent laughed.

"Oh, hi boss . . . what's up?" his demeanor changed as he asked.

"What's up over there?"

"Nothing more than this damned parrot with his feathers all ruffled. He hasn't shut up all morning. I tell you, Vincent, it has been one continuous ruckus around here."

"I should have such problems . . ." Vincent laughed.

"Yeah, I read the newspaper. No biggie. Is that why you called?"

It dawned on Vincent that perhaps he was the only person in town that had not read that morning's paper at an early hour.

"Not really, there has been a slight change of plans on my end. Pick me up at the same location we discussed, but make it Monday at noon."

"Monday . . . one week from today at noon, right?" Gino confirmed.

"You've got it. Oh, by the way, is everything okay with the Quill?"

"As far as I know. We'll see him Friday afternoon for the final pick up. You want me to tell him anything?"

Vincent thought about that question for a couple of seconds before he replied.

"Yeah, tell him how proud of him Anthony is. You know, boost his ego a little."

Vincent knew that he would never see the Quill again, or he would have told him himself.

"Sure thing, boss. Anything else?" Gino queried.

"No, that's it," Vincent replied.

"Okay then, I'll see you Monday at high noon. Bye."

"Good-bye, Gino," Vincent replied before he hung up the telephone.

Moments later, Vincent rejoined Jennifer at the bar. As he slid onto the wooden bar stool Jennifer asked, "Is everything okay?

"Couldn't be better . . . now, let's have that drink, shall we? Tony?" Vincent smiled confidently.

His good friend and favorite bartender walked up as if their previous conversation had never taken place.

"What'll it be, today? Champagne, perhaps?" he nonchalantly asked.

*   *   *

Several hours later and several miles northwest of Ft. Lauderdale, the Quill wiped beads of perspiration from above his bushy eyebrows. He walked into the living room and sat on the sofa. He couldn't believe his ears when he actually heard the rush of air from the compressing sofa cushion. For the first time since he had begun production, the machines were quiescent. He had worked around the clock, with the exception of no more than four hours of sleep per night, like a possessed madman. However, the end result had been well worth the effort, because now his production obligation of fifty million dollars in flawless, twenty dollar bills was complete, and in record time—one week ahead of schedule, to be exact. Fifty-million dollars worth; six hundred and twenty shoe-box sized boxes filled with counterfeit twenties.

The elderly man decided to take the night off from production. What the hell, he thought; I can certainly use the rest. Besides, he reminded himself, after you've printed fifty million, what's another two million? The Quill clasped his wrinkled hands behind his head and pondered the upcoming production run. Because he didn't have to change the serial numbers on Vincent's two million, he estimated that he could knock out the entire amount in two days . . . with machines doing all of the work. "Piece of cake," he said with a smile on his face.

CHAPTER TWENTY-FOUR

The next three days were uneventful. However, that lack of any significant events changed.

FRIDAY . . . 12:38 P.M.

An unmarked, blue, Ford Crown Victoria blew its horn twice before the heavy, iron security gate began to open. An overworked, underpaid, security guard wiped his mouth with a paper napkin as he approached the vehicle; apparently, the vehicle's arrival had caught him during his lunch break. His expression was one of boredom, highlighted with a slight tinge of aggravation that through the years had etched permanent wrinkles into the aged skin on his forehead. Agent Murray watched as the security guard approached the vehicle, his left hand barely gripping a clipboard. Mark rolled down the driver's window just as the guard reached the vehicle. The security guard swung the clipboard up into a position where he could make an entry into the log.

"Afternoon, boys. Which department you from?" he asked.

Agent Murray flashed him his gold and silver badge that identified him as an agent for the Organized Crime Task Force. The guard squinted somewhat while he copied the name printed on Murray's identification. Once the man had finished Agent Murray snapped the black, leather bound wallet which encased his shield and identification closed, and slid it inside the breast pocket of his suit jacket. No sooner had he done so, the weather-beaten man bent over far enough that his eyes were even with the well-dressed gentleman's seated in the front seat. The security guard courteously demanded, "I.D., please." Agent Murray turned toward Wade Jessup and watched as his boss reached into his suit jacket pocket and produced an identical, black wallet. He handed it to Murray, who passed the identification to the guard. The security guard copied the information down with a facial expression that enunciated his sheer boredom with the repetitive task. Neither of those identifications had impressed the aged security guard. After ten faithful years of service at the entry/exit security gate for the underground parking garage of the Federal Building in downtown Ft. Lauderdale, he had seen just about every kind of fancy badge there was to see. After he copied the pertinent information, the guard casually handed the leather wallet back to Agent Murray. Almost as if it had been an afterthought, he leaned down, once again, and peered at the three, suspicious-looking characters seated in the rear of the Ford sedan. A moment later, he turned toward Agent Murray, his eyebrows raised, and queried, "And who are them fellers?"

Agent Murray reached between himself and his superior and grabbed three, official-looking documents from the seat then handed them to the security guard. While the security guard looked over the court orders, Agent Murray patiently explained, "These men are federal prisoners and they are in our custody, for the day. What you're holding are their Writs of Habeas Corpus . . . and as you can see, these three men are scheduled to appear before the Grand Jury at 1:00 p.m."

The security guard skimmed over the documents and grunted before he handed them back to Agent Murray. He made a quick notation on his clip board then pointed in the direction they were to park. "Good enough," he said, then turned and walked back to his little shack where he resumed eating lunch.

Agent Murray wheeled the sedan into a parking spot located on the far end of the underground garage. The very instant he turned off the automobile's ignition, Agent Murray's superior shifted in his seat and turned so that he was facing the three prisoners seated in the rear of the Crown Victoria. Without looking down, his hand found the file folder lying on the seat between Murray and himself. He extracted an eight by ten, color glossy, surveillance photograph of Vincent Panachi and held it up when he said, "Alright, let's go through these pictures, one more time, before you boys get to the Grand Jury. Now, I don't give a good God damn if you ever laid eyes on these men before. What I do care about, though, is your sworn testimonies before this Grand Jury. Read my lips: I *want* indictments for money-laundering and bookmaking, and only your testimonies can do it. I have spoken with the prosecutor pursuing these, and he has assured me that if you boys are cooperative, he will see to it, personally, that you receive the sentence reductions that have been promised to you. I give you my word on that."

Agent Murray's superior paused for a few seconds, for dramatics, to allow ample time for the prisoners to reflect on their freedom. He gazed into their eyes, one at a time, and smiled. The seasoned agent knew that they would swear to anything he asked them to; he had seen that look of desperation in other informant's eyes before. He held the picture up with one hand and pointed at the face in the picture with the other when he asked, "Now, who is this man in this surveillance photograph?"

All three prisoners simultaneously replied, "Vincent Panachi, sir."

"Very good," the agent remarked. Agent Murray's boss quickly shuffled the pictures until he found several that had been taken outside of Anthony Vitale's landlubber party then he held one up. "Now, who might this underworld figure be?" he quizzed the three men.

"Capo Pelligi, sir," they all replied.

Another photograph was held up.

"And this distinguished-looking gentleman?" the agent asked.

"The boss of the crime family, Anthony Vitale, sir," they replied. The rehearsed questions continued for an additional ten minutes before Murray's boss was fully satisfied that they were ready to meet with the Grand Jury.

By 4:20 that afternoon, the Grand Jury had handed down an indictment for one Vincent Panachi. The sworn testimonies by the three felons, already convicted for bookmaking, enabled the prosecutor to successfully bring formal charges against Panachi—one count of bookmaking and one count of money-laundering. His prisoner witnesses did a magnificent job of recalling events and overt acts, in detail, while the prosecutor fed them prearranged questions. Their responses had been clear-cut and precise, when necessary; and long, drawn out stories when otherwise needed. Their testimonies and recollections had been flawless—particularly when one takes into consideration the fact that not one of them had ever seen, nor heard of Vincent Panachi prior to having been approached with a deal by Agent Jessup, the day before.

A combination of the late hour in the day and the end of the work week precluded the agents from leaving the Federal Grand Jury with an indictment in hand. However, they had now set the snare, and by noon Monday, they should be able to spring the trap.

* * *

A nondescript, white van was concealed behind the closed garage door at the Quill's house, and had been there since its arrival a half-hour earlier. Vincent's boys had been busy loading hand-truck after hand-truck full of boxes since the moment they arrived. It was a move that required no explanation, nor instructions from either themselves or the Quill. This trip, however, was somewhat different in that their usual laborious task had been reduced to half the work load—this was their final trip, and it had not been necessary to deliver a van load of supplies to the Quill. Instead, the boys had gone directly to the makeshift print shop bedroom with and empty hand-truck in tow.

Several strands of the Quill's silver-colored hair fell into his eyes when he bent over to check the final load of boxes before they were moved to the garage. After completing his quick count he stood, and brushed the hair from his eyes before making an entry into the ledger. Whether the twenty dollar bills had been counterfeit or not, they were still considered a monetary instrument in the underworld economy. The Quill had kept a running tally of when and what had gone out the door, and had conscientiously entered those figures into a ledger—a ledger that would eventually be turned over to Anthony Vitale. The Quill took a few moments to total his figures. Once he had arrived at a cumulative sum, he turned the ledger around and showed it to Gino.

"Inclusive of your past loads, you should have six hundred and twenty boxes. Is that your count?" the Quill queried.

Gino took the ledger and quickly added the numbers in his mind.

"As a matter of fact, I took an inventory at the house this morning before we left, and your figures agree with mine, Mr. Quill." Gino handed the ledger back to the Quill then in the same movement, waved his hand toward the garage and instructed his helper, "Load it." Before the burly man could answer, Gino quickly added, "I'll handle these suitcases."

"It's on the way, big money," his helper replied. At the same time the burly man tilted the fully loaded hand-truck backwards before skillfully maneuvering it back and forth until it was through the bedroom doorway.

The suitcases that Gino had referred to were the two American Tourister suitcases filled with counterfeit money that Vincent had asked the Quill to handle. As requested, two million dollars in counterfeit, twenty dollar bills had been layered and stuffed into the two large suitcases. The two American Touristers were identical—both in content and construction—with the exception that one had an envelope carefully placed between the layers. The Quill had followed Vincent's instructions to a tee, including the request to place the same serial number on all two million dollars despite the fact that it was against his better judgment. "Whatever he had wants," the Quill had mused. Again, the Quill had only done precisely what had been asked of him.

Gino's helper entered the house from the garage and informed the two men, "Everything's loaded and we're ready to roll."

"Well, my friend, I guess this does it," Gino turned and said to the Quill. Before the elderly gentleman replied, Gino crossed the bedroom and grabbed the two suitcases by their handles.

"You know what to do with those, right?" the Quill asked just before Gino picked up the suitcases.

Gino grunted as he walked past the Quill.

"Vincent filled me in, Mr. Quill. Not to worry . . . I'll handle it from here." Gino got as far as the living room before he set the cases down and turned back towards the Quill. In an afterthought, he said, "Oh yeah, I almost forgot, Vincent asked me to relay Anthony's gratitude for an exceptional job well done."

The elderly counterfeiter *had* done a remarkable job, and it had been much easier for him to manufacture fifty-two million dollars worth of monetary paper than it was for him to accept a simple compliment. The Quill's face flushed red from embarrassment while his eyes dropped toward the floor. Gino noticed his shy reaction.

"You're the greatest, Mr. Quill . . . take care of yourself."

Gino lifted the heavy suitcases and walked them toward the garage.

"Thank you, my friend," the Quill replied.

It was a few minutes past 1 p.m. when the van rolled out of the Quill's driveway, headed toward Ft. Lauderdale.

Twenty-five gut wrenching minutes later, the white van was sitting in the driveway of the golf course house where the two men safely unloaded it within a half hour. Afterwards, Gino surveyed the back bedroom where the six hundred and twenty boxes filled with counterfeit twenties were stored and nodded his head smiling. Apparently there had been some self-satisfaction in knowing that he now had full control of the mother lode.

* * *

That Friday was not any different for Jennifer and Vincent than the rest of the week had been, with one exception. Vincent had kept Jennifer busy with everything from boating, to making mad, passionate love three times a day. They took Jacuzzi baths together each morning, and showered with one another each evening. The two had been inseparable, which was nothing short of disconcerted bad fortune for Jennifer. Jennifer had been patiently waiting throughout the entire week for an opportunity to search Vincent's house. However, about the full extent of Jennifer and Vincent having been away from one another had been when Vincent checked the mailbox. The mail on the isle is delivered to the front door, which time wise left her with little to no opportunity to initiate even the slightest searches.

Vincent's behavior had been frustrating to the agents posted on his island, as well. His daily routine had changed. As a rule, Vincent checked his mailbox no more than twice a week. During the past four days, however, Vincent had checked the box immediately after the postman had delivered the mail. It didn't take a rocket scientist to figure out that Vincent Panachi was expecting something of importance. What that something was had not been as simple for the agents to figure out. Even the task force understood that one does not fuck with the United States Postal Service.

Their assumption had been correct—Vincent had been waiting on the delivery of something important, and it had arrived in Friday morning's mail delivery. Vincent stood on his front porch and lifted the lid on the black-painted mailbox. When he looked inside, he found several pieces of mail that included the usual amount of junk mail. Vincent quickly flipped through the stack. There, next to the last envelope, was the one he had been anxiously searching for. Vincent pulled it from the rear of the stack and placed it up front. He looked at it, once again, and read the upper left hand corner return address. Vincent tapped the envelope against his hand while a smile formed across his face. Jennifer Swords' ticket had arrived, and the last piece of his puzzle was in place. He had nothing left to do but to keep her occupied during the weekend. After that . . . well, after that the outcome of Vincent's plan was in Jennifer's hands.

CHAPTER TWENTY-FIVE

A fter a fun-filled weekend spent boating, Vincent and Jennifer woke up to find Monday morning cloudless and azure-blue in color. It was truly another beautiful day in the winter paradise known as Ft. Lauderdale.

For each of them, the weekend had held its emotional moments that included mood swings which completely crossed the scale from anxiety to exultant gaiety, yet neither dared share those mood swings with the other. For them life had become a carefully evaluated game of chess where their strategies called for twenty-four hours a day of vigilance. Life for Jennifer and Vincent had become a gambit. One way or another, those head games would end, today. Vincent knew it; Jennifer would soon know it; yet neither of them suspected that the other knew anything.

Jennifer and Vincent were having breakfast al-fresco on the wooden deck that surrounded the luxury home's beautiful swimming pool. A fine-china serving platter heaping with fresh fruit and bran muffins was set in the center of the circular table. A pitcher of fresh-squeezed orange juice was off to one side, closest to Vincent.

An agent positioned across the canal watched through binoculars as Vincent refreshed Jennifer's glass with more orange juice. Had this been any other day, Vincent would have probably added a shot or two of chilled, Stolichnaya vodka to each of their orange juices. On this morning, however, there were far too many grown-up things that had to be done. Jennifer was relieved that he had not offered, as she felt exactly the same. The agent watched their every move for five minutes before he lowered his binoculars. He reached for his handheld radio and reported Vincent's whereabouts. However, his mind had been so preoccupied with the knowledge of the impending arrest of Vincent Panachi that he had failed to notice the variation in Vincent and Jennifer's daily habits.

Had he been more observant, the agent would have taken notice that neither of them was drinking that particular morning, and when full-time party persons slack off, there is good reason why. That could have been the Organized Crime Task Force's first indication that this particular Monday was not going to be like the rest. Instead, the surveillance agent had acted in a thoughtless, mechanical, reporting routine. His rote performance as an agent had followed that morning's explicit instructions to a tee—". . . whatever you do, don't lose sight of Panachi. As soon as the arrest warrant is delivered, we're going to take him into custody. Today, he's going down." The agent *had* reported Vincent's whereabouts, but from an investigative standpoint, he had missed the most significant detail of the observation.

Between bites, Jennifer casually reminded Vincent that she had an appointment at the hair dressers late that morning. Vincent nodded his head while he chewed and swallowed a mouthful of bran muffin.

"I remember," he said. Jennifer fought back the temptation to say anything else in hopes that he would share with her his plans for the day. Her patience paid off a minute later when Vincent added, "That's okay, because I've got several appointments today, myself. What time will you be leaving for your hair appointment?" he queried.

"Soon," Jennifer glanced at her diamond-dialed, Rolex watch. "Ten forty-five, I guess . . . it's in Boca, and my appointment is for eleven thirty."

"Well, that'll work because I'll be leaving about eleven thirty. I have no idea when I'll be back, so I'll tell you what . . . I'll leave you a note on the kitchen counter. Look for it when you get in," he replied.

Jennifer flashed him a smile that could have been construed as her being pleased with his being courteous enough to leave her a note. In reality, however, her devious mind was already scheming a systematic plan of action. She would search his bedroom closet first, and then, if she had not found the cash his office would be next.

"Thank you, Vincent . . . that's awful thoughtful of you," she replied. Vincent returned the smile and momentarily wondered if Jennifer would have a smile on her face when she found an airline ticket attached to her note.

Vincent and Jennifer finished breakfast by 10:00 a.m., and just as she told him she would, Jennifer left the house promptly at 10:45 a.m. Vincent watched through the living room's sheer drapes as she drove away. A sudden sharp feeling of emotional distress ran through his mind and heart. He loved Jennifer—there was no mistaking that—but he *had* to find out just what she was made of, and where her loyalties truly lie. The painful thoughts were squeezed from his mind when he recalled the photograph of her with Agent Murray. "What was she doing with him, and why?" Vincent asked himself out loud, again.

*   *   *

Less than two miles away, Agent Mark Murray was pacing the already worn out carpeting in his third floor office. Wade Jessup had called him every half hour since his arrival at the task force's headquarters earlier that morning. Naturally, Murray's superior wanted to know what was happening and precisely when it would happen. Agent Murray had patiently explained to his superior, several times that their hands were tied until the prosecutor delivered the necessary paperwork to make the arrest. Afterwards, Agent Murray had sheepishly dialed the prosecutor's telephone number and informed him of his boss' anxiety. The prosecutor had explained to Agent Murray, more than once, that he also was waiting for the paperwork. He even jokingly reminded Murray that the wheels of justice grind away slowly. He had told him that the paperwork would arrive by noon at the latest, and to stand by for an update.

Murray gently massaged his throbbing temples. A quick check of his wrist watch revealed the time to be five minutes until eleven, and still he had no update. Just the thought of his superior calling, again, in another five minutes, made his nervous headache much worse. He had done all that he could do. "Can't the top floor brass see that?" Agent Murray thought out loud. A split second later, he exclaimed, "What the fuck . . . I'm talking to myself, now?"

The desk top telephone rang on schedule—11:00 a.m., but unfortunately it was his superior and not the prosecutor. Of course, Agent Murray had already known that before he had answered the ringing telephone. Mark's nervous headache was about to become a full fledged migraine, compliments of Vincent Panachi.

*　　*　　*

At the same moment that the telephone in Agent Murray's third floor office was ringing, Gino and the burly Italian helping him were working at a feverish pace loading the boxes filled with counterfeit money, and had been for over a half-hour. Gino paused for a moment while he wiped a bead of sweat from his eyebrow with his right forearm. Meanwhile he checked the expensive watch strapped to his left wrist and confirmed that they were on schedule. The time was 11:02 a.m., and Gino watched while the final hand-truck load of boxes was being carefully wheeled through the golf course house's front doorway.

The golf course drop house was surrounded by a high, wooden fence that assured its occupants absolute privacy. Aside from that tall, bushy palm trees lined the outside perimeter of that fence; their brilliant, emerald green fronds towering over the top of the wooden barrier. A slatted, security door—complete with an electronically operated deadbolt—guarded the luxury house's gateway. That electronic lock was operated by a sophisticated, coded opener that would deter even the best burglar from gaining entry. The white van had been backed up to that gate, and it was through that opening that the previous hand truck loads had been shuttled then loaded.

The arrangement as to who had stayed in the van and who had run the loads had not been prearranged, but they had worked it out for the best. Gino was the smaller of the two, which certainly had come in handy during the stacking of the boxes. In total, there were six hundred and twenty boxes, and even though they were relatively small, there were still significant numbers of them.

The burly Italian pushing the small-wheeled hand truck grunted as the load traversed a slight incline on the concrete pathway that led from the house to the gate. Seconds later, the hand truck passed through the gate and Gino's helper slowly lowered the boxes until they stood upright at the van's rear doorway.

"Is that the last one?" Gino asked.

This time it was the burly Italian who wiped a bead of sweat form his bushy eyebrows. He looked at Gino through the V-shape formed by his forearm and bicep.

"That's it for the boxes. Stack these while I get those two big suitcases," he replied.

"Sounds like a plan," Gino began grabbing the boxes before he had answered. When he turned from stacking the first of the boxes, the burly Italian was already inside of the house.

Five minutes later, Gino's helper shuffled his feet across the concrete walkway while he carried the two American Tourister suitcases toward the waiting van. Gino knew what the contents of the suitcases were, but the burly Italian did not. No doubt from the strained expression on his helper's face, he had wondered. Finally he reached the rear of the van and grunted as he lifted them, one by one. Afterwards he shoved them forward, towards Gino.

"Christ, Gino, how much are in these friggin' things"

Gino let out a muffled grunt himself while he situated the two suitcases for a very short drive.

"A bunch, my friend," he said in a breathless way.

By that time, the burly Italian had recovered his breath.

"A bunch, my ass. Fuck me, Gino. Those are two heavy fuckers. Fooled me, I'll tell you."

Gino was hunched over in the van, which made it difficult to maneuver around the two unwieldy pieces of luggage. However, he did so by turning and twisting his body around the stacks of boxes. Finally, he crawled through the van's rear door then locked it. While he checked the lock he commented over his shoulder, "They're that heavy because they contain two big ones, to be exact."

The burly Italian whistled.

"No wonder," he said.

Gino turned toward him and playfully slapped his helper on one of his beefy shoulders.

"Let's get this load on the highway," Gino said.

Just as the two men got situated in the van—the burly Italian driving and Gino in the front seat—Gino turned toward his helper and said, "We got a couple of stops to make along the way . . ."

* * *

Vincent gathered his composure and turned away from the sheer drapes. Dealing with an out of control emotional moment now was a luxury he surely could not afford. As he crossed the living room toward his office, Vincent reminded himself of the rigorous schedule that must be followed without deviation. Timing, as with all well thought out plans, was everything. In Vincent's particular situation however, the stakes had increased considerably because Vincent would not get a second attempt at success. The Organized Crime Task Force would see to that.

Vincent sat down at this desk and pulled on the bottom right hand drawer. The file drawer silently slid across its well oiled tracks until it opened all the way. Vincent withdrew a manila file folder from the rear of the drawer and placed it on the desk. He opened it and withdrew two envelopes; one contained the airline ticket issued from Beach Side Travel Agency; the second contained a handwritten letter that Vincent had composed during the L-1011 flight from JFK International Airport after meeting with Anthony Vitale. Vincent removed the airline ticket from the travel agency's letterhead envelope and laid it to one side. In the same movement, he picked up the unsealed envelope containing the handwritten letter and gently withdrew it. Vincent remembered the words he had written as if he had written them just yesterday. Nevertheless, he unfolded the one page letter and laid it on the desk. He slowly ran his right hand methodically across the letter's crease marks then read the prose he had written to Jennifer:

> Dear Jennifer,
>
> I'm certain that this letter will surprise you . . . if not shock you. Nevertheless, please read it with an open mind and heart.
>
> There is little doubt in my mind that you have seen the derogatory article published in the *Sun Sentinel* newspaper that has named me as a serious player in the Vitale crime family. If not, I'm certain that the "hair salon grapevine" has informed you of it by now. At any rate, it is apparent—to myself as well as other interested parties—that the Organized Crime Task Force is out to make an example of me, and that is something I just cannot sit back and allow to happen. Therefore, I have left the country for Brazil. As a matter of fact, I am airborne as you are reading this letter.
>
> There was no way of knowing who may have been watching when I left this morning. Therefore, it was necessary for me to leave everything

behind. However, of all the things I have had to leave behind, only three are of any significant importance—two pieces of luggage, and you.

It is no secret that I am in love with you and that I want you to be with me forever. Jennifer, along with this letter you will find a first-class, international airline ticket to Rio de Janeiro. The two pieces of luggage are in the walk-in closet in my office. If you want to be with me and help build new lives for us, be on that flight and bring the two American Tourister suitcases with you. Someone who represents me will meet you upon your arrival and escort you to me.

Should you choose not to come, you may refund the ticket and keep the money. If so, forget the luggage; forget about me; just please don't ever forget about us and the wonderful times we have shared together. I love you.

Vincent

Vincent Carefully lifted the letter from the desk top with both hands and intently stared at it. He rested his forearms against the edge of the desk, yet that support of his upper body weight did not prevent his fingertips from trembling. Vincent noticed the shaking of the paper and put it down as quickly as if it had burnt him; he certainly did not need any visual measurement of the uneasiness and distress he felt about his future uncertainties. The realization that he would soon be leaving his past life behind forever had finally hit home. A sudden, sharp feeling of emotional distress overwhelmed him, however, as with all the emotional flash floods experienced in his past, the anxious moment passed before panic set in. Afterwards, he pointedly stared into nowhere while he simultaneously pondered his past, present, and future.

Vincent picked up the letter and the airline ticket then walked to the kitchen. Along the way he peered into every room; at every piece of furniture; at every piece of artwork. That slow walk through his house was to become a vivid memory upon which Vincent would recall many times during future, reminiscent evenings. When he reached the kitchen he laid the letter and the ticket side by side in a conspicuous place on the kitchen counter, just as he had told Jennifer he would. Vincent looked through the kitchen window at his Scarab Thunder docked behind the house. Knowing that he was looking at his boat for the very last time released yet another quick pang to his heart, but the anguish he felt was short-lived. Vincent was aware that he had lived the good life, and there was no doubt in his mind that he would miss the good times he had experienced in Ft. Lauderdale. However, as Anthony Vitale had so eloquently pointed out, Vincent was hardly being shunned from the crime family and thrown out all alone, with no arrows in his quiver into the cold, cruel world. Vincent would be building his new life with a ten million dollar nest egg—barring no unforeseen disasters. That figure referred to earned dollars for the crime family; which translated into no delivery of the fifty million dollars in counterfeit money to the head of the Colombian drug cartel, then no ten million dollars to Vincent. In the world of the underground economy, this sort of motivation is often described as an incentive deal. No incentive; no deal.

Vincent exhaled a deep breath and turned away from the kitchen window. He glanced up at the clock on the kitchen wall. 11:20 a.m. It was time for him to get moving. From this point on, Anthony Vitale and Vincent Panachi's plans would take on a life of their own. There would be no turning back, and when Vincent walked out that door, it would be forever. Vincent walked through the kitchen and entered the beautiful, formal dining room. He paused for a moment while he admired the expensive, tiered, crystal chandelier. He dragged his hand across the back of a dining room chair—one of a set of six covered in raw silk fabric—when he walked toward the living room. The living room was filled with gorgeous, designer furniture. Vincent paused for a moment in that room, as well, while he reminisced some of the wonderful times he had spent there. He crossed the expansive room and entered the Italian-tiled foyer. The master panel for the house's sophisticated burglar alarm was recessed into the wall perpendicular to the front door. Vincent stopped in front of the electronic panel and quickly punched in a series of numbers on the alarm's touch tone, numerical pad. That series of numbers overrode the system's strategically placed electronic sensors and would prevent them from accidentally tripping the alarm. It was a very sophisticated feature that allowed the occupants of the house to arm certain zones of the house while others were left open for access; for instance, the front portion of the house could be under electronic surveillance while the rear of the house was open for access during a cookout. This time, however, Vincent had punched in the code that overrode the *entire* system, leaving it wide open for entry. There was a method to his madness. Vincent knew that two people would be entering his house after his departure: Jennifer and Gino.

Vincent glanced at his wrist watch while he crossed through room after room toward the garage. 11:28 a.m. That gave him precisely two minutes to leave the house in order to remain on schedule. Vincent withdrew the keys to his Mercedes from his trouser pocket at the same time he entered the two car garage. The Mercedes Benz 500 SL had never looked better to Vincent. He took notice that the leather smelled new when he sat in the luxury automobile. Vincent inserted the key and started the car. Seconds later, he depressed the push-button switch that engaged the garage's overhead, electric door opener. One minute later, the Mercedes 500 SL had backed out of the driveway for the final time.

Naturally, the surveillance agents posted just on the other side of Navarro Isle's tiny bridge had no way of knowing that. Nevertheless, *any* movement from Vincent Panachi was worthwhile reporting, particularly in light of the explicit instructions they had received at this morning's strategy meeting. The sight of Vincent's luxury automobile departing the house startled the two agents enough that they questioned one another as the Mercedes crossed the bridge toward Las Olas Boulevard.

"Holy shit, it's Panachi, and he's leaving. What do we do?" one queried the other.

The agent sitting in the passenger's seat turned toward his partner and suggested, "After this morning's meeting, I suggest we let Murray make that call."

Without waiting for a comment the agent began dialing the discrete telephone number, a private line direct to Murray's office. It was the same line that Murray had monitored throughout the morning, anxiously awaiting updated news form the prosecutor about the arrest warrant paperwork. It was precisely this type of situation that had prompted the surveillance agents to request a cellular telephone in the first place. Now, whatever tactical maneuvers Agent Murray chose, the outcome would be on him, not the field agents.

$$* \qquad * \qquad *$$

When the private line in Agent Murray's office rang, it startled him. Instinctively, he rolled his wrist and checked his watch before he answered. It was 11:30 a.m., and he just knew for certain that this call had to be the prosecutor with good news. Murray took a deep breath and exhaled while the telephone rang another time. He did not want the prosecutor to think that he was some kind of wimp who was cowering in the corner of his office, afraid of his boss. Agent Murray allowed the telephone to ring a third time before he picked up the handset.

"Murray, speaking," he answered.

When the surveillance agent's voice came through the handset's receiver, it was definitely not the voice that Murray had expected to hear.

"Agent Murray, I am calling from our post at Panachi's house. We've got a situation unfolding here, and we need to know what you want us to do," the agent informed him.

The unexpected statement caught Murray off guard. He paused for a few seconds while he gathered his wits.

"What seems to be the problem," he finally queried.

"Sir, Panachi has departed his house, and, as we speak, he is turning westbound onto Las Olas Boulevard. Should we tail him?"

The field agent's words went through Murray like a knife, and he bolted upright in his chair.

"God damn it yes, by all means follow his every move. We should be ready to pick him up any time now."

"Yes, sir. We're rolling now, two car lengths behind him," the field agent replied.

There was a pause across the phone line and Agent Murray heard the familiar clicking of the portable cellular telephone switching from repeater to repeater as the task forces' pursuit vehicle proceeded.

"Stay on the line with me," Murray ordered his men. "I want to know exactly what is happening, as it happens. Got it?"

"Yes, sir. Okay, just a minute he's turned north into the Victoria Park area. We're behind him."

Agent Murray squirmed in his chair and repositioned himself so that he could lean on one elbow while he cradled the telephone.

"Good. Not too close, now we don't want to spook him," Agent Murray coached his men.

"That's affirmative, sir. We're maintaining at least two car lengths behind. Just a minute . . . okay, he's made another turn now to the south. I believe this is the back way to Sunrise Boulevard," the field agent reported.

Mark Murray tilted the telephone's receiver away from his ear while he gently massaged his forehead with his free hand. His headache was worsening, and the throbbing had moved from his temples toward the front of his skull. The phone connection was silent for almost a minute. Murray did not pressure his agents with unnecessary questions, and they obviously had not had anything significant to add since their last observation.

"Okay," the filed agent's voice came through the receiver, "he's made a turn onto Sunrise Boulevard eastbound." Agent Murray listened without interrupting. Seconds later, the field agent updated their observation. "Panachi's crossed the Middle River Bridge. Now he's stopped at the red light in front of the Galleria Mall. Just a second . . . okay . . . okay, he's turned into the mall. I repeat, Panachi has turned into the Galleria Mall."

"Stay on top of him," Agent Murray said. "Shorten your gap or you'll lose him in the parking lot."

"We've got him. He passed up the entrance to the upper level parking decks . . . just a minute . . . okay, he's made a turn."

Several seconds of silence followed, and that made Agent Murray uncomfortable.

"What the hell's happening, guys?" Agent Murray barked into the telephone's mouthpiece.

The field agent's voice sounded strained.

"Just a second, sir . . . okay, Panachi's valet parking the Mercedes. Looks like he's going into the mall. What do you want us to do?" he queried.

"Great," Agent Murray thought out loud then replied, "Okay, listen up. You two split up. I want one agent following Panachi's every move. The other stays with the vehicle."

"Don't you want us to apprehend him?" the field agent asked.

Agent Murray rubbed his forehead with back and forth strokes that disfigured his already creased and wrinkled frown.

"God damn it," he barked, "if we could have taken him into custody, don't you think I would have had you do that already?"

"Yes, sir . . . I suppose so," the field agent meekly answered.

"Okay, call me back with some good news. And, whatever you have to do, do not lose sight of Panachi."

"Absolutely not, sir. We'll call you back, soon."

The cellular connection was broken when the field agent pushed the *end* button.

Three minutes later, the agent that has been on the telephone with Agent Murray followed Vincent into the ground level entrance of a large department store. His partner remained behind, as instructed, and maintained a constant vigil on Vincent Panachi's Mercedes Benz 500 SL.

* * *

At precisely the same moment that Vincent had entered the Galleria Mall department store, with an agent in tow, the receptionist at the prestigious, Boca Raton hair salon was showing Jennifer to her hair stylist's station. Jennifer nodded at the faces she recognized along the way, and as she walked past, the regulars were buzzing with gossip—some of which was about Vincent and the *Sun Sentinel* articles; some speculating as to why they had not seen Jennifer in three weeks or so.

"Are those dark roots I saw when she walked past?" one particularly snooty socialite asked another quite snobbish, Boca Raton, holier-than-thou lady.

"Yes, I saw those, too, but *you* missed her fingernails, didn't you?" the self-righteous member of the fashionable society remarked.

When Jennifer was walking past them, they had been nothing but smiles and compliments. In fact, they had complimented her.

"Darling, you look so wonderful . . . your face is so full of color."

Jennifer has never forgotten those days before she had money, and vividly recalled how those same people had not given her the time of day the year before. Now, she was their long lost friend. Jennifer could have cared less about the two snobbish women, yet seeing them did remind her of one thing—if everything went as planned, she would never have to worry about *her* financial security, ever again.

Darlene greeted her, "Jennifer, dah-ling, where have you been?" The professional stylist did not give Jennifer an opportunity to reply before she added, "Sit down and we'll start you right away." The hair stylist delicately lifted several strands of hair from different areas of her scalp and closely examined them.

She exclaimed, "Oh dah-ling, we're going to have to give you a full treatment today."

Jennifer's voice reflected the unexpected surprise she felt.

"How long will that take?" she queried. Ordinarily, Jennifer could get away with a weekly touchup. However, because she had missed several appointments, she would need the full treatment in order to cover those unsightly dark roots.

"Approximately three hours. But that will give us plenty of time to catch up on girl talk, won't it?"

"But, of course," Jennifer replied as she flashed her smile.

Beneath that smile, however, Jennifer was quiet concerned. Three hours was much longer than she had planned to be at the hair salon, and, without question it would considerably cut into the time she had allocated to search Vincent's house. Jennifer glanced at her diamond-dial watch. It was 11:45 a.m. Three hours. She would just have to live with it, she silently coached herself. Before Jennifer uttered another word her hair stylist called out to the receptionist, "Dah-ling, cancel my next appointment. Ms. Swords will be taking a little longer than we expected, and get the shampooist over here as soon as she is available." Darlene turned to Jennifer and said, "Stay right here, dah-ling, let's see what we can do with those neglected fingernails." Before Jennifer could make a comment, the hair stylist had walked away. Her voice was heard over the roar of the blow dryers as it carried throughout the rear of the elite salon, "Susy, dah-ling, I have an emergency nail job . . . where are you?"

*   *   *

The white van rolled to a stop at Las Olas Boulevard then turned west in the direction of Vincent Panachi's Navarro Isle home. The van full of fifty-two million dollars in counterfeit money drove directly through the surveillance agent's field of view. He did not even notice it until the van crossed the small, narrow bridge that one must cross to enter onto Navarro Isle. The agent also could not see the van pull onto Vincent's driveway and enter the two car garage. The house had obstructed the van's entry from the agent's view, and the agents that had been posted at the frontal view were now off conducting surveillance duty at the Galleria Mall. Had they not left their post at Panachi's house, the Organized Crime Task Force could have taken down the entire load of counterfeit money, along with Vincent Panachi. Apparently, fate had dealt Agent Murray another hand to play.

Once the van was inside of the garage, Gino quickly depressed the tiny electronic switch Vincent had given him, just as he had done seconds beforehand when he had opened the garage's door. The overhead door closed behind them. Gino opened the passenger door as he turned to his helper and said, "This won't take but a few minutes. Stay with the van." Gino did not wait for the burly

Italian's reply. Instead, he closed the door and tracked alongside the van until he stood behind it. Gino opened both rear doors, hunched over then grabbed the first of the two American Tourister suitcases. "Christ," he exclaimed when the heavy suitcase cleared the van's floorboard. He had to half walk, half push the suitcase ahead of him while he slowly shuffled it between the wall and the van. Afterwards, however, he picked it up and carried it in a somewhat normal fashion. Nevertheless, it was quite heavy, and he grunted several times along the way to Vincent's office. Gino was a champion at following directions. Vincent's faithful employee placed the American Tourister suitcase in Vincent's office walk-in closet, just as he had been instructed.

Five minutes later the second suitcase was in place beside the first one, just as Vincent had requested. The two American Touristers were now situated side by side, in plain view, in his office closet. Gino stood beside the luggage and quickly sized up his next task—carefully wipe them down. Gino withdrew a seat-stained handkerchief from his rear pocket and expediently wiped all the finger prints from the two pieces of luggage. Afterwards, he stood there for a moment and admired his handiwork—the two American Touristers were sterile.

After the van backed out of Vincent's driveway and was moving towards the small bridge, Gino let out a deep breath and glanced at his watch. The time was exactly 11:45 a.m., and they were right on schedule. Gino turned to the driver and said, "Alright, that's one stop down. Now, take a right at the stop sign and go west onto Las Olas. I'll give you directions as we go . . ."

No one had been any the wiser that the van had even made the stop, although the agent across the canal from Vincent's house had noticed it leave the island. That, however, was not suspicious. A great number of service-oriented vans travel the island every day. Gino and his cohort in crime had pulled off a smoothie.

* * *

Agent Mark Murray sat behind his desk and stared at the circular wall clock mounted upon the far wall of his tiny office. His eyes were firmly fixed on the timepiece, just as they had been during the past several minutes. The wall clock was not unlike those found in the majority of governmental buildings, whether those buildings were schools or offices; they were standard government issue.

Mark Murray was experiencing a moment of déjà vu. Perhaps he had been hypnotized by the methodical movements of the clock's hands while they slowly ticked away the seconds-and-minutes of the day; like a high school student anxiously awaiting that final movement of the timepiece's hands—the one that would mark the end of that day's school period.

Agent Murray quickly snapped out of his trance when the telephone rang. His eyes did, however, mentally register the exact hour-and-minute of the day before his consciousness returned him to his previous, anxious state of mind. The time was 11:45 a.m., and less than five minutes had passed since Agent Murray had issued the orders to the agents, ". . . *do not lose sight of Panachi.*"

Murray was absolutely certain that this call was the prosecutor with good news. He picked up the telephone's handset.

"Murray, speaking."

"We've got a green light," the prosecutor's voice sounded cheerful when he continued, "The paperwork arrived on my desk just a minute ago. Your team may now take Vincent Panachi into custody."

Agent Murray exhaled an audible sigh of relief.

"Thank you. That's all I needed to hear. We'll handle it from here."

Under the circumstances, Agent Murray was not the least bit interested in making small talk, and cut the prosecutor short before he had a chance to say anything.

"Gotta' go," he added. "I'll be in touch, soon." The telephone went dead in the prosecutor's hand.

Ten minutes passed while Agent Murray searched through his Rolodex file for the numbers of the cellular telephones that had been issued to the field agents. The list of numbers was something that he had never had the occasion to use before now. In his zeal to make certain that Panachi was hemmed in at the Galleria Mall, Agent Murray had forgotten to ask the field agent for his call back number. Murray cursed himself silently under his breath for his moment of incompetence.

The telephone rang. Out of habit Mark Murray quickly glanced up at the wall clock and saw that it was 11:55 a.m. He shifted his gaze to the ringing telephone and smiled through the second ring. Although the timing would have placed him a few minutes earlier than his now routine, on the hour-and-half-hour update checks, Murray was certain that the caller was his superior, and after the way his boss had sweated him throughout the morning, he did not think twice about allowing the telephone to ring a third time before he answered it. Unfortunately, when he did he discovered just how incorrect his assumption had been.

The caller was the field agent who had been inside of the Galleria Mall.

"Agent Murray, you're not going to like this, but we have lost sight of the suspect."

Murray jerked upright in his chair like a bolt of lightening had just passed directly through his spine. He was rigid, as well as momentarily speechless.

"What?" Murray screamed after what had seemed a long pause to the caller.

The field agent had already prepared himself for an outburst of that nature.

"Panachi ducked in-and-out of several large department stores; through department-after-department; up-and-down escalators; I stayed right with him until he disappeared somehow after going into the changing room in the men's department. I don't know how I lost him, but I did," the agent calmly said.

Agent Murray could not believe his ears. He placed his open palm against his forehead and leaned his elbow on the desk top.

"Where are you, now?" Murray asked next.

"Back at his Mercedes. We're watching it like a hawk. He's got to come back here sometime," the field agent's voice exuded hope.

The field agent's analogy did not seem far-fetched to Agent Murray, and he breathed a sigh of relief.

"Okay. Remain in position. When he returns, take him into custody. In the meantime, I am personally going to take up a position outside of Panachi's island home," Agent Murray instructed the field agent.

The field agent breathed a sigh of relief, also. He was certain that the phone call would have included the ass-chewing of the century, but it hadn't.

"We're on top of it, chief," the field agent assured him.

Suddenly, Agent Murray recalled that he had been upset with himself, just minutes before, and said, "Before you hang up, let me have your cellular telephone number . . ."

CHAPTER TWENTY-SIX

V incent Panachi quickly made his way through the ground floor level of Saks Fifth Avenue department store and was not certain if he had been tailed or not. Vincent had too much at stake to leave that possibility to chance, and had reacted under the premise that he had been under surveillance since he departed his house. He was correct.

As Vincent hastily walked past the ladies' lingerie department, he checked his watch, once again. It was precisely 11:59 a.m. His timing had been impeccable; the rear entryway to the large department store was less than fifty yards away, and, as Vincent had painstakingly instructed Gino, the van was supposed to meet him at Saks' rear entry/exit doorway at precisely noon. Vincent had been quite emphatic about the hour he had stressed to Gino, ". . . 12:00 sharp . . . not 11:59; nor 12:01 . . . noon."

Vincent scooted past an elderly, but obviously well kept lady with an armful of shopping bags and exited the haute couture department store precisely as the hands on his Rolex watch shifted to the noon hour. Instinctively, Vincent looked to the right first, then to the left. The white van was approaching from his left and was less than twenty-five feet away. Vincent made out Gino's face through the van's windshield and saw that he was sliding over towards the driver, apparently making room for Vincent. Seconds later, the van screeched to a halt directly in front of Vincent. The heavily laden van rocked forward from the inertia of the abrupt stop, yet Vincent grabbed the door handle and yanked the passenger's door open. Without a word spoken, he stepped into the van. Gino's helper had his head turned in the direction of Vincent, and once he visually confirmed that Vincent was safely inside the van he stepped on the accelerator. The van's tires squealed, once again, and the rapid acceleration threw Vincent backwards against the seat back. They were off and running.

The agents for the Organized Crime Task Force had been none the wiser to Vincent's movements. As the van pulled away from the parking lot, they were still posted in the strategic position where they could watch Vincent Panachi's valet parked, Mercedes Benz 500 SL. They could watch Vincent's Mercedes till the end of time, if they wished, yet it would not move—not at Vincent Panachi's hands anyway.

*　　*　　*

Agent Mark Murray was haphazardly scrambling about his office in a vain attempt to get over to Navarro Isle as soon as possible. In his haste he had momentarily forgotten that his superior would be calling his office any minute for the up-to-the-minute report on the Panachi situation. Too late. The phone rang before Agent Murray got through the office doorway.

What happened during the following few seconds would have made an excellent case study in conditioned reflex for the famous Russian physiologist, Ivan Pavlov. Where Pavlov had been able to condition a dog to salivate at the mere sound of a bell, Murray had conditioned himself to experience sudden overwhelming anxiety at the mere sound of the telephone's ringing bell. A quick glance at the wall clock confirmed what Murray had suspected—it was exactly twelve noon, and Agent Murray knew for certain, this time, whom was on the other end of that call. There was no way he could tell his superior that the field agents under his command had lost Panachi. No, that would never do. Quickly, he thought out his options before answering the phone. Just as he had suspected, it was Wade Jessup.

"Agent Murray, have you heard any news yet?"

Mark Murray placed his free hand on the desk top and leaned on it.

"As a matter of fact, sir, I just got off the phone with the prosecutor. He has informed me that the paperwork we have been waiting for has arrived. I was . . ."

"Good," his superior interrupted, "I want to move quickly on this. If we're lucky we can make the six o'clock evening news with Panachi's arrest."

Before Murray's superior had a chance to ask any more questions, Agent Murray took the opportunity to interpose, "The field agents are in position at their assigned surveillance posts, as we speak, and I was just walking out the door on my way to Panachi's Navarro Isle home.

"Well done . . . keep me informed," his superior said before he hung up the telephone.

Agent Murray replaced the telephone's receiver then spent a few seconds staring at the phone while he reviewed the conversation he had just had with his boss. He hadn't told him the full truth about the situation; but, then again, he had not told him any lies either. "Fuck it," he exclaimed. Seconds later, Agent

Murray was on the elevator that took him from the building's third floor to the ground level parking lot. It would be only a matter of minutes before he was in position at Navarro Isle.

*　　*　　*

The white van exited the Galleria's huge, multilevel parking garage and turned west onto Sunrise Boulevard. The burly Italian who was driving nervously shifted his eyes from side-to-side as he checked the outside rearview mirrors. Vincent and Gino were much calmer. Traffic moved along at a steady pace until Sunrise Boulevard merged with Federal Highway, then it became stop-and-go from red light to red light. Finally the two split at Sears Town. Afterwards, the van had a clear thoroughfare all the way to the northbound entry ramp of Interstate 95.

The van quickly accelerated as it began merging with the other traffic traveling north along the multi-lane expressway. Up until this point, the three men had not engaged in any conversation. There was a time and a place for small talk, and this situation was definitely neither the time, nor the place. Vincent Panachi, was not about to divulge his nervous apprehension to Gino and the burly Italian. Nevertheless, the feeling was real, and his sweaty palms were evidence of that fact. If the truth be known, at that moment Vincent had butterflies in his stomach the size of eagles. This escapade was equivalent to a roll of the dice in the game of craps where the outcome of the throw would drastically affect the rest of the player's life. Suddenly the driver's eyes began rapidly shifting from mirror to mirror. Gino noticed his double take and so did Vincent. They both looked at the driver. Their speechless ride was interrupted when the burly Italian exclaimed, "Oh, fuck . . . there's a cop car coming up behind us . . . quick like . . . with his lights on!"

Gino instinctively turned toward Vincent, his mouth agape. He didn't have to speak a word for Vincent to realize the sudden fear that the Italian had experienced. After all, trying to convince a police officer that you found fifty million dollars in counterfeit, twenty dollar bills would be a feat that even David Copperfield could not pull off. Vincent maintained a calm outward composure, despite the fact that the eagles in his stomach were beginning to flap their wings.

"Just stay cool," Vincent coached the driver, "just a few miles per hour over sixty-five . . . you don't want to look suspicious." Vincent watched as the burly Italian's Adam's apple quickly shifted up-and-down while the nervous man swallowed. Gino remained silent. The trio waited. Finally, after what had seemed like an eternity, the red and blue lighted police car sped past. Vincent, Gino, and the driver simultaneously exhaled a sigh of relief.

As the van progressed northbound, the Oakland Park Boulevard exit sign sped past. Commercial Boulevard was next, and that was their exit. The driver carefully maintained a constant sixty-seven miles per hour until the van neared the exit for Ft. Lauderdale's Executive Airport, Commercial Boulevard, then slowed appropriately.

The van exited the expressway then turned west at the light onto Commercial Boulevard. The midday traffic was considerably less than Vincent recalled from the last time he had driven this thoroughfare during the evening rush hour. Even so, the van was still hemmed in between two large sedans—which suited Vincent and his boys to a tee. The sedans had unwittingly created a protective cocoon where the van could safely travel without fear of another cop car inadvertently swooping down upon them. Despite their unexpected insurance, Vincent's palms continued to perspire profusely.

Several miles and several minutes later, the familiar sign marking the south entrance of Executive Airport came into view. Vincent pointed toward the entrance as he instructed the driver, "Turn right at the sign." One minute later, the driver turned right. Vincent added, "Just stay on this road . . . I'll let you know when to turn." The driver merely nodded his head in acknowledgement while he concentrated on his driving. The driver deftly negotiated the curved roadway while the heavily laden van's weight shifted. Finally, Vincent instructed him, "Okay . . . slow down . . . it's the building just ahead on the right . . . Hangar 24." Seconds later, Vincent added, "This is it . . . turn here then drive around the building to the front."

The white van turned right and entered the large aluminum building's small parking lot. As per Vincent's instructions, the burly Italian continued on and drove around to the dark-green building. Once the van had turned the corner of the far end of the building, Vincent instructed the driver, "Okay . . . the hangar doors are supposed to be open . . . pull in and park behind the left wing, as close to the aircraft's cargo door as possible." The burly Italian merely grunted in acknowledgement to Vincent's instructions. Seconds later, however, the driver braked, carefully accessing the clearance between the open hangar doors before deftly maneuvering the van inside the aircraft hangar.

As soon as the van was completely inside the huge aluminum building, two Colombians quickly closed the sliding hangar doors behind it. Within a matter of seconds, the bright, midday rays of sunlight were replaced by the artificial light emitted from the hangar's powerful, overhead lamps. It was much darker inside the enclosed building, and the sudden transition from the bright sunlight to the inside of the hangar temporarily blinded the van's occupants. The burly Italian did the right thing when he stopped the van, removed his sunglasses, and patiently waited the several seconds it took for his vision to adjust. Before the driver proceeded forward with the van there was a knock at the van's passenger window. Vincent turned to find Carlos Lazarro's face peering through the side window, smiling. Vincent instinctively rolled down the window. Carlos was relaxed as if this day were just another normal business day. He was all business, and consequently did not bother to engage Vincent in small talk. Instead, he pointed toward one of the two twin-engine aircraft hangared inside the building as he leaned forward to see the driver of the van.

"Careful, amigo . . . drive around the wing to the side of the aircraft," Carlos directed him. "My men will give you clearance instructions along the way."

The driver's eyes, as well as Vincent and Gino's, followed towards the direction Carlos had pointed toward. All three could clearly visualize what Carlos had explained. Vincent turned his head slightly and noticed the other Cessna 404 Titan for the first time, but he made no reference of that to Carlos. After all, the aircraft was a part-and-parcel of their family's business; not his.

The driver inched the van forward while he obeyed the visual turn commands issued to him from the same two Colombians that had closed the hangar doors. Three turns and a minute later, the burly Italian gently tapped the van's brakes before placing the van's gear selector in reverse. The two Colombians stood on either side of the rear of the van and gave the burly Italian waving hand directions while he backed the vehicle closer and closer to the aircraft's fuselage. Gino and Vincent watched the driver, and the driver watched the two Colombians, his head swinging back-and-forth from mirror to mirror. Suddenly, the Colombian positioned on the driver's side clenched his fingers to form a fist—the hand signal designated as *STOP*. The driver firmly stepped on the brake pedal and the van came to an immediate halt. The rear of the vehicle was no more than four feet away from the aircraft's open cargo door.

Vincent opened the passenger's door and exited the van. Gino followed. Meanwhile, the burly Italian placed the transmission in park then turned off the ignition.

Vincent and Gino stood alongside the van for a few seconds before they were joined by Carlos Lazarro and an unidentified American. By that time, the van's driver had exited the vehicle, also, and had walked to the rear of the van. Carlos extended his hand to Vincent and said, "Well done, amigo . . . my boys will have your merchandise loaded onto the aircraft within a matter of minutes." Carlos gently withdrew his hand from Vincent's and made a waving gesture toward the unidentified American. "Vincent, say 'Hello' to your pilot, James. He is the best we have, and he has been to the airstrip many times. You'll be in the best of hands."

Vincent and James' eyes met while they momentarily held one another in an inquisitive stare. Finally, the pilot extended his hand and said, "Nice to finally meet you, Mr. Panachi . . . I've been following the articles in the *Sun Sentinel.*"

Vincent accepted James' hand and the two men shook hands. Vincent flashed the seasoned professional pilot a smile and said, "It's nice to meet you, although I'm afraid you have me at a slight disadvantage. I know nothing at all about you."

"Well, sir," the pilot returned the smile, "it will take us precisely seven hours and twenty minutes to reach the jungle airstrip . . . and it's just the two of us along for the ride . . . that should provide you with a chance to get to know me."

Vincent shifted his attention back to Carlos and remarked, "I like him, already," then joked, "you say he's done this sort of thing before, right?" All four men burst out laughing, and the ice was broken.

The fact of the matter was that James had most certainly, ". . . *done this before,*" and his services as a transportation specialist had kept him in Carlos' employ for quite some time. He was in his early forties, yet he did not look it. The years spent amidst unbelievable adventures had been kind to him, and were definitely not something that one could deduce from a first impression. However, if the character lines that formed the tiny crow's feet about his eyes and the tell-tale steaks of grey that blended gently throughout his otherwise golden-brown hair could tell the stories, one would discover that those experiences had left him much wiser than most men equal to him in chronological years. The only saving feature that could possibly have given Vincent a hint at James' vast aeronautical experience was the well-worn, weather-beaten, baseball-style cap with a fifty mission bend curved across its bill. The used-to-be-white hat had the letters *AMR COMBS* embroidered across the front in dark-blue stitching, but to a non-pilot, those letters would have absolutely no meaning whatsoever. James had never, to Carlos' knowledge, ever flown a trip without it. Now, as usual, James' piercing blue eyes peered from beneath the solid bill while he readied himself for his next flight for Carlos. Although Vincent was not a licensed pilot, *his* adventures had him travel extensively by Learjet at least once a month during the past several years while he had shuttled the Vitale crime family's South Florida profits north to Newark, New Jersey. Vincent immediately recognized the letters *AMR COMBS* and knew what they represented. Combs Gate was the company that had built Learjets during a period of time, and those caps had been given to flight crews that had successfully completed their initial factory-approved training in that year's latest model Lear. Vincent also was aware that the factory's trophy hat program had been discontinued a number of years ago. Vincent silently summed up the pilot standing before him and came to the unmistakable conclusion that this middle-aged man was, and had been for quite some time, a seasoned, professional pilot. Vincent's assumption had been one hundred percent correct. Yet even if he had experienced the slightest bit of doubt about James' abilities, it would not have made any difference whatsoever. They *were* going, today. Period.

Carlos cast a glance over his left shoulder and visually confirmed that his men were in the ready position before he raised his left hand and gave them the signal they had patiently waited for. Within seconds, the van's burly Italian driver had not only opened the vehicle's double rear doors, but had climbed into the van's rear compartment and begun passing box-after-box to one of the two Colombians that had been standing beside him just moments earlier. The other Colombian had stepped inside the Cessna Titan and was receiving the boxes of merchandise as quickly as his counterpart could pass them through the doorway. The men had formed a small conveyor line that expedited the transfer of the numerous boxes.

The Cessna Titan's passenger cabin had been stripped of its six, comfortable seats earlier that morning in preparation for today's clandestine flight, and, unbeknownst to Vincent, the pilot in command, James, had overseen those many pre-flight operations. One of the pre-flight duties had included the fueling of the aircraft's six, inboard fuel tanks—tanks that made available 440 gallons of aviation's finest, 100 octane fuel as useable fuel during the flight. This provided the aircraft with phenomenal range and load carrying capabilities; both factors that significantly figured into this particular mission.

Vincent continued looking at James even though James' attention had been diverted toward the loading of the aircraft. Suddenly, the pilot redirected his attention back to the circle of men and said, "Please excuse me, gentlemen." His eyes shifted and met Vincent's.

"Of course," Vincent replied. Vincent watched as the pilot walked behind the van then entered the aircraft. Vincent watched the pilot's hunched over body pass window-after-window as he slowly moved toward the front of the aircraft. Suddenly, the pilot stopped and turned around at the cabin/cockpit bulkhead.

"James is monitoring the weight distribution . . . something to do with weight-and-balance, I believe." Carlos clarified.

Vincent momentarily shifted his curious stare from the aircraft to Carlos, made eye contact with him while he nodded his head that he understood then riveted his eyes upon the Cessna Titan's windows once again. Vincent was truly astonished at the speed in which the boxes were being loaded into the aircraft. While he watched, there was no mistaking the fact that these men had either loaded or unloaded these particular aircraft many times before. Whatever the case may have been, it had certainly honed the two Colombian's proficiency.

Twelve minutes later, the aircraft was fully loaded and the van was completely emptied of all the boxes it had previously contained. Afterwards, both men that had been inside the aircraft exited: the Colombian first, followed by the pilot. James walked directly to Carlos.

"I count six hundred and twenty boxes of merchandise aboard," James said.

Carlos turned and looked at Vincent his eyebrows arched in an inquisitive manner, but did not say a word.

"Six hundred and twenty is the correct count," Vincent remarked.

"Bueno," Carlos replied in his native tongue.

"The aircraft is ready to fly . . . just say when," James quickly added.

Carlos directed his next statement toward the two Colombians who had moved to the front of the aircraft, and were standing along its nose-wheel waiting for instructions.

"Saca el avion del hangar, rapido," Carlos said. Then in a much quieter voice, Carlos translated the order into English for Vincent and James, "Pull the aircraft outside the hangar . . . quickly." To James, Carlos added, "Five minutes, amigo . . . we'll fly in five minutes." To Vincent, Carlos gently placed his right hand on Vincent's left shoulder and said, "Say 'good-bye' to your friends. Five minutes then you must go."

"I understand," Vincent replied.

Seconds later, the sound of a small gasoline-powered motor resounded throughout the huge, aluminum building as one of the Colombians began slowly inching the laden aircraft forward with the assistance of the hand-tractor attached to the Titan's nose-wheel. The other Colombian had already begun opening the hangar's massive, sliding doors.

Vincent spent a few minutes talking with Gino and the burly Italian; both men who had been trusted employees of his for years. Even so, they had no idea that this would be their last conversation with Vincent Panachi. Without having to say good-bye, Vincent easily remained within his five minute time limit before rejoining Carlos. Meanwhile, James was doing the slow-crawl-shuffle alongside the creeping aircraft. Vincent saw that the hangar doors were now fully open, and that the aircraft's elongated nose was already through the doorway. Even by Vincent's estimation, they were but minutes away from departing. A sudden flash of Jennifer shot through his mind like an out-of-control roller coaster, and he winced from the emotional pain that it caused. The Titan stopped, and the pilot entered the aircraft. Vincent marveled at the gleaming, polished fuselage, its wings reflecting the bright, midday sunlight. It was that moment when the realization really hit him hard—fate, and only fate, would determine the outcome of this day.

Carlos walked Vincent to the aircraft's open door where the two men shook hands for the final time. At the same moment, the two Colombians were busy disconnecting the hand-tractor from the aircraft's nose wheel. Vincent thanked Carlos before he boarded the aircraft. James entered the Titan then pulled the split-door closed while Carlos watched through the aircraft's port side windows. The two of them slowly worked their way over and through the maze of boxes stuffed into the passenger/cargo compartment, until finally they reached the cockpit. Less than a minute later, both of the Titan's turbo-supercharged engines emitted an earsplitting roar that slowly faded into the distance when the twin-engine aircraft taxied toward the active runway.

Eight minutes later, Carlos watched as the aircraft climbed straight-out from Executive Airport's Runway 08. Inside the aircraft Vincent was glued to the side window while the Titan's departure path flew over the city of Lauderdale-by-the-Sea and its pristine beaches. Canals and boats were seemingly everywhere, and the ocean below crystalline. The shoreline passed beneath them as Vincent shifted in his seat and craned his neck to better watch it disappear behind them. It was only a matter of minutes before the beach's high-rise condominiums, and the white sand ribbon perimeter that neatly outlines Florida from the air, had been engulfed into the azure-blue ocean beneath them.

South Florida, and the United States for that matter, disappeared behind the aircraft. An entire country, as well as Vincent Panachi's past, had been engulfed by the thousands of square miles of a deep, dark, navy-blue sea beneath the Cessna 404 Titan, and there would not be another landfall until they reached the desolate northern coast of Colombia, South America.

Vincent looked out at the miles of open sea and whispered, "Arrivederci," through pursed lips.

*   *   *

Although Jennifer made the drive from Boca Raton back to Las Olas Isles in a record forty-five minutes, she still considered herself as being short on time in order to thoroughly search the house. It was already 3:30 p.m. when she pulled into the driveway at Vincent Panachi's Navarro Isle home.

Across the tiny bridge, Agent Mark Murray watched through a powerful pair of binoculars as Jennifer exited the automobile. Just the sight of her gave him a hot-shot of jealousy that momentarily increased his heart rate. He quickly adjusted the binoculars' eyepieces until he had her in perfect focus. He noticed that her hair and nails were absolutely perfect; "flawless," was the term he mumbled aloud to himself. Murray watched her every move until she had entered the house through the front door then he lowered the binoculars and looked at the time. He smiled as he marked down 3:30 p.m. next to a notation denoting Jennifer Swords' arrival at the house. This would all become pertinent information he would share with his underlings after they had bagged Panachi coming out of the Galleria Mall. Agent Murray's investigative mind deduced that Jennifer had returned at this late afternoon hour for a specific reason; this was the prearranged hour that she and Vincent had agreed upon to meet back at the house. To Mark Murray, that logic fully explained Vincent's all day shopping spree.

Once Jennifer was inside the house, she noticed that the burglar alarm had apparently not been set when Vincent had left, but thought nothing more of it. As she hurriedly crossed the living room toward the kitchen area, she recalled that morning's conversation, verbatim, when Vincent had informed her, ". . . I have no idea when I'll be back, so I'll tell you what . . . I'll leave you a note on the kitchen counter. Look for it when you get in."

Jennifer set her Gucci purse on top of the kitchen counter, directly next to the letter Vincent had written her. The airline ticket laid beside it. Jennifer noticed the letter first and immediately scooped it up and began reading.

It took several minutes for her to read it—the first time—during which, Jennifer's lower jaw unconsciously dropped in awe. She could not believe her eyes, so she read it, again. Jennifer's heart beat with the rhythm of a jungle drum as she laid down the letter and picked up the airline ticket issued in her name to Rio de Janeiro, Brazil. She stared at the ticket while a thousand different thoughts raced through her mind at one time. This had been the last thing in the world she had expected, and suddenly she was confused. Her emotions momentarily tugged at one another—her basic greed fighting with the feelings of love that she had never felt for any man other than Vincent Panachi. He wanted her forever, yet she didn't want to be under the financial constraints of anyone. She wanted her own financial security. Suddenly, she realized that she did not even know what were in the two suitcases he had described in the letter.

Jennifer laid the ticket on the kitchen counter, just where she had found it, and hurried from the kitchen to Vincent's office. Her hands were trembling when she turned the small handle on the walk-in closet door. Her right hand found the light switch on the first try and the tiny room illuminated. Sitting there, just as Vincent had said they would be, were two American Tourister suitcases, side-by-side. Jennifer stared in bewilderment at them for a couple of seconds while her imagination ran wild with the possibilities of what might be inside those two, large suitcases. After long seconds had passed, she gathered her composure and grabbed the handle of the case situated on her right and pulled hard. The weight of the suitcase took her by surprise, yet she tugged and pulled at it until it was in the office. Jennifer laid it on its side then carefully slid the latches outward. Both latches popped simultaneously. Jennifer leaned over and gently placed her hands along the suitcase's outside edges and eased the top half open. *GASP!* Jennifer could not believe what she was seeing. Stacks and stacks and stacks of twenty dollar bills that filled the entire suitcase from top to bottom and from side to side. She gasped, once again, while she fanned her face with quick up and down sweeps of her right hand. It was too good to be true. Everything she had ever dreamed of all neatly wrapped in one suitcase. *ONE SUITCASE.* The realization hit her like a freight train. Jennifer closed the lid on one suitcase and hurried back inside the closet. She grabbed the second American Tourister, and in her haste half-dragged it across the carpet until she had it in a position where it could be laid flat on the floor and opened. Jennifer hurriedly opened it in an identical manner, with the exception that she flung the top half open the second the latches popped. *GASP!* The second suitcase was stuffed with stacks and stacks and stacks of twenty dollar bills, just as the first had been. Jennifer closed the suitcase's lid as fast as she had opened it, and breathed deep breaths until she had her abnormally rapid breathing back under control.

Whatever struggle there had been in Jennifer's mind between love and greed was over. Greed had won, hands down. Vincent Panachi and Rio de Janeiro were now the last thoughts in Jennifer's greedy mind.

Agent Murray bolted upright in his seat when, not fifteen minutes after Jennifer Swords had entered Vincent's house, she emerged though the front door with a rather large suitcase in tow. Actually, he noted that she was half walking, half dragging the suitcase to her car. Murray adjusted the eyepieces and watched as she placed one end on her car's rear bumper and slid it into the automobile's trunk. Jennifer slammed the trunk lid shut, then re-entered the house.

Murray's mind ran rampant with the possibilities of what was happening when suddenly Jennifer re-emerged through the front door with a second, identical suitcase in tow. Once again, she struggled with the large suitcase, and through sheer perseverance she managed to load the second suitcase into the automobile's trunk. Jennifer ran back into the house only to emerge seconds later, her purse clutched in one hand and the airline ticket in the other. She half ran back to her car and slid behind the steering wheel. Murray's powerful binoculars enlarged the familiar shape of the airline ticket enough that it enabled him to immediately identify it. "Huh," he mused aloud.

Agent Murray watched as Jennifer hurriedly backed out of the driveway and sped away across the tiny bridge, then turned right at the Las Olas intersection. It all fell into place for Agent Murray; Jennifer was leaving Vincent for good, and that explained why she had taken two suitcases full of her belongings. He smiled as her car drove out of sight; not only would he get to arrest Vincent Panachi, but he would also be able to tell him how his girlfriend had moved out on him late that same afternoon. What a day, what a life, Murray happily sang beneath his breath.

Jennifer took several turns until she reached Broward Boulevard then headed west toward the expressway. Once she entered onto Interstate 95 southbound it was a fifteen minute ride to the Ft. Lauderdale International Airport, where the I-595 interchange took her directly to the airport's departing flight's level.

Jennifer pulled up in front of the Delta Airline's curbside, baggage check-in and signaled to a red cap. The well-dressed, black gentleman hurried over to her automobile with a hand cart. Jennifer got out of the car and met him at the trunk.

"I'm going to park the car . . . could you handle these suitcases for me, please?" Jennifer asked.

"Why certainly, ma'am," the Delta red cap courteously replied.

"I don't have my ticket, just yet . . . is that okay?" Jennifer interjected.

The gentleman flashed her a smile and said, "Certainly, ma'am, if you'll just give me your destination, I'll start the routing labels, then all we'll have to do is staple them to your ticket jacket when you get it."

Jennifer flashed him her deadliest smile and said, "Oh, thank you . . . you're so sweet . . . Las Vegas, Nevada is my destination."

The red cap turned and glanced up at the overhead flight monitor and began scanning it.

"There you are," the red cap said, "Flight 711 non-stop from Ft. Lauderdale to Las Vegas, departing in one hour and ten minutes. Missy, you have plenty of time. Just bring me your ticket and I'll handle these suitcases for you."

"Thank you. I'll be right back," Jennifer said as she flashed him another smile.

*   *   *

Delta's Flight 711, a gleaming L-1011, pushed back from the gate on schedule. Aboard were Jennifer Swords and her two checked pieces of luggage. The huge passenger liner departed Runway 9L at precisely 5:27 p.m., Eastern Standard Time.

Just as the L-1011 was lifting off the runway, Agent Murray and his underling agents were beginning to smell the coffee. Panachi had not been spotted since noontime, which unfortunately Murray had just been reminded of by the surveillance agents still posted outside Panachi's Mercedes. Meanwhile, Panachi's Navarro Isle home had remained as silent as a tomb. Agent Murray was beginning to feel the hair on the back of his neck rise. Something was not right, but he'd be damned if he knew what the answer was.

*   *   *

The Cessna 404 Titan was deep into the Caribbean by the time the sun began sinking into the dark, navy-blue sea below. Vincent glanced up at the 24-hour clock recessed into the instrument panel. The clock read 19:28. Vincent turned to James and asked, "7:28?"

The pilot turned toward his VIP passenger and said, "That's correct."

Vincent returned his gaze outside the window and looked west. The sky was golden-orange below and sapphire above. It was by far the most beautiful sunset he had ever witnessed, and one that would remain etched into his memory for the rest of his life.

The island of Hispaniola had passed beneath the aircraft forty-five minutes earlier and left nothing but the vast Caribbean Sea between them and the coast of Colombia. Vincent continued staring at the golden-orange fireball until it dropped into the sea. Soon thereafter, a blanket of darkness shrouded the aircraft as it made its way toward a desolate, foreign shore.

James had turned the panel's lights to their brightest illumination during the last phase of the sunset then had methodically readjusted their back-lit brightness relative to the setting sun with a tiny rheostat switch. The darker it became outside the dimmer the cockpit was illuminated, in order to better preserve James' night vision. Now, it was as dark outside as Vincent had ever seen. However, the sky was filled with thousands of stars that flickered like a million fireflies overhead in outer space. The Cessna Titan flew through the blanket of darkness without its red, green, and white navigation lights illuminated, and consequently Vincent was unable to discern the tips of the aircraft's wings in the total darkness. They were not flying blind—James had turned on the airborne radar. Vincent watched in wonderment as the tiny wand systematically swept back and forth across the radar's small, color screen. The radar screen was like a computer's color monitor, with the exception of being much smaller. It was situated in the center of the instrument panel, which gave Vincent the ability to watch it, too.

Suddenly, a squiggly shaped line appeared at the very top of the radar's screen. James noticed it immediately and calmly made a couple of adjustments to one of the tiny knobs on the bottom of the instrument. Afterwards, they watched as the wand cycled through a few more sweeps. What had been a squiggly line just a few seconds before was now the shape of the approaching shoreline. Before Vincent even asked, James reached over and tapped the screen with his index finger. "Colombia," he said before adding, "We're fifty-five miles out." Vincent did not reply, but instinctively swallowed hard. The eagles in his stomach had been awakened, once again.

James reduced the throttles on the powerful engines, and the harmonic hum that Vincent had grown accustomed to during nearly seven hours immediately changed. The variation of the engine sound was enough to awaken his dulled senses. As the aircraft descended through the black of night, the radar continued to search the darkened sky, and the landfall inched its way down the screen with every passing second. Without thinking Vincent nervously wiped his palms across the thigh of his trousers.

Minutes seemed to pass like hours, and then the aircraft passed over the shoreline of Colombia. Vincent glanced at the altimeter and noted that James had stopped the aircraft's descent at fifteen hundred feet. Still, there was nothing but darkness below. There were none of the telltale signs of civilization that Vincent had spent a lifetime accustomed to seeing; such as automobiles' headlights along a roadway, or even sparsely lit homes scattered about the darkened area. Nothing but darkness. Jungle darkness. Darkness such as Vincent had never known. The darkness continued for another twenty minutes.

Unexpectedly, flickering lights appeared ahead. Vincent sat upright in his seat and strained his neck to see. James, on the other hand, was unruffled. No doubt he had seen the lights before, and had fully expected their sudden appearance. Rather than flying directly toward the flickering lights, however, the pilot began turning the aircraft in a manner which placed the dancing lights off its left, front quarter. They were approaching them at an arcing angle. Vincent knew better than to question James at an intense moment such as this, because it was apparent that the seasoned, professional pilot had his full concentration focused upon the task at hand. Meanwhile, the lights slowly inched across the aircraft's windshield as the plane's relative position to the dancing lights changed. Moments passed then Vincent felt a strange thump, and three green lights suddenly illuminated in front of him. James remarked without turning his head, "Landing gear." Vincent said nothing.

The aircraft banked ever so slightly to the left and what had been nothing more than a maze of staggered, flickering lights just moments before, developed into two distinct parallel rows of dancing lights. The sight of the lighted runway carved out in the middle of a Colombian jungle sent a chill up Vincent's spine. Another foreign sound announced the application of the aircraft's landing flaps. Vincent instinctively reached down and gave his safety belt a reassuring tug, then glanced over at James. His concentration was unworldly, and rightfully so. There are no second chances at a landing made at night on a dirt strip carved out of the middle of a dense, South American jungle.

As the Cessna 404 Titan steadily approached the flickering lights at one hundred knots airspeed, its gentle descent systematically brought the makeshift runway's lights closer and closer. The airstrip was finally so close that Vincent readily identified its lights as dancing flames. Seconds later, the flames dimly illuminated the heavily wooded perimeter of the runway. The Titan was mere feet from the ground—perhaps fifty—and the two lines of flames were approaching rapidly. Without thinking, Vincent tensed, his hand firmly pressed against his thigh.

The dancing lights quickly became evenly spaced burning tar pots, each with a flame that danced eight-to-twelve inches above its lit wick. Simultaneously, the pitch of the engines changed and there was a *THUMP* followed by moderate vibration. The tar pots sped past the side windows like picket fences posted alongside an expressway. James was as cool as any one person could possibly be, yet this was all fresh, new, and very exciting to Vincent. His palms were perspiring and his pulse raced.

The aircraft decelerated smoothly to the end of the dirt runway where James deftly swung it around. Afterwards the fuel supply was cutoff to the fuel—injected engines before they coughed twice and died. James turned to Vincent and commented, "Welcome to Colombia."

When the two men exited the aircraft, Señior Calerro was there to greet Vincent. As a rule, the head of the Colombian drug cartel *never* got near one of their clandestine airstrips. However, he was there that particular night for several reasons: one, there was no cocaine or marijuana anywhere nearby; and secondly, he had handled the logistics of this plan himself, as a personal favor to his American counterpart, Anthony Vitale.

"Buenas Tardes, Señior Panachi," Señior Calerro greeted Vincent. "Welcome to Colombia, although you will not be staying very long." Vincent accepted the gentleman's outstretched hand, and the two men shook hands. Vincent looked at the elderly man. The flames cast a shimmering light that made his face appear weathered, yet strong featured; almost woodsman-like.

"Yes, Anthony has already filled me in," Vincent replied.

Señior Calerro gently withdrew his hand and reached into the breast pocket of his safari jacket. As he withdrew a small packet of papers, he said to Vincent,

"Good. We'll have to make this quick, however, should you have any questions my man in Brazil will be able to answer them for you. He has my full authority to assist you in any way, for anything, although I believe I have thought of everything." Before Vincent could reply, Señior Calerro handed him the packet of papers he was holding and added, "These are your new identity papers; passport—you are now a Colombian citizen, and your name is now Julio Londono. In addition, this morning I personally transferred nine-point-five-million in U.S. dollars into an account at the Banco de Brazilia in Ipanema. The man who will meet you upon your arrival checked the balance this afternoon, the funds have been posted in an account in your name, Señior Londono. Now, there is one more thing . . ." Señior Calerro snapped his fingers and one of his bodyguards hovering nearby immediately produced a full-sized briefcase. Señior Calerro took it and handed it to Vincent. "Enclosed is half a million in one hundred dollar bills. 'Street cake' I believe is what you Americans refer to it as . . ."

Vincent accepted the case then tucked the packet of papers into his hip pocket.

"I don't really know how to thank you for everything you have done, Señior Calerro," Vincent remarked.

The head of the Colombian cartel held up his hands, palms facing outwards.

"It is my pleasure to help in a time of need; besides, I still owe Anthony Vitale two-and-a-half-million on our delivery," Señior Calerro said. He shifted his eyes toward the Titan full of counterfeit twenties, and Vincent understood.

While the two men had been conversing, the workers at the field had been maneuvering a single engine airplane into take-off position at the threshold of the airstrip. Señior Calerro said, "Señior Panachi, my little plane is going to fly you to Bogota where my Learjet is standing by to fly you directly to Brazil. You will be in Rio de Janeiro within a matter of hours. I wish you happiness in your new life." The head of the cartel extended his hand, and the two men shook hands.

"Thank you . . . I mean Gracias, Señior Calerro."

"Bueno, Julio . . . , bueno," he replied.

One hour and ten minutes later, Vincent Panachi, traveling as Señior Julio Londono, departed the Bogota International Airport for Rio de Janeiro, Brazil in Señior Calerro's personal Learjet.

*   *   *

At the same moment that the Learjet departed Bogota, Colombia en route to Rio de Janeiro, Jennifer Swords was checking into the Mirage Hotel in Las Vegas, Nevada. She presented her gold American Express card, a credit card she had kept since her marriage to Dr. Mitchell Swords, to the young lady at the Mirage's front desk. The hotel clerk queried, "Standard, deluxe, or suite, Ms. Swords?"

Jennifer was flying high; with three drinks during the flight and hours spent dreaming of all the things she could buy and do now that she had her very own wealth, it was no wonder. *Nothing* was more important than knowing that to Jennifer Swords. She flashed the clerk a self-confident smile.

"A suite, of course," Jennifer arrogantly replied.

The clerk merely returned the smile and informed her, "Yes, of course . . . I show we have a suite available for three days at eighteen-hundred a night. I'm sure that meets with your approval, Ms. Swords." The front desk clerk at the Mirage Hotel had seen almost every variety of haughty, nouveau riche, want-to-be enter through those elegant lobby doors, and Jennifer Swords' excessively high parvenu, brimmed over with self-importance, was far more entertaining than aggravating to the experienced hotel employee. After all, she had seen them come and go; all full of themselves until they lost their new found wealth at the unforgiving gaming tables.

"That will be fine," Jennifer snootily replied.

The front desk clerk smiled, completing the necessary paperwork before ranging the bell for the bellman.

A handsome, young man in his mid-twenties hustled over to the front desk and asked, "Bags, ma'am?"

Jennifer quickly turned around in a manner that caused her lengthy hair to swing.

"The two American Touristers are mine," she replied before quickly adding "that's all."

Jennifer said it so nonchalantly that it gave one the impression that she traveled with a near entourage. The bellman deftly set her bags on a hand truck and gently leaned it back until it was balanced.

"If you are ready, ma'am, I'll show you to your suite."

"That will be fine, thank you," Jennifer replied to the bellman.

Away they went toward Jennifer's suite.

The bellman was a professional, and when employed at one of the world's foremost hotels one is expected to be. He was informative, yet not unduly inquisitive. He pointed out the hotel's hot spots along the way, and noted the marvel and excitement in Jennifer's eyes. Their timing had been such that they just happened to be in the vicinity of the lobby's unbelievable volcano when it erupted, just as it does every fifteen minutes like clockwork. Jennifer watched in awe at the different colors.

Ten minutes later she was comfortably stretched out across the king-sized bed in the suite's luxurious bedroom. The two American Touristers stood upright at the foot of the bed. Jennifer decided champagne would be in order, so she reached to the nightstand and telephoned the twenty-four-hour-a-day room service. A cheerful voice was more than happy to take her order for a bottle of Dom Perignon, and promised it would arrive within ten minutes. Jennifer thanked her, hung up the telephone then rolled over onto her back. The ceiling overhead the bed was mirrored, and Jennifer spent a few moments admiring herself. The bedside lamp's soft lighting reflected off her diamond necklace. Although she was unable to read the word *STILLETTO* in the mirror's reflection, she knew what it was and what it meant. Jennifer had never felt stronger. She had it all. Everything.

Five minutes later, the door bell rang and the champagne arrived. Jennifer signed the check with a flourish, and, recalling the numerous times she had seen Vincent tip handsomely for services rendered, she added a fifty dollar tip. *She* wanted to be recognized as a big tipper, and was by the room service delivery boy.

"Thank you, Ms. Swords . . . please, let me know, personally, if there is *anything* I can do for you during your stay here at the Mirage," the delivery boy said.

"I will," she smiled and said. She dismissed him as if he were her personal servant, but for a fifty buck tip, the room service delivery boy admitted to himself that he would put up with her obnoxious, super-ego antics.

Jennifer finished off the bottle of Dom Perignon within the half-hour then decided it was the appropriate time to make her debut at the gambling tables downstairs. She manhandled one of the large suitcases until she was able to lay it flat on top of the bed, its weight badly wrinkling the expensive bedspread where it sunk inches into the mattress. Jennifer unsnapped the matching latches and flipped the top half of the suitcase over onto the bed. Piles-and-piles of money were all she could see; it was all she wanted to see, because this wasn't just money, it was *her* money. Jennifer admired it without touching any for a full minute before she extracted a rubber band wrapped handful and shoved it into her purse. She closed the suitcase's lid then re-latched it. Because of the struggle she had experienced with it earlier, Jennifer decided to leave it lying flat on the bed. That way, she reasoned, it would be easier for her to replace the gambling earnings she was certain that she would soon possess.

With her purse containing approximately ten-thousand dollars in counterfeit twenty dollar bills, Jennifer leisurely strolled into the hotel's casino. She slowly cruised the crowded casino floor once before settling in at an empty seat at one of the blackjack tables. She glided onto the stool as if she were the hottest thing in the casino.

"Chips, madam?" the croupier asked.

"Yes, please," Jennifer calmly replied. She reached into her purse and extracted a wad of the twenties an inch thick and said, "One hundred dollar chips will be fine."

"Cash in, blacks," the croupier called over his shoulder.

The pit boss heard the croupier and walked over as the younger man quickly counted out the twenty, black chips. The counterfeit twenty dollar bills were deposited into the cash slot box, and the chips were given to Jennifer.

Jennifer played several hands of blackjack; winning a few, and losing a few, but having a good time at it. She felt elegant sitting there at the blackjack table with so many wealthy persons. She ordered a cocktail from the skimpily clad cocktail waitress that had been around just minutes after she sat down at the gaming table. Life was grand. Of course she would have no reason to notice the pit boss make the hourly change of the case box at her croupier's station, but, at any rate, she hadn't noticed it. Unfortunately, her twenties had been the last deposit to enter that cash box, and the stack of one hundred of them—two thousand dollars worth—were unmistakably lying on top of the rest of the cash in that box. There had been little mystery to the pit boss as to which player at that blackjack table the counterfeit bills had come from. With all those skeletons in their closets that the casinos of Las Vegas already have, the last thing in the world that they want to become involved in is the laundering of counterfeit bills, of any denomination.

A very sharp cashier in the cage took notice of the bills and checked several of the serial numbers, one against another. Naturally, they were identical. She depressed a small button at her station that summoned the same pit boss who had delivered that particular cash box, just moments before. Within seconds the pit boss responded to the not so routine alarm. The cashier showed him the bills, along with the matching numbers. Together they matched all the bills with the identical serial numbers. They were top quality, but nevertheless counterfeit, and definitely something the Mirage Hotel and Casino could in no way be associated with. In addition, the last thing they wanted or needed was publicity of this nature. It had the air of mob money about it, and anything whatsoever that implied the mob was to be avoided like the plague. The casino's pit bosses had been briefed beforehand for just such an occurrence, and it was the management's policy to avoid conflict, at all cost. "Just get them away from the gaming tables . . . quietly. Let them pass it at another casino," the pit bosses had been instructed by the upper-level management.

The pit boss scooped three bills into his hand and headed back to the blackjack table. When he got there he leaned over and whispered something in the croupier's ear. The croupier never missed a beat during his deal, but afterwards he leaned across the table, toward Jennifer, and said, "The management would like to buy you a bottle of champagne. If you would meet the pit boss standing behind me outside the cashier's cage, he would like to make the proper arrangements."

"Oh, how sweet," Jennifer gushed, "pass me by on this deal, please." She scooped up her chips and slowly strutted over to the distinguished looking gentleman standing alongside the brightly lit cashier's cage.

The pit boss was very experienced at handling situations in a dignified, discreet manner. He smiled as the attractive blond approaching him, expertly putting her at ease. Jennifer returned the smile and outstretched her hand when she finally reached him.

"Hi . . . Jennifer Swords," she introduced herself as she shook his hand. The pit boss introduced himself, but his name blurred past her. Jennifer queried, "You asked to see me?" The pit boss expertly withdrew his hand from hers and casually slipped it into his trouser pocket. His eyes never left hers during the smooth movement, yet his fingers found the three counterfeit bills he had stuffed inside the pocket without a moment's hesitation.

"Yes, Ms. Swords, I did. I'm certain that you inadvertently came by these, but I thought it my duty to warn you that somehow you have come into possession of counterfeit money."

The pit boss carefully withdrew his hand clutching the three counterfeit twenty dollar bills from his trouser pocket and handed them to her. Jennifer accepted the bills without thinking. She had heard his words, but the ramification had not yet hit her. As she held the bills between her fingertips, the pit boss patiently explained to her why the bills were worthless. He even showed her the matching serial numbers. Other than that, the average person could have never told the difference between the fake and the real Federal Reserve Notes. It did, however, preclude her from ever being able to deposit the bills, spend more than one at a time, buy anything substantial, etc. For all practical purposes, the counterfeit bills were worthless—all because of the serial numbers.

Jennifer maintained her composure and reacted to the pit boss' discovery just as if she had unknowingly received the twenties in her change, somehow, somewhere. After a five minute lecture on how the casino just could not allow that sort of thing to happen, Jennifer politely excused herself. Of course, there had been no mention of the management supplying her with a complimentary bottle of fine champagne. On the contrary, she had passed the state of embarrassment several minutes earlier. Now, she felt the sudden urge to get sick.

Jennifer left the casino in a hurry and passed by the volcano without hesitating a single second to enjoy its magnificent eruption. She felt lightheaded while she waited what seemed like hours for the elevator to arrive at the lobby level. Finally an elevator car arrived, its six-foot-by-six foot square packed with potential winners headed to the hotel's casino. Jennifer entered the elevator and was the sole occupant during the ride to her fourteenth floor suite. Her hands were trembling as she attempted to insert the credit card sized plastic card into the suite's electronic lock. Finally, she was able to open the door.

Jennifer ran into the bedroom and sat beside the suitcase that was already lying on the king-sized bed. Her trembling fingers quickly found the suitcase's latches, and she unsnapped them with a popping sound. Jennifer's hands found the sides of the suitcase and flung the top half open. The mountain of cash lay before her eyes. Jennifer grasped a handful and tore several from their rubber band bindings. Quickly, she laid them side by side on top of the expensive bedspread then scanned their serial numbers one by one and compared them. "THEY ARE ALL THE SAME," she screamed in near panic. Jennifer began tearing through the suitcase like a mad person, ripping a bill from this stack and that stack, comparing serial numbers, one against another. Positively, all the serial numbers were identical.

In a fit of frustration, Jennifer dug deeper into the layers of cash. Suddenly, her fingertips struck a foreign object—something much larger and stiffer than dollar bills. Jennifer grasped it between two fingers and pulled it from between the layers. Needless to say, she was surprised to see that it was an envelope. Her hands trembled when she flipped it over so that she could better open it. The paper tore with ease, and Jennifer slipped the single-paged letter from its envelope. Her mouth fell open when she saw that it was addressed to her. Her eyes swept back and forth across the page as she read it. It read:

Dear Jennifer,

If you are reading this letter it means that you obviously chose to take the money and run. Well, it was the wrong choice. Why? Because things are not always as they appear. For example, what appeared to be all the money you could ever need in a lifetime has turned out to be worthless. That's right; if you haven't figured it out already, check the serial numbers on ALL the bills. You will find that they are one in the same.

Another thing that is not as it appears is my hasty departure. My leaving was something that had been planned for quite some time. I only wish that I could have shared those plans with you with a clear conscience, but alas, I was not certain that you could be trusted. I knew that you were somehow connected with Agent Mark Murray of the Organized Crime Task Force, yet in what way I am still not certain. Therefore, I had to test you in some way to see exactly where your loyalties laid. Apparently, since you are reading this letter, they did not lie with us.

I have loved you, and more than likely will for some time to come. However, I did not leave empty handed. I have ten million dollars with which to begin my new life, in REAL money. Somehow, someway, the memory of you and us will fade away. Good-bye . . .

Jennifer re-read the letter once again, and tears quickly swelled in her eyes at the realization of what she had done. She had won it all—love, money, financial security; everything that she had dreamt of since her childhood, but she had lost it to greed. Jennifer's hands began trembling so badly that it was impossible for her to read the letter any more, so she threw it onto the bedspread. Jennifer looked at the piles of worthless money while tears streamed from her eyes and ran down her flushed cheeks. In a moment of desperation, she darted across the bedroom to her purse and ripped it open. The airline ticket to Rio de Janeiro that Vincent had left her with the letter was inside. She rummaged through the purse until she found it and snatched it from the bottom of the purse. Her eyes quickly scanned the flight itinerary and found the arrival time that the travel agency had so neatly typed in for her convenience. Jennifer gasped; even the Concorde could not have gotten her to Rio in time to make it appear that she had arrived on that particular flight. The VARIG Brazilian Airlines' flight was scheduled to arrive at Rio de Janeiro's Galeao International Airport within the half hour. Jennifer stared at the ticket and winced at the thought of what could have been was to be lost forever in less than thirty minutes, and there was not a damn thing she could do to prevent it.

Jennifer dropped the airline ticket and threw herself across the bed as an emotional wave of depression overcame her. Her tears flowed freely now that the reality of the situation had set in. Jennifer whimpered while she turned over onto her back. Her vision was somewhat blurred through her tear-filled eyes, yet Jennifer still made out the unmistakable reflection of her diamond-studded necklace in the overhead mirror, once again. She stared at it for a few seconds, then, in a fit of fury, Jennifer yanked the chain from her neck. The necklace broke in her hand. Her breathing became labored, almost to the point of hyperventilating, while she cried her eyes out. In her hand, Jennifer clutched her favorite piece of jewelry—the necklace that spelled the word *STILETTO* in pave diamonds. It was all over, and she knew it. Vincent Panachi had slipped through her web.

*　　*　　*

Exactly thirty-three minutes later, Señior Calerro's Learjet—Colombian registration HK-GBV—landed safely at Rio de Janeiro's Galeao International Airport. The new, improved Vincent Panachi, aka Julio Londono, was the sole passenger on that international flight, and, just as Señior Calerro had promised, his personal representative had been there to meet him.

As soon as the Learjet's two turbojet engines spooled down, a Mercedes Benz sedan pulled up alongside the aircraft. A distinguished looking gentleman, well past his sixtieth birthday, emerged from the luxury sedan and motioned to Vincent to get in. Julio Londono did just that, and before the gentleman had even introduced himself, Vincent looked at his watch and asked, "Could you take me to VARIG Brazilian Airlines' International Arrivals area, please?"

"But, of course. However, if you are referring to the inbound flight from Miami, that flight has already arrived, not five minutes ahead of the Learjet. By now the passengers should be clearing through Customs," the elderly gentleman replied in perfect English.

There was a moment of silence before Vincent turned toward the gentleman and introduced himself. Everything was so new, and it had happened so quickly, that Vincent was momentarily overwhelmed by it all. That feeling passed within seconds, however, and Vincent politely introduced himself.

"Julio Londono," he said as he courteously outstretched his right hand to shake hands with the elderly gentleman. The distinguished looking gentleman had been clutching the Mercedes' leather bound steering wheel in the classic ten and two o'clock position. He released his grip from the two o'clock position and accepted Vincent's offered hand with his right hand, and the two men shook hands.

"Yes, I know. My name is Raul, and I am at your disposal for anything that you may require. It will be my pleasure to help you smoothly transition into your new life, Julio. By the way, no Customs clearance is necessary for you."

The sedan pulled alongside the curb and stopped just outside the Customs' passenger arrival area. Vincent craned his neck as he watched a seemingly endless line of tourists stream from the building. Raul noticed Julio's eyes darting back-and-forth while he frantically searched the crowd for Jennifer. Vincent wanted her to be on that flight so bad. Raul watched Julio's anticipative behavior for nearly a minute before he queried, "May I assist you in any way?"

Vincent turned toward the man and replied, "Yes, Raul, you may. Please. I am looking for an American woman by the name of Jennifer Swords who was supposed to be on that Miami flight."

"Well, that is simple enough. My cousin is working passenger arrivals tonight. Give me a few minutes to check and I'll tell you if she was on the flight," Raul remarked.

Raul got out of the luxury sedan and entered the Customs building, where he remained for approximately ten minutes before returning to the Mercedes.

"I'm sorry, my friend, but your Jennifer Swords was not listed on the flight's passenger manifest. Perhaps she is traveling under another name?" he asked.

Vincent stared straight ahead into the steadily moving stream of passengers disembarking from the Customs building. The realization hit hard, but he maintained a steadfast composure while he turned to Raul.

"No . . . she's not coming," Vincent said.

The two men shared a silent stare that lasted a full minute. After that, what was there to say? Raul understood the heart-stricken look without having to pry, for he himself, just like every other human being that has experienced love, had faced that distraught feeling when love is lost. Finally, Raul reassuringly patted Julio on the shoulder and suggested, "How would you like to see your new penthouse apartment . . . compliments of Señior Calerro?"

The suggestion snapped Vincent back to reality. "I'd like that, thank you."

Without hesitation, Raul dropped the Mercedes into gear and sped away towards the bright lights of *The Marvelous City*, Rio de Janeiro.

Raul patiently explained that the city was build around lush, green mountains connected by thirteen different tunnels. No sooner than he had informed Vincent of that fact, the Mercedes Benz entered into the Botafogo Tunnel. Thirty seconds later, the multilane, paved highway emerged from a hole in the side of a mountain where the many lights of world famous Copacabana Beach illuminated the sky.

Minutes later, the sedan entered another tunnel. This time, the vehicle emerged from the mountain at Ipanema Beach. The brightly lit roadway paralleled the Atlantic Ocean for several miles, during which they entered into the posh residential community of Leblon.

Raul slowed the vehicle and turned into the parking garage of an ocean front, high-rise condominium. The building appeared to be brand new, and was. After they parked the sedan, Raul showed Julio through the security-manned lobby then escorted him to a penthouse-level apartment.

Vincent had seen some beautiful apartments in Ft. Lauderdale, but nothing that could compare to that penthouse. The living room had views of the ocean and Sugar Loaf Mountain. Lights below twinkled in every direction. Raul cheerfully informed him that there was a rooftop swimming pool above him, and a city filled with some of the world's most beautiful women below him.

Raul placed his arm around Vincent and reminded him, "Life is beautiful, Julio, and at my young age I make a point of living every day as if it were my last."

Vincent pondered the elderly gentleman's philosophical statement for close to a minute, during which thoughts of Jennifer breezed through his mind. The realization finally settled into Vincent's psyche—Jennifer Swords was gone; Vincent Panachi was gone; and a new world and new life lay at Julio's fingertips. Vincent mumbled something under his breath, "Don't live in the past . . . don't live in the past . . ."

Raul heard Vincent's unintelligible mumbling and said, "Pardon me?"

Vincent turned toward his new found friend and said, "Thank you, Raul . . . thank you. I understand fully, now. Life is beautiful, and I want to live it to its fullest."

EPILOGUE

THREE MONTHS LATER . . .

The Organized Crime Task Force had failed miserably in their attempts to bring Vincent Panachi to justice, and after the fiasco of that fateful Monday, the investigation had been abandoned by the powerful men who occupied the top floor offices of the task force's Broward Boulevard headquarters. Naturally, Wade Jessup had shielded himself from their wrath by offering Agent Mark Murray as the sacrificial scapegoat to his superiors.

Unfortunately even Ms. Phyllis Lloyd, the *Sun Sentinel*'s crack investigative reporter, had turned against him. She had not forgotten Agent Murray's reaction that afternoon when he had shown her around the task force's surveillance condominium. She vividly recalled when Murray had spotted the unidentified female accompanying their primary suspect in the organized crime family investigation, Vincent Panachi. Ms. Lloyd, being a crack investigative reporter, began her own thorough investigation based upon that one suspicious thread of evidence revealed when Murray had acted so strangely. It had taken her several weeks, but eventually she had unraveled the circumstances that hadgiven rise to his suspicious behavior. After all, an investigative reporter of her stature had her own information grapevine in which she could readily access. First came the name: Jennifer Swords. Several days afterwards, Ms. Lloyd had received an anonymous tip that outlined Agent Murray's affair and subsequent infatuation with Jennifer.

Thirty days to the date after that fateful Monday, the *Sun Sentinel* ran a follow-up feature article on the organized crime stronghold articles that they had previously published. This article, however, had a little different slant to it. Ms. Phyllis Lloyd had speculated, in print, that the Organized Crime Task Force's lead agent in the investigation had intentionally bungled the investigation in order to protect his ex-girlfriend, Jennifer Swords.

After that article had appeared, it was the unanimous decision of the powers that be who occupied the top floor offices of task force's headquarters building that Agent Mark Murray be suspended from duty, without pay, until he had successfully passed a thorough psychological examination. Agent Murray had gone in peace, yet he did not need a psychologist to analyze his mental problems. He knew what had indirectly caused all of his problems, to date—his love for one woman; a woman incapable of returning that love—Jennifer Swords.

The newspaper article had been read far and wide. As a matter of fact, Detectives Earnest Polk and Jack Farmer of the Palm Beach Sheriff's Department had become somewhat of celebrities themselves. They had carried that newspaper article with them for several days after its publication, telling almost anyone who would listen how they had worked with, "that city boy investigator during them black-tuxedo-wearing murders we had out here." The Palm Beach Coroner, Dr. Kramer, had also read the article, but he had made it a point to offer nothing but a standard reply when asked: "No comment." To him, the mutilated bodies of Slick Nick and the Maitre'd had been routine autopsies which he had no desire to relive. Period.

*　　*　　*

Señior Calerro and Anthony Vitale met with one another at Ft. Lauderdale's Harbour Beach Marriott Hotel just weeks after that fateful Monday. The atmosphere had been more of a meeting of old friends rather than the business meet that had been scheduled. Señior Calerro had graciously settled up with Anthony Vitale on the two-point-five million owed, then the rest of the day Señior Calerro had answered Anthony's many questions about Vincent and how he was getting along in his new life. The smooth business transaction, combined with the unselfish manner in which Señior Calerro had assisted Vincent, made for a lifelong friendship between the two crime family bosses.

As soon as Anthony Vitale had returned to Newark, New Jersey, he had taken care of the Quill with a cool million dollar payment for professional services rendered.

One month later the Quill bought himself an estate in upstate New Jersey and retired, as he had so eloquently informed the head of the Vitale crime family. The Quill retired with the satisfaction of knowing that his handiwork was admired by many persons in-and-around Colombia, South America.

Anthony Vitale helped another of his trusted employees retire by dispatching Capo Pelligi to Ft. Lauderdale, Florida to oversee the family's operations there. Within a matter of weeks afterwards, the golf course house was in full swing, once again. Under the Capo's guidance and watchful eye, Gino and the burly Italian that roomed there with him continued the business as usual.

At the request of Anthony Vitale, Salvatore Santori, the crime family's Consiglio, traveled to Florida a number of times during those three months. There he had eventually demonstrated his unique ability, once again, at finding the right pocket to pad. Afterwards, the Vitale crime family had the protection it should have had before the affair with Vincent even began. As the Consiglio had assured Anthony Vitale, "It is something that will never happen to the family again." Monthly payoffs assured that history would not repeat itself.

Anthony Vitale now lives his life in peace in his palatial mansion outside Newark, New Jersey. He has made peace with the world, and the world has made peace with him. He has not attended a birthday celebration in Ft. Lauderdale, Florida since Vincent's departure; without him, he felt, it just would not be the same.

* * *

It had been almost two months and three weeks since the Cessna 404 Titan returned to Hangar 24 at Ft. Lauderdale's Executive Airport. James had completed another successful trip for Carlos Lazarro, and had been amply rewarded for his gallant efforts.

* * *

Carlos and the beautiful receptionist finally got married and were expecting their first—although unexpected—child.

* * *

Raul had become Vincent's mentor over the period of the past few months. It seems that the elderly gentleman had taken to Vincent as the son that he had never had. He had certainly helped Vincent in every imaginable way. Of course, to Raul it was not Vincent; it was Julio Londono he had taken the liking to.

Over the months, Vincent had settled into his new lifestyle quite comfortably. Raul had helped him purchase a new Mercedes Benz then given him directions to areas of interest and worthwhile sights to check out. The beautiful beaches had been among them.

Julio Londono was spending the majority of his time working on his tan. His days were spent at Rio's best beach, in Sao Conrado at Praia de Pepino, where it is isolated from the rest of the city by a long ocean side cliff. Vincent spends days sitting at the clear, warm water's edge, sipping chilled coconuts sold by local beach boys while he watches hang gliders that launch from the rocky cliff side above soar lazily overhead. Jennifer Swords, just like the name Vincent Panachi, were thoughts he has long since pushed from his mind.

Julio Londono is happy, healthy, and wealthy; and lives his life in complete freedom—both mentally and physically—in a posh neighborhood outside of Rio de Janeiro, Brazil, South America.

*   *   *

Jennifer Swords had not been spotted on the social scene in Ft. Lauderdale since that fateful Monday. Finally, after nearly three months, she reappeared for the first time at Shylock's. Naturally, the notoriety that she had received from Ms. Phyllis Lloyd's follow-up feature article in the *Sun Sentinel* had played an important part in her self-imposed exile from society, but that had not been the only determining factor considered. After experiencing weeks of sleepless nights spent crying, Jennifer had decided to undergo the knife once again. This time the plastic surgery was to eliminate the multiple wrinkles that had formed beneath her eyes over the past several weeks. It appeared that Jennifer's vanity knew no bounds, yet she considered the outpatient operation as nothing more than the cost of doing business—her business. Jennifer Swords had to remain desirable to the opposite sex.

The operation had been successful. The plastic surgeon who had performed the operation was an associate of Jennifer's ex-husband, and he had filled her in on Dr. Swords' life after divorce. It seemed that he was happy, prosperous, and stable—everything that Jennifer Swords wasn't, yet yearned to be.

It was during her post-operative recovery when Jennifer had decided upon her next tactical move. Jennifer reached for the telephone and dialed her ex-husband at this office. The receptionist placed her on hold then several minutes later Dr. Mitchell Swords' voice came over the line. "Jennifer?" he asked, his tone revealing the disbelief he felt.

Jennifer began spinning another web. "I've been thinking about you . . . about us . . . a lot lately. Would you like to meet for a drink and talk about it?" Without hesitating, he had agreed.

Jennifer sat at the lower bar at Shylock's, at Tony's station of course. Naturally, Tony had read the follow-up article in the newspaper, but that had been months ago. He placed a paper cocktail napkin in front of Jennifer and said, "How nice to see you, Jennifer. You look great. Younger, I think.

"Oh, thank you, Tony," Jennifer gushed.

"Vincent meeting you? I haven't seen him in awhile," Tony said.

The mention of Vincent's name sent a pang through her heart, and Jennifer struggled to maintain her composure. She loved him; she knew that now, but it was too late. Vincent was gone. Jennifer replied, "I thought maybe you had seen him . . . we sort of broke up."

Before Tony could reply to that statement, an older gentleman leaned over and kissed Jennifer on the cheek. Jennifer turned and flashed the well dressed man

369

a smile, then turned to Tony and said, "Tony, I'd like you to meet my wonderful ex-husband, Dr. Mitchell Swords."

The shy plastic surgeon extended his hand across the bar and shook hands with Tony.

"It's a pleasure," Tony said.

"Likewise," the meek and mild mannered doctor said.

"Something to drink today?" the bartender asked.

"Before Dr. Mitchell Swords could reply, Jennifer interjected, "Champagne, please. The best you have." She turned to her ex-husband and said, "It's a very special day for us." Dr. Mitchell Swords merely blushed in response. Two bottles of champagne and several hours later, Jennifer Swords had lured Dr. Swords into her web, once again.

Jennifer Swords and Dr. Mitchell Swords were remarried three months later, and the good doctor presented her with a brand new Mercedes Benz as a wedding present. Throughout the years he has continued to shower Jennifer with expensive gifts; and, in return, she has continued to keep him half-crazed with her sexual persuasion.

When Jennifer Swords remarried Dr. Mitchell Swords, it was a ceremony that took her back to where it had all started. Jennifer Swords had gone full circle, but some things never changed. At best, she was pacified; but never satisfied.

To this day, Jennifer Swords has never forgotten, nor gotten over, the one man in her life who had satisfied her in every way—

VINCENT PANACHI

Printed in the United States
78181LV00001B/1-6

9 781425 711467